Off Season

Off Season

Anne Rivers Siddons

GRAND CENTRAL
PUBLISHING

NEW YORK   BOSTON

Grand Central Publishing
Hachette Book Group USA
237 Park Avenue
New York, NY 10017

Visit our Web site at www.HachetteBookGroupUSA.com.

Printed in the United States of America

First Edition: August 2008
10 9 8 7 6 5 4 3 2 1

Grand Central Publishing is a division of Hachette Book Group USA, Inc.
The Grand Central Publishing name and logo is a trademark of
Hachette Book Group USA, Inc.

Library of Congress Cataloging-in-Publication Data

Siddons, Anne Rivers.
   Off season / Anne Rivers Siddons.—1st ed.
       p.   cm.
      Summary: "Anne Rivers Siddons tells the beautiful, tragic, and
redemptive story of a woman who searches for meaning after her husband dies"—
Provided by publisher.
      ISBN-13: 978-0-446-52787-3 (regular ed.)
      ISBN-10: 0-446-52787-4 (regular ed.)
      ISBN-13: 978-0-446-50548-2 (large print ed.)
      ISBN-10: 0-446-50548-X (large print ed.)   1. Widows—Fiction.
   2. Self-realization in women—Fiction.   3. Psychological fiction.   I. Title.

   PS3569.I28O35   2008
   813'.54—dc22

                                                          2008010090

For Cynthia and David,
who know why, or should

After the first death, there is no other.
—DYLAN THOMAS

Prologue

From where you leave Interstate 95 at Bangor to trace the jumble of state and county roads over to the coast around Sedgwick, your driving time can range from an hour or so in fine, bright weather to an anxious, creeping three and a half in dense fog. On this day in early July, I made it in just over an hour, a shorter time than, if I remembered correctly, Cam ever had.

"See there," I said to him in the backseat. "You always drove because you said I poked along, and I did better today than you ever did on your best one."

He did not answer, of course, because he was dead, was now fine, silvery dust in the dark bronze urn I had chosen, nestled between piles of books and old Silas's basket, which was lined with the rotting old sweater Silas guarded fiercely. It smelled of salt and pine and wood smoke and now, of course, Silas.

Silas answered, though.

"Rowp." "*When are you going to stop this damned car and let me out? I'm hungry. I need to take a piss.*"

It was Cam who'd invented Silese, swearing that it was possible to tell what was on the cat's mind by listening closely to his rusty grumble. Silas had never, to my knowledge, purred. On this strange afternoon of sun and flying cloud-shadow and whipping wisps of fog,

I felt I could translate him as well as Cam ever had. Or at least it amused me to think so. Probably neither one of us had it right. Silas could have been cursing us vilely in Esperanto, for all we knew.

I'd been talking chattily and often giddily to Cam all during the two-day drive from Virginia. In fact, I had been doing so ever since the last of the guests left the—what would you call it? a reception?—my daughters and best friend, Kitty Howard, had put together while I was at the short service at the crematorium. I literally had had to push Betsy and Alice out of the house and into their husbands' rental cars to go back to their motel and have a shower and some dinner. Betsy claimed she was allergic to Silas, but I knew her bond lawyer husband did not want cat hair on his four-hundred-dollar khakis. Both of my girls were puffed and smeared with tears, and clearly terrified that I did not wear the stigmata of widowhood. "Denial" and "Doesn't know what she's doing" hung in the air like room deodorant.

I was sure they were right, and just as sure that the gut-wrenching grief and corrosive tears and lassitude all lay ahead, waiting just out of sight. But for now the witless chatter to a dead man and a cat served me well. Neither was likely to fuss or hover.

"I'll call you both the minute the meltdown starts," I said, and in the end it was staunch Kitty who had taken them by their New York–thin arms and pulled them along after her.

"Let her be," she drawled in the Tidewater lilt I had always loved. "If she wants to burn incense and dance naked around the urn, it's her business. Wait till you get here yourselves before you start quoting proper widowhood protocol."

They left, I am sure, to sit around their motel table with pomegranate martinis and discuss who would take on dear old mum if she flipped out totally, and what to do with that monstrous old pile of a house on McCall's Point and the Maine house that, though not old by Maine cottage standards, was sinking deeper into the piney earth and leaf mold every year. And, of course, about Silas.

"Don't you even *think* the word *euthanasia*," I yelled at the door that had slammed behind them. And then I began to laugh, maniacally, until my breath stopped and the laughing slid over into sobbing. It was what I had been doing ever since Cam died, although mercifully in no one's presence, except for Silas. Once or twice he got up from his fetid sweater and trundled over and gave my face a usually peremptory lap, reeking rankly of Kitty Rations seafood dinner, the only kind of food he will eat. But usually he just sat there regarding me as I laughed and wept and finally slept.

"Seems like as good a way as any," he said in Silese.

I think I made the decision to drive up to Edgewater, the Maine cottage my family had owned since before I was born, after one of these middle-of-the-night explosions. These last few days I had been muffling them with my pillow because Betsy had come back with her two children "to stay for a little while and help cheer Gammy up," which I think consisted of lurking silently around corners and outside my bedroom door to see if a stray whimper, sob, or howl could be heard. That and the children chasing Silas until he turned at bay and bit one of them soundly. After the ensuing hysterics and the trips to the doctor over in Reston, and the mutterings about "that monster is not safe," my way seemed clear as cool water.

The next morning at breakfast I told Betsy that I was going up to Edgewater for the summer to see to some things up there and get my bearings, and would be home in the early fall. And there were to be no uninvited guests.

I could have recited beforehand what she said: "Who'll look after you? You can't just isolate yourself way up there in those woods and not see anybody. What if you fell or something? How would anybody know?" (For that, read "What if you set fire to the place; you could burn it and you to a crisp and then we couldn't even sell it.") "You know Daddy said he never wanted you to be up there by yourself."

Betsy was not a selfish child, or even a thoughtless one; she adored Cam and had not yet learned that there are many, many ways to hurt and grieve, although few to mitigate either.

"Well, I won't be by myself, will I?" I said mildly. "Daddy will sure as shootin' be with me every minute of the day. You know that is where he wanted his ashes to be spread, and we'll do that at the end of the summer, and everybody can come up then. Meanwhile, I'll have him closer to me than I did lots of times . . . before."

"That's sick," Betsy wailed. But when she saw that she was only annoying me, she packed her clothes and her children and left for New York in a well-bred huff.

"I'll have to make it up to her sometime," I said to Silas.

"Murf." *Let her work it out.*

And so in a couple of days I had loaded the car and given the keys to Deeanne, our heartbroken housekeeper, and to Kitty, and now here I was, almost within sight of the turnoff into the dense spruce and pine and ash woods that blanket this stretch of coast, about to turn left onto the dusty, unpaved lane that led deep into them and down a steep small hill. Here I was, about five minutes from the moment I could stand beside the old green house in its clearing in the forest, the lawn trimmed neatly by Toby or Laurie, and look down from the top of the piled-stone seawall and watch the bay playing about the rocks, creaming and swelling and falling, glittering far to the west where the afternoon sun was lowering. I would smell the clean, fishy, kelpy sun-on-dried-rocks smell, and I would hear the sea breathe.

On the outer shores of Maine the sea howls, and roars, and smashes itself on its cliffs; it booms and shouts and sings. But our bay is protected by the bulk of Little Deer Isle and Deer Isle, and below on the rocks of Edgewater, it breathes. In and out, in and out, sighing, hushing, soothing. Soon, I knew, my own breathing would fall into its rhythm, and I would be one with it. Again, I felt tears of joy well up in my eyes, and my throat tighten with it. I had wept, I think I remember, with this same joy every time we had come to Edgewater since I was very small.

"Why are you crying?" my mother might say.

"I want to hear the ocean breathing."

And somehow, always, the sea breathed to me.

I pulled the car into the unkempt driveway and skidded to a stop, spurting gravel, and was out of it and on the path around the house before I remembered Silas. I could hear him moaning spectrally from his nest in the sweater and started back, then I trotted on.

"I'll die from thirst and hunger, and this is how I'll sound to you in your dreams every night. Every night—don't think I won't."

"You weigh too much already," I shouted back at him. "The vet says you need to lose five pounds. Good a time as any to start."

I didn't hear his reply because I came abruptly to the seawall, took a deep breath, and looked down. Edgewater is built on a small cliff, the last petulant spasm of the last great glacier in the Pleistocene Age. It tumbles down to the water in a crazy quilt of fierce black and gray stone outcroppings, smooth boulders both small and enormous, petrified trees, and a skimpy apron of beach. A headland of red Maine granite guards the left side of the crescent; when the setting sun touches it, it looks primeval, supernormal, on fire inside. There are two enormous kelp beds that float on the water, making for slimy swimming at high tide and a stinking miasma at low tide. I love all of it.

But all I saw now was a solid wall of cold, wet white fog, one of the impenetrable summer fogs that haunt this coast and dampen bedclothes and shoes and tempers. This one stopped, as they almost always did, just at the seawall, and it was eerie, I thought, not for the first time, that you could stand on firm, sun-warmed grass and look into empty, piled-up white eternity.

Worst of all, I could not hear the sea. The fog hushed its breathing as totally as if the bay were comatose and someone had just pulled the plug. I felt something near panic clench my stomach, and my chest began to tighten as in the beginning of an asthma attack. For a moment I could not breathe.

I turned, suddenly cold and afraid, grabbed Silas, sweater and all, and floundered up the fog-slimed wooden steps to the porch that wrapped around Edgewater, and pushed open the heavy wooden door and the screened one behind it, and stood still, listening to silence and looking at darkness.

"Ngow!" Silas growled. *"Get some light and heat in here!"*

I dumped him, sweater and all, onto the faded old tartan sofa that had sat in front of the big stone fireplace since I could remember, dug out the matches that were always kept in a weatherproof tin on the mantel, and lit the fire. It was a fine one of sweet, dried wood—birch, I thought. I knew Toby had come in earlier in the day and opened the house and laid the fire. It gave a kind of booming burp and a great whoosh, and then a small cave of room was flooded with light and the sweet smell of wood smoke. Silas muttered a grudging thanks and found his hollow at the end of the sofa, glared at me until I laid the old sweater down, turned around three times, and settled lumpily in for a nap. *"Wake me when there's food,"* I was sure he said.

I should have turned on the electric lights and brought in the suitcases and put away the perishables and thought about dinner. But I didn't. I wasn't breathing well. I picked up Cam's urn and put it on the stone mantel and sat down on the rump-strung sofa to regard it. It looked well there, catching the firelight, looking as if it might have been there as long as the house had stood.

"Are you warm enough?" I said to him, and then thought, *Well, of course, you've just been in a place a thousand times warmer. It ought to last you awhile.* Then insane, idiot laughter bubbled up, choking me, followed by great, vomit-like sobs, and I threw myself down length-wise on the sofa because I could no longer get breath in and out of my lungs.

I'm going to die, I thought, sucking in decades-old dust, but instead I slept. I slept without moving until the fire was embers and the room cold, and then sat up abruptly with a voice in my ears.

"Lilly, get up," it said. "Get up and go look. The fog is gone."

"Really," I said fuzzily. It was not until I was out on the porch, looking up at the huge blind white eye of the moon (*"Strawberry Moon,"* said Silas, who had accompanied me), that I even wondered whose the voice was. Silas's? Cam's, in a dream? Not quite, but one I knew, a voice of this place, though of an earlier time. A voice with laughter in it, a good voice.

I walked through the dew-cold grass to the lip of the seawall, and there was the bay, a sheet of burning-cold silver all the way out to Great Spruce Head Island. I saw none of the lights I was accustomed to from the summer colony on Little Deer; tonight it was just me and Silas and the bay and the moon.

"Listen," the voice said again. (Cam, almost certainly.)

I did, and took a deep, hungry breath, and the sea breathed with me.

Before

CHAPTER

1

There were seven of us at Edgewater that summer, if you count my brother Jeebs. None of us did, really. Jeebs was thirteen and gone into another orbit of his own; he entered ours only when he had nothing else to do, and then grudgingly.

That left Harriet Randall, aged eleven; Ben and Carolyn Forrest, who were twins, aged ten; Cecie Wentworth, aged eleven; Peter Cornish, aged twelve; and Joby Gardiner, eleven. And of course, me. Elizabeth Allen Constable but called, by my own creed, Lilly and nothing else. I was eleven that summer of 1962 and stonily determined not to be confused with my mother, who was Elizabeth, too.

My mother: Elizabeth Potter Constable; painter, activist (in her own words), great beauty. She was sporadic and only adequate at the first two, but at the third she was spectacularly successful. Turned heads followed Liz Constable wherever she went.

It was the apogee of the frenzied Jackie Kennedy mythology, and even up here in this rural saltmeadow world almost untouched by fashion for a century, women wore their hair in carefully tousled bouffants and put on crisp white sleeveless blouses and Bermuda shorts to go to the post office or general store (which were one and the same). The yacht club cocktail-and-chowder suppers looked like a Norman Rockwell magazine cover of an idyllic girls' camp. Into the middle of all the matched Lilly Pulitzer wrap skirts and T-shirts, the huge sunglasses pushed casually above foreheads to form chic headbands, my mother would drift barefoot like an idle racing sloop, her hair in its uncombed little Greek-boy tousle of curls, her white pants smeared with paint, the striped French matelot T-shirt she had affected since a trip to Cannes when she was sixteen daubed with it. There would not be a vestige of makeup on her pure medieval features, only a flush of sunburn on her high cheekbones and a slick of Chap Stick on her full, tender mouth—a Piero della Francesca mouth, according to Brooks Burns, two cottages down, who was a classical scholar and eighty years old, and had been in love with my mother, according to my father, since she came here as a bride.

"Eyes like summer rain on the ocean," he would say. "Eyes like clear pond ice."

"Eyes like a frozen February crust over Eggemoggin Reach," I might have added, "especially when those black brows come together over them."

But I doubted that anyone but my father and Jeebs and I had seen that. My mother's brows were two silky black slashes set straight over her eyes, which were clear, light-spilling gray and fringed with black lashes. With her sun-streaked copper curls they were striking; you expected slender sienna arches. I had those brows, I was often told, and the gray eyes, too, but even to me they often looked stormy and sulky instead of mythic. I had seen my mother, in her studio just before she came out to join us for an evening, slick her eyebrows with some sort of cream, and lightly redden her cheeks, and finger-tousle her hair before the old seashell mirror that hung beside the studio door. Once or twice I saw her daub a sunset smear on her cheek or forehead, or stain her shirt lightly with it. The result was a careless beauty seemingly preoccupied with things more important than her looks. It served her well.

I spied on my mother shamelessly during the summer. I'm still not quite sure why. I think I was looking for revelations, epiphanies, a map for knowing where the real woman and mother lay. It seemed that if I found it, I would have the map for myself, could chart a course by it. But I never did, and after that summer I did not spy on her again. Instead, I set about trying to become the direct antithesis of the woman in her mirror. It got me in endless trouble with her, though not so much with my father.

"Let her be," he would tell her from the rocking chair on the porch that was his regular summertime emplacement. "You wouldn't want a perfect little copy of you, would you? I would think one is enough."

"She could do worse," I heard my mother say once, tightly, in the days when I still eavesdropped.

"Not much," I thought my father murmured from the rocker, but I was never sure of that.

And yet she was not all artifice. All the children from the cottages around us flocked to ours as naturally as thirsty birds to a birdbath. All the cottages down on this particular cove were members of the Middle Harbor Yacht Club, in the old Retreat Colony up the road, and had full privilege to join the brown, scabby-kneed colony children on the dock and in the tenders and small Beetle Cats in the harbor, or playing Ping-Pong in the raffish old clubhouse, or camping out on the islands in the bay across the harbor. And sometimes we did, but summer friendships are cemented early and tightly, and we came to be regarded as privileged outlanders, "too good for us," hanging around only with each other at Liz Constable's cottage. My mother really loved children, or, perhaps, I thought that summer, the children of others, and never seemed annoyed or bored with our endless and obscure yelping games, or the little flotilla of kayaks and Shellback dinghies that were tied up all summer beside my family's old Friend-ship sloop at the end of our dock. We were the only cottage in our settlement that had a deepwater dock. All the others kept their boats at the yacht club.

Mother vanished for long periods during the day, into her studio or at the desk in her bedroom, writing letters or phoning on behalf of her causes. They were good New England liberal causes, my father often said: birth-control information for young girls, Martin Luther King, Jr., and his incendiary young civil rights battle, meals for the infirm and disenfranchised of Hancock County, cleaning up the effluent-fouled streams and bays nearby.

I know she was serious about these causes. I had seen her in tears over some social injustice or other featured on the flickery old black-and-white television in the cottage living room. And I know that there were people in the colony, women mainly, who found her indiscreet and vaguely threatening and her causes as unseemly in our little nineteenth-century fiefdom as a fart at the Chowder Race. I know too that she honestly did not care a finger flick what people thought of her activism or her painting. But she did care, secretly and profoundly, about maintaining her role as a careless natural beauty, a warm, funny woman far above artifice and agendas. I could never fathom the why of that as a child; complexity is largely beyond children.

But I still can't today.

At noon Clara Anderson, who "did" for us mornings and who was the third generation of her family to do so for mine, would make a tray of bologna and cheese sandwiches and lemonade and put it on the big side screened porch, and we would rush in and wolf them down and be off again in a chattering swarm, out to the water or to the badminton and croquet courts my grandfather had carved out of the woods behind the cottage.

The other cottage mothers in our cove knew where to call if they had need of their children. So far as I knew, none of them ever worried that their offspring might be a bother to my mother, or that they might be in any way unsafe. Of course it was Clara who had the day-to-day burden of us, but she too liked children and had three of her own, and in our defense we had not yet absorbed any of the early-blooming horrors creeping into the cities then: drugs, alcohol, promiscuity, revolution. In Carter's Cove, as our little settlement was called, all that came much later. The only really malicious thing I can remember us doing was setting off cherry bombs in the shabby small bathroom of the yacht club's steward, a tight-faced fireplug-shaped young man from one of the original colony families who had not been accepted at Yale and was coldly mean-spirited to our crowd because we were not "his" kids. When our parents found out about it, we were forced to pick blueberries and wash windows and mow lawns to earn enough money for a new and vastly superior toilet. It struck us as only fair, and so we did not grouse too much about it, except that the steward got a far better toilet out of the deal and smirked at us all summer.

"Why were you so down on your mother that summer?" Cam asked me once. We had been together two months and were still in the stage where the necessity to know everything about each other, tell everything about ourselves, was paramount. On weekends, over coffee in one of the many small, dark cafés; at dinners of pizzas and cheeseburgers and an occasional salad; at night in the carapace of his old Porsche Carrera between kisses so profoundly consuming that they left us both sweating and gasping, we talked and we talked and we talked. Everything we said to each other was miraculous: the fact that he had been in the National Spelling Bee and lost by misspelling "mackerel" (I don't eat it to this day). The fact that I had once dyed my hair green with food coloring before the Cornwell Country Day production of *Peter Pan.* ("Were you Wendy?" "No, I was the dog, Nana. A green sheepdog. I was a great hit.")

So when he asked me about my mother and my feelings toward

her that summer, I did not hesitate to spill out to him the thing I had never told anyone. Not my various best friends, certainly not Jeebs. Not my father, of course. No one.

"One day early that summer I went running up to her studio to ask her something," I said. "I forget what. Whether we could go somewhere or other, I think. The stairs and the third-floor hall were covered in sisal matting, and I was barefoot and was sure she couldn't hear me. It was lunchtime. We were never around her at lunchtime.

"Anyway, I got to the door of her studio and it was closed, but it always was, so in my adopted mode as supersleuth I eased the door open and looked in. She was . . . she was standing in front of her easel, facing me, and she had her shirt unbuttoned to the waist and was holding it open, and old Brooks Burns was standing in front of her with his hands all over her breasts, crawling like old spiders. Every now and then he'd bend over and smack one of them, or suck at it. He was making a kind of whistling noise in his throat; I thought maybe he was dying. She was smiling at him. It was . . . a sweet smile. Tender, like she'd give a child. After a while she said something to him and kissed him on the cheek, still smiling, and buttoned up her blouse and turned back to her easel and picked up her brush. He stood there awhile, gasping like a gaffed fish, and started to turn and leave. I was out of there and down the steps before I could get a deep breath. Then I went into the bathroom and threw up, and stayed in my bed under the covers all that day. I couldn't let anyone in, not Clara, not my father, not my summer best friend, Cecie Wentworth.

"After dinner, my mother came in with a tray of toast and milk and started to sit down beside me and—I don't know—feel my forehead or feed me or something. I said, 'No,' and turned over facing the wall. In a minute I heard her set the tray down and go out of my room and shut the door."

18

Cam was silent for a while, tracing the line of my jaw with his fingertip. Then he said, "You never cut her much slack, did you?"

"Slack? My God! That old . . . satyr! You should have seen it."

"Did it ever occur to you that she might have been doing him an exceedingly kind thing?"

"Not once," I said, knowing the truth of what he said. Tears burned in my eyes. "Never once."

The memory of that day stuck like a burr in my brain. I tried to dislodge it; I was not prepared to give up my grand and secret anomie. But I could feel it begin to trickle away like sand out of a sieve.

"Well," Cam said, "I know if I was old and you showed me your beautiful boobs it would be an act of spectacular kindness."

"That's different."

"Why is it?"

I did not answer, and presently he said, "Was she like that? I mean when you were back home, in school and all that?"

I remember that I stared at him for a long moment. It was something that had never occurred to me. "No," I said slowly, thinking back to the winters in Washington that followed those summers. "No, she wasn't. She was different at Edgewater. Come to think of it, we all were."

"Why do you think that was?"

"It was just . . . simpler there. Nothing changed. In our colony, in all those old colonies, not much had changed since the first people came there. Nothing much was new. If somebody painted a veranda or built a porch or bought a new piece of furniture, no matter how broken-down the old one was, people talked about it for weeks. New people hardly ever came in, except to visit. We ate the same things at the same time that our parents and grandparents had, or so my father said, and the grown-ups went to the same porches for cocktails and the club had the same regattas with the same boats every year, and it

19

seemed to me that we even wore the same things every summer that I could remember, things we'd left at Edgewater. And we played the same games, children's games that we wouldn't have been caught dead playing at home. It was like all of us slipped back into some kind of idyllic summer time warp; it was like time stopped. I wonder why I never thought about that before. It was a whole other life and nobody seemed to know or question it."

"So what do you think was responsible for all that? It sounds like Brigadoon."

"The ocean," I said suddenly, as sure of that as I had ever been of anything in my life. "The bay. The water."

He laughed. "You sound like a sea nymph or a kelpie. Couldn't it have been that you were all the same people you were all year, and the place, and the water, and all the old associates just called out different parts of you? Parts that just weren't . . . winter parts? People don't have two different selves, Lil. There are countless sides to all of us."

"No. We were different people there. I'm sure of that."

I was obscurely annoyed at him. He was undoubtedly right; Cam was always, among a thousand other things, my voice of pure reason. But I knew what I knew. I was different at Edgewater; I had always been different there. Back in Washington I was very much a child of my time; that sweet, smug, late fifties and early sixties world shaped me like potter's clay. I was touched by most of it. But in those Maine summers I was a creature of water and wind and tides and rock, a much simpler being, awkwardly pure and without artifice except for that last summer, when I became a spy, and there was something essentially artless even about that. Cam was wrong. The sea changed me.

I remember that I began to feel the sea recede as soon as we pulled out of the gravel driveway at Edgewater. By the time we crossed the Piscataqua River into New Hampshire, the breath of the bay was as faint as that of a dying child. By the time we reached Washington,

D.C., it was gone, though its cadence whispered to me for months, a ghost without enough strength to do a proper haunting. In the first few humid, swaddling days before my classes at the National Cathedral School for Girls began, I was like a timid, newly caged wild thing: scarcely remembering but feeling in every cell the world I had lost, sniffing and tasting the somehow familiar cage into which I had been put, creature of neither, creature of both. My mother never failed to say that I was impossible in those few days; a changeling. My father simply touched my tangled curls and said, "It's not easy when you first come back, is it? But in a few days you'll be right at home at Cathedral, and then before you know it it'll be time to go back to Maine again."

I was nine or ten when I realized that it must be hard for him, too, newly returned to the most urban fortress of George Washington University, where he taught Chaucer, Shakespeare, and the Lake Poets to juniors and seniors who had not had the grades or the wherewithal to attend one of the Ivies. George Washington has a lustrous academic name now, but it was not always so. I am certain that my father never minded that. He was essentially a content man, perhaps a happy one. He was easy in his skin and confident in his calling, and a born family man. I have seen him angry, but never at us, though he must have been sometimes. His blue eyes often narrowed at injustice, unfairness, cruelty. But I have also seen them fill with tears as he looked at us around the dinner table or together in the sun at Edgewater. I think he was a very good man. I wish I had inherited more of that, instead of his wide mouth and light, straight stature.

I think my mother minded about his academic station and his ambition, or lack of it, though. The winter before that summer had changed everything. My mother's best friend, Tatty Glover, had come for tea, bringing her daughter Charlotte to play with me. She was slightly older than I, and I thought her timorous, whiny, and a sissy. I can see that I must have intimidated her. I was impulsive, clamorous, a taker of risks and scorner of softness. I shudder to think now what those obligatory play sessions at our house must have cost her.

It was raining and I was bored with the pretty pink, green, and white bower that was my bedroom. Charlotte did not know how to play board games; she was afraid to climb on the gym set my parents had set up in the cavernous, white-painted basement for Jeebs and me. Jeebs had never paid it the least smattering of attention, being gone into the concerti and fugues of numbers inside his head by the time he was eight or nine. That left it to me—and to my father. He was delighted with it, and spent as much time as possible with me on the bars and swings. He was small, slender, firmly muscled in shoulders and arms and legs; indeed, he had the build of a gymnast. My mother was surprisingly amicable about our basement sessions on the gym set. She would only say, smiling, that she hoped all had gone well with the Flying Wallendas that day. Most of the summers of my childhood, when my mother and I and Jeebs were at Edgewater and my father's duties kept him in Washington, I wondered if, there alone in the big house on Kalorama Circle, my father swung and leaped and thumped and laughed in the silent white Olympic ring of his basement.

So it was that day, petulant and disgusted with the shrinking Charlotte, that I said, "Okay, then, you think of something. What do you like to do at home? Comb your dolls' hair?"

It was a nasty thing to say to a child I had already intimidated, and I knew it. I was half prepared for tears. Charlotte had employed them more than once to be allowed to go home early from our house. Instead, she looked at me out of brown eyes that could only be described as sly.

"Let's go listen to our mothers. Hide and listen. I do that all the time. It's fun!"

I stared at her for a moment as if she had lost her wits. Who cared what grown-up women said over tea in a Washington drawing room? On the other hand, there were thirty more minutes left of our enforced confinement. I followed her sulkily downstairs.

Our drawing room—my mother always called it that—opened off a large, high-ceilinged central hall, the focal point of which was a beautiful, curved mahogany staircase that rose three stories to the top of the house. Jeebs and I had worn out the patina on the railings, sliding down them until my mother or Lucille caught us. The drawing room was divided from the hall by heavy velvet drapes that were fastened back on either side with golden ropes and rosette holders. The flowing folds made a perfect hiding place, as secret and secure as a duck blind in a swamp. We crept into the velvet shelter, crouched down, and settled ourselves to listen.

At first the mumbled conversation was boring in the extreme; I could not make out the words themselves. I started to fidget, and Charlotte shushed me, and then I heard. It was Tatty Glover talking.

"What on earth more do you need, Liz?" she said, her voice smooth and oily and laced with humor that wasn't really humor. I did not like Tatty then any more than I did her daughter, although I could not have said why. My affection for her came much later.

"I mean, you've got this fabulous big old house on one of the best streets in Washington, and the summer house in Maine, and the Chevy Chase Club, and the Sulgrave Club, and George has the Metropolitan Club, and a distinguished career as a professor—your children, well look at them. Jeebs is an Einstein already and number one in his class at Saint Albans, and Lilly is at Cathedral and is going to be a pretty thing. I can name thirty of our friends who are green with envy of you. What else is missing?"

Over the chink of china I heard my mother's low voice. "It's just that it was all here, Tatty," she said. "There's not a piece of it that's

23

ours; we didn't choose any of it. It came lock, stock, and barrel from George's parents and grandparents. The only things we've paid for are the cars and the children's educations, and if you think that's easy on a college professor's salary, especially George's, well, think again."

"You're not saying you're poor," Tatty said. "I can't believe I'm hearing this. Everybody knows how . . . well off the old judge was."

My mother snorted. "Well," she said, "Mother Emily made short order of all that when the judge died. Every bit of it went to Susannah and Gregory and the damned Colonial Dames. I guess she figured George would be president of the university sooner or later, so the houses and the clubs and all that would do us."

"And they haven't?"

"Oh, of course they have. I don't mean to sound bitter or greedy. There's just nothing of . . . *me* in this house. When I look in the mirror I always expect I'll see old Emily Constable smirking at me under her blue wig."

"Well, hang some of your paintings. Or sell some. Get a job. Take in sewing. God, Liz. I'd swap my life for yours any day."

"You know not what you say, Tatty," my mother said. "Enough of this. I'll shut up. It's just that we were at dinner at the club last night and Jackie walked in with her sister and that movie star, the Lawford one, I think, and it was like someone set off roman candles. The energy, the pure style, the sense of joie de vivre—it made me want to come home and burn the drapes and the antimacassars. I want to be part of that. I want to know those people."

"You will, eventually, what with your good works and all," Tatty said. "You and George will be dining at the White House and never play bridge with any of us again. Look, I've got to run. See you Thursday?"

"Yes," Mother murmured, her voice subdued. "Look, don't go telling anybody I'm whining about being poor. I'm just antsy, and it's

February and George has some excruciating faculty dinner I've got to go to tonight, and I hate Earl Grey and Lucille knows it, and I've got cramps . . ."

"You don't have to explain. Jackie Kennedy does that to you. I saw her at the Sulgrave last week and wanted to come home and shred my entire wardrobe and buy a Mercedes convertible. So instead I ate a whole box of chocolates."

There was the sound of laughter and the gathering of coats and scarves.

"Charlotte? Time to go, dear," called Tatty Glover, and Charlotte and I ran silently back up the stairs and into my room.

"You're not so rich, are you?" She twinkled at me. Charlotte was famous for her twinkle. "I guess you think you are, but you heard what your mother said. Y'all don't have anything of your own. It was all your grandparents'. I guess that must have really surprised your mother. My mother says she only married your father for his money."

A red mist of rage struck me nearly blind. I had felt it before, but not often; it frightened me. I thought while it blinded me I might do something really terrible: smash, hurt, kill. I turned my head away from Charlotte Glover and clenched my teeth until my jaw throbbed.

"Your mother doesn't know shit," I said, summoning the worst word I could think of besides "fuck." "My mother married my father because he loved her the first time he saw her and courted her a year before she said she'd marry him. He said she was so beautiful that it was one of God's miracles that she ever said she'd marry him, and he was the luckiest man alive. And she says she knew the minute she laid eyes on him that he was the one she wanted to be with the rest of her life. They talk about it all the time."

"That's not what my mother says," Charlotte sang, and scurried down to take her mother's hand and smirk back up at me. Before I could think of a scathing reply, they were gone out into the early blue dusk and damp of Kalorama Circle, their lilting good-byes lingering after them.

My mother let out a long breath of relief and said, "Finally. I thought they'd never go home. I've got to get dressed for that thing of your father's tonight. Did you have a good time with Charlotte?"

"No," I said. "I hate her. She makes me itch."

My mother laughed and came up the stairs and ruffled my hair. "You hit the nail right on the head," she said. "She makes me itch, too. I think you're going to grow up to be a writer. Would you like that?"

"Are writers rich?" I said.

"Some of them are, I guess. Why, do you want to be rich?"

"I think so," I said. "I didn't know we were poor. Charlotte told me. She said you must have thought Daddy was rich, though, because her mother said you only married him for his money."

"Did she, now." My mother's soft mouth curled into a smile I had never seen. I thought fleetingly that I hoped never to see it directed at me.

"And how would her mother happen to know that, do you suppose?"

"Don't know," I said. It had never occurred to me to question the provenance of the knowledge of grown-ups. I thought that great knowledge simply came with adulthood, like driver's licenses and the right to drink liquor.

"Well," she said, kneeling and putting her arms around me and pulling my face onto her shoulder so that I could smell the lovely perfume she always wore, Vetiver—it came from Paris. "I am rich, my funny little girl. We are all rich. I have your father, who is the love of my life, and I have my children, especially my little lionhearted girl who's going to be a writer and get very rich, and we have a really wonderful life. I want you to remember all that the next time some horrible little brat like Charlotte Glover says something nasty about me. Or about any of us. We have us. We don't need anything else."

She rose and went swiftly up the stairs and presently I heard the sound of water thundering through the old pipes into the cavernous claw-footed bathtub in her bathroom. I knew it would be deep with billowing lavender-scented foam.

"That's not what you said today," I whispered to the empty stairs, but I knew she had spoken the truth. I knew that she loved us, or at least in that moment I knew it, as fully as I ever have. She was rarely so demonstrative with me. I glowed with her touch. It was the first time it had ever occurred to me that one could feel two different ways about anything, as she seemed to about her life, and I shoved the knowledge down deep, where I pushed all the things I could not yet deal with.

When my father came home that night I met him at the door, dancing with impatience.

"Tell me how you met Mama," I said. "Tell about when you first knew her."

"Can I take off my hat and coat first?" he said, smiling. "Lilly, I've told you that story a thousand times. What's going on? Have you forgotten it already?"

"No, I just like it," I said. "Tell me, Daddy."

He poured himself a glass of whiskey from the decanter on the mahogany trolley beside the drawing-room fire, and sat down in his old leather chair and motioned to me, and I ran across the room and jumped into his lap.

"Well," he said, sipping whiskey and looking at me through the amber glass, "you know that I had just graduated from Princeton and gone to work at the university. I was very young and I was really only a teaching assistant then, but it was the tail end of the Depression and the job was a plum for me. I was twenty-one and full of myself and a burning desire to fill young heads with the beauty of the English language. I couldn't have asked for a better job, and I guess I still can't."

"But Granddaddy didn't like it. He wanted you to be a judge like he was."

I had heard the story many times.

"No, he didn't. He wanted me to go on to Harvard Law like he had, carry on the family tradition and all that. Luckily my brother Gregory came along and filled that position beautifully, so the heat was off me a little. Anyway, the start of my second year at the university, the dean of the department hired a new secretary to replace the old battle-ax who had ruled over us all, and—"

"It was Mother!" I shouted.

"It was your mother," he agreed, hugging me lightly. "Well, the minute I saw her I was a goner, along with everybody else in the department and half the students, but she was very reserved and proper and wouldn't give anyone the time of day. Lord, she was pretty! I used to stand just outside her office and watch her work. She was quick and quiet and very good at her job; for the first time in living memory the department ran like clockwork. I don't think I ever would have worked up the courage to ask her out if I'd known how young she was."

"Tell how young!"

"She was barely eighteen," he said. "But she never seemed young in the silly sort of way that some young girls do. She had just graduated from high school and the aunt and uncle she lived with couldn't afford college and probably wouldn't have sent her anyway—they were none too gracious about taking her in when her parents were killed in a trolley accident, when she was only ten—and so she knew she'd have to get a job. Well, she'd wanted to go to college in the worst kind of way, and she figured the next best thing would be to work for one, and George Washington was easier for her to get to on the trolley than any other school in D.C., so she marched right in and up to the English

28

Department and asked to see the head, and the dean hired her that day. I still don't know how she got past the old gorgon who was her predecessor. But your mother had her ways. Still does, don't you think?"

"And then . . ."

"And then the rest is history," he said, kissing the top of my head and depositing me on the floor. "We eventually got married and had Jeebs and you and moved into this house when my parents were gone, and here we are. If there's a happier ending to a story than that, I haven't heard it."

"But Grandmother and Granddaddy didn't like her at first . . ."

"No," he said slowly. "But it wasn't that they didn't like her. They just had never met anybody like her, a very young girl from a not-so-well-off family who was making her own way in the world. They had wanted me to marry a society girl, you know, the kind you see in the papers, and have a huge wedding and all that stuff. But then Gregory did that; he married Susannah Carter of the Virginia Carters, and they immediately set about producing gilded offspring, and so I was off the hook again. Besides, when they really got to know her, they both came to like and love your mother. My father told me the day before he died that he couldn't have asked for a more loving and appropriate wife for me than your mother, and he reckoned he'd been a hardheaded old fool about her in the beginning."

"And you said . . ."

"And I said yes. You hop down now, Lilly. I've got to get changed."

I got down, but lingered, still troubled. Then I said, "If somebody tells you a lie about somebody else and you know it's not true, what should you do about it?"

"Depends on the lie, I guess," he said, "and who told about whom. Did somebody tell you a lie?"

"Yes. And I knew it was. I was really, really mad. I thought I might hit her."

29

"Did you?"

"No."

"Good. It's rarely a solution. Who told you a lie, and about whom?"

"That stupid Charlotte Glover. It was about Mama. She said her mother told her."

"Ah, the Glover ladies," he said, smiling and sighing. "A pair of she-hounds in full spate, as they've always been. You did the right thing. It wouldn't have done a bit of good to swat Charlotte. Her kind never learns."

"I can still go back and hit her, you know," I said.

"Heaven forbid," he said. "Then you'd become just like her. You don't want that, do you?"

"No. But maybe a little poke . . ."

"No pokes," he said, and went out of the drawing room and up the stairs. It struck me only later that he had not asked what Charlotte Glover had said about my mother.

"You must have been a handful," Cam said. "I don't see much of that side of you."

It was the same season, the season of the great tide of talking, and we were sitting in a small café on M Street that had cheap hamburgers. Since I lived at home and Cam shared a ramshackle apartment with a med student at Johns Hopkins, cafés and the breath-fogged Porsche were about the only places we spent much time together. Yet we two were a universe. There was no room there for others. Nor had I visited his family in the big old country house on the James River, near Williamsburg. The McCalls had a pied-à-terre in Alexandria and a summer place in the Caribbean, but since the Judge's retirement they spent most of their time at River House. I knew the family had money, but I had not yet thought much about it. Almost everybody our family knew in Washington "had money," or that even more luminous asset, "family." Cam and I were still wrapped tightly in the glove of ourselves; our contexts would come later.

"I rarely saw the lovely and talented Charlotte again, though I got regular bulletins about her," I said. "Her mother still came to visit, but not nearly so often, and my mother dropped their weekly bridge game. Not many of her friends made the cut. She started to paint in earnest after that afternoon, and I became a spy."

"Did you lose any friends in the brouhaha? If it had been my mother, I would have been fiercely forbidden any consorting with the offspring of the enemy. Amelia McCall didn't take no shit from anybody. Still doesn't."

"Oh, no, I had my own crowd," I said, thinking back. "There was a little bunch of us from Cathedral who were inseparable. We snubbed everybody else who might have been benighted enough to want to join us. I can see now that we were obnoxious and mean-spirited, but back then that little coven was the central fact of our lives. We called ourselves the T Club, and told our parents that the T stood for Thursday, since our once-a-month formal meetings always took place on Thursday afternoons after hockey practice. We were together constantly, but that Thursday was not to be missed."

"What did the T stand for?"

"Thieves. We stole things and brought them to the meetings and voted on who'd made the best heist."

He laughed. The deep dimple that creased his left cheek flashed, and I felt my stomach go warm.

"What in God's name did a bunch of eleven-year-olds steal?"

"Well, sexy things, I guess, or things we thought were sexy. I stole a bra from Woodward and Lothrop. It was one of those padded, pointed things that looked like the bumper of a 'fifty-two Stude-baker. I wore it to the meeting and won the prize for the month. I

31

didn't need a bra for another two years and I never wore it, but I still have it."

"What on earth for?"

I leaned against him in the wire chair next to me and rubbed against his shoulder.

"To see if it would get guys like you excited when I got older."

I felt his thumb trace my nipple and my breath came up into my throat.

"You don't need to do that," he murmured. "Christ, we're going to have to find a place. So what else did you-all steal?"

"Margaret Canfield stole a package of rubbers from Peoples Drug Store at Chevy Chase Circle. We spent the whole meeting trying to decide quite what you did with them. Christine Dawson stole a copy of *Playboy* from the same drugstore. It had just come out. It was wrapped in brown paper: she had to sneak behind the counter to get it. We laughed knowingly at the cartoons, but I don't think any of them really made sense to us. By the time spring came we had quite a collection of erotica. I don't remember where we kept it. I usually dropped out in the spring."

"Why?"

"I'm not sure. Things just . . . changed. I wanted to be alone; I spent a lot of time in my room, reading or listening to records. The thought of the club—or, rather, the things we stole—made me feel a little sick. I usually got asthma about that time, too. I remember my mother saying to my father after one of my attacks that it was time to go to Edgewater."

"So the sea could breathe with you."

"And when we got there, and it did, I was different again. I was a child, a real one. There was nothing left of that thieving little pseudo-sophisticate. I didn't even remember her."

He held up a finger for the check and turned to kiss me lightly.

It morphed into a rather unseemly kiss for a public place, as they all did. When he drew away from me he was grinning.

"What?"

"I was just thinking of your little gang at Edgewater, and their names: Randall, Wentworth, Gardiner, Constable—almost a caricature of the entire WASP gene pool. Names that ring in New England history. I'll bet a black or a Buddhist or a Jew, or even a Catholic, never set foot on the soil of Carter's Cove. I bet the earth would have crumbled."

Before my next breath, thick, lightless silence fell down over me like a glass bell jar. Sound imploded; I could feel the wind of it on my face. I could hear nothing; I could see only dimly. My throat closed and my breath gargled in my chest. In the foggy airlessness I heard sounds: the hollow thudding of running feet on our dock at Edgewater; faint, anguished cries; the high crooning of the wind in the tops of the pointed firs; the bay, which was not breathing now, but howling out its anger. I smelled blowing salt fog and felt rain stinging my face, and saw flashlights and lanterns bobbing in the darkness. I heard a child crying, wildly, inconsolably, and knew it was me. The whole thing was torn from someplace so deeply buried inside of me that I thought if I could touch it, it would be sticky with my blood and viscera.

By the time Cam was on his feet and pounding me on the back, I could begin to breathe again, and sat taking deep, sobbing gulps of stale air, coughing. People were looking at us. A few had half risen from their chairs.

"Lilly, what in the name of God! We need to get you to a doctor."

"No," I protested, taking deeper, slower breaths. My sight cleared and my ears no longer rang with awfulness. I felt, simply, hollowed out, forever hollowed and empty.

"I swallowed the wrong way. I'm okay. What were we talking about? Oh, yeah—well, as a matter of fact, we did have a Jew at Edgewater once. But at first you couldn't really tell, and he didn't stay long."

CHAPTER

2

Though I told Cam, in one of those confession-filled winter nights when we were first together, that the summers at Edgewater were perfect, seamless, and endless in their salt-steeped sameness, it was not true. That summer of 1962, even before I became a spy in my mother's house, the changes began. Some were so small, almost infinitesimal, they hardly rippled the skin of consciousness. But some rang like bells. The first of these came on our first day at the cottage, one of the very first of the gilded days that hung like heavy fruit just within our grasp. On this day, after I had dashed to the seawall and had been given breath, flying came back to me.

From the first moment of my life I remember, I knew that people could fly. I knew it in a way deeper and wider than dreams, though I often dreamed of flying, too. I knew it by the dying stir in the streaks of sunlight, in which golden dust motes danced, made by the bars of my crib, the light, soft wafts of air left by people who had flown in to visit me and then departed. My mother? My nurse? My father, or brother? A stranger? I never knew, only that someone had been there and flown away, someone who left comfort and beneficence in his or her wake. It did not seem to matter a great deal who it was.

I knew it in the little warm wind smelling of high space that eddied

34

around my carriage or, later, around myself and a companion when we were playing in my backyard, or, perhaps, in nearby Rock Creek Park. The air above and about me then would seem alive with unseen wings and the almost palpable brushings of fabric and fleeting human fingers. Before I could talk, my mother and father told me later, I would often point into middle air or a sun dazzle and smile and crow and cry out, "Fy! Fy!"

It was a long time before they figured out I was saying "Fly." And when they did, I gather there was no little concern about me. It is one thing to have a baby daughter who sees iridescent dust motes dancing in sunlight, or scudding clouds, and believes that they are corporeal beings flying by. It is quite another when that daughter gains years and speech and presumably intelligence a bit higher than normal, and still insists that people fly. My delight in my airborne entourage might have been downright eerie, but I recall that it was a calm, matter-of-fact delight, such as a child would feel at the appearance of a pet puppy or kitten. After a while, my parents gave up trying to disabuse me of my extraterrestrial notions and simply chatted with me when I brought them up, or questioned me gently and with real interest. Once I overheard my father say to my mother, "If she is still talking about it when she is sixteen it'll be the time to worry. Right now I'm sort of enjoying it. It's quite a lovely turn of fancy."

I don't remember what my mother said to that. At any rate, no one whisked me to a child's shrink, or consulted with my teachers and attendants in preschool or kindergarten. So my flying visitants were largely the property of my family, and a few chosen and gullible friends, and remained so until well into grade school. I've always felt fortunate that my parents, whom I came later to know were considered by some to be eccentric and far too permissive when it came to child-rearing, were as they were. Flying was a wide gilt skein of joy in the fabric of my childhood.

"Do you see them fly?" my father would say, leaning over my bed at story time and smiling at me.

"No, but I see where they've been, and I almost see them. I don't think they let you really see them. People would talk about them and then they couldn't do it anymore!" I said.

"Good point," he would say. "Do other people ever see them? Can everybody do it? Can you?"

"I don't think everybody can," I said once, slowly. "Maybe they could once, but now I think not so many people can. Maybe you forget. Or maybe some just never could do it. I can, I think, but I don't really remember it after I have, just the way it felt. But you know, Jeebs could never do it."

My father laughed heartily, and said he thought I had that right. He related the conversation at supper the next night and Jeebs, who was fed up to the gills with a sister who prattled constantly about flying, said waspishly, "I bet I could, too, if I wanted to. It's just aerodynamics. But everybody knows that people can't fly and never could, or we'd know about it. You're crazy as a loon, Lilly."

My mother laughed too, and gave my curls a little twist, and reached out and pushed Jeebs's soft, heavy, dark hair off his glasses. Even then Jeebs looked like a scientist, a miniature one, his intense dark eyes behind the thick, round lenses focused almost permanently inside his head.

"My dear Dr. Jeebs," she said, "you have many and singular talents, and will one day no doubt win a Nobel Prize in something no one has ever heard of, but I do not think you could ever fly. Lilly, on the other hand . . ." and her voice faded away, and her smile widened.

Love and wings bloomed inside me.

Children forget quickly and without regret, but somehow they rarely lose the forgotten thing. It sinks quietly deep inside them and drifts into the maw of childhood as neatly as a tender new bone into a forming skeleton, and there it stays: part of the fabric of Child. After a time I did not talk so much about flying; I did not, after all, ever see my ethereal visitants, and other and newer furniture of childhood was brighter and clearer. Occasionally I said, as casually as I might say anything unremarkable and of my world, "Back when people could fly . . ." but my family and the few friends who knew of my celestial predilection usually ignored me. And every now and then I would dream of flying. I dreamed more than once of swimming through a pink and blue mist, turning and diving and rising as in water rather than air but knowing in the dream that I was flying, so full of rapture and transcendence that I would wake with tears on my face at losing the dream. After those dreams it occurred to me that you could fly without wings if you chose, simply by swimming into the air, and I was much comforted by this. I had always been puzzled by where the wings were kept.

By that summer of 1962 flying was, to me, perhaps a once-a-year dream, or something brought sharply alive for a snip of a second by a curl of fragrance in the air, a taste, melting instantly. So when I whistled for Wilma on that first day and ran from the seawall over the rock promontory to the left of the cove and up it to where the rocks crested in a sort of red-granite crow's nest, high above the beach and the house and the bay, it was not to look farther up, but down.

There it was, the familiar sweep; from the firs and rooftops of Retreat Colony to the far left, and the masts in Center Harbor and the boatyard beyond, and the sweep of water where Eggemoggin Reach became Jericho and then Blue Hill Bay, down the coast to the right, where the chimneys of the old cottages of which ours was one broke the forest, and the sea stretched, glittering in small dimpled cat's-paws where little winds broke it, over and under the great green Deer Isle Bridge, and where Deer Isle lies, and beyond it all to the low, sweet body of Great Owls Head Island. It was a locally famous and much-recommended view; almost everyone's visitors were driven to climb the rocks and gaze at it, especially when sunset stained everything silver and magenta and lavender and a furious, hungry pink. I had always regarded it as my own. I was the only one of our small crowd who bothered to come to the top of the headland; the others contented themselves with diving from its lower rocks into the bay. Mr. Carl Forshee, who owned the old cedar cottage that lay just behind the headland and whose property it was, feared for our safety (and lawsuits, my mother said), and drove us away whenever he caught us swimming from it. But in the end he could not stem the tide of small brown bodies silver with seawater arching off his rocks, so he simply put up a sign that said ANYONE SWIMMING FROM THESE ROCKS WILL BE PROSECUTED and left it at that. We swam. He did not prosecute.

My father might have come with me on this ritual first climb to the rooftop of our world; he was taking a summer's sabbatical at Edgewater to pursue his work on the songs and ballads of John Donne, of which none were known to exist but which he was stubbornly certain did somewhere, and he was determined to unearth and preserve them.

"If you did, would we be rich?" I asked him once.

He looked at me in surprise.

"I have no idea, Lilly. But the world would be richer by far for the finding of them."

Since that made little sense to me, I did not pursue it, and learned to leave him alone when he was deep in Donne. He was on this glowing, pulsing first day, so I climbed the staircase to the top of our summer world with only panting, scrabbling Wilma for company.

For some reason, I shut my eyes before I looked. Then I opened them, and the world of my summers wheeled around me. I drew in a breath; down below on earth, you smelled clean, still-cold, kelpy sea and warming rock and newly mown grass and smoke from the dying fires of the cold morning. Not much in the way of flowers bloomed this early in June, but there was a fresh acrid smell of new vegetation and the smoky musk of wild lupines, and somebody's breakfast bacon always seemed to linger. But up there you smelled only wind and empty space and the deeper, darker body odors of the great Atlantic, off beyond the outer ledges and islands. A wild smell, the old one.

The day was so clear that everything—the horizon, the far curve of Great Owls Head, Deer Isle—was edged in blue. The sky was the tender, almost crooning blue of early summer; I knew that the great clarion cobalt that stained earth and water would not come until some pre-autumn day in late August. But it was still enough to steep everything in the absolute purity of blue. The dimples of the cat's-paws spoke of winds to come; this time of year it usually started up a little after lunch, setting all the colony flags to snapping and driving our mothers indoors for sweaters. But now it was calm. The sun seemed stronger here. I shucked off my hated cardigan and kicked off my sandals and gripped the grainy pinnacle of granite with my long toes. Pure, bottomless, meaningless joy gripped me so hard that my head swam with it and I clenched my eyes shut, watching the whorls of light pinwheel behind them. It was not a new feeling; children have it fairly often, I think. But I do not remember that it came back to me after that day. Wilma leaned against me and thumped his tail and I opened my eyes again.

Down below, precisely in the center of the symmetrical cove that cradled our beach and land, my grandfather's house sat like a jewel in a rajah's turban. It was painted a strange pea green, with dark red trim and black shutters, and it had grown from a simple two-story New England colonial to a jumble of wings and ells and porches and terraces that looked crumpled and thrown down as from a giant's hand. But somehow it was not awkward. It looked as if it had sprung, mushroom-like, from the sandy earth and the forest behind it after one rain, organic and right. It looked no age at all, but at the same time far older than I knew it was, fully as old as the oldest cottage in our little enclave or the larger one over at Retreat. Only our car and station wagon stood in the driveway now, but I knew that soon it would be thronged with the cars of visitors and the trucks of deliverymen and the wagons and bicycles of all of us. Already a kite and upset croquet set lay on the side lawn. Shoes littered the deck by the kitchen door. Screened doors slammed and the snap of sails filling with wind echoed off the water and the sound of the Palestrina to which my father always worked curled up with the dying smoke from our fireplace.

Edgewater. It had always been here. I had always been here.

"It's a real Bar Harbor day," I said to Wilma, who thumped his tail and went back to licking his balls luxuriously. Wilma was all male, unmistakably and irrevocably male. He was rawboned, lank, flop eared, often stinky, and always happy. He was my dog and would be no one else's; I had found him when he was a small puppy, tottering around a garbage can in the kindergarten play yard, starved and crawling with fleas.

Even then he was happy; his small, generic tan-and-brown face lit into a wide white smile when he saw me, and he pranced over to me, weaving a little from weakness and rubbery puppy legs, and sat down on my shoe. The matter was settled then and there. I took him home wrapped in my sweater, crooning to him, and fed him a mush of carrots and onions and potatoes from last night's pot roast, and was pouring milk into my Grandmother Constable's delicate Haviland consommé cup when my mother arrived in the kitchen.

"No. Absolutely not," she said, looking at the puppy, who gave her a milky grin and began gnawing at the fleas on his feet.

"You'll have to take him back to wherever you found him. He's probably carrying plague or something even worse." And when I set up a howl, she said hastily, "I bet his mommy misses him. You don't want to take him away from his mommy, do you?"

"He's got no mommy," I wailed. "Look at him! Does he look like he's got a mommy?"

There was no rebuttal to this; the puppy was the most patently motherless creature anyone had ever seen.

"Well, we'll have to take him somewhere," my mother said. "You better get used to that."

"Will not!" I cried. "Will not! Will not willnot willnot willnot willnot . . ."

It had risen to a dirge of anger and tragedy that was positively Aristotelian in tenor and volume when my father came into the kitchen. He looked at me, feet planted on the kitchen floor, eyes screwed shut, mouth open, cheeks stained with rage; looked at the tatty puppy already asleep on my shoulder, and said, "What a fine puppy. I'll bet it'll be a grand grown-up, a real watchdog. A female, is she? Wilma, you've named her?"

It was soon apparent that Wilma was a boy dog, but by then it was too late; Wilma he became and Wilma he stayed. He turned into a huge, flat-pawed, tongue-lolling, tail-whipping black-and-tan dog with what seemed to be more than a little wolf in him. His teeth were white and saber-sharp, his growl and bark were formidable, his yellow eyes under his thick tan eyebrows could look murder at you. But Wilma never murdered, seldom if ever barked, and growled only once, to my knowledge, when I was about to reach down and pick up a baby porcupine. Wilma was a lover, not a fighter, and even if he would win no Best in Shows, he was a great favorite with my small crowd at Edgewater. He would follow us anywhere, grinning and larruping, would accept huge hugs and from any one of us, no matter how rib-crushing, and was seldom more than a yard or two from my side. He even slept with me in my narrow iron cot at night, not flinching when I rolled over on him or shoved him out of my space. Cleaned up and well fed, he was really quite a presentable dog, though never handsome, and only seldom did he fart in company. But when he did he could clear a room in five seconds. I remember a Thanksgiving when I was about nine, when there must have been twenty people clustered in front of the fire, chatting genteelly and sipping sherry and waiting for dinner. My prepossessing Constable grandparents were among them. All of a sudden, the crowd surged swiftly away from the fire en masse, like some many-celled sea organism scuttling along the sandy bottom. I was watching from the kitchen, having begged a turkey drumstick from a harried Lucille, sweating in her white apron and cap. I knew what had happened. When the crowd dispersed, there was Wilma, lying contentedly on the hearth rug, nodding with warmth and the comfort of the post-fart condition.

Wilma seldom joined us for state occasions after that.

A Bar Harbor day was a day so clear that there were sharp blue lines around everything: horizon, hills, mountains, trees, faraway islands. On such days the ladies of the colony would announce a trip to Bar Harbor, about an hour's drive away, to drift along the main street and try to sift some gold from the dross of tourist displays in windows: moose heads on towels, pillows stuffed with pine and balsam, whale ashtrays, stumps carved into stodgy black bears. No one from Carter's Cove ever bought anything in the town, but the ritual had to be observed. Everyone then went to Testa's for Bloody Marys and lobster salad. Afterward there might be a visit to the glorious Abby Aldrich Rockefeller Garden in Seal Harbor. I remember that the gardens were still open to the public then. And then the obligatory drive around the outer loop road to watch the sea battering furiously at Mount Desert, with a stop at Thunder Hole to see if the incoming tide would boom and thunder under the hollow rocks when it rushed in and send up a huge spray of white, salty foam. Then a stop at Jordan Pond, at the pond house, for tea and popovers that tasted to me like encrusted air. And then home, into the sunset that would soon bloom over our cove and would, on such a day, be breath stopping, a conflagration of purple, orange, pink, vermillion, all shot with gold.

"It's the prettiest one ever," someone would say, and everyone else would mutter assent, and then, in a day or so, one even more spectacular would bloom in the west and the chorus would begin again. The sunsets of Carter's Cove were the exclamation points to our days, the gifts given us whether deserved or not. Few of us did not walk out to see the sunsets. They were our earthly treasure.

After such a day, we usually had two or three days of wind and rain and fog. The natives around us called those perfect days weather breeders, and they were seldom wrong. I was glad for the storms. I could stay huddled in a moldy blanket in some upstairs nook or on the living room couch in front of the fire with Wilma, reading, reading. And best of all, there would be no chance at all of going to Bar Harbor. I hated Bar Harbor. I hated all of Mount Desert. I did not care that it was considered one of the world's great scenic attractions. There the sea did not breathe with me, but roared and bellowed and hissed and threatened, and I would come home with my entire body aching from muscles stiffened against the Mount Desert sea.

I was just considering going down to see who was around and what sort of sandwiches Clara had set out for us when I heard my mother's voice from the lawn below, pitched so that I could not claim not to have heard her.

"Lilly? Come on down. Peaches is here, and we're having a little party for her."

"Peaches is a shitass," I told Wilma, and he grinned and stretched and rose, and we started unwillingly down into the summer of Peaches Davenport.

43

I hated Peaches. I had hated her ever since I'd first heard of her, a couple of months before we came to Edgewater. My mother had kept Jeebs and me at the dinner table after dessert one evening and said she had something to tell us: that a new little girl would be spending the summer at Edgewater, and she wanted us to be especially kind because the child had just gone through a terrible tragedy. Her name was Roberta Davenport, but she'd always been called Peaches because of her pretty coloring. She was the granddaughter of a retired Episcopal canon from Baltimore and his gentle, otherworldly wife. The Davenports summered in a big old Victorian down the shore from us toward Sedgwick, and in all the time I had known them, I had never known children to be in the house. Young grown-ups, yes: their son and his wife, and their daughter and her college friends, were in and out, though not often. Someone had told me it was because old Mrs. Davenport suffered from Nerves, and children caused her great distress. She was kind and interested when she encountered the children of Carter's Cove, but in an abstracted way, and never paused to chat or came in to visit in our houses, as all the other grown-ups did.

"He's just a saint, to put up with all those vapors and 'conditions,'" my friend Cecie Wentworth's silly mother said to my mother once, back in my spying days. "She keeps him so cloistered away, even up here, and he's such a masculine, vigorous man. You know he'd rather be out sailing or hiking or whatever with the other men."

Canon Davenport, in fact, was a vigorous and masculine man. He was tall, broad, tanned even though he was ostensibly cloistered, pitch-black of hair and mustache even at his age, which I thought to be middle seventies or somewhere near it—at death's door, practically. He had a cultivated, resounding voice that could be heard from one end of Carter's Cove to the other, and a narrow white smile like a wolverine's. I could not imagine him dispensing compassion and Christly love from a pulpit.

"Peaches is going to be living with them now," my mother said. "Her mother and father, the Davenports' son and his wife, were killed at a railroad crossing in Baltimore last year. Of course the canon and his wife took her in and, as I understand it, really brought Peaches back to life. She was very ill with shock and grief; I gather she's a rather sensitive child. But she's doing much better now, and the Davenports thought a summer in the Maine air, with children her own age, might be just the thing for her. I gather she's scarcely been out of their sight since the accident. I want you two to be especially nice to her, include her in your games, take her sailing and swimming, all that. Lilly, she's just your age, eleven, and I think you might even know her, or at least have met her at some little party or other. Her best friend is Charlotte Glover—you know, Tatty's little girl."

A flash of corkscrew curls and sly, knowing eyes swam in my head, and I shook it furiously.

"Elizabeth," my mother said in the "you're in trouble" voice I seldom heard, "you will be nice to that little girl or you will go to camp this summer and not set foot at Edgewater. I mean it. No matter what that poor child is like, she's been through something you cannot even imagine, and she needs young friends around her. The Davenports are lovely people, but they're elderly. It's not enough for a young girl."

"Okay," I said sulkily. "I'll ask her to go everywhere we go. But you can't make me like her."

My mother stared levelly at me for a long moment, and then said, "I don't ask that. But one unkindness on your part and I will know it. Don't think I won't."

I didn't think she wouldn't. My mother's astonishing, chatoyant gray eyes could see through solid walls and beyond to the horizon. I had no doubt of that.

"All right," she said. "Jeebs?"

45

"Yeah," Jeebs said, far away in some airborne equation. "Okay. No big deal."

Although I knew he would emerge from the summer without the slightest notion of who Peaches Davenport was, and knew that my mother knew it, apparently she was satisfied. "Good," she said. "They get there the same day we do. We'll have a little luncheon for her."

Until I heard my mother's voice that morning, I had buried the coming of Peaches deep. Mulish obstinacy flooded me. I would nod to the little waif, wolf a sandwich, summon my special gang, and sail my Beetle Cat over to Sunderson's Island, where, Clara had told me that morning, the ospreys were back in the nest on the big fir, and you could just see the babies. Peaches could practice her waifdom on the timid Forrest twins, and on Harriet Randall, who stuttered badly and often found reasons not to join us in our summer maraudings. They should be a gracious plenty for her.

My summer best friend, Cecie Wentworth, met me halfway down the slope. She was sweating and panting, as if she'd been running. I knew she'd climbed up from the beach.

"She's got on a *dress*," Cecie gasped, "and a ribbon in her hair, and shoes! And she's white as a sheet and she gets tears in her eyes when she talks to you. *If* she talks to you. So far she hasn't talked to anybody but the boys. They're reacting like flies caught in honey. It's really awful! What are we going to do with her all summer?"

"Nothing," I said, hugging her. I had not seen her since last summer; she went to Holton Arms and our crowds didn't overlap. In fact, I'm not sure we would have even liked each other if they had. Cecie was tall and willowy and going-to-be-pretty-but-not-yet, and an accomplished equestrienne. We could not have been less alike. But what we had together was Carter's Cove, and the breathing reach, and the rocks and the pointed firs and the sun and the winds and the birds that rode them, and when we saw each other for the first time each June, we clamped together with the same sharp little click that those Scottie dogs, the black-and-white ones with magnets, did. After that, no one could have parted us. A best friend is as crucial to a child as air to breathe and food to eat. A child's heart and mind are not yet deep and dark enough to hold secrets. They must be shared, or they will implode.

"We can pretend we don't see her," Cecie said. "Just look right through her all summer. 'What girl? I don't see any girl.'"

"Our mothers would kill us," I said. "We need to do secret stuff. Stuff nobody sees us do, so we can't get blamed for it."

"Like what?"

"Oh, like putting spiders in her bed. I know where there's some wolf spiders back in the woods as big as pancakes."

"Do they bite?"

"Well, I guess they bite something; they have to eat. I don't think they bite people, though. But they're hairy. And they jump."

Cecie shuddered.

"Wouldn't just plain old short-sheeting do? I learned how to do that at camp."

"Not good enough. We could take her kayaking and give her Jeebs's old kayak. It's got a slow leak that you can't see, but it fills up pretty quick. We can always say we didn't know."

"What if she can't swim?"

"Well, we can haul her out and half drown her in the process and still get credit for being heroes. Yeah. I like that."

"We'll probably think of some other good stuff as the summer goes on," Cecie said. "Meanwhile, let's just be sweet as sugar and cut out of there as fast as we can. Daddy said he heard the ospreys are back over on Sunderson's. There are babies."

"Yeah. That's what I heard, too. I think most of the boys will come with us. Peachie-Pie probably won't want to get her dress dirty, so she'll be stuck with the old Davenports. They can look at those old pictures you put in the what's-it."

On the rare occasions when Mrs. Davenport was forced to include children at one of her occasions, she herded them into the big screened porch and gave them ancient photographs of unknown Davenports on long-ago vacations in places like the pyramids of Egypt, or Niagara Falls, that one looked at through a viewing contraption you held up to your eyes. We had all seen them a myriad of times. It was considered extreme punishment.

We stumbled down toward the base of the cliff, scattering stones as we went. Wilma cut off the path, nose in the sedge, snuffling after some unseen wild creature. I didn't call him back; he had never caught anything.

We slid out onto the stony beach and looked up toward Edgewater. There was a small group of people on the lawn, both children and grown-ups. The umbrella table had been set up, and Clara was coming down from the terrace bearing a cake plate. Laughter hung in the water-clear air.

"Let 'em eat cake," I muttered.

My mother saw us and gestured.

"Come on, you two. Peaches has been waiting to meet you."

"I just bet," Cecie said.

We climbed over the little cliff path and swung our legs over the seawall and walked barefoot through the cool, silky early-summer grass toward the group. They were in a circle, grown-ups at the rear, my crowd and Jeebs at the front. They were all laughing and chattering, even the twins, who rarely ever laughed. Even the older Davenports. My father stood behind my mother, smiling a little bemusedly. He saw us and grinned. There was something in the grin that I didn't know.

When we reached the circle, I could see that a girl sat in its center on one of our Adirondack chairs that were sparkling green with the new paint Seth or Clara had administered, as they did every year. The first thing you noticed was her hair. It looked like a fire on her head, a conflagration of strawberry blond—dark gold in the morning sun. It hung in ringlets to her shoulders, which were bare and gardenia white in her blue-flowered sundress. The rest of her was white, too, satiny, sunless, perfect white, unblemished by scabs and scars and smears of Maine dirt. Her small white feet, with tiny, iridescent toenails, were slipped into blue leather sandals that matched her dress. Her hands, similarly pristine, were clasped loosely in her lap. She lifted her head at our approach, and I could see why they called her Peaches. She was exquisite, like a Titian miniature, her skin delicately flushed with apricot, her mouth like a little strawberry, just ripened. She had the bluest eyes and the longest eyelashes I had ever seen. When she smiled, twin dimples studded her cheeks. Her teeth were pearls.

My hatred flamed and danced.

"Peaches," my mother said, "the dirtiest one is my daughter, Lilly, and that's her friend Cecie Wentworth. I wish I could say that they don't usually look this way, but in fact they do. Girls, this is Peaches Davenport."

"H'lo," Cecie and I mumbled.

"I'm so pleased to meet you," Peaches said. Her voice was like a little bell. "I've heard so much about you. Grandmother and Grandfather told me you were just my age. I think I'll be going to school with you this fall at Cathedral. I went to a French school at home . . ."

Her voice faltered and the incredible eyes filmed over with a sheen of tears. She looked down at her hands.

We all remembered the tragedy then. It would have been hard to forget it. Sympathetic murmurs from the grown-ups hung in the air, and the boys in my crowd cleared their throats and moved closer to her. They were mesmerized, as though Peaches were a cobra.

She looked up again, brightly, though small tears still trembled on her eyelashes.

"Well . . . good," I said, lamely.

"Actually, I go to Holton Arms," Cecie said pleasantly.

"Oh, I'm sorry," Peaches said. "But I'll bet it's a good school. Like Cathedral, almost."

"Oh, yeah," Cecie said in a voice I had never heard, dry and puckered. "Almost."

Clara set down the cake, a splendid one, angel cake frosted with chocolate and adorned with strawberries, and Mother said, "Now, who's ready for some cake?"

The boys surged toward the table, and then stopped and looked at Peaches. She did not move from her chair.

"Clara," Mother said, "if you'll just slice it, I think one of the boys will be glad to take a piece to Peaches. The rest of us can serve ourselves. And there's lemonade, too."

"I'll get it," several boys' voices chorused.

"I've got it," a deeper voice said. Jeebs. Jeebs, looking at Peaches Davenport as if she were something perfect and Pythagorean. And he got a plate of cake and a glass of lemonade and brought it to Peaches and put it down on the arm of her chair.

"Why, thank you . . . is it Jeebs? Why do they call you that?" she asked, smiling her pointed kitten's smile up at him.

"It's my initials," Jeebs said, blushing maroon. I stared. I had never seen Jeebs blush in my life. "GBS, for George Bayard Semmes."

"Semmes?" Peaches raised a silky eyebrow. "Aren't you a Constable? I thought . . ."

"I have three surnames," Jeebs said, going from maroon to the black-red of an old-fashioned velvet drape.

"Oh, how wonderful," Peaches trilled. "I've never known anybody with three names before. Nobody will ever forget you, will they?"

50

Jeebs choked.

None of my crowd had even acknowledged Cecie and me. I said, in a voice that sounded false and silly even to me, "Hey, y'all, the ospreys are back on Sunderson's and they've got babies. Let's sail over there after lunch and see them."

I waited for the chorus of enthusiastic agreement. None came. Somehow, over the past two summers, I had become something of the group's leader, daring to go places, do things, that some of the others, perhaps, would not. It was not a conscious thing; it was just that somehow, during the years of gymnastics with my father in the basement at home, I had lost fear. Where I led, the children of Carter's Cove usually followed. Their silence puzzled and then stung, as I understood it.

"I mean Peaches, too," I said.

"Oh, my dear . . . boats? I think it's a little soon for Peaches to try boats," old Mrs. Davenport said. "I had thought you young people might come over after lunch and look at the slides Peaches made of her vacation in Europe last summer. They're really lovely—Paris and London and Rome, and the Riviera, and all the castles on the Rhine."

There was another silence.

"They're the last ones I have of my mother and father," Peaches said softly, the sheen of tears glistening in her eyes again. "They were killed soon after we got home last summer."

She dropped her lids again. Her grandmother and grandfather made small sounds of distress. All the boys at once exclaimed, "Great, let's do that!"

I simply stared at them. No one would meet my eyes. My mother smiled fixedly. Glancing at my father, I saw that his eyebrows were drawn together in sort of a perplexed half frown.

"Well," I said, my voice sounding loud and strident, "Cecie and I are going to go. Maybe we can see the slides another time."

My mother opened her mouth to protest just at the moment

when Wilma burst out of the thicket and bounded up the beach to the lawn, barking his joy at the sheer splendor of the morning, and at all his people gathered on his lawn. He cleared the seawall in one mighty jump and plunged into the crowd, tail wagging madly.

Peaches began to scream. She shut her eyes and screwed up her face and clapped her hands over it and screamed and screamed and screamed. She was drawn up in the chair into a knot, and her heels drummed the wood, and her head jerked back and forth. The screams were high and pierced the blue morning like a knife. I had never heard anything like them. I could only stand and stare. Wilma looked at the writhing shape in the chair and bounded in to join the game. He jumped up and licked Peaches' covered face, barking in exultation.

"Gethimoffgethimoffgethimoffget him off!" Peaches screamed.

Several of the crowd started toward them, but Jeebs stepped in and grabbed Wilma by his collar and jerked him back furiously across the lawn and into the house. Wilma yelped in surprise and pain. None of us had ever hurt him before. I felt red fury surge behind my eyes.

"You let go of him, Jeebs Constable! He's my dog, and you're hurting him. You know he wouldn't hurt her, he was just playing . . ."

I began to cry, embarrassing myself profoundly, and started after Jeebs and Wilma, whose howls of grief at being shut into the house away from his people rang down the reach.

"I didn't realize you had a large dog," Canon Davenport said icily. "I trust he can be confined while Peaches is here? She is terrified of dogs."

"How could you not know we had Wilma?" I sobbed furiously. "He's been coming up here as long as I have. He wouldn't hurt a fly!"

"Lilly," my father said quietly, putting a hand on my shoulder. "It won't hurt Wilma to be inside for a little while. I'm sure we can work something out."

"Well, you just work it out, then," I bawled, and turned and ran, over the seawall and down the beach to the base of the cliff. As I started up it, stumbling and sniveling, I heard my mother cry, "Lilly Elizabeth Constable, you come right back here and apologize," and my father saying, "Let her go, Elizabeth. That was hard on her, too."

I turned and looked back. The crowd had tightened around Peaches as she was led, sobbing, back into the safety of the Davenports' grand old Rolls-Royce. Wilma howled and howled. I turned and plunged into the undergrowth that fringed the cliff bottom and began to climb.

The sun was higher now, toward noon. Soon it would be the highest it would ever be this year; the summer solstice was approaching. I had always loved the notion of the solstice. It swam with magic as old as time, with forest things not of our world dancing in moonlit glades, of something wild and enormous and ancient walking the world.

The sun was directly overhead this noon, and an erratic little wind had sprung off the water, puffing and stopping, then blowing again, each time a little longer and stronger. It blew before it a strange mist, a radiant light-struck mist that was only the sun through ordinary June sea fog, but looked otherworldly, portentous. I was a little frightened by it; it obscured everything below me, and the summit of the cliff appeared and disappeared into it. But I climbed on. I wanted the solitude of the cliff top. If there was magic there, I wanted that too.

About a third of the way to the top I stopped. A figure was moving above me on the cliff, a figure that seemed impossibly tall and slender, made of the same luminous mist that crowned the cliff. A figure that was coming down. I froze.

Out of the fog came a boy. When he saw me, he stopped. He was no older than Jeebs, I thought, but you could hardly tell in the blowing mist. The sun breaking through picked up a shock of white-blond hair over his forehead; long, tanned legs in faded plaid shorts; gold-tanned arms with sliding muscles, covered, as the legs were, with tiny gold hairs. Big, bony feet bare in disreputable Top-Siders, a worn blue Shetland sweater tied around his waist over a white T-shirt, and a face—a carved, planed, tanned face of such beauty that you wanted to avert your eyes, or weep. Around him the swirling air tossed the mist; it was as though invisible wings were beating it. My breath stopped, and then started again. All fear left me. It was almost as though I had always known I would find him here.

After a moment, he spoke. His voice was harsh New England, but it had music in it.

"Hello," he said. "Is this your cliff?"

"Yes," I said stupidly. Then, "No. I mean I come here a lot but it doesn't belong to me. But everybody climbs it."

"Good," he said, and smiled. His teeth were very white and the smile was a little crooked, and one front tooth was chipped. I felt giddy with relief. He was human; he needed orthodontia as much as any of us.

"I'm Jon Lowell," he said. "I just got here."

"I'm Lilly Constable. Did you fly?"

He looked at me keenly for a moment, and then the grin widened. "Not the way I think you mean. But this would be a great place for it, wouldn't it? I flew in on Delta from Boston last night. I wish it had been the other way."

"I think people used to," I said, wondering if there was any way I could stop my tongue. "Sometimes I think they still can."

"Wouldn't be surprised," Jon Lowell said. "So do you live here, or visit, or what?"

"My folks have a house just down there on the cove. Edgewater. I've been coming here all my life."

"Lucky you. We've rented a place down near that big bridge. My folks are looking for a summer place up here. I've been to the shore around Boston—Martha's Vineyard and Nantucket—but I've never been to Maine. I was afraid it was really going to be the sticks."

"Sometimes it is," I said, unable to look away from him. "There's a bigger colony, Retreat, up the road a little, but Carter's Cove doesn't usually have many people. I've never met anybody who rented a house."

"And I've never met anybody who could fly."

Without speaking, we turned and walked together down the path toward the beach. We did not touch, of course, but, looking down at the path, I saw that our shadows did.

CHAPTER

3

When Jon Lowell and I came out onto our beach, I saw that my mother and father were sitting in the two Adirondack chairs that were always set alone under the huge pine that guarded the cliff down to the shore. Mostly people sat in the cluster of little chairs and tables under the shade of the big firs down where the seawall leveled out, with lunches or lemonade or evening drinks. But when they were alone, my parents always went to the Adirondacks. I liked them, too. Sitting in one gave you the feeling that you were surveying your own domain, both monarch and chatelaine of it.

They were sipping drinks and talking, their heads turned toward one another. When we started up the path to our cliff, my mother saw us and stopped talking. She lifted her hand to shade her eyes against the brilliant dazzle of the reach. The wind had blown the strange, radiant fog out to sea and the water was the tender, faultless blue of an early June flat "ca'am," as Clara would have put it. Here and there little patches of dimpled water broke the surface as the wind eddied and dropped. The sun had moved just far enough west so that anyone or anything to the east was lost in diamonds. Mother shook her head slightly, as if to clear it, and said, "Well, hello. Where have you been?"

She was looking at Jon Lowell.

"Up there," Jon said hesitantly, gesturing up at the high cliff top we had just left.

My mother ran her hand over her eyes and squinted back at us.

"I'm sorry," she said, smiling. "For a minute you looked like somebody we know, or have seen Lilly with. I'm Elizabeth Constable, Lilly's mother, and you must think I'm a stark raving lunatic."

Jon looked at her, taking in the sunglasses that held the copper-streaked hair off her face, the stormy eyes, the perfect, carved medieval features. She wore one of the striped French jerseys she liked, and fresh white pants, and her feet were bare. She looked spectacular, stunning. I thought what it must be like to be seeing her for the first time, as Jon was, and a lick of the same hatred I had felt for Peaches Davenport seared my stomach and then calmed. You might as well hate a rainbow, or a new moon.

"No ma'am," Jon said, smiling his chipped smile. "I sure don't think that."

"Mama and Daddy, this is Jonathan Lowell. Jon," I said. "He was up on Mr. Forshee's cliff when I went up there. He and his folks have just gotten here from—where did you say?" I asked, looking at him. He grinned and my stomach prickled.

"It has to be Boston," my father said, smiling and offering his hand to Jon. "Lowell, I mean. I'm George Constable, the father of this"—he looked at me and lifted his hands and smiled again—"I was going to say young lady."

Jon shook his hand gravely and said, "No, sir, actually we're from western New York, a little town called Rockville. My father has some quarries there, and I guess the Lowells have pretty much always lived around there. My grandfather and great-grandfather had the quarries before we did."

I dropped down on the cool grass beside my father's chair and he gestured for Jon to sit, too. Jon did, a coil of bony grace. His tanned, scarred knees and big, muscular hands looked almost dangerous in the deep shade of the pine.

"So how did you find your way down east?" my mother inquired. "And particularly to Carter's Cove? Almost nobody ever comes looking for us."

"Well, we've spent summers all around New England, but never in Maine, and my mother was tired of the crowds on Nantucket and the Vineyard. Dad met Canon Davenport at some Episcopal conference in New York several years ago, and they kept in touch, and the canon called this winter and said he knew of a house for rent in the same little summer place where they went. So we ended up renting it, and we just got in last night."

"Oh, you must mean the old Poston place," my mother said. "I'm so glad there are finally people in it. Old Mrs. Poston never came back after her husband died, and her children are all on the West Coast and never get here. I've always thought it was a wonderful old house."

"With the emphasis on old," my father said. "I don't think anything's been done to it since right after the Korean War. Are you falling through floors and swatting mosquitoes all night?"

"No, sir, just a few sort of big spiders. One got into the bathtub with my mother last night. My dad said she walked on water getting out."

"Bet it was a wolf spider," I said. "There's lots of them around here. They won't hurt you."

"They won't have to," Jon said. "You'd die of a heart attack before they ever touched you."

We all laughed, and Jon said, "Speaking of my folks, I ought to go home. I told my mother I'd just be gone an hour or so and it's been—lots longer than that." He looked at me with a small smile. I felt myself flushing, and knew that the unbecoming fuchsia red was staining my face and chest.

"I sort of thought we might take the Beetle Cat over to Sunderson's and see the ospreys," I said, not looking at him. "Nobody else wanted to go, and you can see the babies by now."

"Oh, gosh, I'd like that," Jon Lowell said. "I've seen ospreys from way off, but they don't hang around the beaches we go to. They're beautiful."

"Yes, they are," my father said softly. I knew that of all the birds in this water world of ours, he loved the ospreys best. There had been a young eagle around for a couple of summers, a heart-stopping sight, but the ospreys were at the core of my father's heart.

"Real family birds," he would say. "They'll die defending their young, but they don't go after anything but fish. And they'll keep coming back to the same nest year after year, until something destroys it. The ospreys on Sunderson's were there for years until a bunch of the local boys shot up their nest. They've never come back until this summer. That's why everybody is so anxious to see them and the babies."

"Who would do that?" Jon said, real shock in his blue eyes.

"We don't know. The police never found out, if they even tried, and none of the Mainers ever said, at least not to us summer folks."

"And nobody ever was . . . punished for that?"

"I didn't say that," my father said. "Seth and Clara Anderson, the couple who've helped our family out since forever, just said 'We look after our own,' so I gather they've been called to account one way or another."

"Are you a sailor, Jon?" my mother asked.

"No ma'am," he said. "I'd really like to be, but I've been sort of involved in tennis every summer since I can remember."

"Well," my mother said, "why don't you kids grab a sandwich and take poor Wilma and go over to Sunderson's, and I'll call the Davenports and Jon's parents and ask them for drinks tonight. And

I'll tell them where you are, Jon. I'd love to meet our new neighbors. And they don't have to worry about your going out with Lilly. She's been sailing since she could toddle."

"Will Peaches be coming?" I said, too casually.

"Of course she's coming," Mother said. "They'd hardly leave her alone, would they?"

"That would be too much to ask," I said, under my voice.

"Lilly . . ." my mother began, but before she could finish I jumped up and yelled "Come on" to Jon Lowell, and we dashed into the house, grabbed a couple of wilting ham and cucumber sandwiches, liberated the frantic and joyful Wilma, and pounded down our long, weathered dock where our two boats, Jeebs's and my stubby Beetle Cat, and the graceful old Friendship sloop that was the pride of my father's heart, bobbed on a little freshening wind.

From the muddy shingle beach of Sunderson's Island much of the shoreline of Eggemoggin Reach was visible, from the rusted green Deer Isle Bridge down to the rocky shores of Center Harbor that jutted out to the end of the sweep. If not for those pitted glacial boulders, you would have been able to see all the way to Naskeag Point, where the reach became Jericho Bay.

"That's why they call it a reach," I said to Jon as we tossed the Beetle Cat's anchor overboard and sloshed through the shallow, freezing water to the beach. "If you set your sail down at the bridge, you can sail all the way to Jericho without resetting it—that is, if the wind is right. It's supposed to be one of the best sailing lanes in the world."

"Wow," Jon said. "I'd love to do that."

"One day we will," I said.

He smiled at me but did not reply. I felt the dreaded fuchsia burn start again. Would he think I was assuming we'd be together all summer long?

"It looks like a movie," he said, pointing to the line of tiny cottages on the far shore with the dark woods behind them.

"I know," I said. "It looks like we're miles away, but it's only about a mile. See, there's your house." I pointed to the old gray cedar-shingled pile of the Poston house, where Jon's family was staying. Even with the blue station wagon parked in its driveway and the window shutters open, it still looked empty. For some reason I felt a small shudder.

"And there's the canon's house, and our house, and on down to Mr. Forshee's cliff. That's where we were this morning. With no people around, it looks like a toy village, doesn't it? Oh, I take that back. There's the famous Peaches Davenport coming out on the canon's porch."

Jon shaded his eyes and looked at her.

"Why's she got on a dress?" he asked. Peaches wore a soft green sundress and sandals to match. Her flaming hair was tied into a ponytail by a silly scarf. I thought she must have hundreds of pairs of sandals.

"I don't know," I said. "I guess she doesn't want anybody to forget she's a girl."

"That would be hard to do," he said. "She looks like she's pretty from here."

"Oh, she *is* pretty," I said. "And she's had a great tragedy. Her parents were killed in an automobile accident last fall, and she's living with the Davenports now. I don't think she wants anybody to forget the tragedy."

He looked at me.

"You don't like her, do you?" he said.

Briefly I considered lying, but knew, without knowing how, that he would know I was.

"No," I said finally. "I'm really sorry about her folks, but she's . . .

61

sneaky. Or something. She doesn't mean what she says, and she's always batting her eyelashes at the boys and ignoring the girls. She really doesn't like me. And she had such a screaming fit when she saw Wilma that we had to shut him up in the house. It's not fair. Everybody up here knows Wilma has never hurt anybody in his life."

Hearing his name, Wilma, who had been happily nosing in the unfamiliar detritus along the tide line, came prancing up to us with a decaying crab in his mouth, grinning his wide white grin and wagging his tail. It was hard to tell which smell was worse, wet dog or dead crab.

Wilma laid his crab down at Jon's feet and jumped up and put one gargantuan paw on each of Jon's shoulders and licked his face exultantly.

"God, Wilma!" Jon protested, but he hugged the dripping dog to his chest and rumpled the floppy ears. Wilma dropped to the sand at Jon's feet and rolled on his back in an excess of love and pleasure. "It's hard to see why anybody would be afraid of him," he remarked, ruffling Wilma's wet stomach. "Maybe she just got a whiff of his breath."

"No," I said. "I have never seen such a fit. Daddy says we're going to have to keep him in the house when Peaches is around, which is almost always. Poor Wilma doesn't understand. Nobody's ever penned him up before. I don't know what we're going to do. I wish he'd bite Peaches. Then maybe they'd take her home."

"Tell you what," Jon said. "There's a big fenced-in place behind our cottage. I think somebody said the lady who lived there raised Rottweilers—it's really huge. Our dogs love it. They'd love Wilma, too. They love everybody. Why don't I take Wilma home with me when he's not with you-all? He can come in the house and sleep in my room, and I'll play with him outside. Then when it's time to go to bed I'll bring him home."

"That would be wonderful," I said, almost in tears with gratitude and deliverance. "But wouldn't your parents mind? And what if Peaches starts coming to your house?"

"My mother and dad love our dogs," he said. "They're Bernese mountain dogs. They make Wilma look like a Chihuahua. And Peaches isn't coming to my house. I can promise you that."

"How do you know?" I said, feeling something very like adoration swell in my chest.

"Because nobody who doesn't like you and Wilma is," he said, and smiled again.

"Come on," I said, not trusting myself to look at him. "Let's go find the ospreys."

Sunderson's Island lies about a mile from our shore down toward the Deer Island Bridge. I don't know if anybody remembers who the Sundersons were; even Seth and Clara Anderson professed not to know precisely.

"Seems to me like there were some Sundersons over at Stonington once, but that was a time ago," Clara said. "I don't think there are any of them left around here. They may still own the island, but nobody's ever seen anybody over there much but you colony kids."

This was true. Sunderson's was a great dome of rock, almost perfectly round, that thrust out of the still-shallow water of the reach. It was one of the really enormous boulders left by the petulant glacier, my father said, and there was no telling how large the bottom of it was. Because it was rock, not much except scrub undergrowth and a few small valiant pines could grow in its thin topsoil. One of these was the lone pine at the top that the ospreys chose for their nest. Pretty smart, my father said. Nothing much could surprise or ambush them. The rest of the dome was covered with velvety moss of a vivid emerald I had never seen anywhere but on the island. It was about four or five inches deep, and so soft that the temptation to take a nap on it in the sun was all but irresistible. You paid the price in vicious chigger bites, but on a still, sunny afternoon with no sound but the soft breathing of the reach, many of us kids were willing to pay it. You could combat the vicious mosquitoes and the satanic blackflies with a thick, evil concoction the lobstermen and clam diggers brewed. "All of you will have deformed children," my mother said once, but she used it too. But there was nothing to be done about the chiggers except the application of colorless nail polish over the fiery red welts, and that was after the fact. Still, we sprawled in the sun on the moss, and I suspect that the older ones of us did more than sprawl. Furtively scratched behinds invariably drew lifted brows from adults. I don't think I ever noticed.

I had brought the mosquito and blackfly repellent with me, and Jon and I slathered it on.

"We smell at least as bad as Wilma," Jon said, his perfect golden nose wrinkled.

"You'll be glad we do," I said. "Blackflies actually take little chunks out of you when they bite."

We neared the top and found the ospreys' tree and the new nest, but there were no ospreys to be seen. We could hear the babies, though. Frantic, shrill, insistent, their cries pierced the still afternoon like tiny silver blades.

"Wow," Jon said. "What if you had to listen to that all day?"

"Maybe to their parents it's beautiful," I said, "like any parents would think their babies' sounds were."

"Where do you think the big ospreys are?" Jon said.

"Off getting dinner," I said. "They'll be back soon. They don't stay gone long."

"I'd be on my way to Miami by now," he said, and I laughed. I laughed a lot when I was with Jon. I didn't think about it then, but he was funny almost like an adult is funny: wry, smart, interested.

Not just interested for a little while. Jon was interested in everything. Somehow I knew he would never give me a frog on my bicep, or a snigger, or pull a mean trick on me and bawl with laughter.

"Let's sit down and wait," I said. "If we're still and quiet we won't spook them when they come."

We sank down into the velvety moss and in one accord lay back and stretched out on it. It was sun warmed, but a little cool wind had sprung up, and the warmth was soothing. Wilma came from wherever he had been foraging, covered with a thicket of sticky green burrs and grinning his foolish grin. He sprawled down beside us. In less than five minutes we were all drifting toward sleep.

I had been born with what my mother called the Unfortunate Hostess gene. I could be peacefully silent with people I knew well, but I felt an irresistible urge to chatter in the presence of newcomers. Silent, dead air seemed wrong, insulting. But with Jon I felt no urge at all except to slide into warm sleep beside him. Sleep came as it often does outdoors: the sun hammered down on you, sounds faded out, insect drones grew stronger and lulled, you began to breathe in their rhythm, and that of the sea under it, and then all sound was gone.

I don't know how long we slept, but the sun was lowering into the west over the Deer Island Bridge when we woke. The reach was a blinding sheet of glitter. I'm still not sure if it was Wilma's low, eerie growl that woke me, or the shadow. I think they came at the same time. I know only that Jon and I both came awake and sat up in one motion. Somehow it seemed important to be very still and quiet. I had never heard Wilma make a noise like that, and was just turning toward him when the great shadow swept over us, the shadow of huge, flat wings that seemed to block out the sun and go on and on. We looked up and saw the eagle. He was utterly silent, not making the harsh, creaking *kak kak kak* I was familiar with when our own young eagle made his sweeping rounds over the reach. This was not a young eagle; it was enormous, gargantuan. The great wings were making slowly decreasing circles over the nest. The baby ospreys fell silent. So did Wilma. For a long time I could not get my breath, and then I began to scream.

"Get out of here," I shrieked. "Go on, get away, get away!"

Wilma began to bark fiercely just as the eagle slowed over the nest. I could easily see the massive yellow beak, the silvery white head and tail, the great talons stretching down. For a long moment it seemed to hover in the air. And then, as it beat its great wings downward, Jon grabbed me from behind and turned me into his chest.

"Don't look, Lilly," he said sharply. "Don't look!"

I began to cry loudly, my head pressed into his shoulder. He had put on his sweater, and even as the horror and grief of the nest attack swallowed me, I was aware of the smell of him in every atom of my body: damp wool, salt, wood smoke, sweaty and somehow sweet flesh.

And then he was shaking me and crying, "Look, Lilly! Oh, look!"

I screwed up my eyes and shook my head, but he turned me around and I did look, and my breath left me.

They came out of the dying sun like arrows shot from twin archers, flying fast and low and level, screaming their rage. Two ospreys, so close that we could make out the beautiful autocratic crested heads, the black cheek patches, the black wrist patches on their long, cocked-back wings. The wings were the way I always identified ospreys when they wheeled over the reach; no other bird I knew flew with that graceful crook. That and their cranky, rather annoyed whistles, almost too high for such a large bird.

But they were not whistling now. They were shrieking, a frenzied *cheereek*, *cheereek*. It made your blood thicken and chill to hear them. The eagle stopped his slow downward circling, rode the air, and looked at them. Before he could move his massive wings in another beat, they were on him.

Later Jon and I could not say precisely what we saw, except that in an eyeblink the eagle was out over the reach, beating for the far shore, and the ospreys were diving at him, screaming. One came at him from above, one dived and came from below. They did it over and over again as the eagle picked up speed with his great wings and finally outran them. He vanished into the dark woods behind the cottages. The ospreys turned back over the reach.

They did not come directly to the nest, and I was just saying "I hope he didn't hurt them. I didn't see them touch, did you?" when Jon grinned.

"Suppertime," he said, pointing. And there they were, touching down into their nest, mouths full of wriggling silvery fish. Finally we saw the babies; their scraggly heads and huge, yawning beaks appeared above the nest rim. The parents sank down into it, and sound ceased again, except for soft whistles and the occasional "cheep." I wept for a long time.

It was late afternoon when we got back to our beach. The sun was just flaring into one of the great fiery Penobscot Bay sunsets when I came into the dock. I knew we were late, and that they were probably worried about us. My father was walking quickly down the dock, and before he even reached us I was saying, "It was my fault, Daddy—you wouldn't believe what we just saw."

He looked at me for a moment. I knew that my nose was still running, and my cheeks were streaked with drying tears. He looked at Jon, not smiling.

"An eagle was about to get the baby ospreys, Mr. Constable. The parents weren't there, and he was just circling down to the nest when they came out of nowhere like they'd been shot out of a gun just screaming, and they dived at him, one on top and one on the bottom, until they ran him clear back over here into the woods. I'm really sorry."

My father smiled.

"Don't be," he said. "You've just seen one of the most wonderful things in the world, and maybe one of the rarest. You'll tell your children about it. I wish I could have seen it. I'm not down to fuss at you. Lilly, you need to take Wilma quickly around the side of the house and put him in the front door. Peaches is getting a little upset."

I looked up at our seawall. Canon Davenport was on his feet scowling down at us, and Peaches was cowering behind him and beginning to scream.

"I'm taking Wilma home with me, Mr. Constable," Jon said. "We've got these two big old Bernese mountain dogs who love every dog they've ever seen, and a great big fenced backyard, and I'm going to put Wilma there until . . . after supper. I'll bring him home before bedtime. He can stay all summer, if you'd like him to."

"You are an officer and a gentleman, Jon," he said. "You've probably saved my summer. A lot of people's summer, for that matter."

"No problem," Jon said, and whistled to the dripping, capering Wilma, who followed him, gamboling, up the gangplank and to the dirt road that bound all our cottages together, and out of sight.

As we reached the seawall, a pretty woman with Jon's yellow hair tied back in a ponytail and freckles on her snub nose asked, "Where is that son of mine?"

"He's taking Wilma over to your house, Mrs. Lowell," I said. "If you don't mind, he'll probably stay with y'all a lot this summer."

"Not at all. Charles and Gordon will love to have company."

"Charles and Gordon?"

"Our two dogs. I know. It's ridiculous. Don't ask."

She smiled, and all of a sudden I liked her very much.

She cupped her hands and raised her voice.

"Jon?"

"Yes ma'am?" came floating faintly back from the direction of the road.

"Take a quick bath and change your clothes. You looked like a pirate getting out of that boat."

"Yes ma'am," he called back.

"You too, Lilly," my mother said, not smiling. I knew she was annoyed at my lateness and my bedraggled shorts and hair. "We're going inside now and will light the fire. I always forget how quickly it still gets chilly in June. Hurry up—I need you to pass some things for me."

The canon was standing next to a tall, darkly tanned man with Jon's planed features but somehow without his light. Jon's father, I knew.

"Where is he taking that dog?" the canon said forbiddingly. Behind him, Peaches gave a great rattling sniff, but did not scream anymore.

"He's taking him over to our place, Canon Davenport," Jon's mother said. "We've got a huge fenced dog pen and two big idiots of dogs who'll love to have a new playmate."

"More big dogs? I hope they can't jump that fence," the canon said.

"Not unless they have wings," Mrs. Lowell said sweetly, smiling at Peaches, who was edging out from behind her grandfather. She was all in white tonight, and seemed dipped in pearl, nacreous like, I thought ungenerously, the inside of a dead oyster's shell. Her apricot hair brushed her shoulders.

"Hey Lilly," she said. "My goodness, did you-all have an accident?"

"No," I said.

"Well, I mean you're so wet and all, and you've got this green stuff all over your shorts—"

"I know what you mean," I said, and turned and went across the chilly lawn and into the house, shaking with anger.

"Peaches, dear, it's not really kind to remark on people's appearances," I could hear Mrs. Davenport start sweetly. I did not hear Peaches reply. I could imagine it, though.

It is almost always dark in the old cottages in Retreat and Carter's Cove. Very few of them have ever been winterized, so that the walls and ceilings are of dark pine boards and beams, without insulation or plaster. I always loved Edgewater best at this time of day. All those years of long winters and smoke from our many fireplaces had stained the old pine a beautiful, dark honey gold, and the last of the fire from the dying sunset down the reach burned pure gold on them.

By that summer, a few wealthy people from Boston and New York had found the colony, and had bought up seaside land down the Naskeag Road and built huge, rambling houses that cost nearly a million dollars and sent everybody's taxes skyrocketing. They were not loved, nor were the cottages. They did not look like cottages. They looked like big, rich suburban houses. I had never been in one, though I think my parents had, once or twice, for drinks and dinner. I knew I would hate them. Insulated and plastered and painted against the Maine winters, they had no glowing, smoky gold walls that smelled of all the fires of summer, no narrow, dim staircases and dark magical corners.

I ran up our steep, creaking stairs to the second-floor bathroom that Jeebs and I shared reluctantly and took a very brief, bone-chilling bath, then jumped out of the old claw-footed tub and toweled myself dry and raw. Everyone else had had baths, I thought; the hot water was feeble, and died soon. I ran into my room, purple with cold, and reached for my clean shorts and a sweater, and then stopped. In the back of my closet I found the single skirt I had at Edgewater, a flowing, paisley affair my mother had bought me, remarking that if someone died or got married at least I'd have something besides pants. I put it back. Besides loathing the skirt, I was damned if I would put on a skirt just because Peaches Davenport had one on. I rummaged for a moment in the faded, clean clothes, most of which had been left in my closet here year after year, and then stopped. My hand felt a silky linen, unlike anything I was apt to have, and pulled out the beautifully tailored white linen pants my mother had bought for me, too. They were crisp and fell perfectly. I had hidden and then forgotten them as I had the skirt. I took them out and put them on. Then I found the heavy navy turtleneck cable-knit sweater that had been a present from my Constable grandmother one Christmas, which I had never worn because it scratched. I pulled it over my head and then went into my mother's room to look at myself in her full-length mirror.

I did not know the person who looked back. She was slender where I had been knobby, softly curved where I was flat, very nearly elegant. I goggled. I pushed at my unruly curls and then went to my mother's dresser and took out one of her white headbands and bound my hair back with it, and looked again. For a moment I thought I was looking at my mother. I did not know how to feel about this, so I poked at my hair some more until tendrils broke free from the band and curled onto my cheeks. My face was tanned, and flushed with sunburn from the afternoon. Gingerly I picked up my mother's single lipstick, a hectic pink, from her dresser and dabbed it on my mouth. I looked grotesque, like a flesh-eating Kewpie doll, so I wiped it off. But a faint stain remained, and I smoothed a little cold cream over it, and turned and ran out of the room and started downstairs. Then I went back and slid my feet into my mother's white espadrilles. They fit perfectly. Not knowing in the least who I was, I crept downstairs and into the living room.

Except for the clothes everyone wore, I might have been walking into the room as it had been fifty or sixty years ago. My father, sentimentally, had never allowed many changes at Edgewater, so the room was full of spavined old wicker armchairs, faded blowsy chintz settees, fussy, tottering little tables, and two or three small, frayed Oriental rugs that had been old when my grandmother brought them to the cottage. On shelves and the mantel of the stone fireplace sat china trinkets and dried flowers and brownish photos in curly frames that showed people in long skirts and hats and high-buttoned suits on the decks of steamers, or at what seemed to be dances in fern-filled drawing rooms; there were a few grim portraits of no one I knew, and a shot of two people in 1890s dress posing on the colony's little clay tennis court with racquets poised, smiling for the camera. My father insisted they were his mother and father, but my mother demurred. "Your mother never picked up a tennis racquet in her life except to smack a bug."

In only two instances had my mother stood firm. "We are going to have one comfortable place to sit," she said, "and this house is going to have light in it."

So the huge tartan sofa came, before I was born, I think, for I seemed to remember it always, and solid, simple lamps sat about, making pools of light in the black-gold dusk and warming corners and chairs and tables and faces sweetly. Of all the rooms in my life, it was this one I loved the most.

The fire snickered and whispered. My father was just bringing out a fresh tray of drinks, and something baking in the kitchen smelled wonderful. Everyone looked at me when I entered. Conversation stopped.

Then my mother said, "Why, Lilly. How nice you look."

There were murmurs from the other adults, and from Peaches, "Isn't that a winter sweater? Gosh, you must be burning up."

"You looked so much like your mother for a moment it was almost frightening," my father said, smiling at me.

In the corner by the fire, with Peaches planted firmly at his feet, Jon, in fresh khakis and a blue oxford-cloth shirt, said, "Wow."

My face flamed, but I thought that the dancing firelight would mask it. I walked over to the end of the sofa and sat down beside my father. "It's really nice to have you all here," I said.

My mother and father stared. "Nice going," my father whispered to me. My mother introduced me to Jon's parents, Claire and Arthur Lowell.

"But I guess you've figured that out already," Mrs. Lowell said. "Jon is the spitting image of his father, and thank God for that. Arthur always says I look like a little yellow hen, and no boy needs that." She smiled fondly at Jon, who gave her a brief, sweet smile and moved his leg surreptitiously to dislodge Peaches' cheek from it. I looked at his mother incredulously. Jon looked like his father? I looked again. Arthur Lowell was tall, bronzed, with abundant chestnut hair and sculpted features that were, I could see now, rather like Jon's. But his eyes were dark brown, almost opaque, and his dark brows were thick and straight over them. Jon's eyes were the dancing diamond blue of his mother's. I would never have thought that there was a resemblance to this dusky man if his mother had not pointed it out. Lean, erect, still almost to the point of stiffness, Jon's father reminded me of nothing so much as a high-ranking military officer.

"It's nice to meet the young temptress who had my son out all day long." He smiled at me. I blushed. Jon made a soft strangled noise. Peaches sniffed.

"I just told everybody about your afternoon with the eagle and the ospreys," my father said. "You're lucky, Jon. You'll remember that all your life."

"Yeah," Jon said, "I truly will."

"What was the eagle going to do?" Peaches asked querulously.

"He was going to eat the baby ospreys," I said. "Eagles will grab almost anything small that's moving and fly off with them. I've even heard they eat babies," I said, smiling sweetly at her.

"Lilly," my mother said. "That's an old wives' tale and you know it."

"Well, I've heard it a lot," I said. "And I've seen our eagle stalking things."

"Your eagle?" Peaches whispered.

"Yeah. He stays in those big pines out on the rocks. We see him a lot."

Peaches edged closer to her grandfather on her other side. "Does he come out in daylight?" she quavered.

"Sometimes, sweetie," my mother said. "But he's a young eagle, almost a baby, and there's no way he could pick up a kitten, even. You don't have anything to worry about as far as he's concerned. He's very beautiful, in fact."

"I don't want to see him, Grandpa," Peaches said in a small, fretful voice.

"Well," her grandmother said, "we'll be going to visit all the places I told you about, mostly, so you won't see him. No eagles at Jordan Pond, or in Bar Harbor, or at that pretty sandy beach on Mount Desert. No eagles at the beautiful flower gardens or the museums and stores." She lifted her face and looked at me, and then Jon.

"You missed Peaches' lovely slide show this afternoon," she said, "but we hope you'll come with us to tea at Jordan Pond tomorrow afternoon. Most of the other children are going."

"I told Jon we'd take the bicycles and ride up to Caterpillar Hill tomorrow," I said. "But of course, if he would rather—"

"Did you enjoy sailing today, Jon?" my father asked hastily.

"Oh, man! I'd really love to learn," Jon said.

"We heard they gave lessons at the club in the colony yacht," Jon's mother said. "I thought I'd call tomorrow."

"Let George teach him," my mother said quickly. "That idiot steward at the club couldn't sail a rubber ducky in a bathtub. George has won most of the sailing awards we give over the years, but he's just about stopped competing."

"Got too vicious for me." My father smiled. "But I'd be more than glad to teach Jon, if you'd like. Our Beetle Cat is the perfect boat to learn in."

"That would be great!" Jon said.

"It's very generous of you," his mother said warmly. "We want him to learn. But I would like him to meet some of the colony young people. I mean, if we buy here . . ."

"I don't want to right now, Mom," Jon said. "I don't even know the ones around here yet. Well, except Lilly—"

"You know me," Peaches chimed, and smiled winsomely.

In the firelight she really was lovely. I looked over at Jon, and the sheer beauty of him struck me silent. What a pair they would make.

"We're anxious for Peaches to make a lot of new little friends, too," Mrs. Davenport said. "I know the Randolphs and the Simmonses, and Ambassador Fielding and his family are at the colony, and there are several little girls Peaches should know. I think the ambassador's granddaughter Shirley is going to Cathedral next year. Not that the Carter's Cove children aren't perfectly charming."

"Well," my mother said, "I think I heard there are dances every Wednesday night."

"Oh, I *love* to dance," Peaches cried. "I took lessons at home, and I'm going to Mrs.—what's her name, Grandma?"

"Miss Walker," her grandmother said. "The Shippens' granddaughter, you know. All the Washington children go. I'm sure you and George Junior go, don't you, Lilly?"

"Jeebs goes," I said shortly. Guns, knives, cannons, missiles could not drive me to Miss Walker's notorious dancing school.

"But you don't?"

"No," I said, and then, "My father and I have a real gymnasium in our basement, with trapezes and high bars and everything. That's what we do. We're good, too."

"Oh, that's funny," Peaches trilled. "You're a circus!"

"The dances are square dances," I said. "You know, like hillbillies do."

"Oh," Mrs. Davenport said. "Not like junior cotillions, then."

"We're pretty rustic down here," my mother said, smiling.

"Bucolic," Jon's father said. "Just what we all need. Jon's been hitting the balls pretty hard this year."

"You're a tennis player, I hear," the canon said magisterially to Jon. "I used to play a bit myself."

The thought of Canon Davenport playing tennis with anyone but God was patently absurd. I looked at Jon. In the firelight his face was still, his eyes shuttered by his gold-tipped lashes.

"Jon is the second-ranked New York State amateur player in his age group," his father said. "He has what it takes to play professional tennis, if he wants to. He gets special lessons at Eaglebrook, and has a great coach in Albany. I practice with him too. We usually play every day. I want him to let up a little, try some sailing and all, but we're going to have to play a couple of hours most days. I hear there's a court in the colony."

"Yes, and it's a disaster," my mother said. "Nobody who hasn't been coming here a thousand years can get near it. Tell you what, though— the twins' family has a good clay court, and I'm sure they'd be more than happy to let you play in the afternoons. I never see anybody on it. I'll ask for you."

"Thank you," Arthur Lowell said.

"I'm taking lessons," Peaches said. "I'll come play with you, Jon."

"Well, young lady, I'm afraid it has to be just Jon and me," Jon's father said. "I drill him pretty hard. He doesn't need distractions. But maybe one weekend we can all play."

Far, far back in Peaches' luminous eyes I saw a storm begin.

"Well, Jon," my father said. "You want to get an early start in the morning on that sailing?"

"Oh, yeah!" Jon looked at his parents.

"Of course," his father said. "It's very generous of you. He needs to be home by lunchtime, though. I like him to rest an hour or two after lunch, before we start practice."

Jon said nothing, looked at no one.

"I want to learn," Peaches said loudly. "I want to learn to sail!"

"No sailing this year, darling," her grandmother said with the first note of firmness I had ever heard in her voice.

"Nine o'clock?" my father said.

"Yes sir," Jon said.

The storm grew nearer.

"Well, on that note we should get home," Claire Lowell said. "We need to check on the dogs and get to bed early. It's been a long day."

"You all must be tired," Mrs. Davenport said, "but perhaps Jon would like to stop in for a bite of supper with us? We're having a crab casserole that Peaches likes."

"Thanks, Mrs. Davenport," Jon said, smiling at her, "but I promised I'd bring Wilma back after dinner."

The canon bent a stern eye on Jon.

"You're not going to let that animal out, are you?"

"I had a real trauma with a big dog," Peaches announced importantly, looking up under her eyelashes at Jon.

"Did it bite you?"

"No. But it came up real close to me . . ."

Jon stared.

"Don't worry about Wilma, Canon," my father said with just a bit of an edge in his voice. "We'll see to it that the dog situation works out well for everybody."

"Except the dog," I said under my voice.

"Right. Except for the dog," my father said in his normal voice, and everyone smiled, thinking he had made a joke. Everybody, I thought, but Jon.

Everyone left shortly after that. It was not quite full dark, but it soon would be. The nights were longer now than they would be again until this time next year, and the mornings were born at four-thirty, when the gulls woke the crows and the crows woke everyone else.

Jon hesitated. "You coming sailing with us tomorrow?" he asked.

"I might," I said, looking only into the red teeth of the fading fire.

"Well, you can't," Peaches snapped. "Your daddy said it was just one person at a time."

"I know." I smiled at her. "I just thought I might take out the big boat and follow along, see how things were going."

"Can you sail the big one?" Jon asked. There was awe in his voice.

"Oh, sure," I said, not daring to look at my father. As a matter of fact, I could sail the Friendship, but I had never been allowed to take her out alone.

My father was silent.

"Boy, I'd sure like to learn to sail that one," Jon said reverently. "I think it's the prettiest boat I ever saw."

"Later, maybe." My father smiled. "*Much* later. She's one of the sweetest of the old boats to handle, but the bay can get tricky very quickly. We'll see. And by the way, a lot of people have called the Friendships the most beautiful boats under sail, even now. You have a good eye."

Jon's white, chipped grin lit the dusk, and then they were all gone.

I heard Peaches' voice reach storm pitch. I knew it was not going to be a particularly peaceful meal in the Davenports' house.

"See you after supper, with Wilma," Jon called back.

"Okay."

At dinner that night, at the old scarred round pine table that had fed generations of Constables, my mother served thick, buttery clam chowder from the general store, and she and my father had white wine. Jeebs had left to spend the weekend with a St. Albans friend whose family summered on Little Cranberry Island. Mother lit candles and the fire snored in its dying. It was our customary first-night dinner, and I would have missed it if we had not had it. But I could hardly eat a bite; there was a little prickling dam in my midsection that would not let the food pass. My face burned, too, from the sun and wind and whatever else lights young faces when their attention turns away from themselves and fastens on another person for the first time.

"Are you sick?" my mother wondered, reaching over to feel my face.

"No," I said. "We ate the sandwiches pretty late."

"I liked the Lowells a lot, didn't you?" my father said. "They'd make a good addition to Carter's Cove. I hope they stay."

My mother looked down at her plate.

"I wouldn't count on it," she said. "That old pile they're in would cost a fortune to renovate."

"Well, from what the canon tells me, that's not a problem," my father said. "I gather the quarries make a small fortune. I mean, Eaglebrook, and Yale, and that station wagon . . ."

"That station wagon is a bit much, I think," my mother said. "I mean, a sky-blue Lincoln up here in this mud pit?"

"What about you, Lillybelle," my father taunted, using my old childhood nickname. I hated it.

"I really like them," I said neutrally. "Especially Mrs. Lowell. She's funny."

"Ah," my father said. "And what about Jon? I can't imagine you dressing up like that for a bunch of grown-ups."

"I didn't want that Peaches to think I always looked like a doofus," I said.

"Point taken," my father said. "It's going to be a long summer with Peaches, I fear. But anyway, you surely looked pretty."

"Thank you," I mumbled. My hands were beginning to shake. I clenched them in my lap.

"I think he is a very nice boy," my mother said. "Polite, natural, certainly not silly like most kids his age. If he grows up to look like his father, he'll be something."

I lifted my eyes and stared at her. Grows up to look like his father? Couldn't she see what Jon looked like now? How could she miss that rangy golden beauty, that perfect Michelangelo face, saved only by the chipped tooth from the inanity of perfection? "I like the way he looks," I said.

"Well, of course," Mother said. "When he grows into his ears and nose and hands and feet, he'll be a handsome young man. We'd better keep him away from all those colony mamas up here without their husbands."

"I like the way his mother looks better," I said.

"Actually, I do, too," my father said. "Herr Lowell is just a bit too Light Brigade for me."

"I'm going outside and wait for Wilma," I said.

"Take your sweater," my mother called after me.

I went out and sat down on the edge of the porch and looked out over the reach, toward Deer Isle and Great Spruce Head, beyond it. There was no moon yet tonight, and I could barely make out the shape of Little Deer Isle. I could see the lights of the colony there, though, and, far out on the reach, the riding lights of two or three boats already anchored there.

The stars were out, though. They almost always shocked me when I saw them for the first time at Edgewater every year. Huge, burning silver chrysanthemums hanging so close you could almost touch them; the silver peppering of smaller stars, the diamond-dusted arc of the Milky Way. The constellations were as clear as if someone had drawn them in silver chalk. I saw the Big and Little Dippers, the Belt of Orion, and Deneb, Altair, and Vega, the stars by which seamen and airmen navigated for centuries. My father had tried, without success, to teach me celestial navigation. Now, I thought, I'd like to learn. Jon would like it, too. Low on the horizon Venus burned like a torch. I leaned against the porch railing and waited.

I heard the jingle of Wilma's chain, and then the frenzied scudding of his big feet on the gravel drive, and then he was up the steps and pawing and licking and snuffling me all over, ecstatic. Jon trotted behind him.

"I thought I was going to have to ride him over here," he said, gasping for breath. "He had a great time with us, but when we started home he went berserk."

Over his blue shirt he had put on the same old sweater he had worn all day, and I wanted to lean over and bury my face in wet wool and smoke and salt.

"Is he going to be a problem this summer?" I asked.

"Not at our house. The Berneses love him, and so does my mother. He had a nap on the sofa with his head in her lap before we came."

"I hope your father will like him."

"Oh, he does. He just doesn't show his feelings very much."

We sat silent for a small space of time, looking at the star-pricked bay. Phosphorescence danced on the frills of its little waves. You hardly ever saw it except on the moonless nights. The reach was larky tonight, almost playful. It seemed to be laughing softly.

My skin prickled, and I felt as if the hairs on my arms were reaching out toward Jon.

"Well, I better take Wilma on in before he starts barking and the canon comes down with a gun," I said.

"Or holy water," Jon said. "I'd like to take all three of them down under Peaches' window and let them bark," he said. "Or read her *The Hound of the Baskervilles* out loud. In a dark room."

I burst out laughing, charmed once more with his quick, quirky humor.

Finally he got to his feet and said, "I need to get back," and turned to go. I sat still, hugging Wilma. Then he turned back, fishing in his pocket.

"Brought you a present," he said, taking my hand and putting something in it and closing my fingers over it. I opened them. It was a feather, a small, silvery white breast feather of an osprey.

"Thanks," I said over the hammering of my heart. "I'll keep it always."

"I can always get you another one," he said.

"No, I want this one."

He faded away into the dark, around the side of the house. I sat staring at the place he had been. It seemed to me that he left a hole in the skin of the world.

I went in and loosed the maddened Wilma into the living room, where my parents were sitting with coffee before the frail fire. I heard him scrabbling and whimpering with joy, and heard them talking to him, and turned and went upstairs to my bedroom. I was suddenly so tired I could hardly slip out of the linen slacks and the sweater, and left them in a pile on the floor beside my bed and dived deep under the down quilts.

But I did not sleep. I lay on my back staring at the dark ceiling. I don't remember thinking anything at all.

At some point later Wilma came thumping into my room and scrabbled into bed with me and curled himself up against my ribs and under my chin. There was a lot of Wilma. I could feel the warmth of him against my entire left side.

I turned over and took him into my arms and held him against me, and felt him shudder and groan with luxurious pleasure.

I started to cry, fat, warm, silent tears.

"I love you, dog," I whispered. And then, "I love him."

This was simply too much to get my mind around, and so I stopped crying and let sleep come with the smell of wet dog in my nostrils and, down farther, perhaps in my heart, the smell of smoky wool and the dry scent of the osprey feather still clasped in my hand.

CHAPTER

4

When I came downstairs the next morning, it was still and quiet and dim. I had slept hard and long and did not know what time it was. Last night's blaze of stars had given way this morning to lowering gray clouds and airlessness. Later in the summer such a day would produce stunning heat, but now it was only heavy and thick. It sat on your skin like soap scum. I knew it wouldn't last, though; by tomorrow one of early June's great thunderstorms would boom through like an infantry barrage and everything would be blue and nearly transparent again. Whoever had said "If you don't like the weather in Maine, wait a few minutes" was right. It was one reason we came so early and stayed until Labor Day. Back in Washington, when the great, sullen heat set in, it would not break until almost October.

I could hear no sounds of human habitation, and I felt groggy and disoriented. I don't think I had been alone at Edgewater much until now, and the feeling was fairly ominous, as though it were a different house, much older and larger, and I a different person. Down deep, uneasiness stirred. It was more than the quiet and the aloneness, I knew, but for a moment I could not think what it was. Then I did. I remembered the whole of the day before and Jon and the osprey feather, and that I had fallen asleep thinking *I love him.*

84

The uneasiness spiked up into near panic. Kids didn't love other kids, not the way I meant. That came, I presumed, much later. Kids simply did not love kids. Kids love their parents in the offhand way they always had, or their dogs, or their best friend, or geometry. That love had nothing at all to do with what I had felt in the darkness last night. The enormity of it frightened me profoundly. It was too big a leap; it asked too much; it implied an inevitability I knew nothing about. Feeling like a child in a kindergarten play, I called out into the echoing silence: "Anybody here?"

"In the kitchen," Cecie's voice replied. There was an edge of annoyance in it. I went shambling into the kitchen in my old madras shorts and a GW sweatshirt of my father's. Cecie sat at the scarred kitchen table dragging cold butter across cold toast. Always, on the second morning of our summers in Carter's Cove, and on many other mornings, she and I had early breakfast together at my house, planning the day while the other cove kids drifted into the house and my mother whisked in and out, asking about everybody's winter and settling down to do her morning telephoning, and Clara bustled about coaxing fresh toast out of the rusting old toaster and smacking her own homemade blueberry jam down into the middle of the table. This morning rang with difference.

"Where is everybody?" I asked. I looked around the kitchen to see if more food lurked about but none did, so I sat down opposite Cecie and took a piece of limp, cold toast. A glass of orange juice sat at my place, but it was stale and tasted of its cardboard carton, and I pushed it and the toast aside. I was vaguely affronted. No one had ever failed to provide me with a hot breakfast before.

"Out doing whatever you do in the middle of the morning," Cecie said snappishly. "It's almost ten-thirty. Your mother's painting and said she'd kill anyone who disturbed her, and Clara's gone to Ellsworth to take Seth to the foot doctor, and all the others left after you hadn't come down by nine-thirty and went over to the Davenports'. Peaches is having a little luncheon party at Jordan Pond."

"What did they do that for?" I said stupidly. I could not imagine my summertime coterie not there and ready for adventure, much less gone all the way over to Mount Desert to eat popovers in their good clothes. This was the morning in the summers when we always planned our courses of action for the next three months, laid out our goals and itineraries: the serious harassment of the yacht club steward, finally being allowed to ride our bicycles across the Deer Isle Bridge to Little Deer Isle, or whether or not this would be the summer we rebelled against the parent-mandated participation in the Saturday Beetle Cat regattas over at Middle Harbor. The theory was that we would acquire sportsmanship and new friends and priceless future contacts along with sailing acumen, but we hated the regattas. It was not that we were poor sailors; most of us could outsail the colony young of our ages, largely because of the proximity of the Shellbacks and Beetle Cats tied up at our dock. We just wanted our own regatta. There were almost enough of us for that.

It was the full flowering of Camelot, the New Frontier, and the glamour and rigor of the young Kennedy administration brought with it strong feelings. The Republicans among us in the summers loathed the Kennedys. The fewer Democrats loved them. It never struck me as worthy of note until later that most of the Carter's Cove crowd, with the exception of Canon Davenport and old Brooks Burns, were Democrats. I'm still not sure what that signified, but I had heard my father say he was damned if he was going to the yacht club teas and listening to all those fat-necked old Captains of Industry bellow about shanty Irish and Not Our Kind and looming welfare states. The fact that they all summered in one of the latter, he said, hadn't occurred to a single one of them. After that I vocally castigated Republicans, although I could not have told you why.

It was, too, a time of exploration and flaming new cultural concepts, and the sound of tumbling mores was loud in the land. I am sure that most of our parents worried about our going baying after the rock music and the burgeoning hair and the beginning-to-be-whispered-about emergence of a terrifying substance called marijuana. They might as well not have worried, at least not there or then. We were as innocent of worldly knowledge and ambitions as a school of sprats. If we yearned after rebellion, it was against sailing regattas and good clothes.

"Well," said Cecie now, rather prissily, "you weren't here and Mrs. Doo-doo Davenport came in the minute everybody got here saying she had hot pancakes and real maple syrup, and I guess everybody figured if they were going to eat at all, they'd have to do it over there. Besides, Clara never makes anything but toast anyway. And from pancakes to popovers isn't such a big jump if you don't have anything else to do. We all thought we were going to sail over to Sunderson's and see the baby ospreys, but I guess you already did that yesterday with that new kid. He's out getting a sailing lesson from your dad. That left me. I'd starve before I ate anything of Peaches Davenport's."

Guilt smote me, for I had indeed suggested that we all take our Beetle Cats over to the island this morning. And there was another feeling, too, somewhere in my chest. Jon. I felt a sudden absolute need to hear someone speak his name. "You mean that Jon guy?" I said, striving for nonchalance and missing.

"Yeah," Cecie said. "That Jon guy. The one you spent all afternoon and last night with. Nobody else has met him or even seen him. What is he, spastic or something? They don't let him out?"

Anger rose in my throat, hot and bitter. I swallowed it. "He's not spastic. He's nice. They just got here, Cecie. Mother asked them for drinks, them and the Davenports and that goon Peaches, and we just talked and stuff. He's keeping Wilma over at their place in the daytime because they've got two big dogs and a fenced yard, and Peaches goes crazy when she sees Wilma. You'll like him when you meet him. His mother, too. She's neat. I don't think anybody much likes his dad. He's really uptight."

She was silent for a while, and then she said, "Don't tell me he likes Peaches. Just don't tell me that."

"I'd like to read her *The Hound of the Baskervilles* out loud. In a dark room," I heard Jon saying again, his voice full of laughter.

"No. He can't stand her. That's one reason I like him."

"One?" Cecie said, and I knew I had not yet been forgiven for my abandonment of her yesterday afternoon. I was suddenly weary of innuendo and quivering feelings. I did not reply.

We sat in silence a while longer, and I looked over at her. She was staring out the kitchen window at the reach, and in the dim, aqueous light I saw what I had not seen the morning before when we'd met on the cliff top: Cecie had passed the going-to-be-pretty stage and was there. Sometime over the past winter she had grown taller and even slimmer, and there was the definite beginning of breasts under her T-shirt. Her profile, in the underwater light, was defined and clean; she had lost the little wrappings of childhood fat under her chin and on her neck, and her hair shone mahogany. Her soft mouth was pinker than I remembered; could it be she was wearing lip gloss? Her skin was winter pale, just flushed with the first of summer, her bare legs porcelain. I stared, and then looked down at my own legs. They were scabby and bruised, and glistened with tiny bronze hairs. Why had I never noticed?

"Cecie," I said idiotically, "do you think I'm hairy?"

"Hairy?"

"Yeah. You know, hair all over me."

"I think you're nuts. But I don't think you're any hairier than you've ever been. What, did somebody say you were?"

"No. I was just looking at my legs. And yours. You don't have any hair on yours, and I do."

"Well," Cecie said a little uncomfortably, "I shave them. Mother said it was time."

Time. Time to shave your legs, time to wear lip gloss. Cecie was only two months older than I was, but the gulf between shaved legs and unshaved ones seemed unbreachable. I wondered if my mother was ever going to tell me when it was time to begin to let childhood slough off. Somehow I did not think so.

"Is it hard?" I said.

"No. You just have to be real careful. I'll show you, if you want me to."

"Yeah, I do."

We made an appointment for the ritual virgin shaving the next morning. I could think of nothing to say. I had always been the leader of the pack, the instigator. But I sensed that now we were moving into an uncharted country whose map I did not have. I hated the feeling.

Then Cecie said, "Here comes your dad and the famous Jon, just tying up at the dock. Let's go down so I can meet him and see what's making you act so silly."

"I am *not* silly," I said indignantly, but thought to myself that I probably was. All of a sudden I did not like anybody in my world. But then . . . Jon. Jon would be there, standing on the end of my dock in the wind and new sun just sliding out from behind the scudding clouds. I rose and followed Cecie out of the kitchen.

They had tied up and were climbing onto the end of the dock when Cecie and I got there. My father, in a battered parka and frayed old Top-Siders, waved. He was grinning widely, and I thought again how distinguished he was, and how glad I was that I had his rangy build and quick smile. Or did I alone see his beauty, and the goodness

89

and sweetness of his face? I was beginning to distrust my own perceptions this shifting, sliding summer.

"He did wonderfully," he called. "He's a natural. I let him bring us home by himself, and in this chop, too."

Behind him, Jon grinned hugely. His golden face was already darker, with wind and light, if not sun, and his streaked-gilt hair fell over his eyes. I thought it would be sun bleached to vermeil by the time the summer was over. Again I was grateful for the chipped front tooth. Without it he would be, simply, unbelievable.

I turned to look at Cecie, to see her face as she saw him for the first time. It was calm and pleasant, Cecie's meeting-new-people face, but that was all. No awe. No widening of her sherry-brown eyes. What was the *matter* with everybody?

"Well," my father said, "a gathering of young Olympians. A tennis star who sails like Odysseus. A horsewoman who is half-centaur. And my daughter, who is—"

"The star of the flying trapezes," Jon finished. I was absurdly pleased that he had remembered my telling him about my father's and my gymnasium in our basement at home.

I introduced Jon and Cecie, and we all walked up the dock toward the seawall. It was a sweet, calm morning, and I am sure I was the only one who felt the inklings and oddments in the air. The other three talked pleasantly of Jon's sailing prowess and Cecie's family's winter. My father said that my mother would call her parents soon and arrange for drinks or dinner. Cecie said she knew they'd like that. Jon said he hoped his family would get to know hers, too. I said nothing. I was afraid my voice would rend the taut skin of this strange world.

When we got to the seawall Jon's father was standing under the big pine looking down at us. He wore perfectly creased khakis and a beautiful oatmeal cashmere sweater over a blue oxford-cloth shirt, and gleaming loafers. In comparison, we four looked like scurvy-ridden survivors of a shipwreck.

Jon's father smiled. It did not reach his dark, opaque eyes. "You're more than an hour late, Jon," he said in a neutral voice. "Your mother has had lunch waiting for quite a while. We were getting worried."

"My fault entirely," my father said. "He was doing so well that I wanted to try him out a bit longer. He's a natural sailor. We'll be more attentive next time."

"Jon is a tennis player first and foremost," Arthur Lowell said. "His training routine is very strict, and much as I'd like to let it slide a bit this summer, we simply can't afford to. Next year will be a very big competition year for him. So we'll need to be a bit more careful about schedules. Jon, go up and have your lunch, so you can get in at least two hours' rest before our match. I'll be right along."

Jon's face tightened. The joy of the morning drained out of it. He looked at my father, and then at me, helplessly.

"I thought maybe we could still ride up Caterpillar Hill," he said to me. "It shouldn't take too long, should it?"

"Definitely *not* before tennis practice," his father said. "Another time, perhaps."

Jon opened his mouth to say something else, and then shut it.

"Yes sir," he said finally. Both of the Lowells turned and walked up the hill toward the road and their cottage. Neither looked back.

On the dock we were all silent, and then Cecie said, "Well. You want to go cycling with me, Lilly? I hear there's a really big boat up at the boatyard, being worked on. We could go see it."

All of a sudden exhaustion swamped me.

"Tomorrow, okay? I don't know what's the matter with me, but I'm so sleepy I can't hold my head up."

After a moment Cecie said, "Sure."

My father said nothing at all.

91

CHAPTER

5

"Look," Jon said. "Is that the moon? I never saw it so clear in the daytime before."

"Yeah," I said, looking up into the sky, going milky blue now with the coming evening and with a huge shrouded white moon hanging low. "Seth and Clara call it a Ghost Moon. Sometimes you can see moons in the daytime, but I don't remember why. That's the Strawberry Moon. The moon of June. I guess because the strawberries are ripe. It's full, too, or almost. And the tide will be full in when it rises, so it will be a really, really high tide. They happen once or twice a year, around the summer and winter solstices. Clara says mariners call them moon tides. Tonight's the solstice; well, you know. Mother's having a party for it. She said y'all are coming."

"Yeah. My mother's really excited about it. She says she never knew anyone who gave parties for the summer solstice before and from now on she's going to give them, too. She really likes your mother."

"Mom likes her, too," I said. "I don't think I ever met anybody she likes in the same way."

"How do you mean?"

"Oh . . . well, your mom's somebody who would understand a party for the solstice, I guess. Somebody who doesn't get snarky when Mom talks about magic. Tonight is powerful magic, she says. The

92

solstice, the full moon, *and* the moon tide. Earth magic. It's very old. Dad says people have always believed in it."

"Does your mother believe in it?" Jon said.

"Oh, not really. It's just that it's nature and all, you know, and she cares a lot about that stuff. And she likes celebrations. Dad says she's half witch, and sometimes I think she agrees with him. Her ancestors were Scots from the Highlands, and sometimes she laughs and says she has the sight. She says magic is just as necessary for human beings as food and shelter, but most of us have forgotten it."

"I like that," Jon said. "Sometimes I almost feel it—you know, like the ospreys and all. And people flying . . ." He grinned at me. "That would be magic, wouldn't it?"

"Yeah," I said, raising my arm to lie across my eyes so that the sun and drowning glitter from the water would not blind me. We were lying on our backs in a tangle of blueberry bushes a little way down the slope of Caterpillar Hill, and from there the entire panorama of earth and sky and water wheeled before us in almost a 360-degree circle. From here you could see over to Blue Hill and Blue Hill Bay, to the mountains of Mount Desert, to Deer Isle and all the inner and outer islands, to the great swell of the peninsula that rose to meet the sky above the Camden Hills. It was a very popular scenic spot for tourists, and there were almost always cars drawn up on the little overlook and people with cameras and artist's easels on its brow. But there were none now, and there had been very few since midmorning. Just at this moment, at the huge and mystical turning of the year, we had the great hill to ourselves.

It was, perhaps, a kind of magic that Jon was here with me. For many days, his time had been filled only with sailing with my father, lunch and resting at his house—whatever that meant—tennis with his father, dinner with his parents, and evenings at home. I saw him only from the dock, to wave at, or at night when he brought Wilma home, and then he could not stay. His father waited up for him. We did not even have time to talk, but once he picked me up in his arms and whirled me around on our dew-wet starlit front lawn, with Wilma capering and jangling around us, and said, as he put me down, "I miss you."

"Me too," I had responded, tears prickling in my eyes. "When do you think—"

"I don't know," he said, turning his face away from me, and then back. "But pretty soon. Mom is really pissed with Dad about all this resting-at-home shit—'scuse me, Lilly, crap—and says she's going to talk to him about it. She's the one who told me to skip the routine and go do whatever I wanted to with whomever I wanted to when he went to New York Monday. I think she's going to have it out with him when he gets back."

I smiled into the red darkness of my own flesh, under the sun. "I hope so. This has been a good week, hasn't it?"

"The best."

During our first weeks of June, I had done the things I always did in early summer at Edgewater. Cecie and I had indeed had the great virginal leg shaving, in the old claw-footed bathtub in our upstairs bathroom. It was pitted and stained with decades of Maine's mineral-rich water, and so short you had to lie on your back with your legs hanging over the end if you wanted to wash your hair under the faucet. It belched and gurgled and finally spat out icy water that took eons to warm up, so only the patient at Edgewater ever had hot baths. I sat on the side with my feet and legs in it and Cecie crouched in it with the water dribbling, armed with a can of her father's shaving cream and a rusted razor, which she assured me had a new blade. I closed my eyes until she was done, waiting to feel the stinging bite of the blade, but when she said "There, now you've got sexy legs," only my red-blond stubble whirled away down the drain, no threads of blood among it.

For days I felt naked and somehow indecent without my leg hair, and wore only blue jeans, but then a vicious little heat spell settled in and I pulled out my soft, faded old shorts. Looking down, I saw long, tanned legs that shone in the sun from the furtive sluicings of my mother's Jergens lotion that I employed as per Cecie's instructions. I held up one, and then the other, and then laced up my sneakers and crept out into the morning where the others waited restlessly for me. We had at last been given permission to ride our bikes as far as the top of Caterpillar Hill, and everybody was milling around in our front yard, balancing on their bikes and making circles on my mother's flower beds. Some were still chewing on Clara's toast.

When Cecie and I appeared, they jeered at our lateness and straightened up their bikes, waiting, I knew, for me to walk my blue Schwinn to the top of our driveway so we could move out. With my damp, naked legs catching the little wind off the reach, I was stricken with such self-consciousness that I could not move. Peter Cornish, whom we had overheard our mothers say would probably be in some kind of sexual trouble before he was sixteen, stared at my legs and said suddenly and loudly, "Lilly's shaved her legs! Look, everybody, Lilly's shaved her legs!"

Everybody stared.

Since it would have been ridiculous to protest that I had not, I wound one leg around the other and stood like a stork, staring belligerently around the group.

"Well, at least I *can* shave," I said. "That's more than you guys can say."

"Well, you don't have to get snotty," Peter said. "Did you think nobody would notice? God, Lilly, we look at your legs every day. They're what hold you up—how could we not? But I have to admit they look kind of . . . nice now. Like you could lick something sweet off them."

My face flamed all the way to my collarbones and I mounted my bike and pushed off up the little dirt road. I knew everyone would follow. It had always been the natural order of things at Edgewater and I thought little about it, except for sometimes feeling a sneaking conceit that I was the leader.

But on this day I would have given anything I had to be at the back of the pack, hairy legs pumping like pistons, wind from the others' slipstreams in my hair.

It had always been the best day of the summer, this first bicycle excursion. After a year of structured city outings and fretting about how we looked, the piney wind in our hair and the young June sun biting our pale limbs red was nirvana. But somehow this one died at birth.

We dropped our bikes on their sides in the great, low tangle of the blueberry barrens that swept from the top of Caterpillar Hill, around massive boulders and outcroppings of glacial rock, down to the lip of the reach. In another month the barrens would swarm with pickers, mostly migrant workers from Canada, many of them Acadians with the soft, indecipherable patois of Arcady. Sometimes they had small tents or shacks in which they slept, and occasionally we might spy, far away from them on the fringes of the barren, two or three of the small, thin bears who had shambled among us when we first came to Edgewater, looting garbage cans and terrifying newcomers but doing little harm. When the blueberries ripened I think all the bears in our part of Hancock County headed for the barrens and, for the rest of the summer, gorged on sun-fermented blueberries until they trundled tipsily into the woods to their lairs and slept their benders off, only to start again the next day. My father often said he wished the more notorious drinkers of his acquaintance would behave as well.

In the late fall the barrens turned an electric purple red, a color

I have never seen anywhere else; it seemed to be lit from within. But I did not see it so until much later.

We ate the sandwiches Clara had left for us and balled up the waxed paper and put it in our bicycle baskets and waited for the alchemy to catch up with us, the giddiness that would seize us and propel us, wild as woods colts with joy, through the rest of the summer.

It did not come.

I don't think they were waiting for me to give the "Gentlemen, start your engines" sign, it was just that somehow no one spoke or moved, and the silence spun out, until finally Carolyn Forrest said, timidly—for Carolyn was an enthusiastic follower but had never, that I could recall, initiated any action—"Clara's dog has got puppies. Do y'all want to go see them? Clara says they're real pretty, little wolf-dog puppies, but Daddy says they're illegal in Maine because their daddy was a wolf and they'd always have a wild streak. So I can't have one of them but I'm going to get a puppy this summer anyway. But it might just be fun to see wolf-dog puppies."

"If you're going to get a puppy you better check with Peaches first and see if she hollers," Joby Gardiner said. "But let's go see them. I've never seen a wolf-dog."

"Where is Peaches?" Cecie asked. "I didn't hear any screaming and Mrs. Davenport didn't invite me to one of Peaches' little dos."

"She's going with her grandparents down to Rockland to the art museum," Peter said. "We all got invited but I said we'd already promised to ride up Caterpillar Hill with Lilly. That's when she screeched. Her grandparents don't want her on a bicycle yet. Didn't you get invited, Lilly?"

"No," I said, both overjoyed and stung. Who was Peaches Davenport to exclude me from outings in my own domain?

"She's mad at you because she thinks that Jon guy has a crush on you." Peter smirked. "Well, everybody else thinks so, too. Is there something you want to tell us, Lilly? Like spending a whole afternoon over on Sunderson's with him?"

I was suddenly furious.

"I wouldn't tell you crap, Peter Cornish," I said. "You don't know what you're talking about. You never do."

"Well, I know that Peaches has a crush on the guy and thinks you do, too. If I were you I'd watch my back, Lilly."

After that I did not want to see wolf-dog puppies or much of anything else, so I coasted on home while the rest went swooping past me and down into the village, to Seth and Clara's house on the road to the public harbor. By that time it was nearing two o'clock. The Beetle Cat was tied up at our dock, so I knew Jon's sailing lesson was over and he was gone. The house was quiet and still, with that fathomless midafternoon, dust-moted silence old houses sometimes get, and I could find no one about. Clara had long finished in the kitchen and everything was shined and put away; my father was closeted in his study in pursuit of a warbling John Donne, and I knew that my mother was upstairs in her studio. She had been painting feverishly for a week or so, in one of the fits that sometimes took her, and had forbidden anyone to disturb her. No one had.

But I felt, suddenly, that I could not bear this echoing tomb of a house, and so I crept up the stairs and pushed open the door to her studio. The first thing I saw was the tweed-clad back of Brooks Burns. The second was what he was doing. I backed away from the door, my breath gagging in my throat, and ran silently down the stairs out into the air and light of afternoon. I sat on the seawall for a long time, struggling to find the rhythm of the sea's breathing, thinking nothing at all. When I finally got my breath and stood up, I knew that my world had changed, and I felt like I was floating over an abyss that had no bottom.

I wanted with all the force of my being to run to someone for comfort and the restoration of my world, and knew even in the wanting that there was no one. I wanted—I wanted Jon.

But I knew I would never tell him what I had seen. I thought I would never tell anybody. There was no one I could tell who would not, like me, be changed. I sat on the wall for a long time.

It was then that I began to spy on my mother.

I never went back to the studio. I was very careful about my covert routine. I am sure no one saw me. But that summer I learned more about my beautiful mother than I had in the past eleven years of my life, though nothing that would explain what I had seen in the studio that first day. Chiefly, I think, I began to learn about being a woman. But I did not know it then.

For the next two weeks I seldom went out with the group to bicycle or swim or sail. No, I told my mother, I didn't feel ill in any way. No, I had not had a squabble with anyone. No, no one had said anything that hurt my feelings. I just—an inspiration took me—felt like reading. There were some things I had brought from home that I was dying to read.

"About what?"

"Mythology," I said, having no idea where the word had come from but hearing in it the absolute rightness, the sure balm for my naked, quivering heart.

"Mythology?" Her straight, silky brows knotted. I stared into her face. I do not think I looked at her breasts for the rest of the summer, and for a long time after.

"Yes, I'm reading"—my mind fastened on a dusty old book I had seen in the attic, how many years ago I did not remember—"*The Golden Bough.*"

My mother looked at my father. He looked at me for a moment, and then smiled.

"Yes. A fine work, even if it is nearly undecipherable and overwhelmingly ponderous. If it speaks to you, Lilly, by all means dive in. It doesn't speak to many people."

And so, with my father's blessing, I spent long days in the attic lair I had fixed up with two broken Morris chairs, a rickety table, and a frayed old Oriental rug set under a window that gave onto the sea. I was giddy on Sir James George Frazer and spying on my mother. My father was right. The great, seminal book of the old religions and folklore and magic did speak to me. I never forgot it; I sometimes went back to it many years later. I think that learning about the wild, fire-shot, naked ancient world was the thing that saved me from total obsession with my mother.

And then Jon came back, and I forgot both in the joy of being with him.

At the beginning of this week, his father's overall manager of the quarries died of a heart attack and left in his shadow such a tangled mess of mismanagement and perhaps even larceny that there was nothing for it but for Arthur Lowell to go back to Rockville, New York, and pick up the pieces.

He was grim faced and furious. I learned later that Jon got the brunt of much of his anger. At first he wanted to take Jon with him as far as Eaglebrook and put him into the summer program so that he could keep up his tennis with the instructor there. When his wife said, simply, "He is not going," he sought to find an instructor in Ellsworth or Bangor who might, for whatever sum necessary, come and drill Jon in his absence.

Claire Lowell simply looked at him.

"All right, by God," he snapped finally. "But you see that he practices every day with somebody who's a match for him. Get that doddering old pro over at the colony. Or there must be somebody around here who can give him at least a decent game."

"The Forrest twins' father is good, Arthur, and I know he'd be happy to play with Jon. Go on, or we won't be able to afford tennis lessons or anything else." All this Jon told me on the first day we came together. He had, he said, listened from the kitchen. I wanted to hug him. So someone else did it, too.

And so, finally, Claire Lowell drove her husband to Bangor, where he caught a rattletrap commuter flight to New York, and on the morning after he went, my father said to Jon, "I need a week or two to myself right now. I'm on to something promising with Donne, I think. Can we pick up sailing a bit later?"

Minutes after he spoke, Jon and I were on mine and Jeebs's bicycles, heading out.

"Won't Jeebs want his?" Jon asked me that first morning, swinging onto Jeebs's old 'cycle with his rangy athlete's grace.

"He hasn't ridden it in ages," I said. "He's going around with some kids from the colony this summer. One of them has a car."

"Great." He grinned, and his smile lit the world.

We rode everywhere. We spent hours on the twisting dirt tracks off Reach Road toward the west, most of which ended in ramshackle, unpainted, falling-down houses with high-piled firewood and corpses of long-dead cars and abandoned lobster traps and buoys. Only occasionally did we see anyone around them, and the ones we did see were dark and almost feral looking, not offering the one-lifted-finger wave that is the traditional acknowledgment of another in Maine. We did not linger around these houses. Maine was a sporadically poor state behind the prosperous, white-painted saltwater farms that lined the front roads and the beetling old summer cottages down on the shore. We were deep in this other Maine when we came into the purview of these houses, and knew on our skins we were not wanted. We would lift our forefingers slightly, nod, and pedal briskly back the way we had come.

We went down to Naskeag Point, where, I told Jon, rumor had

101

it that there were, in the rocks fringing the shore, the petrified tracks of one of the Viking longboats that were said to have discovered this beautiful point centuries before. I had never seen them, and the Mainers I knew usually just shrugged and said, "Makes a good tale, doesn't it?"

But I knew in my soul that the tracks were there, and I never ceased looking for them.

We went halfway to Blue Hill and back, singing as our wheels burred sweetly on the long hills down. We went down to Sedgwick and bought ice-cream bars and sharp cheddar cheese said to be the best in Maine at the teeming little general store there. When I learned later that the cheese came from Vermont, I simply chose to disbelieve it.

This day I had been saving for last, for this first Friday of our liberation. This Friday we came up to Caterpillar Hill.

Never think that the very young cannot love. Never think that. They love with a fierce, direct love. This first love is one-celled and consuming, the lovers unable yet either to fear for or save themselves, untrammeled yet by experience, unleavened with wiles and prudence. I simply loved Jon Lowell with all my heart and soul, and it never occurred to me that he might not love me. I think that on that day we were both still easy with it. What came after hung blooming in the air far ahead of us, but we did not yet need to touch it. It would ripen; it would last. It was, then, simply enough to be together, to talk endlessly, to laugh at everything and nothing, to drown with pure joy in our alikeness. I read no more Frazer. Jon played no more tennis. So far, no one seemed to mind. We did not touch.

Now we lay side by side in the springy blueberry barrens of Caterpillar Hill, full of lunch and drowsiness and as near-perfect contentment as I could ever remember. My mother's solstice party loomed, exotic and gleaming, ahead of us. The molten golden week lay behind. It was a moment out of time, the kind you remember when you are very old, though I did not know that then.

"It feels like when we get up we'll leave outlines of ourselves, like an X-ray, or a photograph the sun took," I said drowsily.

"Yeah," Jon said, just as drowsily. "We can come back in fifty years and here we'll still be."

Happiness such as I had never known flooded me. "We can come back in fifty years . . ." After a few minutes I asked, "Do you like tennis?"

"No," he answered. "Why did you ask me that?"

I did not know. The words were simply out of my mouth before I thought about them.

"I guess because you never talk about it," I said finally. "And it doesn't sound like much fun if you have to do all that stuff your father makes you do just to play it. I mean, do you really want to be a tennis professional when you"—I almost said "grow up," but stopped. I often forgot he was not grown up.

"No. I want to be an archaeologist, I think. I loved studying it at school. We saw a lot of artifacts in museums around Boston, and we went on one or two little digs. I found a piece of blue-and-white pottery that my teacher said was probably from the earliest Colonial period in Massachusetts. He thinks it was a piece of a teapot. I remember that it felt so funny in my hands when he said that that I almost dropped it. Hot and quivery, almost alive. I could almost see the woman who made the tea in it. It was . . . a great feeling. I knew then that was what I wanted to do. I was supposed to go on a real dig this summer with this guy from Harvard who sometimes takes a prep-school student with him. The dig was in Peru, around where the last Incas were supposed to have lived."

He did not continue, so I said, "But your father wouldn't let you."

"No."

"Couldn't your mother have helped you persuade him? I mean, I know she's on your side."

"I never told her I wanted to go."

I lay silently in the sun, trying to get inside his mind. Then I said, "My father says I can do anything I want to. He says nobody ought to put a kid's mind in a cage."

"So what do you want to do, then?" he asked.

"I don't know," I said, feeling foolish. "There's lots that would be fun, I think. A writer, maybe. Or something with animals, or the moon and stars, or . . . oh, I don't know. Maybe I'll just run away and join the circus."

He laughed, behind the screen of his own upraised arms. "I bet you could, if you wanted to. You aren't afraid of much, are you, Lilly?"

"Well . . . not yet. There's probably a lot of stuff I will be afraid of later, but it hasn't happened yet." And then I thought, *But it has. Love has happened to me. And I don't know what to do with it.*

"Are you afraid of your father?" I asked. It never struck me then that the question might be impertinent, too personal. This was Jon. I wanted to know this.

"I guess I am," he said slowly, still not looking at me. "I don't mean that he'll do something to hurt me. I'm afraid of hurting him. I think about that all the time."

"How on earth could you hurt your father?" I asked in astonishment, sitting up to look down at him.

He did not answer. He rolled over so that his face rested on his crossed arms in the blueberry brush, so that the sun hammered his back. Then he said, "I had a brother, Lilly. A big brother, almost ten years older than me. My dad says I was a surprise, but my mother says she'd been planning for me for a long time. It doesn't matter. Sib was . . . everything. Almost from the minute he was born, he was everything. He was so good-looking by the time he was ten or twelve that he was almost—unbelievable. I don't think he even noticed, although he couldn't beat girls off him. His grades were fantastic. He was a born musician. He won every essay contest he entered. He was president of everything they had at Deerfield. And there wasn't a sport he couldn't do, if he wanted to. He was phenomenal at tennis, so good that Deerfield gave him a full four-year tennis scholarship, which they almost never do, and he'd already been accepted at Yale by his junior year at Deerfield. There were scholarships waiting for him there, too, and my dad said that some of his old fraternity brothers told him in confidence that Sib could probably have his choice of fraternities, probably even Skull and Bones. My dad almost flipped over that. He didn't make it."

"What on earth is Skull and Bones?"

"I don't know. Some kind of secret club a few guys get to join."

"Will you be in it?"

"If Dad has his way I will. I hope I am. Then everything will be all right."

"Why isn't it all right now?" I wanted to know. "If he wants you to be the best tennis player in the world, you probably could be. What else does he want you to be? King?"

"No," Jon said into his arms. "Sib."

I could think of nothing else to say, but felt the darkness coiled deep in this conversation.

He rolled over onto his back and looked at me. The dying sun turned his eyebrows pure gold and poured over the strong, straight features. I noticed for the first time that there was a tiny round scar, an indentation like a period, at the corner of his mouth. In the sun his skin was poreless, a golden hide. My heart twisted with love for him.

"Arthur Sibley Lowell," he said and grinned slightly. The grin was crooked. "I idolized him. I followed him every step he took. I must have driven him nuts, but he never tried to get rid of me. He always made time for me. It was my dad who shooed me away so Sib could practice, or whatever."

Something inside me began to chill, slowly, as if cold water crept up my limbs toward my heart.

"You said . . . you said you *had* a brother."

"Sib died when he was seventeen and I was seven. It was an accident. I thought my father would probably go crazy from it. He went down to the quarry office and didn't come home until real late every night. I almost never saw him. My mother was torn to pieces too, of course, but she would hold me for hours or sing me to sleep, and she never, ever stopped saying that it wasn't anybody's fault, and that my father would realize that in time."

"I don't understand," I said. "If it was an accident—"

"I caused it, Lilly," he said. His voice was guttural and his face twisted briefly and then relaxed into passivity.

"He'd just graduated from Deerfield, and his graduation present was one of the first Corvettes. It was bright red, a great car. He tinkered with it constantly when he wasn't driving it. I was crazy about that car. I was forbidden to ride in it yet, but he was going to take me for a ride right before he went away to Yale. Dad told me never to touch it, not even to get near it. I remember once thinking, *If Sib died, I bet I'd get that car* . . ."

I reached over and put my hand over his. It was warm and smooth, with hard little sailing calluses in the palm and older tennis ones along the outside of it. He did not move it for a moment, and then he curled his fingers around mine and squeezed them so hard I almost felt the bones crack. But I said nothing, only squeezed back.

"I've wished Jeebs would kick off a million times," I said. "I've even told him I wished he would. Everybody does that, Jon."

"I know. I even knew it then. It still hurts, though. It really hurts."

He looked at me. "I've never told anybody about it.

"So anyway, one day in the summer just before he was going to Yale—I remember that because his trunks were all over everywhere and Mom was filling them up with new underwear and sheets and stuff, and he was laughing at her. He was out at the driveway where it runs into the street, waiting for some friend of his to come pick him up. They had dates that night. It's a long, steep driveway and it curves right at the end. He was lying down at the bottom of it. He used to do that when somebody who was coming to get him was really late, make believe he'd waited so long he'd gone to sleep. There wasn't anybody around, so I crawled into the front seat of the Corvette and fiddled around with the dashboard, and somehow I let off the brakes. I . . . couldn't . . . I couldn't figure out how to put them on again. I remember that I was scared to death nothing would stop me until I hit the street, and I'd be killed, and nobody would care because they'd told me not to play in the car in the first place. It seemed like a long time, and the car went faster and faster, and I started to yell, and then—"

"Don't," I said. "Don't." I began to cry silently. I did not think I could bear that terrible old pain for him.

"I don't remember a lot about the year after that," he said. "I know my mother was almost always with me. I know I started at Eaglebrook, and I know the tennis lessons started, but I don't really remember them. Just what people told me."

"And so he started right in making you . . ."

"Into Sib. Yeah. I doubt if he even realized it. Mother does, but she doesn't know I hate the tennis and all the rest of it. If she did I think she'd come right down on him. But nobody's wanted to hurt him any more after . . . that. It doesn't hurt me to play tennis right now, I don't guess. I can always change things when I get to Yale. Maybe I won't even go to Yale. Maybe I'll go to—Ole Miss or somewhere. I'll be eighteen then. I can pick my own classes and maybe even what I want to do. I don't have to go on to law school and come home and run the business. I know that here." He touched his forehead. "I just don't know it . . . here." He touched the Lacoste shirt over his heart. "In here, I still feel like I have to give him back Sib, or at least try. I know nobody could do that, not really, but I just know that I have to try."

I did not say any more. My tears dried themselves on my face, in the little evening wind that sprang up with the turn of the tide. The air was cooling slightly. It was time to go.

We got up and packed our picnic things and pushed the bicycles onto the main road. I looked back to where we had been lying. I truly thought for a second that I could see the outline of our bodies there, in the blueberry bushes.

We were swooping side by side down the crest of Caterpillar Hill when I said, "Boy, I guess it's a good thing your dad isn't going to be here for the famous solstice party. He'd probably call the sheriff on all of us."

Jon did not look at me.

"He's coming home this afternoon," he said. "He called early this morning. Some piece of equipment or other didn't come in and he's coming back for a week or two till it does. Mom's gone over to get him at Bangor. They may be back by now."

108

I said nothing. We rode steadily until we reached the cutoff onto Reach Road and home. By then the sky was turning lavender and the Strawberry Moon was swelling yellow, and I knew that if I went back to look, there would be no X-rays of Jon and me in the blueberry barrens of Caterpillar Hill.

CHAPTER

6

From the top of the back roof overhang, it was possible to see and hear everything that went on on the lawn, the veranda, the driveway, and a stretch of the lane that connected the cottages. At six o'clock that evening I went into my parents' room and climbed out their window to the roof and sat there with my arms wrapped around my drawn-up knees. My mother's solstice party was not due to start for another half hour, but I knew that she and my father and Clara and her daughter and granddaughter, who were known to be good with parties, would be either in the kitchen or out on the green lawn by the seawall, preparing to honor the gods older by far than ours.

From my perch I could see my father stringing Japanese lanterns from the great pines and firs surrounding the little glade by the seawall, and my mother setting candles on the small round tables she used for outdoor parties. These were covered not with their customary color-splashed cloths but with some sort of white, drifting stuff that I suspected was the old organdy curtains that had once hung in the guest bedroom. The tables were garlanded in greenery, and there was a small bouquet of what looked to be ferns, ivy and balsam sprigs, silvery woods moss, and the last of the wild pink and purple lupines. The effect was surprisingly pretty, I thought. Only the colors of the sea and sky and the woods, all lit by tiny flickering flames and the wash of vermillion from the sunset far to the west, and the rising radiance of the voluptuous Strawberry Moon. Even the green darkness of the deep woods around us would be moon soaked tonight. Shadows would be sharp and ink black. I remembered my earlier fancy that all the small wild things danced on our lawn in the light of such a moon. It did not seem foolish now. Just as my mother had said it would, magic was waking in the woods, and it would soon walk with us on the lawn.

I was scrubbed and dressed in a sleeveless white blouse and the long, sheer paisley skirt my mother had brought me back from India a few years before, telling me that it would make a lovely summer party skirt. I had finally capitulated and put it on this evening for the first time, and was surprised how nice it felt brushing against my bare legs and billowing in the little tidal breeze. I had piled my hair on top of my head while it was still damp, because I could not subdue the curls that summer humidity by the sea had spawned, and stabbed it with a few of Mother's hairpins. It was already springing loose and wisping around my face, but I did not care. I had put on no lip gloss nor stolen any blush, and I smelled simply of soap and mineral-infused water. I had not even looked at myself after I had dressed. This evening did not feel like a party to me. There was a dullness in my heart and a weariness in my limbs. It had been so since Jon told me his father was coming home, this afternoon on Caterpillar Hill. Whatever we had, Jon and I, would soon be lost to strictures and schedules and sternness. Suddenly I wanted to cry.

I wish we'd never had it, I thought, sniffling. Presently I saw Claire Lowell walking across our lawn from the lane, dressed in something long and blue and carrying a huge bouquet of white daisies and some kind of shiny green leaves. I leaned forward to see if Jon had accompanied her. He was not there. My whole body shuddered suddenly with hatred for Arthur Lowell. What sort of man was it whose mere presence blighted an entire summer?

I sat back, realizing that Jon's mother was talking and I could hear her. I sat very still.

". . . stole them out of that pasture we pass on the way to Blue Hill," she was saying, laughter in her voice. "It was covered with them and I've never seen a living soul around there . . . Yes, Arthur's home now, but he's pretty tired from the trip, and he and Jon have been playing tennis for over two hours. I don't mind telling you he was furious that Jon hadn't played all week."

". . . partly our fault," I heard my mother say. "George had research to do and I think he thought Jon needed a little downtime from sailing anyway. I knew Jon was off with Lilly on their bikes most every day, but they were . . . having such a good time."

"I'm delighted he had that time," Claire Lowell said, putting her bouquet into Clara's waiting arms and smiling at her. "Something smells wonderful in the kitchen, Clara," she said.

"Crab quiche." Clara smiled in return. "My own recipe. Those folks up at the inn want me to make it for them, but I didn't want to be tied down every night."

"I will eat a dozen slices," Claire Lowell said. And then, to my mother, "I told Jon it was okay to skip the tennis for a while," she said. "It's almost all he ever does. I know he's awfully good and he needs to practice, but this is . . . obsessive and excessive on Arthur's part. I never saw him quite so rigid about it before this summer. We had a pretty unpleasant scene about it, to tell you the truth. He said he didn't want Jon spending so much time with any girls, including Lilly, and I said I was delighted that he had Lilly for a friend. Jon's never made many friends because he's never had much free time, and Lilly's just the sort of friend I'd always hoped he'd have. Arthur said he hoped friend was all it was—oh, God. I shouldn't be babbling to you about this, Liz. But it was just such an ugly thing to say. I hope Jon didn't hear it, but I think he may have. He didn't say a word on the way over here, and he usually talks a lot, to me."

Jon was here, then. My fury blew away as suddenly as it had come, and I got up and crawled back through the window to go and find him.

"We all love Jon," I heard my mother say. "Not just Lilly, though I know she adores him. Do you think people are talking about the time they spend together, or anything like that? I never even thought about it."

"Oh, of course not! It's not as though they were seventeen or eighteen yet. When I was Lilly's age my best friend was literally the boy next door, and we spent every waking minute together, and no-body minded at all. I still keep up with him," Mrs. Lowell said. "I think Arthur is terrified that something or someone will take Jon away from tennis, and I'd give a good deal if something would. He needs a real life. He's never said, but there are times I think Jon is just plain tired of tennis."

That's all you know, I thought smugly.

"Well, you can tell Arthur he's got nothing to worry about," my mother said, laughter in her voice. "Lilly hasn't even gotten her period yet. Is Arthur coming tonight, by the way?"

"No. He said he was damned if he'd go to some kind of magic witch party, and I told him our house could use a little of both, and he went upstairs to his office and closed the door. I'm hoping he'll be asleep by the time we get back."

I hardly heard the rest of the sentence. My entire body flamed with embarrassment and violation, and I swung into the room and ran down the hall to my bathroom and scrubbed my face with cold water. Then I sat down on the end of my bed, my heart rocketing in my chest. I sat waiting for it to find the rhythm of the sea so I could breathe again, but it was a long time before it did.

I knew about periods, of course; everybody in my crowd did, and talked of them endlessly in bored voices, but in truth I did not think anyone had gotten hers yet. We would have known. There would have been no end of ersatz agony and preening. I had always thought about my first period as something that would mean I was nearly grown up, waiting far ahead in some golden-mist–shrouded future along with getting my driver's license and being able to vote. It was nothing I had to deal with now, nothing I had to think about yet.

But suddenly the gilded mist turned dull red and roiled. Small tadpole shapes swam in it, and it smelled somehow of low tide. It terrified me. I wanted with all my heart to go back to the first day at Edgewater, before I had met Jon coming out of the sun at the top of the cliff. I wanted cold green water and sunlight tingling on my shoulders and dew pricking my bare feet and Wilma larruping around my ankles and nothing on my mind or in my world but seeing Cecie for the first time and what we might have for dessert that night. I wanted simplicity. I wanted only childhood.

But then there would be no Jon.

I laid my hot face down on my folded arms. Red darkness danced behind my eyelids. Was this what it was, then: love? Was this what love meant? Having to give up so much self that you did not even recognize who was left in order to have this stabbing, sweet, wild new joy? How did people ever choose?

But then, how could they not?

I was overwhelmed with complexity and choice and joy and pain and fear, and suddenly I wanted not Jon, but my father. I ran out of the room and out of the house and down onto the lawn, still barefoot, and looked around for him. I did not see him. I did not see Jon.

"How pretty you look." Jon's mother smiled at me. "I like your hair up, and that long skirt . . . a proper solstice princess."

"You do look nice, sweetie," my mother said, looking at me long and closely. "But do you feel all right? You're flushed."

"Too much sun," I said, hoping my voice would not wobble. "Where's Daddy?"

My mother gestured.

"Down at the dock with Jon," she said.

I looked. They stood at the end of the dock, their backs to us, silhouetted against the mothy, luminous darkness that came just before summer moonrise. Jon's head was bowed, and my father's arm was around his shoulder. He was saying something to Jon, but of course I could not hear what.

"Just getting a little pep talk, I think," Claire Lowell said. "His father wasn't too pleased that he missed tennis this week."

Just then Jon turned and looked up the long dock at me. In the dusk I could see that his yellow head lifted and his teeth flashed white. I could see the chipped tooth in my mind without seeing it at all. He lifted his hand in salute. I felt my mouth curve up in an answering smile. My arm lifted and waved back.

Jon. Of course. Jon.

No choice.

I started across the lawn toward him. By the time I reached the edge of the dock I was trotting. He walked quickly up the dock, his long legs cutting the distance. When we met, I turned suddenly shy and dropped my eyes. We did not speak for a long moment, and then I said, still looking down, "Hey."

"Hey," he said.

Whatever we might have had at this meeting exploded softly into the air, shards of it tinkling to the ground.

Finally I looked at him. His face was shadowed in the failing light, but I could see that his eyes were red.

"Are you crying?" I blurted.

"No," he said. "Come on. Here comes Clara with a plate of something. Whatever it is, I want some. I'm starved. I haven't eaten since those sandwiches at noon."

We turned and walked together over the lawn to the buffet table, already spread with hors d'oeuvres and hot bread and a great platter of cheeses with crackers. There seemed to be no one about yet but our mothers. My father had gone in to change, I supposed, and Clara had disappeared back into the house.

The two women smiled at us. That was how they seemed to me tonight. Two women; powerfully and totally whole, archetypal in the flickering light of the candles and the strengthening radiance of the moon. Below the seawall the sea murmured and slapped, almost reaching the top. I had never seen it this full, and remembered what I had told Jon that afternoon.

"Moon tide," I said.

"Yes," my mother said, smiling at me. "Prettiest one I've seen since I started coming here. Fix yourselves a plate before the ravening horde gets here. The chowder isn't out yet, but this will hold you."

"Fill your plate, Jon. You haven't eaten," Claire Lowell said, looking keenly at her son. He turned away to the table.

"Where is everybody?" I asked, my mouth full of hot crab dip.

"They'll be along," my mother said. "I told everybody except Claire seven, so we could admire our handiwork and commune with the old spirits. If we did that in front of this bunch they'd shove us in Saint Elizabeth's before you could say Aphrodite. I think the only old spirits this crowd communes with are single malt. Listen—I think I hear the outriders now."

It was the custom in the colony and its environs for every family to give one large party a summer, inviting literally everyone. My mother dutifully followed the custom, but this was not her large party.

116

This party was just for the families in Carter's Cove. She had given it on this night for years, and so far as I knew no one had ever suspected they were paying homage to pagan deities, even though it was done in fun. Well, half-fun, anyway. As my father said, Canon Davenport would attempt to exorcise us if he suspected.

At this party the children of all the cove's families were included, something my mother never did except on this night.

"The only children I want to see at a party are the ones passing trays," she had said once, when we were leaving a large dinner party that had been completely hijacked by racing, shrieking children.

I listened and heard them too: the children of Carter's Cove, my summer cadre, pounding down our driveway en masse, laughing and yelling at everything and nothing. My heart lifted suddenly and flew out to meet them. Childhood was coming back to me in one drowning rush. I ran to meet them at the edge of the lawn. Jon was close behind me. Before the first of their parents arrived, we had fallen into linked-arm lines opposite each other on our lawn. Red Rover was about to begin.

There is something magical about playing outdoors by moonlight so bright that you need nothing else. It is as if you have drunk the moonlight; you are giddy with it. Since early childhood on this night, the children of this cove had played games of childhood: Kick the Can, Red Rover, Statues, Giant Step. Back at our winter homes and schools we would not have been caught dead playing them, but in this place, and certainly on this night, childhood claimed us once more, perhaps all the sweeter because deep down we knew that we were leaving it, that we all had one foot on the farther shore. I thought about this a good deal much later, but this was not a night for reflection. This night was for young bodies and new grass and the great sphere of the Strawberry Moon, fully emerged now and ruling all the earth. It was immense, luminous, so close you could see the pits and shadows, the great lunar seas and valleys and mountains where, before any of us were fully grown, men of earth would walk. It was hardly possible to look away from it for any length of time. My father said later that he could never remember a moon that seemed so near the earth. The adults, all of whom had arrived in the middle of our games, sat quietly, drinking cocktails and nibbling quiche and smoked salmon, looking up at the moon. It was obvious that this party was not only for my mother's friends, but also for the great moon of the strawberries.

When at last we were limp and panting from our exertions, we went in a pack to the buffet table to fill our plates. As bidden by my mother, I said hello to all the parents there, all except Jon's known to me since childhood. When I came to Cecie's mother and father, I stopped still.

"Where's Cecie?" I said. It was only then that I realized that she had not been in the pack on the lawn.

"She's at a new equestrian camp in Virginia," Mrs. Wentworth said. "She left a couple of days ago; a spot opened up and her instructor called us. She really wanted Cecie to go. Cecie said to tell you good-bye if she didn't see you."

"I . . . but . . ." I stammered, shame nearly choking me. I had not thought of Cecie since the beginning of the week, when Jon had been liberated.

"It was very sudden," Mrs. Wentworth said, smiling. "We hardly had time to get her packed and on the plane. She knows you'll understand. She's going to write you."

The borrowed childhood sluiced off me like water. I had totally forgotten my best friend for Jon. That other thing, that thing that was stealing my soul like aborigines believe a camera will steal theirs, was back. I mumbled something and went to sit on the seawall with my plate. Jon followed me.

"What's the matter?" he asked.

"I didn't do anything with Cecie all this week, and now she's gone to camp, and she didn't say good-bye."

"That's my fault," Jon said softly.

"No," I said, looking up at him. "It's mine. I just plain forgot about Cecie. I wanted to be with you."

He swallowed a great mouthful of buttered bread and grinned at me. "Me too," he said.

"Is all that over now that your dad's back?" I said.

"No. I'm not going to let it be over. I'll play tennis with him, but I'm going to see you, too, and there's no way he can stop me."

"He could make you go home."

"Well, he can't make my mother go home. So it just ain't going to happen. She loves it here. She's not about to leave. She said so. She may seem a little . . . ditzy at times, but she's tough when she needs to be."

"You were crying this afternoon, weren't you?" I said. In this enabling moonlight I felt that I could say anything to him.

"Yeah," he said, so softly I could barely hear him. "I just got so . . . mad at him. I wanted to yell 'You can make me play tennis till we both drop dead, but you still won't get Sib back. Don't you see that? Don't you see *me*?'"

"Did you say it?"

"No. It was the first time I'd ever really wanted to, and that scared me. I wanted—I wanted to talk to your dad.

"He said that there'd come a time when I'd feel like I could talk to Dad, and it would be a great thing for both of us, but he didn't think the time had come yet. He said that there was an awful lot for my dad to get used to, and it was starting now, and that things might get worse before they got better, but they *would* get better. I asked him how he knew that, and he said he'd been both a kid and a dad, and as it turned out, being a dad was better than being a kid. That for him it was the best thing in the world. Your father is fantastic, Lilly. I wish he was mine."

"But . . ."

"I know. If he was we wouldn't be sitting here. Not like this."

Before I could say "Like what?" there was a stir among the adults up on the terrace, and we heard the booming voice of Canon Davenport, followed by the sweet, tired treble of his wife. All my muscles tensed. I hadn't noticed that the Davenports were not here. I had not even noticed that Peaches was absent.

". . . all the godforsaken way down to Freeport for it," the canon boomed.

"Well, it was a pretty ride." Mrs. Davenport sighed. "And Peaches had her heart set on it. I think it will be fun for the children. She says she got it especially for Jon."

"I'm sure he'll be very glad to hear that," I heard Jon's mother say formally.

"Where is Jon?" Peaches' trill cut the soft envelope of moonlight. "I want to show it to him right now."

"Let's have some dinner first, darling," her grandmother began.

"No. Now."

"Oh, God." Jon breathed wearily and got to his feet. "Let's get out of here."

I got up too, and took his outstretched hand. Such a big hand. Warm.

"Where are we going?"

He thought for a moment, and then pointed to the uppermost cliff of Mr. Forshee's headland. It shone in the moonlight like marble, or snow. "Up there."

Still holding hands, we ran, crouched over like marauding Indians, through the outer rim of the circle of light from the house and the lanterns, down onto our beach, all but covered now with the soft-breathing sea, and along it to where the cliff's wild underbrush began and the headland cast its black shadow. We stopped for a moment, breathing hard, and then we began to climb.

Jon reached the top ahead of me, and held out his hand. I took it and stood looking up at him for a moment. He seemed lined with cold fire; the white moonlight ran over him like wild honey. I smiled. When I had first seen him, it seemed as though he had just stepped out of the sun. Now he was newly moon-born.

I told him what I had been thinking. He grinned at me.

"Just wait till you see me coming out of a poolroom or a bar. I bet I look good in neon."

"You'll never go in places like that," I said, sitting down and leaning back against a smooth-worn boulder left there more than ten million years before. It had a slight concavity that fit my back and head nearly perfectly. I sat back in the flood of the moon and looked at Jon, who sat beside me. The last glacier had left him a seat, too. At that moment we reigned over heaven and earth.

"I might," he said. "I'm going a million places besides tennis courts when I'm on my own. I'll see every one of the seven wonders of the world. I'm going to run the Boston Marathon, swim the Bosporus, and walk the Silk Road. I might even check out up there." He gestured at the moon.

"Have you got room for two?" I said, feeling uneasy. He had made no mention of me in his journeys.

"Well, sure," he said, looking at me seriously. "I mean us."

Something inside me swelled with joy. Something else took one step back, whimpering "Wait a minute." Aloud, I said nothing.

The moonlight was an elemental force that pressed upon us until we lay back on the rock, much as we had lain side by side in the blueberry barrens on Caterpillar Hill that afternoon. It seemed right, the only thing to do up here where the entire world burned silver, from the small mountain that was Blue Hill in the west to the sweep up to the Camden Hills and the entire open sea beyond them in the east. I did not want to stand up in the face of all that. It felt like—what was the word my father had used a night or so ago, talking about Jon's father?—hubris. This was no night and no place for hubris. This was a night for awe.

It was cold on the cliff. I had the fancy that the moon was pouring her cold radiance directly through us. Shivering, I burrowed against Jon's shoulder, and he put his arm around me. Wherever our skin touched there was heat.

We lay in silence for a while, and then I said, "Your father doesn't like me. I heard your mother talking to mine, and she was telling Mom what he said about you being around girls, and especially around me. I don't understand that, Jon. I've hardly ever even spoken to him."

He sighed, a long sigh.

"He doesn't dislike you, Lilly. He's afraid of you."

"*Afraid* of me?" The idea seemed incredible to me, almost laughable.

"Yeah. You're a leader. People just naturally follow you, at least kids do. He's seen that. It scares him. He doesn't want me around anyone who takes me away from—"

"Tennis?" I said.

"Yeah. Tennis and—the life he's got planned for me. You know, Eaglebrook and then Deerfield and Yale and the right clubs and the right kind of friends." He paused. "The right kind of girls."

"What kind are they?" I whispered, knowing that whatever they were, I was not and never would be one of them.

"Well, smart, nice girls from the right families and the right schools, girls who are respectful and charming to their elders and never get into trouble of any kind and get to be deb of the year and marry the right kind of boy and have the big house and showplace gardens and the right kind of children. Two, preferably. Never more than three. And the kids go to the right nursery and preschools and prep schools and so on . . . into eternity, I guess."

"Pretty girls?"

"Oh, yeah, that helps. Blond, with long hair and headbands and pearl necklaces their grandmothers gave them. Blue eyes." He grinned over at me. "Good at one or two sports, preferably tennis. But of course not too good. Just enough to give me what he calls a good game."

I lay back in the crook of his arm, silenced by the recitation. Then I said, "I don't fit any of that. None of it. I guess he's afraid you're hanging around with the second string."

"No. He's afraid I'm going to do more than hang around you. He's afraid I'm going to—oh, marry you, I guess. That would be a disaster, in his book. That would make me . . . not Sib."

In my mind the word *marry* ran to and fro wringing its hands.

"When do you think he's going to realize you're not Sib?" I said.

"When I marry you, I guess."

"Jon," I said faintly.

"Well, we are, aren't we? Going to get married sometime or other? I thought you knew that."

"I didn't—well, I guess maybe I did, Jon. I don't know how to think about being married and I certainly don't know how to think about having kids. I'm still a kid myself. You are, too."

"No," he said, looking at me. I could feel his eyes inside me, in the marrow of my bones. "We're not kids. I've always known that. The others are kids. We're not."

I turned my face into his shoulder, out of the light of the consuming moon, the great moon that made changelings of people who,

123

only a week before, had been kids but were no more. He put both arms around me and pulled me against him. I felt the warmth of his long body in every molecule, every atom.

"Have you ever had a boyfriend?" he asked, into my wind-tangled hair.

"I . . . don't think so," I said doubtfully. "I mean, Peter is my friend, even though he's a jerk, and Ben and Joby—"

"No, I mean a boyfriend. Somebody you liked a lot, or maybe even loved."

"No," I whispered, feeling somehow ashamed, as if I had failed a crucial test. And then, "Have you ever had a girlfriend?"

"Well, a couple of times, I guess. I mean, they were girls I kissed in the movies and stuff like that."

He did not go on. Kissed and stuff like that. What stuff?

"Are they . . . is one of them still your girlfriend?"

"Of course not," he said, into my hair again. "I wouldn't be here if one was, would I?"

I did not know how to respond. I did not know the etiquette of having girlfriends. Or boyfriends, for that matter. My crowd at home talked endlessly of love affairs and passion and the sweetness of forbidden lust, but in truth we knew only what we could imagine, which was not much, or what we had read in books, which none of us would have dared to do or even think of doing.

"So what happened to them?" I said. It was something I thought I should know, so as to avoid making the same missteps and losing him. The way ahead, the years to come with Jon, seemed so fraught with perils and land mines and dos and don'ts that I simply lay against his shoulder in despair. I would never get it right. I would never learn all the rules.

"I don't really know," he said slowly. "They just . . . didn't change.

They were both just the kind of girls my dad approved of, pretty and from—you know—good families, and shoo-ins to be Junior Leaguers and debutantes and all that, but they were just the same on the day we broke up as the day we met. I just got the feeling that if I got hooked up with one of them she'd never change, and I knew I would. It didn't seem like much of a life to me. My dad was really pissed when I broke up with the last one. Barbara. Buffy, everybody called her. You'd have thought I'd left her at the altar, or something. God, I was barely twelve then."

"Do you think I'll change?" I mumbled into his sweater. It was the one he had worn when he first met me, on the day we sailed over to Sunderson's Island and saw the ospreys. Scratchy, damp, smelling of saltwater and wood smoke and something else that I knew now to be Jon himself. Jon's flesh. It felt wonderful, safe. Like home.

"Lilly, you change practically every day I'm with you. It's one of the things I . . . like about you."

I knew he meant to say "love." I was glad he had not. It seemed a delicate and endearing thing to do, to know that even if I felt love I could not yet make my mouth say it.

"Have you ever kissed anybody?" he asked, this time into my neck, which flamed so red I knew his mouth would feel its heat.

"No," I answered. And then, wanting suddenly to be totally honest with him even though it embarrassed me beyond words, I said, "Well, at home we used to practice kissing our arms, and once Cecie and I tried kissing each other, but it felt awful. It felt like you ought to swish out your mouth and then spit. And we didn't know where to put our noses."

He laughed, and then, very gently, very slowly, turned my head to his and bent and touched his lips to mine. For a moment, just touched. It felt . . . it felt like slow fire, slipping into my mouth and down into the middle of me. He lifted his head and looked down at me, and I reached up and pulled his face down to mine, my hands tangled in his hair. It was like holding the color yellow.

The next kiss was not slow. Soft and deep, but not slow. I could feel myself sliding away, following my breath into his mouth and beyond. There was no question where to put my nose. None at all. There were no more questions about anything.

"I'm going to tell."

It was a soft hiss, like that of a snake. One you had not seen in the long grass and had stepped on. My blood ran frost cold even before I broke away from Jon and looked up at her.

Peaches Davenport stood there in the moonlight, the moon striking fire from some kind of little stones sewn into her violet dress and at her ears. The dress was stained from her scramble up the cliff, and her lavender shoes, with tiny high heels and bows, were ruined.

"You're doing the nasty and I'm going to tell." The hiss gave way to furious shrillness.

"My grandpa said you go to hell if you do the nasty before you get married, and you-all sure don't look married to me. You just look nasty."

I could not speak.

Jon could.

"Get out of here, Peaches," he said in a slow, cold voice I had never heard. "Get on out of here before I throw your prissy little ass off this cliff."

She turned abruptly, jerkily, like a malevolent marionette, and began to pick her way back down the cliff through the underbrush.

"You said 'ass' and you were doing the nasty," she shrilled at us. There were outraged tears in her voice. "And the minute I get back down I'm going to tell."

She did.

CHAPTER

7

I never knew how she did it; precisely what she said, or to whom. Jon and I, frozen in disbelief and fury, didn't move until we heard both our mothers calling us from the bottom of the headland to come down. Their voices were tight and calm. The only other sounds were the unmistakable rustles and murmurings of people leaving a place and Peaches' treble shrieking. Precisely what she was shrieking I never really knew. My mother told me later that she had not wanted to go home when her outraged grandparents attempted to take her.

"Probably wanted to stay around and admire the aftermath of her handiwork," my father said grimly. By that time Peaches Davenport was persona non grata in more houses than ours. Dad told me, perhaps by way of comfort, for I was utterly devastated, nearly flattened, by the fallout from her betrayal, that none of the Carter's Cove kids would play with her, and her grandmother was busily arranging outings with the colony children. And, I thought bleakly, drawing their mothers aside to whisper in their ears the "whole dreadful business," as Canon Davenport had put it during the acrid parental confrontation that had followed.

Jon and I had had time to tell my parents and his mother, tearfully on my part, that we were doing nothing wrong. That we were simply sitting on the top rocks watching the moon and talking when Peaches had materialized beside us.

"Honey," my father said, "she said Jon was lying on top of you. If that's not true, then we'll dismiss her as the little liar I suspect she is. But you have to tell us the truth now."

I did not speak. Across our living room, beside the fire, Jon sat cross-legged on the rug at his mother's feet, staring into the flames, unmoving. Her hand was playing softly through his hair, just as mine had been earlier.

Jon raised his head and looked around the big, fire-lit room as if memorizing it, and then at my parents.

"I was kissing her," he said. "And I wasn't lying on top of her. I was propped up beside her. I kissed her one time, and if Peaches hadn't snuck up there I probably would have done it again. But that's all it was. I . . . . I like Lilly an awful lot. I wanted to be with her as much as I could this summer. But I guess that's out of the question now, isn't it?"

"Peaches is just jealous." I sobbed. "She's always wanted Jon to be her boyfriend. She's chased him all summer. Whatever she said we were doing, it was just exactly what we told you. I know she's messed the whole thing up. I know that. I know you're not going to let me see Jon anymore. I know his dad will take him home."

"You let me handle his dad, Lilly," Claire Lowell said, her voice calm. "If we leave now, maybe I can get to him before the canon does. I do think you two better not see each other for a while, until we can straighten all this out. The Davenports ought to take that little witch home right now, but I can just imagine the fit she'd throw. Neither of them will lift a finger to discipline her. It's not the end of the world, or even the summer."

Jon got up from the rug and followed her out of the room. He gave me one last despairing look, and then he was gone into the darkness of the hallway.

I sat crying softly on the sofa for a long time. My mother and father sat beside me. Both had their arms around me. I will always love them for that.

"We trust you, Lilly," my mother said. "You've never given us reason not to. But you're only eleven years old. That's a bit young to be kissing anybody, especially somebody you just met. You've got years and years; there will be so many boys."

"No." I wept. "There won't. There's only going to be Jon. I—I'm going to marry him. He wants me to. He's not going to change his mind and neither am I."

In the silence that spun out, only the fire snickering sleepily behind the screen made any noise. I could almost feel the look my parents exchanged over my head.

Then my father said, "Well, you could do a lot worse. Jon's a fine boy. Just promise me you'll wait until you can pay your own rent. I don't want to be giving the bride away next summer."

I hiccupped. "His father will take him home as soon as he can pack. I heard Mrs. Lowell when she told Mother what he thinks of me."

"Honey . . ." my mother began.

"I'll bet there will be a next summer," my father said, tightening his arms around me. "I'd hate to try to take Claire Lowell anywhere she didn't want to go. Go on up to bed now. I'm going over to the Lowells' in the morning and try to talk some sense into Arthur. Maybe he'll fall on his sword. I need to bring Wilma home, too. I miss him, Peaches be damned.

"I doubt we'll see much of Peaches," my father went on, grinning. "Damned shame, isn't it?"

"George, we need to try to remember the terrible loss she's had," my mother said.

"Her parents. Yeah. Maybe they committed suicide rather than spend another day with Peaches."

"George!" But she didn't sound terribly shocked.

I crawled into bed thinking that I would probably cry all night. But I didn't. I slid into a great orb of moonlight in which floated crystal islands, and a low voice whispered in my ear. I could not understand what it was saying, but it was a comforting voice. I woke once, got up and retrieved the osprey feather from the little jewelry box where I had put it, and went back to sleep.

He kissed me, I thought. *He kissed me. There's not anything anybody can do about that.*

The next morning one of the first of the July fogs had rolled in, thick and solid as cotton.

"Going to be a long one," Clara said, pouring coffee. "The first one always is. I remember one—oh, back before you were born, Lilly—that lasted twenty-two days. None of the lobstermen could get out. Lost most of the summer haul that year."

I finished breakfast and went up to the third floor to my lair. It was cold and fog-clammy, and I wrapped myself in the old quilt I kept there and picked up *The Golden Bough*. I knew it would sustain me, and after it there were others, and still others. Endless books. I wondered what Jon would do with his long hours of house arrest. He certainly couldn't play tennis. Each day I woke thinking, *This will be the day I hear they are leaving.* But they did not. I knew Arthur Lowell was absolutely furious; my father's face told me that when he returned with Wilma the morning after the solstice party. But he would not talk about it, beyond saying, "The man's an enormous fool."

On the eleventh day the fog lifted a bit, enough to let the sun sidle out for a few hours, and I went out into it, so glad to see steaming earth and water and sky that I simply sat on the seawall, eyes closed, face turned up to the sun, letting it recast the bones under my skin. Beside me Wilma jingled and snuffled, and then curled up on the still-wet grass and went to sleep. I drowsed, too.

"Wake up, sleepyhead," said a voice that had lingered in my ear these long days, and I started, and looked up, and there was Jon, grinning at me.

Wilma gave a joyful woof and jumped up on Jon's shoulders, so that I had to push him out of the way to get my arms around Jon. I buried my head in his shoulder. He hugged me hard.

"How?" I quavered, trying not to cry. "How?"

"Dad went home," he said simply. "Mother and I are staying on till September."

"Is he still mad?"

"Oh, yeah, but he'll get over it. He'll stay down at the quarry office and take it out on the guys there. It'll be okay."

"Didn't he want you to come with him?"

"Yeah. But Mom and I both said no. I don't think I've ever said that to him before."

"So what did he say then?"

"Nothing. He went to bed. Next morning I heard the car leave real early."

"Well," I said. "So what should we do today?"

"Go take a look at the ospreys?"

"It's awfully foggy," I said doubtfully.

"Not now it isn't."

"None of the boats went out. I don't think we're done with it yet."

"Whatever. Want to play Chinese checkers? I found an old set over at the cottage."

Just then Claire Lowell appeared, her arms full of early yellow daylilies.

"Hey, sweetie," she said to me, "is your mom here? I wanted to congratulate her."

"What for?" I said.

"Big surprise," Claire Lowell said. "I'll let her tell you."

My mother came out of the cottage and down the terrace steps then, smiling.

"What on earth?" she said. And then, in a different voice, "Hello, Peaches."

We all stared. Peaches had come silently up behind Jon's mother and none of us had seen her. I could not believe she was standing in my yard, smiling sunnily, not after what she had done, but there she was, in a pink sweater and apple green clam diggers, looking angelic enough to ascend that moment into heaven.

"Hey," Peaches said. Her voice was lyrical, light and sweet.

"Hey, Jon."

He stared at her a moment longer, and then said, "Hey, Peaches."

She did not look at me, or speak.

"I've got my surprise for you all set up," she said to him. "Grandpa finished it last night. I want you to come see it right now. You'll just love it."

No one said anything. Peaches merely looked up at Jon, her dimples flashing.

"I'm going to play Chinese checkers with Lilly," Jon said. "Probably all day. Maybe tomorrow too. Maybe the rest of the summer."

Peaches did not reply, but a frown knit her silky brows and her rosy mouth turned corner-down. I flinched. I knew that look.

But she did not speak.

Finally Jon's mother said, "Well, if nobody else is going to tell you, I will, because it's wonderful. Lilly, your mother is having a one-woman show of her paintings over at the yacht club next Saturday. Mr. Brooks Burns arranged it as a surprise for her. Aren't you proud? Nobody's ever had an art showing over there, I'm told."

More likely as a little thank-you, I thought meanly, remembering the old hands on my mother's breasts. But I said nothing.

"Gosh, that's fabulous, Mrs. Constable," Jon said. "I can't wait to see it."

"Well, you can't," Peaches said.

We all looked at her.

"What?" Jon said.

Peaches' face was red and tight with triumph.

"You can't because you're Jewish. They don't let Jews in the yacht club."

"Peaches, where on earth did you get that?" Claire Lowell said. "It's not true! What on earth has gotten into you?"

"Yes, it is too true," Peaches said. My mother reached for her, but she dodged away and stood staring up at Jon, fists on her hips.

"I know it's true because I heard my grandmother on the telephone talking to Mrs. Constable, way long ago. She said you didn't know it, and she doubted your mother did either, because your dad made such a big thing out of the Episcopals and Yale and all that, but that your grandfather had changed his name when he was real young. It used to be Lowenstein. Jon Arthur Lowenstein. Granddaddy knew all about it. He said he'd always known, but he liked your dad and wasn't going to upset the apple cart. But you can't go to the yacht club and that's that."

"That's a lie . . ." There was no breath behind Jon's words.

My father moved in and put his arm around Jon's shoulders. Claire Lowell simply stood stock-still, white as paper, and stared at Peaches Davenport.

"That will do, Peaches," my father said. His voice was flat and cold.

"Well, it's better to know, isn't it?" she fluted. "What if he'd tried to go to the yacht club and they'd told him he couldn't come in because he was a Jew?"

"You're a goddamned liar!" Jon roared suddenly. It was not a boy's voice. Peaches stepped back, but she went on.

"Why do you think Mrs. Constable got Mr. Constable to give you sailing lessons instead of the guy at the club? Why do you think she said the Forrests' tennis court was better? She didn't want your feelings to be hurt, and I don't either. Listen, it's okay with me. I don't care who's a Jew and who isn't—"

"Peaches," my father said in the same iron-cold voice, "go home. Go home right now."

"I don't want—"

"GO HOME!"

She turned and ran. We watched her go out of sight. The fog was curling in again; we lost her to the mist before she reached the road home.

Jon turned around very slowly and looked at his mother. "Mother?" he whispered.

"I didn't know," she said, so softly we could hardly hear her. "I didn't know."

"Jon, you must not think it makes a particle of difference to anyone who knows you," my father said. He started to lay his arm over Jon's shoulder again, but Jon shrugged it off.

I looked at my mother. Her hands were over her mouth and her ocean eyes were stormy gray. So it was true, then. But what difference did it make? Jon was Jon, would always be Jon. What did it matter if he was a Jew or a Catholic, or an extraterrestrial or anything at all?

"*Why didn't he tell me?*" It was a cry of such primal agony and fury that I could not, for a moment, believe it came from Jon. His face was bleached white around his mouth, and veins stood out on his temples.

"*Why didn't he tell me?*"

"Honey, because he didn't want you to be hurt in any way," his mother began. There were tears running down her cheeks. "Or me either. I'm sure that's why he never told us. There are some really stupid people who care about things like that, and they can do awful things because of it—keep you out of things you might want to join, talk about you to people whose influence might have helped you, things that shouldn't matter a bit in the world, but do, to some terrible people. I know he must have wanted to protect you—".

"No!"

We all stared at Jon. His mother put her hand on his arm and he jerked it away.

"It wasn't me he wanted to protect." He was whispering now, a raw, guttural whisper. "It was Sib. He couldn't stand for anybody to know Sib was a Jew. Not even a dead Jew. It wouldn't have mattered to Sib, it wouldn't have mattered to you or me, but it mattered to him! It mattered more to him than the truth!"

He turned suddenly, gave an incoherent cry, and vaulted over the seawall and ran down the dock to where the Beetle Cat sulked and wallowed in the thick slow sea. In an eyeblink he was down to it and had cast off the lines that held it, and was paddling out into the open water.

"No!" I felt in my throat that I was screaming, but could not hear my words. "No!"

My father ran down the dock after him.

"Jon, come back," he called. "We'll work this out—Jon! You can't sail in this fog, nobody could!"

Claire Lowell gave a wordless cry of terrible grief and fear; I heard it in my ears for weeks after. My mother cried after my father, "Call him back, George! Call him back!"

I looked out over the sea. The thick bank of fog that had shrouded us for days was rolling back in. You could not see any of the islands; we could barely make out the Beetle Cat, Jon's figure crouched in it. And then we could not see it at all.

"Daddy!" I screamed. "Daddy! Take the Friendship and go after him! I'll help, I'll come too!"

My mother had her arms around Claire Lowell. I ran to her and she put one around me, too, and pulled me against her so that my face was in her shoulder. As it had been, not so long ago, in Jon's.

"He can't take the sloop out, honey," she said. "Jon will see that he can't sail it and turn around. Just wait a minute . . ."

My father came striding back up the dock.

"I'm going to the general store to see if any of the lobster fleet is out. They'll have the marine band on. Take Claire inside and call the Coast Guard. He could easily turn back any minute, or just drop the sail and sit still until somebody finds him. But we can't take that chance."

He ran on past us and up into the clearing where the Jeep was parked. There was no sound in the smothering fog. And then we heard, lost far out in the fog, the distinct snap of a sail finding wind, and filling.

I don't remember much of that afternoon. Clara came and made coffee and put out sandwiches, but I don't think anyone ate them. Jon's mother sat stiff beside the fire in our living room, crying softly. My mother sat with her arms around her, whispering in her ear every now and then, giving her small hugs, but she did not speak. Even Wilma was quiet, curled at my feet where I sat on the window seat, staring out at the fog. My fist was closed tight around the osprey feather. My father did not come back until much later. I knew he had been at the general store all afternoon listening on the marine band on the radio that was kept on at all times, so that a lobsterman in trouble might rouse other lobstermen to come to his aid. Mrs. Beatrice Glenn, the store's owner, knew all the boats by name and call number. The store was the first place you went when there was trouble at sea. The radio picked up the Coast Guard's signal, too. By now, I knew that they would have long been out on the sea from the station at Castine. I knew that they would stay out until they found Jon. I knew, but it did not help the sick terror.

It was just after dark when my father came into the living room. The fog was so thick that we had not heard the Jeep come into the driveway. His step was slow and he did not speak. He did not have to.

I saw that he opened his mouth and spoke to the two women by the fire, but I heard nothing. Nothing but the terrible ripping sound as the fabric of the world was rent, and the cold, windy sucking of the infinite black void beyond it, where everything vanished: the moon and the sun and the cold music of the stars and the wings of children, the warmth of fires and the shapes of islands and the swift, darting white bellies of ospreys, and the soft curl of a feather, and the taste of summer strawberries and the smell of wood smoke and the breathing of the sea. And Jon.

Gone.

After

CHAPTER

8

In the early fall of 1963, the year after we left Edgewater, my mother finally received her invitation to luncheon at the White House. It was not for some little duty affair for Democratic women, either, as she pointed out radiantly, showing us her heavy cream vellum invitation with *The White House* engraved on it. It was for "six women who have made a difference through the arts," and it was signed by Jacqueline Bouvier Kennedy. The other five women were unnamed, but my mother's friend Tatty Glover told her that *her* friend, Tish Baldridge, had told her that three of the others were Mahalia Jackson, Joan Baez, and Margot Fonteyn. Tish had not been sure who the other two were; probably writers or journalists, Tatty said. But it was generally known in the West Wing that the President planned to drop in unannounced.

"Just unofficially," Tatty said Tish said. "He couldn't very well seem to play favorites or anything."

It was the first time since we had left Edgewater in the early dawn hours of last midsummer that I had seen my mother really smile, or heard the little growl of lusty pleasure she got in her voice when she was very excited. It was the first time, I think, that I had seen any of us really smile, much less seem exuberantly excited about anything. For a moment it was like hearing birds sing again, but only for a moment.

The piercing sweetness of the sound whistled in the air of the library and hurt my ears and I snapped the helmet tighter.

Late into the white, fog-felted night when my father had come home with the Coast Guardsmen but not Jon, I woke, still muffled in the damp old sofa blanket and lying in my father's arms as I had been when I'd finally cried myself to sleep. My father had not moved; was still lying on his side with his arms around me. But they were slack in sleep now, with exhaustion and pain, and he did not stir as I wiggled out of my swaddling and stumbled into the middle of the living room. The fire had burned down to pallid joyless ashes, and the room was cold and clammy with fog. I could not remember at first what had jerked me out of sleep and thrown me out into the room. But then I did, and pain so huge and pulsing that I could almost feel it stretching my skin doubled me over, and I knelt on the threadbare old hearth rug, thinking that surely one must die of this kind of agony, and wishing that it would hurry with me.

Frantic with the pain and the fear of living even another minute with it, my mind battered and scrambled, casting about for someone, something, that could take it from me, I did not care how. Something that would smother me with warm softness so that the pain died with my breath. Something that could puncture my heart and let the roiling toxin rush out. Someone to come and take me into his arms and say, "It's all right. They found him and he's just fine."

But there was no one. My father was sodden with his own anguish. Clara had at last gone, heavily and red-eyed, home, when no more coffee was wanted, or the clam chowder she had kept hot. Jeebs was off cruising the Cranberry Islands with his sail-gifted friend, and in any case I would never have run to Jeebs. We had little connection now.

My mother had taken Claire Lowell home, and was staying with her until her sister and brother-in-law could come from their summer home in Vermont. I knew that by now someone would have reached

Arthur Lowell in his sere bedroom or cold quarry office, but I did not care who had, or when he could reach Carter's Cove. Arthur Lowell died in my mind that night far more inevitably than his son ever did. Canon and Mrs. Davenport left my mind completely, taking Peaches with them.

Still crouched on the hearth rug, gasping for breath and biting my knuckles so hard against screaming out, or retching, that they bled, I had a silent implosive vision of what it would take to enable me to live. I scrambled to my feet and in what seemed an instant was up in my attic lair, breathing in dust and summers immemorial, pawing through my books. I jerked them out of their shelves; they lay in heaps on the floor, spines cracking, pages torn, until my dirty hands fell on the one I remembered. Even as it lay closed in my hands I felt the stretching pain ease a little, the gagging panic recede. Jules Verne's *20,000 Leagues Under the Sea* had been, I think, my grandfather's book, old when I had first read it, yellowed and warped now by wet sea air and the hundreds of times I had leafed through it. I held it hard against my chest. I had always loved it, and now it was going to save me.

The page I remembered presented itself to me as if it had been waiting. It was smeared and grubby with what looked to be small chocolate fingerprints. I even remembered the time I had put them there: hot cocoa on a night of howling winds that shook the house, and fusillades of rain.

"Heavy, waterproof suits, made of seamless rubber and constructed in such a way as to be able to bear up under considerable pressure," I read. I could have almost recited it.

It was like strong yet supple armor. The suit consisted of trousers and a jacket. The trousers ended in thick shoes with heavy lead soles. The fabric of the jacket was held firm by copper plates which protected the chest against the water

143

pressure and allowed the lungs to function freely; its sleeves ended in gloves that were supple enough for the wearer to perform any normal operation with his hands. . . . The top part of the jackets ended in a threaded copper collar onto which metal helmets could be screwed. Three holes covered by thick glass permitted us to see in any direction merely by turning our heads inside the helmet.

I could not have said why the passage had always called out to me. The writing was banal, and the picture it painted of the suits was almost industrial, certainly not beautiful. But those suits had lived in my earliest dreams, and they were always dreams of lightness and safety. Somewhere deep inside me, the suits had always waited.

I read the passage over and over. I pored over the illustrations of the men in the suits. I pulled out my old quilt and lay down on the floor, wrapping it around me, and read and read and read. When I had entered the attic I remembered being as cold as I had ever been in my life. When, around four in the morning, with predawn washing the window, I woke, I was warm and dry and nimble and supple, and the suit fit me as if every inch of it had been made for me. Terrible pain still stalked the house, roared like a tiger, slashed at the suit and helmet, but it did not quite reach me. It never did again until many years later, when I heard, dimly, a laugh so joyous and summery that I tossed away the helmet and tore away the suit and left it puddled on the earth behind me like a discarded snakeskin.

No one could see my suit, I knew, but I thought perhaps my father and maybe my mother knew it was there. But for a long while no one commented on it. It muted the world, which I knew now to be a killing place as well as a life-giving one, just enough so that I could walk in it without much fear or even much pain. Without much joy, either, but for a long time I considered the suit to be a fair trade for the world.

Even I knew that my suit was ridiculous: ludicrous, a clown's disguise, a Halloween thing. Sometimes it made me laugh a little, thinking what would happen if the people in my world could see it. I imagined it suddenly blooming into visibility in my classes, after school at the record shop, at the Chevy Chase Club's Sunday family brunches. Would people point and laugh? Run away from me? Pretend not to notice at all? On the whole, I thought the latter would be the most common reaction; especially at the club. Somehow it seemed the eeriest, the most awful, thing of all. But as time went by I thought less and less of it, and clumped through my days if not happily, then almost contentedly. It never occurred to me that I, in my suit, walked very closely with a kind of madness. It served.

Of our flight into Egypt with that dawn I remember almost nothing, except that my father, thinking I was sleeping, carried me out to the car and settled me in the backseat with a blanket and Wilma, who was, for once, silent and still. Wilma knew. Of course he did. The whole way home he slept.

It is a very long drive from Maine to Washington, and we made it in a day. I don't remember much about that day except that I slept a lot and re-read *The Catcher in the Rye*, and ate the Howard Johnson's sandwiches my parents bought, and stumbled sleepily into rest stops or to walk Wilma. I don't recall that my parents talked much, either, but they must have, of course. How could they not? I do remember once coming up out of sticky hot sleep and hearing my mother say in a low voice thick with tears, ". . . can't imagine what will happen to her. She's lost everything. Both her boys. Her husband, really; he was never who she thought he was. The whole life she lived . . ."

"Maybe she'll find a better new one," my father said heavily. His voice had changed. It had somehow, in the space of that day, gone from sometimes a boy's to an old man's. "God knows she's got a clean slate now. She could live any way she wanted."

"No. She's lost all she wanted. Would you want to start a whole new life if you'd lost what she has? I wouldn't. I couldn't! I think I'd find a way to die. I think she will too."

"Oh, Liz," he said. His voice trembled. "Don't even say that. Don't ever. We'll keep in touch with her. She could come visit us. I thought you both had a lot in common, really; that she'd get to be a really good friend."

"No. We'd have been very good friends, but not now. She won't come and we won't keep in touch. Remember when the Garrisons' daughter was killed in that awful accident in the school parking lot? Janet said once that she simply could not force herself to see anyone who was there, who might have even seen the accident. Sometimes she'd just turn the car around and go back home when she saw one of Delia's classmates' mother's cars coming toward her. She never went back to Saint Margaret's. Soon after that is when they moved out to Reston. Do you think Claire Lowell would ever want to lay eyes on us again? I don't mean that she'd be angry, it's just that she couldn't stand what it called back. It was our boat, remember?"

"Do you think I will ever in my life forget that for one moment?" my father whispered.

I don't remember any more conversation between them until we reached our house on Kalorama Circle, late into a hot night, hulking dark against the moon-bleached night sky, looking bruised and swollen and without breath. But I breathed in its lifelessness almost gratefully. Once I would have choked for the breath of the sea, but I knew now that the sea that could give breath could also take it, and I turned my whole being gratefully into the hot, still city.

We did not go back to Edgewater, at least my mother and father never did, and it was many years before I did, and somehow then it was a different house on a different ocean, and therefore possible.

My father came into my bedroom one afternoon a week or so after we had left Edgewater in that awful dawn, looked around, and went to my windows and rolled up the shades. I had not opened them since we got home. I had never spent a summer in our house in the city; I could not imagine seeing our quiet lawn and my mother's garden in the searing light of midsummer, and I felt that to do so would let in some inexorable sun-scorched reality with which I could not deal. Always, my summer windows had framed rocks and islands and sea and sky. I felt that a wilting rose garden and dingy white cast-iron lawn furniture would send me plummeting out into endless space.

The high white sun of afternoon flooded in, and I rolled over on my bed, where I had been reading a copy of *The Tropic of Cancer* I had gotten last winter from a member of the Thieves Club and kept under my bed. The Shirelles wailing "Will You Love Me Tomorrow?" cut the thick, stale air. I pitched Henry Miller under the bed, turned off the Shirelles (my father was appalled at most of the music of the day), and hid my face against the invading light with my forearm.

My father came over and sat down on the side of my bed. Like me, he was at loose ends in the city in midsummer. He had toiled in the browning garden, watered futilely in the evenings, fixed whatever flapped or rattled, and was close, as my mother said, to giving up and running for his office.

Watching him from beneath my folded arm, it struck me that he walked differently now. The bouncy stride he usually had in the city was gone; so was the loose, long sort of lope he had at Edgewater, going down the dock or across the lawn to the rocks. The precise, padding athlete's gait that he used in our basement, getting ready to mount the high bars, was gone, too. Now he walked on the balls of his feet, almost on tiptoe, as if ready for flight. If I could have cried within the helmet, I would have, would have wept for my young father who had lost his walk. That I had lost mine also did not occur to me then.

"What are you doing shut up here in the dark, Lillybelle?" he said, brushing the disheveled curls off my forehead. "You look like a mole in a hole. Want to walk over to the drugstore with me and get a milk-shake or something? I've got to pick up something for your mother. Or even better, when I get back why don't we go give the high bars and the trapeze a workout? You haven't even been down there."

"Oh, Daddy, it's too hot to go out," I said fretfully. "I like it up here in the shade. I'm reading."

"What are you reading?" he said, looking around for the book that was not there.

"Oh, *The Golden Bough*. It's around here someplace."

"You know, Lilly," he said slowly, looking not at me but out the window where the branches of the big dogwood screened out the sun, "sometimes there's such a thing as too much magic. It's good when your feet are planted on the earth, but if they're not you could just— vanish into a cloud of magic and not come out. We'd hate to lose you to a flock of summoning spells."

I looked at him.

"Why did you say that?"

"I don't know, it just popped into my head. Come on down to the gym with me, Lil. It'll be good to be up in the air again, won't it?"

After a long while, I whispered, "I can't."

"Why not, baby?"

"My feet are too heavy," I muttered, thinking of the plated boots.

I hoped he would not press it; I could not tell him about the diver's suit. Somehow or other, they would take it away.

He didn't. He just looked at me for a while longer and said, "Maybe tomorrow we'll go down to the National Gallery. It's been a long time since we've been downtown. I'll take you to lunch at the Metropolitan Club."

"Okay," I said, forcing a smile. It even felt false. I could imagine what it looked like. He went out of the room, leaving me pointing my silly rictus at the ceiling. I dug *The Tropic of Cancer* back out.

That night at dinner my mother said, "Lilly, we've been talking, and we think it might be fun for you to go to camp, or take some lessons in something you like. There's a lot of summer left, and I'm going to be painting, and your dad's got his research. I know most of your crowd are off somewhere with their parents, but there's lots going on in Washington that you might like to try. Art lessons, maybe. Or riding, like Cecie. Or something at the club—their summer program is supposed to be good. Tennis . . ." Her voice trailed off. I could not look at either one of them. My cold salmon looked thick and dead on my plate. I could not get any breath into my lungs.

"Swimming, maybe?" my father said. "There's a new instructor everybody says is a shoo-in to qualify for the Olympics."

He paused, looking at me. "You can't just sit in your room until school starts, Lilly," he said gently. "You may not think so now, but you can't afford to waste a summer. Nobody can, not even somebody as young as you. I remember how it felt, thinking that you had all the time in the world left, but that's not always true. You know that. Don't throw these summers away, darling."

It was the closest he had ever come to talking about Jon, and the closest he ever would, for a very long time. I saw tears in his eyes. Incredibly, I felt them on my own cheeks, even inside the hermetic sphere of the helmet.

"Please don't," I whispered.

And all of a sudden I wanted water more than anything in the world; clear, cool, infinite water that would close over me and give me weightlessness, water through which radiant shafts of sunlight would dance dreamily, never touching the bottom, water in which I could, as the old *Book of Common Prayer* says, "live, move and have my being." I could stay on the half-lit bottom forever, floating languidly through the underwater forests and canyons and mountains, as Pierre Arronax had done. All the fantastic and beautiful creatures of the waters of the world could come and bump at my helmet's huge glass eyes but could not come in. I could live on plankton, on krill, as whales do. I would be a creature of water and light, but not of cold, opaque green water, lightless just inches below its surface. Different water, water that did not steal from you.

"Swimming," I said. "I'd like to take swimming lessons. I'd really like to do that."

"Well, you know, darling, you can already swim," my mother said. "You might be bored in the beginning lessons."

"No. I wouldn't. I want to learn to really swim, to swim like—oh, you know champion swimmers do, to be really, really good at it."

"You couldn't just want to be that good a swimmer," my mother said. "You'd really, really have to work at it, probably for a long time. I didn't think you were that interested."

"I am now," I said. "Please, it's what I want most to do. I promise I'll work harder at it than I ever have at anything."

"Well, we'd hope you'd relax enough to enjoy it, too." My mother smiled. "But of course, if that's what you want to do, we'll see about signing you up tomorrow. I just hope it's not too late to get a class with the new instructor."

"He'll take me," I said. "But could we call right now, instead of tomorrow?"

And so it was that the next Monday, at 10 A.M., I stood on the apron of the pool at the Chevy Chase Club with perhaps fifteen other girls my age, not caring that my old swimsuit bore the stigmata of another, a northern, sun, while all the other aspirants were sleek as seals in new ruffled one- and two-piece suits, staring up at the bronzed, tanned young man who was going to give me, instead of wings, fins and gills. His name was Charles Rowley, but I never thought of him as anything but Nemo.

"This is an intermediate class, so I assume that you can all swim to some extent or another," Nemo said. "When I point to you, dive or jump into the pool and swim a length and back."

He looked at a clipboard and then up at the first girl in line, in candy-striped pink ruffles.

"Melanie Porter," he said, and pointed at her. Melanie Porter made a little face, giggled, and jumped prettily into the deep end of the pool, feet together, toes pointed. She hardly made a splash, but by the time she had done her Esther Williams face-out-of-the-water crawl two lengths, she was gasping. He gave her a hand out of the pool, and then pointed at the next girl, in a one-piece suit of violet that matched her eyes, cut very low in front and back.

"Margaret Cassidy," he said, and pointed.

"Everybody calls me Meggie," she said, smiling widely, and flung herself into the pool in a flat, stomach-blasting dive. She thrashed her way through her two lengths and emerged with a red face and reddened breasts that bobbled now over the top of her suit.

He said nothing, and then looked at me and then at the clipboard. "Lilly Constable," he said.

I walked to the edge of the pool and felt my muscles respond to the green-blue water below me as if to magnets. I went into it in a clean, perfect racing dive, which I had never in my life been able to do before, and let myself glide deep. This was it, then, the cool, silent world lit from above with gold-filtered sun rays, endless, caressing. My leaden feet felt strong and feather light. The helmet, unneeded, floated away. I felt joyously one with the dolphin, the sailfish, and went the length of the Chevy Chase Club pool and back without going to the surface. Only when I lifted my tangled wet, curly head out of the water did I notice I was gasping for breath. Nemo gave me a long, neutral look and then pointed to the next girl.

"Cissy Stringfellow," he said.

When the last girl had demonstrated her prowess and we stood in a ragged, dripping line before him, he said, "Well, we have a good bit of work to do, I think. Class meets back here Wednesday morning, same time. Get yourselves a club racing suit before you come. I can't teach ruffles and bouncing boobs. Lilly Constable, stay, please."

The other girls filed out, some snickering because they thought I would be reprimanded, some obviously concerned that I might become an early favorite, even in my patched and pilled old suit. I did not notice them. It was about to begin.

"Where did you take lessons?" Nemo asked, studying me.

"I never took any," I mumbled. I wondered if that would disqualify me for the class. It was, after all, an intermediate class.

"You had to learn that racing dive somewhere," he said. "And your underwater butterfly is pretty impressive, even if it was grandstanding. If you're going to be in my class you can't stay under that long again. I don't teach drowning."

"I wasn't . . ." I began, and then stopped. I couldn't have explained where the dive and the underwater prowess came from if I tried.

"I used to swim a lot in the summers," I said, clearing my throat. "It was in Maine."

"Well, you'll have to go along with the rest of the class," he said. "I don't do special lessons, and underwater swimming is not on the agenda."

"Okay," I said, looking at my feet. They were still brown from the high sun of Maine, and scarred from its beach rocks.

"That doesn't mean you can't stay after class and swim any way you want to," he said, grinning. He had very white teeth. "It's a free pool, so to speak. If I'm still around maybe we can do some under-water stuff sometimes."

"Okay," I said again, my heart swelling into my throat with joy.

And so I went underwater, to stay for a summer, and a winter, at the club's indoor pool and the Georgetown YWCA. Early the next summer, 1963, my parents rented a villa on the beach in St. Thomas, and my father found a snorkeling instructor for me, and Jules Verne's world came alive for me in the warm, transparent sunlit blue and green water. For two months I was seldom out of it. I remember that summer as a nearly perfect one. I had the glorious water. My father was deep in his research once more. And my mother painted.

The summer before, when Mother was still fiddling around with florals and landscapes and an occasional portrait, Flora, our new young housekeeper (maid, not to put too fine a point on it, my father said), came late to work, and with a bloody handkerchief wrapped around her head. There was blood spotting her immaculately ironed blouse, too, and a huge, ugly bruise blooming on one high cheekbone. Flora was our beloved old Johnnie Mae's niece, brought onboard and meticulously trained by her aunt, and we loved her. She was sweet-tempered, funny, and so smart that my father began giving her books of poetry to take home and peruse. When she tottered into our kitchen, it was like seeing a despoiled Madonna. My father jumped up and led her to a chair, my mother came with a wet towel and ban-dages, and I burst into tears. Something whole and sweet in my world had been broken. At the time, I did not know what.

My grim-faced parents took Flora to our doctor on Massachusetts Avenue. She came back with seven stitches, bandaged arms and hands, seemingly stricken to stone. I don't think she said a word, not that I heard. My father drove her home to Johnnie Mae's little house in the projects.

My mother's face was blazing. Her eyes were so dark that they seemed black, and I could hear her breathing across the room, where I cowered at the breakfast table.

"What happened to Flora?" I asked faintly, not wanting to know.

"She was waiting at the bus stop for her bus, and a car full of white men came by very fast and threw Coca-Cola bottles at her," my mother said between clenched teeth.

"*Why?*"

"Because there was one of her and a car full of them, and because she's black, and because there was no one to stop them," she said.

"Isn't there some kind of law?"

"Yes. There is. And it's about as useful to black people as socks on a rooster," my mother said, and wheeled around and went out of the kitchen and upstairs to her studio. She did not come back down until late that afternoon. When she did, she held up the canvas she had been working on. No one said anything. The painting was beyond words.

It was Flora's face, very close up, the detail amazing. I did not know what you would call the style of painting; it was not so much representational as a sort of tender caricature. There was no doubt that it was pretty Flora, but her caramel skin was mottled and bruised and the stitches were very black and savage against her skin, and where there had been blood my mother had simply let scarlet watercolor dribble. And the eyes—Flora's eyes—were white-ringed with terror and pain. You could not look away from them. I was silent, still. Flora's face seemed to burn into my retinas, and I literally felt her fear flood my eyes with tears and thicken my throat. I knew I was looking at a work of amazing skill and emotional import.

My mother had painted this?

Finally my father spoke.

"It is stunning, Elizabeth," he said, his voice gruff and thick. "I think you have found something inside you that will make you an artist of real importance. I never dreamed . . ."

"Neither did I," my mother said, her voice flat and cold. "Until I understood about real evil. Those murderous fools changed a face I loved into something . . . broken and shamed. The cuts will heal. Her eyes won't."

She turned and went back upstairs. My father put together a supper of scrambled eggs for us. Mother called out that she did not want any. The light in her studio burned very late. I could not sleep until I saw it go out. Hate and rage and sheer monstrousness walked our house that night. I knew, huddled into my pretty flowered comforter, that we would never really be safe there again.

After that my mother took her car and went out every day and came back with more sketches of the beautiful, terrible faces. I remember a small black face trying to reach a drinking fountain that said WHITES ONLY. Reflected in the store window in front of him, his mother reached out to snatch him away, her eyes cut sideways, to see where danger might lie.

A white child in a flounced and ribboned bower of a carriage being wheeled across the Potomac Bridge stared out at a woman and a small boy on foot, crossing the bridge also. They were black. The woman pushing the carriage was black, too, dressed in starched black and white, and the Scottie she was walking along with the child shone ebony in the sun and wore a plaid collar.

A beautifully dressed white matron, eyes staring straight ahead, hands so tightly on the steering wheel that her knuckles were blanched, drove a small sports car along a street that was obviously far from her own streets, thick with lounging black men and tired black women with shopping bags. They all stared at the car, and at the tired, fat black woman in the backseat who had fallen asleep, her mouth open. The fear and the hate on the street were palpable.

My mother painted far into the nights. Flora's older cousin Emma came at five now, to make our dinner and then walk home with Flora, who would not walk alone after dark on the streets of Washington ever again. We did not see much of each other in those fall and winter days of 1962; my father had buried himself in John Donne and my mother painted her faces and I slid deeply and dreamily underwater. My father had found a scuba-diving instructor at a Y near the university, and I was there almost every day after classes. Though I did well in my classes, school never again seemed so real to me as the living water; I literally forgot about the T Club and stole no more objects of erotica. My club mates finally dropped me, and I made no new friends except the girls I met at the Y.

In my father's house in those months, everyone was deep inside himself, walking in his own world. Whenever we met, it was as travelers on the same safari might, all in search of different prey but bound by the familiar rituals of food and sleep, reporting equably and with vague affection on our days.

It did not seem a strange way to live to me then, and even looking back it doesn't. Families are bound by myriad different cords, and as long as they hold, the family is safe. Ours held.

Late the next August of 1963, my mother joined 250,000 others, black and white, in the great March on Washington for Jobs and Freedom from the Washington Monument to the Lincoln Memorial. When she came home she disappeared into her studio for three days, eating the meals that Emma brought her on a tray. She slept, if she did, on the sagging daybed in her studio. When the three days were over there were six or seven unforgettable faces lined up against her studio wall: Joan Baez, Odetta, Bob Dylan, and Mahalia Jackson. All the faces were suffused with a kind of radiance, a dignity, a joy so intense that it was almost tangible.

The last painting was of Dr. Martin Luther King, Jr., almost at the precise moment, my mother said, when he uttered the words that galvanized a nation: "I have a dream . . ."

I have seen no portrait of Dr. King since that came close to the power and the sheer love, the transcendence, of the one my mother did on the evening of August 28, 1963. It was so far beyond technique—for my mother had little of that—that it rendered technique obsolete.

Many people wept when they saw those paintings. One of them was Katharine Graham, who was lunching at the Sulgrave Club on the day the club hung a few of my mother's paintings in the lobby. The next month the paintings had all been featured in the *Washington Post* under the title "Faces Now."

At the first of September the invitation to luncheon at the White House came. It was set for the first Tuesday in December. After November 22 in Dallas, of course, there could be no luncheon. But my mother could not have attended, even if there had been one. By then she had had the first two of her chemotherapies and the glorious, gilt-streaked copper hair was very largely gone.

CHAPTER

9

They told me, of course. They must have; you cannot hide the toxin of fear and anguish that leaches into the viscera of a family when serious illness comes. But, looking back, I simply cannot remember the moment when anyone spoke to me of my mother's cancer. I knew, dimly, that there was a new darkness in the house, but down in my sunlit, silent world at the bottom of pools, nothing but the reality of water and movement seemed to touch me.

There was no talk of illness at dinner or whenever, more and more infrequently, we came together. I knew that my mother was seeing a doctor downtown rather frequently, and that she had recently had what she called a little surgery, a woman thing, just a nuisance. She would not let me come to the hospital, and whenever I lingered around her bed when she was back home she shooed me out, saying she needed a nap before dinner. Flora and Emma stayed later, and brought my mother trays in bed, and when I protested that, fretfully, she said that she had been feeding the masses all her life, practically, and was by God going to have a little pampering now.

My father was quieter, and spent a lot of time in her room with her, but I had no sense that he had lost interest in me and my affairs. We talked of swimming and literature, and occasionally we took small after-dinner strolls with Wilma jingling along behind or in front of us. They were pleasant; late fall is a lovely time in Washington, mellow and still burnished. In the streetlights the big houses around ours looked solid and invulnerable, windows lit and wood smoke drifting out of many of them. I scuffed leaves and Wilma sniffed and scrabbled and panted contentedly. I sensed nothing of my father's anguish. Or if I did, I pulled the helmet closer and all was well again, dreamlike.

I don't know how long I could have clutched my denial to me, but after a morning in late October it was no longer possible. Stuffing towels and goggles and my swimsuit into my gym bag in my small, upper back bedroom, I heard a scream so terrible that I seemed to feel it in my bones, in my teeth. It turned my legs and arms to water. I could not stand. I sagged onto my bed, hands trembling so hard I could not hold my gym bag and dropped it onto the floor. Dimly, I heard my father's footsteps start up the basement steps, heard Wilma whine in the kitchen, and then bark. I threw my bag back on the bed and ran down the hall to my mother's bedroom. She was not in it, but I could hear water running in the adjacent bathroom and my mother crying softly. Sick with fear, I put my head around the door.

She was leaning on the washbasin, her arms stiff, her head bent low, as if she was going to vomit. I started toward her, and then stopped. The basin was full of shining copper and gold coils of hair. More of it lay on the floor beneath. It looked like nothing so much as a beautiful, dead animal. I screamed and screamed and screamed.

"Lilly."

I looked up at my mother. Her voice was calm again, but her beautiful, narrow head was bald, or nearly; patches of the glorious hair still clung to her skull. Her head was white, bone white. In places it gleamed like porcelain. I stared at her, incredibly, still beautiful, but a corpse. I saw my mother dead, yet moving and breathing. My hands flew to my own head, I suppose to see if my hair, so like hers, was still there. My mother closed her eyes and took me into her arms, where I stood rigid with fear. The specter of sickness raised its dead-eyed head and stared at me, smirking. I pulled away, slowly, staring. The illness, where was it? In her decimated head, her arms, her stomach? But I knew it was her breast, and I think now I had always known that. In the breast she pressed me to. I backed farther away. Could it leap into me?

"It isn't contagious, you know, Lilly. We talked about that, remember?" Her voice was fully her own, light and sweet and still a bit husky, as if she was about to laugh.

"I told you I'd probably lose some hair. The medicine they give me does that. It'll grow back. Come on, darling, let me get dressed and we'll have some hot chocolate in the garden room. You can miss a morning of school. I'll write you a note."

Still, I could not look at this beautiful woman in my mother's bathroom. Wilma came pattering in, his toenails clicking, and leaned against my mother and thumped his tail. My father was behind him. My mind flew to *The Golden Bough*. My father's face gazed as if he had gazed upon the face of Medusa.

"Oh, darling," he said. His voice was strangled in his throat. He went to her and took her in his arms and held her against him. She leaned into him, her eyes closed.

"Can I have your hair?" I said suddenly.

"Lilly, really. That's simply not appropriate," my father said crossly.

But my mother smiled at me over his shoulder.

"Of course you can. You can sleep with your old mum's hair right under your nose, if you want to. You can make a mustache out of it. Why do you want it?"

"I want to put it in something like a pillow, and keep it."

"Well, as long as you're careful who sits on me."

Normalcy was slowly seeping back into the bathroom.

"So what happens now?" I said. "How long does this stuff go on? Till Christmas? We're still going to St. Thomas, aren't we?"

We'd leased the same villa on the beach in St. Thomas for Christmas, and I could not wait. We were ten steps away from an azure world that floated me in its heart.

We all loved it, all but Jeebs. Jeebs was so entrenched in the earth and its bones and the soaring space inside his mind that water and sky were no longer in his lexicon. Later in the summer that we came home from Edgewater he had gone to a math camp in Massachusetts and returned with his heart's bags already packed. That winter, his last at St. Albans middle school, he had begged for and gotten private tutoring in esoteric mathematics and gone, on his school breaks, to special programs for gifted students at MIT and Harvard. He had been at the latter when we had gone to St. Thomas early this summer, and he planned to attend another one for the two weeks before he started high school at Groton. Set for St. Albans high school, my father's old school, he had changed his mind and lobbied passionately for Groton.

"Why?" my father asked, genuinely puzzled. Jeebs had never expressed much interest one way or another in where he would go to high school and college. My father was leaning toward George Washington for him, and I knew that my mother rather liked Georgetown. But I had never heard Jeebs state a preference.

"Because you almost automatically get into Harvard or MIT from there, and there's nowhere else I want to go," Jeebs said as if my parents should have known this.

"That's a lot of money, darling," my mother said. My father said nothing, but I knew money would be foremost in his mind. It had recently dawned on me that we were not rich; that we simply lived like the rich. Almost everything I took for granted as simply privileged and special had come from someone else.

"I'm a shoo-in for a full scholarship, if I want it," Jeebs said briskly. "All my instructors say so. It never occurred to me that I'd need to, but I can apply anytime. It's no problem." *For me, even if it is for you,* hung in the air among us all, unsaid. All of a sudden I wanted to kick Jeebs. He stank, these days, of pretense and elitism, two qualities that had always been vigorously discouraged in my family.

I wondered then if Jeebs did not know about my mother's illness, or if he simply did not care. Unfairly, I preferred the former. I wanted to know something of overpowering import that this new Jeebs did not know. I liked thinking that my parents simply had not told Jeebs yet. It made me feel grown-up and competent, the chatelaine of cancer on Kalorama Circle.

"Is Jeebs coming home?" I asked as we stood in the bathoom.

"Yes," my mother said. "He's staying home over Christmas. It's time for a family powwow."

"So we're not going to the villa?" I said, putting as much pathos into my voice as possible. I felt, suddenly and savagely, that I wanted to punish my mother for her illness.

"Not at Christmas," my mother said. Her voice was cool and remote, as it became whenever I intentionally wounded her. "We really need to have this family discussion. Maybe at spring break. It'll be nicer weather then."

"Well, I don't want to have some stupid family powwow," I said, almost in tears of rage and contrition and what I know now to have been fear. "I'm not going to it if we have it."

"Yes, you are," my father said, his voice suddenly steely. I had rarely heard that voice before. "You can't live underwater anymore, Lilly. Your mother needs us now. This is a family affair."

"What is?" I shouted, daring him to say it. It was, finally, my mother who answered.

"Cancer, Lilly," she said. "I don't think you quite took it in when we told you. I have breast cancer, and we need to name it and talk about it and decide together how we're going to handle it. I'll need all your help."

"Will I have to stop swimming?"

"No."

"Well, I won't stop swimming. How long does this last?"

"We don't know. I just started treatment. We'll know more about that later."

"I'll bet I will have to stop."

My father roared at me, but my mother laughed. "I wouldn't do that to you for the world, my little selkie."

"What's that?"

"A seal who turns into a woman and then back into a seal," she said. "Who can't really live away from the water."

"Well, okay then," I said sniffily, knowing I had been childish and cruel. I began to cry. Wilma leaned his head against my leg, and I reached down and patted him.

"I'm sorry, Mama," I said, choking on the words.

"Don't be. The last thing I want for any of you is to give up your loves. I don't plan to give up mine."

My father made a small, strangled sound, and she pulled her robe tight around her and went to him and slipped her arm around his waist, and they walked out of the bathroom together. I looked furtively at the swell of her breasts under her satin robe. Which one was it? Surely there would be a difference. But there wasn't. Not then, anyway.

The still gray time that is Washington at Thanksgiving came wheeling past. We were accustomed to having Thanksgiving dinner at the Chevy Chase Club, because neither of my parents had living mothers and fathers, and my father's brother had a large family of his own and tended to take his brood to the huge old hunting lodge in

Arkansas, where Gregory's in-laws held impossibly lavish four-day celebrations, with servants and cooks and legendary bird-hunting trips, and everyone dressed formally for the game dinners that followed.

I had always liked having just us, together again, in the beautiful old dining room we knew so well, with, as my mother once said a bit ironically, everyone who was anyone in Washington around us; course after course of traditional holiday food, sumptuous desserts, the great Christmas tree in the lobby already shining, and elegant old Frost to greet us at the door.

Frost never forgot anyone's name. I always wondered how he did it.

It was my custom to save a fat drumstick for Wilma, but we didn't go to the club that Thanksgiving, and so I saved the drumstick from the turkey that Flora and Emma cooked and gave it to him in my bedroom. He was as happy to get a home-cooked drumstick as he had ever been to receive a Chevy Chase one, and capered all over the house with it, dragging grease and seasoning over every available rug. My parents, who had come into the sitting room after complimenting Flora and Emma effusively, had lit the fire and put a little Haydn quartet on the record player. Rain had begun to tick against the diamond-paned sitting-room windows, and the fire snickered softly and smelled faintly of the old apple tree that had died in the backyard over the summer, and the Haydn rippled and purled sweetly. Wilma brought his bone and curled up on the fire rug and attacked it, and I sat on the little corner settee and looked at my family and listened to the music and smelled the sweet smoke and was unaccountably very happy. Right then, just for that moment out of careening time, we were all stopped and stilled in pure grace, and nothing could touch us. My mother lifted her head and looked at me and smiled, and I knew that she felt the magic too. My father had his head back against his chair and his eyes closed; he frequently napped thus after meals. I did not, somehow, believe he was asleep, but if he was, I hoped his dreams were as sweet as this room on this day.

The weeks before Christmas had always been a giddy, heart-lifting time to me on Kalorama Circle. It had always been a time of decorations going up, of vanilla and cinnamon swirling out of the kitchen, of fresh pine greenery and the sharp fragrance of poinsettia with which my mother forested the drawing room, of carols on the radio and baroque music on the phonograph, of the first melting chocolate cherry from the drugstore box that always sat on the table behind the big sofa, discreetly shielded by its more elegant Godiva companions; of the cold fragrance of the big fir that came in fresh from the lot behind the Avalon Theatre; of tissue paper crackling and boxes stowed in bedroom closets and, always, laughter from the drawing room as my parents' friends came for Christmas eggnog or Tom and Jerrys; and sometimes the whisper of fat wet snowflakes against the diamond panes of the big front windows.

A long time later I told Cam about those Christmases and he said, "Pure Norman Rockwell. Do you know how lucky you were?"

"I didn't then," I said. "I do now."

The Christmases had always included nighttime drives to see the decorations on the embassies, and, of course, the great tree on the lawn of the White House. But we did not go that year. For one thing, my mother loathed Lyndon Johnson and said to my father that he had probably hung bull testicles all over the tree.

But it was more than just the hulking new Texas President. Something had happened when John Kennedy was shot, something that seemed to leach joy and safety out of the world. Terrible things that had never before seemed possible, now were. I think of it as the time when America hunched its shoulders and lowered its head, waiting for the next blow. They were not long in coming.

"Aren't y'all going to have any parties?" I remember saying to my mother. I pretended to hate them, as I was usually pressed into wait-ress service dressed in my holiday best. But I missed the before-party bustle, and the hum of adult laughter from the drawing room, and the smell of perfume on cold fur coats in the upstairs bedroom. I always sniffed furs at my mother's winter parties.

"No. Not until after Christmas. I've put the word out. I just want to be quiet this year, no visitors, and then right after Christmas we'll have a big party and ask everybody. I'll have to decide what to do about my hair. Maybe you can go wig shopping with me."

"Maybe we can have a wig made out of your hair. I've still got it. It's in my underwear drawer."

She laughed.

"Not a bad idea at all, Lilly. Maybe we will."

But she never did. She wore turbans or scarves at home, and one of her signature slouch hats when, infrequently, we went out. I never thought about her bald head anymore. She became just my mother who had a penchant for scarves and turbans, as if she had always worn them.

Given time, a child can fit almost any horror into his or her world. We did not have such elaborate decorations that year, but there was the customary magnolia wreath on the door, and my father brought home the fresh fir from our accustomed lot, and we decorated it. This had always been a pinnacle moment for me in the landscape of Christ-mas, accompanied by laughter and reminiscences about the prove-nance of this battered ornament and that, and hot cocoa. We even draped Wilma in tinsel, hastily removing it before he ate it.

But that year was quiet, even with the crackling fire and the car-ols and, of course, Wilma. My father brought down the boxes of lights and ornaments, and he and I decked the tree under Mother's direction. She seemed to have little energy, but in the evening she was usually the weariest. When we were nearly done, we stepped back to survey the tree. It was beautiful, a bit smaller this year but a lovely shape, so fresh that the scent of fir sap joined that of the needles and the fire logs in the room. My father paused over the box and lifted out the decoration that we almost always put on last, a long chain of translucent colored sea glass we had gathered from the beach at Edgewater over the years. He stopped and looked at my mother. She shook her head almost imperceptibly, and he laid the chain back in the box. I said nothing, but my heart was hammering with relief and something else I could not name when the chain disappeared in the box again. We did not speak of it.

Two weeks before Christmas, I woke in the night and heard my parents arguing. They were all the way down the hall from me, and both our doors were closed, but I could still hear my father shouting indistinguishably, and my mother's voice, higher, and with an edge of hysteria in it that I had never heard before.

"No!" she shouted. "I absolutely will not! I will not have my son come home from school and find me puking my guts out for three days! I won't spend Christmas with my family tiptoeing outside my door and eating Christmas dinner alone, and listening to me throw up every five minutes. I'll do it after the holidays, but I will not do it now!"

They finally stopped shouting and the after-midnight silence fell down over the house again. It was a long time before I went to sleep. It took me many minutes to concoct a scenario that fit what I had heard. I finally settled on one of the painful trips to the dentist that often made my mother nauseated for a day or two, and fell asleep with Wilma twitching and warm beside me. No one mentioned it; I would have died rather than ask.

Jeebs came home a week before Christmas. My father met him at Union Station on a raw gray day slashed with blowing sleet, and they came puffing and stamping into the house in the late afternoon.

My mother and I were waiting for them in the sitting room, where the tree and fire were lit and Wilma groaned happily in deep doggy sleep on the hearth rug. The rug was grubby and frayed with the years of Wilma, but my mother always said there was no use replacing it while Wilma was in residence. She began to smile when she heard the footsteps, and rose from her chair.

Jeebs came into the room, and she stopped, and we both stared. He was inches taller, and wore an astonishing costume of corduroy knickers, a moth-eaten velvet coat with dull, frayed satin lapels, and round granny glasses on his snub nose. He had striped woolen stockings and what appeared to be unlaced combat boots on his feet, and his hair fell into his eyes so that he had to keep brushing it back off the glasses. He stopped still and stared back at us as if daring us to say a word. Behind him, my father's mouth quirked with laughter, but his voice was level and placid.

"Behold the prodigal son," he said.

Jeebs scowled. He had not, I knew, wanted to come home for Christmas, having been invited to ski with a classmate at his parents' lodge in Aspen. But my father had put his foot down. Jeebs glanced at my mother's pretty red satin turban, and then looked quickly away, as if he had inadvertently beheld something obscene.

Mother rose and went to him and put her arms around him. She had to stand on tiptoe to do it.

"Hi, baby," she said. "I'm so glad you're home."

Jeebs took a step backward.

"Grotties don't hug," he said.

"Well, this Grottie damned well better hug his mother at Christmas or he'll find himself matriculating at Harry Truman High next semester," my father said, his voice shaking with rage. Harry Truman High was in the heart of the projects, and spawned more juvenile crime than any other institution of higher learning in Washington.

Jeebs hugged my mother gingerly, and, when her arms dropped, stepped back once more.

"Well, look at you," my mother said, her voice just a little too high. "I rather had in mind blazers and white shirts and ties."

"Everybody wears this stuff when they're off campus, Mother," Jeebs said. For the first time he looked uncomfortable in his moth-eaten finery. "We get 'em at thrift shops and sometimes costume shops."

"Should save a bit on clothes," my father said dryly.

"I'll go up and change," Jeebs said. "Am I still in my old room?"

"Darling, where else would you be? Of course you are. No one's touched it except to clean it since you left."

Jeebs muttered something and went upstairs. He left his luggage where he had dropped it in the hall. When he came back down he was in the khakis and crewneck we were accustomed to, and somehow had become Jeebs again, not just a Grottie.

We had the family powwow late that afternoon, by the tree in the sitting room. It did not go well. I was just beginning to understand the import of my mother's illness and was struck dumb by it, and Jeebs stubbornly refused to confront it at all.

It was, as we had been told, cancer, my father said, and my mother had had her left breast and some tissue from her underarm removed. There was no sign of cancer in the lymphatic glands that the surgeons had removed, but it had been a tumor of some size and had apparently been there for quite a while, so, to be sure, my mother was getting chemotherapy treatment, and would later receive radiation.

"The treatment is sometimes worse than the disease," my father said. "Chemotherapy destroys the malignant cells, but it destroys the white blood cells that fight it, too. Your mother will possibly be very sick for a few days after she gets the chemo, very weak and nauseated.

She hasn't been so far, but they say that the third treatment is when the sickness usually starts, and she'll be getting that . . . soon."

He paused, and all of a sudden I understood what they had been arguing about. She had been due a treatment now, and had refused to have it until after Jeebs had come home and Christmas was over.

"After the first course of chemotherapy they'll take another look at her and see where we are. We all hope that there'll be a remission. The doctors think it's highly possible. But if there isn't, we'll do another course. We very much hope that after this course, or between others, she'll feel much better and gain weight and some of her hair will begin to come back. But it could be a rough time, especially for her, and really for all of us. We may have to make some changes. I may take some time off from the university. We'll probably have an overnight nurse from time to time. Jeebs, we may have to ask you to come home for a bit now and then. We—"

"Wait! No! I can't leave school my first year; it's when the college admissions are fixed! Everybody says so! Harvard tracks you from the very beginning!"

Jeebs was on his feet, his face blanched white.

"Jeebs, if your grades are good enough I'm sure both Groton and Harvard will see fit to make an occasional exception for serious family illness," my father said in a dangerously level voice.

My mother said nothing.

"But I mean . . . it'll be over soon, won't it?" Jeebs squeaked. "I mean, with all that chemo stuff and all—isn't it just a matter of time till it's over?"

"A matter of time, yes," my father said. "But it could be a very long time. You can't just turn cancer on and off. You live with it—if you're lucky, a very long time—but no one can predict how long. The waiting is hard and the ups and downs are even harder. Cancer can be a fatal disease, Jeebs. We don't think it will be in your mother's case. But you can't just go on thinking it's something temporary that will work out after a while, because it's not."

"You mean we might not ever really *know*?"

My mother spoke for the first time.

"We might not for a very long time, darling," she said.

"Well, I can't leave school," Jeebs said mulishly, not looking at anyone.

"Then you might as well go apply for all those scholarships," my father said tightly. "Because I'm not paying for a son who won't come home to help out when he's needed."

"Fine," Jeebs said furiously, tears beginning to run down his cheeks. "Fine. I'll do just that."

He turned and ran upstairs. No one spoke for a long time. Then my mother said, "It's a terrible shock for him. He's never had to face anything like this before. Neither of you darlings have. I hate it for you, *hate* it. But you've got to know, and to be realistic about it. Otherwise it will hurt you even more."

Presently Jeebs came back downstairs. He was wearing his baroque traveling uniform and stood in the hall beside his bags.

"I'm going to Aspen with Dubby's family," he said. "I just called him, and he'll meet me in Denver. I'm going on the train. I've got enough money for that. I don't believe any of this crap. You can't make me. And don't worry about taking me to the station. I've called a cab, and I'll wait for it outside."

And he turned and went out the front door and slammed it. Shortly we heard the soft honk of the cab's horn, and the door slamming as Jeebs got in. We listened until it was out of hearing range.

This time it was my father who had tears on his face. "I don't believe we raised a son who could do that," he whispered.

171

"Darling, he's scared to death," my mother said, her voice clear and strong. "He'll be back. Wait and see. Give him time to adjust."

"I hate him," I said, beginning to cry in earnest. "I hope he falls off a mountain and dies."

No one said anything more. Wilma came and slurped at my tear-stained face with his huge tongue. The fire and the old mantel clock ticked. The late afternoon slid into the tender blue of an early winter night.

Jeebs did not come home, and it was a long time before he called. By then a lot of things had changed.

CHAPTER

10

It was the worst Christmas I can remember. None of us seemed to know what to do for one another. My mother smiled brilliantly at us across the Christmas dinner table, and said that she didn't believe she'd ever had better dressing than the oyster pecan dressing that was Emma's specialty.

"Or better sweet potato casserole, either," my father said heartily. "Is it candied or something?"

As a matter of fact, I knew that he loathed sweet potatoes; and they were on our holiday table only because Jeebs loved them.

There would be a silence, and then they would both begin to talk at once, and fall silent. My father would smile his stretched smile at my mother and say, "Go ahead. You were first," and she would giggle, a strange little sound as sharp as broken glass and as elusive as spilled mercury, and shake her head and say that she couldn't remember what she had been going to say. They would both look at me, and I would stuff and stuff my mouth with turkey and green bean casserole so I would not have to speak. I don't think I could have. Anger at Jeebs burned in my throat like bile. At Jeebs and at my parents, too. Why couldn't we all talk about it, say that Jeebs was an insufferable little shit and we were better off without him, and go on with this Christmas as we had in Christmases past?

But I knew that was not going to happen, so I said nothing and waited mutely until the apple and mince pies, both with dollops of whipped cream on them, were brought from the kitchen and served, so I could bolt mine down and plead fatigue and flee to the sanctuary of my room. After I was safely there, Wilma groaning happily with a full stomach from a comfortable nest in my bedclothes, I could hear them talking downstairs in the sitting room. I could tell from the absence of light cast into the hallway and on the stairs that they probably were sitting with only the lights from the tree and fire. They often did that on Christmas night, and I had always loved knowing they were there in that warm, magical radiance and I was snug and warm up here in my bed, with days and days of holiday left to me. But tonight my mother was crying; I could hear her soft, strangled little sobs, and my father's voice, also soft but deeper, going on and on. Finally both voices ceased, and I heard them start up the stairs toward their bedroom, and I turned over and buried my head in Wilma's side. It was a long time until I slept.

A couple of days after Christmas my mother went back to the hospital for her third and, she hoped, last chemotherapy treatment. It was the last one in this series, she told me before she went, and she had been told it would probably make her quite sick, but when the sickness was over they hoped, *she* hoped, that she would begin to feel stronger and better than she had in a long time, and we could get back to the business of living.

"It's been awful for you. I know it has," she said. "I've hated every minute of it. But this could very well do the trick, and I would count the long tiredness and the silly hair loss and the famous nausea well worth it, if we can have our lives back."

"When will you know?" I said.

"We've talked about this, baby. It may be a long time. We may never really know. The thing is just to feel better, be stronger. And the doctors believe that can happen, and your father and I do, too."

"So maybe we could still go to St. Thomas?"

I had gotten, from my parents, a glistening black wet suit and tanks and goggles for scuba diving, and a certificate for instruction at the Central YWCA downtown. I was beside myself to put them on and sink into my green crystal world and not have to come up for ages and ages.

"Maybe we could. We can surely shoot for early summer. I'd love that myself."

"Will Jeebs go with us?" I asked, holding my breath.

"If he wants to," my mother said. "I hope he will."

"How can you want him to go, after what he did? How can you just—"

"Because he's my child and I love him," she said, smiling a little, though not at me. "And because he's desperately sorry about the way he acted."

"How do you know?"

"I just know," my mother said. "Jeebs is not as strong as you are, Lilly. I think I've always known that. He can think of nothing but to run away when he's frightened and sad. But he'll be okay, in his own time. We mustn't push him."

Well, I think we should shun him like the Amish do, I thought, but did not say. I had no intention of forgiving my brother his treachery at Christmas, and felt achingly guilty that my mother thought I was strong. What would she think of me if she knew about the diver's suit and the helmet? They, truly, were for escape as surely as the physical act of Jeebs's flight.

My mother was right: the third chemotherapy treatment made her sicker than I had known a human being could be. My father brought her home; she had insisted, saying she could throw up as well in her own bedroom as in the hospital. She was trembling, and holding on to his arm when they went up the stairs, and she slipped gratefully into the fresh, pretty linens that Flora had ironed to perfection, smelling of the lavender soap my mother always loved. The room was cool and dusky with the winter sun shut out by the curtains, and there were bowls of hyacinths and lilacs, my mother's favorites, set about. The instant she smelled the flowers, she vomited violently all over her cream wool dress and alligator pumps, and she did not stop vomiting for three days. It was a visceral, savage vomiting; after half a day of it I thought it must surely tear her slender body apart, erode her throat, and I ran upstairs to my room and put on my albums of the Beach Boys and let the sounds of California surf wash over my ears and my heart.

But over it all I could still hear the brutal retching, the agonized heavings of a body trying to expel sickness even when there was nothing left to expel. Between bouts I heard my mother crying softly, and the equally soft voice of my father, talking, talking, talking. Late that night she was still vomiting and crying, and my father was still speaking softly, and I pulled the covers over my head and fixed Wilma in a death grip—he was whining softly—and finally slept. I dreamed we were all on a ship going to Europe, and were all seasick in vast, wave-roughened water, but knew that when we reached calmer water it would all be over. When I woke, rather late the next morning, we had not reached calmer water and my mother was still vomiting.

My father came into my bedroom, hollow-eyed and stricken.

"Did you get any sleep, Puddin'?" he asked. His voice was hoarse.

"I think so," I mumbled. "But I bet you didn't. I bet she didn't. How can she live through all this? Won't it just . . . tear her to pieces?"

"They say not," he said, trying to smile and failing. His jaw was blue with whiskers, and I realized that I had not seen him unshaved for a very long time.

"It sounds it, but the doctors say that when it's over, it's over. She may not even remember it very well."

I knew I would never forget the sound of my mother struggling to expel her cancer, and that he would not, either.

"What can we do?" I said, beginning to cry. He sat down on the side of my bed and scratched Wilma's fat speckled stomach and pushed my tangled hair off my face.

"Be here. Just be here. Let her know no one is going to leave her. She thinks she's going to die from this nausea, and she keeps saying, 'Don't let me die alone. Stay with me.' So that's what we'll do."

"You have to sleep sometime, Daddy," I said. "I'm scared you'll get sick, too."

"I can sleep when she does," he said, smiling. It was a real smile. "I've got years and years to sleep."

"What do you talk to her about?"

"Mostly I read to her. I think it helps a little; at least when I stop, she gestures for me to go on."

"What are you reading?"

"Well, I've gone through most of the Penrod and Sam books. She used to love those when she was a kid. And some of *The Little Colonel*. I don't know why that doesn't make her sicker. And we're starting on *The Jungle Book*. That's a good one. We both love that. Sometimes she whispers along with me, when she recognizes a passage. 'We be of one blood, Thou and I.' 'Mark my trail!' Mowgli and Akela and Baloo and Shere Khan are the only ones who can get her to sleep a little."

"I used to love that book too," I said.

"That's what she said.

"Flora is cleaning her up a little, and Emma has taken her a little tray of bouillon and crackers. I doubt that she can keep them down, but she needs to try. She's terribly weak."

"Is she going to die?" I quavered, hearing the terrible storm of viscera starting again.

"No, baby. But she'll probably wish she could, before this is over."

"And this is supposed to cure her? It's awful; why can't they find another way?"

"This is the best thing they've got. It sounds like it's destroying everything in her, but it destroys cancer cells too. And after it has, you just . . . build everything else back up."

"I wouldn't ever want anybody to do that to me. I'd rather die."

"No, you wouldn't, Lilly. When it comes right down to it, nobody would rather die. If I didn't think it would help her, I'd never let her go through this again. But the thing is, it *does* stop. Meanwhile, all we can do is go through it with her. I'm pleased and honored to do that."

He smiled again, and went away to take a shower, and I lay listening to the dreadful sounds from my mother's room and then picked up *20,000 Leagues Under the Sea* and immersed myself in Captain Nemo's mad and radiant plans for great cities under the sea.

"I'd live there," I whispered to Wilma. "I'd live there in a minute; I'd be the first one to go. You could come with me and be the first dog at the bottom of the sea."

He whined and thumped his tail and put his head back down on his paws. He did not sleep. Like me, he simply listened to the agony emanating from the big bedroom down the hall.

Days later, while my mother drifted in and out of an exhausted sleep, a letter came from the financial officer of the Groton School. My father opened it, and smiled a little.

"Jeebs is as good as his word," he said. "Full scholarship. Grotty shouldn't cost us a penny from now on out."

"Is there anything from him?"

"No. I imagine he rather likes the statement the official notification makes. Sort of 'See? I told you so.' I expect we'll hear from him before long."

"He ought to know how sick Mother is! He ought to think he did it! We ought to call him and tell him."

"No," he said. His face was serious and his voice was firm. "Your mother would never forgive us. Now that he's shown us he can do it all by himself, I expect he'll call. And when he does, no one is to mention this little siege of nausea to him. He's frightened enough as it is."

He left my room and I sat seething. Jeebs had behaved unforgivably, and all he got was sympathy and understanding. What would have happened to me if I'd literally run away from my ill and terrifying mother?

I found out the next day.

All through the previous night, and this morning, until about noon, my mother retched and cried, retched and cried. And my father stayed beside her, reading, reading, reading. Late in the afternoon the raging sickness seemed to abate a little; I heard the vomiting less often, and the crying stopped.

The day after this one, Monday, was the day I returned to school, and I was packing up my swim bag and shuffling through the books we were supposed to have read over the holidays. I had read nothing but Jules Verne. My father came into my room, freshly shaved and in clean clothes, his face ravaged but smiling, and said, "Your mother's sleeping right now, and I really think the worst of it is over. I have to go over to the office for about an hour. I wish you'd go see her when

179

she wakes up. She's been asking for you. Maybe you could read a little to her this afternoon. What are you reading now?"

Silently I held up Jules Verne, feeling my stomach go cold with fear. I could not, could *not* go into that malodorous room and look at my corpse of a mother. I would die if I had to.

"That looks good. I think she'd like that," my father said.

"Well, Daddy, you see, there's this . . . I have a swim meet tonight." I gestured at my packed bag.

"Before school even starts?"

"It's a makeup," I lied fluently. "With Cold Farm. We won't be eligible for the regular schedule until we make it up. I thought I told you."

"Maybe you did," he said distractedly. "Well, you can read to your mother tomorrow. I'll drop you . . . where?"

"At the Cold Farm pool house. But you don't have to drop me. Helena Boykin and Shirley Tate are meeting me at the corner, and we're going to take the bus. It goes right past Cold Farm. Mr. Boykin said he'd bring us home."

"Well, go along then, and good luck," he said. "I'll tell your mother. Don't be out late."

"No sir," I said, and grabbed up my bag and my coat and scarf and ran downstairs.

I went out into the cold, clear night and closed the door firmly enough so that they could hear it. Then I walked down to the bus stop on Rock Creek Parkway and took a bus to Chevy Chase Circle and sat through two showings of *Breakfast at Tiffany's* at the Avalon Theatre. When I caught the bus back it was nearly eleven, and if it occurred to me that I had never been out so late before alone, it did not bother me at all. I was drifting along Fifth Avenue with Holly Golightly, eating Cracker Jacks and looking like a startled gazelle in the fabulous store windows I passed.

"I'm home," I shouted up the stairs, and went straight to my room. I threw my swimsuit and towel over a chair and dampened my hair under the shower, and was just into my flannel pajamas when my father came in.

"We were getting worried," he said. "Who won?"

"Oh, Cold Farm," I said yawning elaborately. "They always do. All their swimmers are eighteen and built like whales. I don't know why we bother."

He smiled.

"Well, get to bed. School day tomorrow. I told your mother you'd read *20,000 Leagues* to her when you got home. She's looking forward to it."

"How is she?"

"Better. She had one more session of vomiting right after you left, but nothing since then. And she ate a little bouillon, and she's sound asleep now. I think we've turned the corner."

"I hope so," I said in Holly's voice and floated to my father and kissed his cheek, and drifted into bed. He looked at me for a moment, and then smiled and went out.

After the door had closed, Holly Golightly gave me a little flutter-fingered wave, turned, and glided out of my room, still munching Cracker Jacks, her tiara slightly askew. I was alone except for Wilma, who apparently had not seen or smelled Holly. I twisted and tossed with guilt for most of the night.

The next afternoon when I got home from school, I picked up Jules Verne and went down the hall to my mother's room, my heart pounding in my throat. I rapped softly on the door. Perhaps she was asleep; perhaps—

"Come in," she called, in almost her old voice. I went in. She was propped up on a pile of fresh, lacy pillows, in a coral nightgown I had

181

never seen, a matching turban on her head. She was still deathly pale and lines that had never been there before cut her face, but she had put on a little dusting of pink blush, and there was light coral lipstick on her mouth. She wore eye makeup, too. I felt giddy with relief. All right, so she was thin almost to the point of transparency, and there were great yellow bruises on her hands and arms, but she was still my beautiful mother, and still very much alive. A little tray of cookies and a teapot sat on her bedside table. There was a book facedown on the coverlet beside her. I glanced at it: *The Tropic of Cancer*.

I wanted to laugh aloud. She saw me suppress it.

"Nothing like a little Henry Miller to get the juices going," she said. "One day you might want to read it, if you're feeling a little juiceless."

I said nothing and she looked at me more closely. "Unless, of course, you already have."

I shrugged and she laughed.

"Come in, darling, and let me get a look at you." She stared at me until I began to fidget, and then said, "Still a pretty girl. Maybe even prettier. I'm glad to see there are no gills. What have you brought to read to me?"

I held out Jules Verne and she laughed again.

"Why am I not surprised? Well, I'll enjoy that. It's been years since I read it."

I read the chapter that had always fascinated me most; the most seductive evocation of what might be found underneath the sea if one could only get there, the passage where Captain Nemo takes Arronax into the forest of Crespo Island. At first I faltered over the words, but then their power took over and I lost myself in the fecund magic of the undersea forest.

When I had finished, she was silent for a little while, and then looked at me, smiling her strange, oblique kitten's smile.

"It's very beautiful, isn't it? No wonder you want so badly to live under the sea. But you must remember to come back, darling. As an old poet I like, Robert Frost, said, 'Earth's the right place for love.'"

Does she know about the suit and the helmet and all? I wondered. *No. There's no way that she could.*

"Pass the cookie tray, sweetie, and pour us a cup of tea. Maybe tomorrow we'll press on."

We ate the cookies and drank tea by the light of the fading afternoon, until Flora came in to turn on the lamps and I heard the front door slam as my father returned from the university.

"Thank you, Lilly," my mother said.

"Thank you, Mama."

I could not have said for what.

Washington's cranky and erratic spring seldom comes breathing in when it is expected, so that cherry blossoms and tourists freeze simultaneously along the mall. But this year it slipped in early, and as Easter approached, Washington's legendary flowering trees and shrubs were in full plumage. Rock Creek Park was a cave of shining new green, Georgetown's window boxes and pot gardens blazed with color, and the suburban enclaves like Spring Valley were massed with surging azaleas and camellias and tulips. The skies over Washington were a soft, washed blue, and the Potomac ran clear and singing.

"I never saw a prettier spring here," my mother said one noon in the garden behind our house. My father had bought her a little umbrella table with four chairs, and our sometimes gardener, Randolph, had mowed and trimmed and fertilized, and set pots of blooming annuals around the perimeter of the little brick patio where the umbrella table sat. She loved the garden and the table and chairs, and spent most afternoons there in fair weather. Today she and I were having lunch there, it being the beginning of Easter holidays. We sat drinking lemonade and waiting for our tuna salad to come, and I could not stop looking at my mother.

She had been right. There had been no more sickness after that first bestial three days back in January. She had gained a bit of weight, so that the hollows in her face were filling in, and the faint flush on her cheeks was natural. Her hair was beginning to come back, too; a soft fuzz of copper that promised curls later on. She still covered her head sometimes, but did not always bother. Today she wore a broad-brimmed straw hat she had bought last summer in St. Thomas. It had cutout work around the brim, and in its flickering shadow her face looked mysterious and beautiful, like a saint's in a niche. I loved that hat. In it she was a young girl on a holiday in the sun.

Flora came with lunch, smiling, and said, "Y'all finish that now, Miss Lizabeth. We got fresh strawberries for dessert."

"Oh, Flora, are the strawberries out? How wonderful."

"They's out in California," Flora said, and went back into the house. We both laughed. From under the table Wilma thumped his ropy tail. He did not aspire to tuna fish, or he would have been mobbing the table.

"Your father tells me Jeebs called last night," she said.

"Yes ma'am," I said, not looking at her. Jeebs had indeed called, in response to my father's letter of congratulations and the handsome check he had sent for Jeebs's birthday. He was not coming home for Easter, he said, but was rather going to Bermuda with his roommate's family, who had a house there.

"But I'll try to get home early in May," he said. "Tell Mom hello for me."

"Would you like to speak to her?" my father had said. "I don't think she's asleep yet."

"No, just tell her I called and said hello, and . . . wanted to know how she was doing."

"She's much better. She's through with the chemo for now, and she's up and about and feeling good. But I know she'd want to talk to you."

"I'll see her in May," Jeebs said, and hung up soon after.

I was furious with him, but my father only said, "It's a start, Lilly. By summer we'll all be back to normal, God willing. For Jeebs, it's a pretty big step."

I thought it was less than a baby step, but said nothing. Now my mother said, across the table, "I'm sorry I missed him. I really wanted to talk to him."

"We thought you were asleep, and he said he'd be home in May, anyway," I said, and then heard myself rushing on: "But he said to give you his love and tell you he was sorry about Christmas, and he couldn't wait to see you . . ."

I fell silent. She was grinning at me under the hat brim, a young girl's impudent grin.

"He said no such thing and you know it," she said, "but I love you for saying he did. You've come quite a way with me, haven't you?"

"I don't know what—"

"You saw us that day at Edgewater, didn't you?" she said gently. "Mr. Burns and me, in my studio?"

She did not have to explain further. The image of her head thrown back and her beautiful breasts bared to the groping, spidery old hands came surging up from wherever I had buried it, so clearly that I almost gagged, and closed my eyes.

"Yes," I whispered. And then, "You meant me to see it, didn't you?"

"Yes, I did. You were as good as the CIA about spying on me that summer. I was pretty sure you'd see."

"Why?"

"Because I wanted you to learn something about being kind. You weren't a kind child, Lilly; well, children hardly ever are. But you were such a natural leader, and things fell so neatly into your lap, that I was afraid that somehow you might never learn it—"

"You think that was kind?" I roared. "I think it was sickening! Those old hands all over you; for a long time I thought it was him who gave you cancer with his old yellow hands."

"But you did learn about kindness, Lilly. Somewhere along the way you did. You couldn't have told me that lovely lie about Jeebs if you hadn't. It's one lie I'll always treasure. And you mustn't think Mr. Burns gave me . . . anything. In fact, he may just have saved my life. It was he who found the lump, that day."

But as it turned out, Mr. Brooks Burns did not save my mother's life. Three days after our lunch she developed a troublesome cough, and then shortness of breath, and was admitted to the hospital so that her doctors might draw some fluid from her lungs.

"It's not unusual when you've been bedridden as long as I was," she said. "They don't even expect me to be there overnight."

So I went, instead, to swim practice, and it was Flora who told me when I got home, eyes brimming with tears, to get a cab down to the hospital because my mother was in a bad way.

"Yo' daddy already there," she said. "And he done call Mr. Jeebs and he on his way. You tell yo' dad we got lamb chops and mashed potatoes tonight, do he want to come home for a minute and have his supper."

I don't remember the cab ride to the hospital. I do know that I was singing to myself, over and over, witlessly, "Moon River, wider than a mile . . ."

When I ran into the intensive-care waiting room my father was sitting on a sofa, staring at the wall. His face was a perfect blank.

"Where's Mama?" I said, my voice high and quavering.

"She's in there," he said, pointing to a room whose door was closed and bore a sign that said NO SMOKING. OXYGEN IN USE.

I started for the door, but he called me back.

"We can't go in, Lilly. She's on a ventilator, and they've got her hooked up to a million tubes. There's a nurse with her all the time, and the doctor looks in every hour."

"*Why? What happened?*"

"During the procedure she aspirated some of the fluid back into her lungs, and pneumonia set in before they even got her back to her room. They're giving her everything they've got for it, but she hasn't got many white cells left to fight with, and it—doesn't look very good."

"But she's not going to *die*! People don't die of pneumonia now."

"Lilly, she isn't getting better. She's slipping in and out of a coma. The doctor says we ought to . . . speak with her now, if we're going to. I've called Jeebs—" He stopped. His face was slack and blasted. He did not look at all like my father.

A nurse put her head out of the room's door and motioned to us.

"She's awake now, I think. She's not in any pain. But she's very, very tired. She wanted to see you, but I can't let you stay more than a very few minutes."

We tiptoed into the room and looked down at the slight mound that was my mother under the starched covers. She was lying with her eyes closed, and we could hear the long, monotonous sigh of the respirator, and the slight hiss of the oxygen unit. I felt a momentary crazy stab of relief. There had been a mistake. This was not my mother. Only a few days ago I had sat under a garden umbrella and laughed with my mother in the noon sunlight. This woman had never laughed. This woman had never breathed.

She opened her eyes and turned her head and looked at us. A very faint smile stretched her cracked lips.

"What a crock," she whispered. "George, darling . . ." and she moved a claw-like yellow hand very slightly and he lifted it slowly to his lips and kissed it. Tears slipped from his closed eyes.

My mother looked at me.

"Pretty girl," she whispered. "My pretty girl . . ."

It was the last thing she said to any of us. She slipped deeply into a coma and did not stir again, and she died the next morning just at dawn, barely thirty minutes before Jeebs got there.

We all sat together in a private lounge, looking at one another. Nobody seemed to know what to do next. The doctor had said he would come and speak with us in a little while, but it had been over an hour and we had not heard from him. I did not know if my mother was still in the hospital room or not; I had no wish to go and see. We simply sat. Jeebs cried quietly; my father had put his hand on Jeebs's knee but otherwise had not moved.

"I should call Campbell's, I guess," he said finally, thickly. "I guess that's the next thing you do."

"You mean so they can come get her and—do all that stuff to her?" I said.

"Honey, yes," he said. "They'll have to, you know."

"No," I said. "They don't have to. She wanted to be cremated and her ashes to be taken—you know—up there, and scattered over the ocean."

"That's ridiculous, Lilly," he said, in what sounded like mere annoyance. "Of course she doesn't want to be cremated. We don't cremate our loved ones. She'll be . . . at Oak Hill, like everyone in this family always has been and will be."

"I heard her say it," I said, beginning to cry. "I heard her. She was sitting on the lawn chairs talking to . . . to Mrs.—you know, his mother . . ."

"Jon's mother? Mrs. Lowell?" he said incredulously. We might have been talking about some happening or other at a near-forgotten vacation.

"Yes." I wept. "She said so. She *said* so, Daddy. The night of the summer solstice."

He snorted in exasperation and we fell into silence again. Presently the people from Campbell's Funeral Home came and took my mother away, although I did not see this, and we three went back to the house on Kalorama Circle where, now, my mother no longer lived. Still we did not talk. Jeebs went, sobbing, upstairs to his room. My father went out to the kitchen and spoke with Flora and Emma in the same dry, dead voice he had used all morning, and I heard them begin to wail.

A little later, I heard my father go down the basement steps and heard, for the first time in a very long time, the rhythmic thump of the trampoline and the metallic jingle of the chains that held the balance bar.

I went swimming.

CHAPTER

11

The night after my mother's memorial service, I woke in the deep predawn hours, in the grip of a terror such as I had never known. If I had read Sartre or Camus, I would perhaps have had a name for it: existential terror. But I didn't know about Sartre. Not then. All I knew was that if I moved a muscle, made a sound, I would be sucked out of bed and through the roof and up into the whistling, limitless black space beyond the stars, and there I would die. Or I would step out of my bed and fall instantly into the bottomless abyss that yawned hungrily beneath the manicured crust of suburban lawns and cherry-tree-lined malls. The abyss had always been there; somehow I had always known that. If you fell into it, you would never stop falling; you would smell the rotting exhalations of its wet black lungs, feel the pulsing of its swollen, indifferent heart, but you would never reach the actual limits of the abyss.

All this I knew in an instant, in my bed in my room on the second floor of the house where I had been born, and I thought that the terror would follow me all the days of my life. There was no enclosing sky above me, and no solid earth beneath me.

I pressed my face into my pillow and willed the helmet to lock into place, but it did not, and I was not surprised. For the first time I had not really thought it would. The helmet kept the world at bay. This

190

dark thing was not of the world. It encompassed planets, galaxies, the universe. It was everywhere and nowhere. *Alone,* I thought. *This is what alone means.* I needed not helmets, but the touch of human flesh.

I got out of bed and stumbled down the dark hall toward my parents' bedroom, but even as I pushed the door open I knew they were not there. Well, not my mother, of course. But neither was my father. Wilma was, curled tightly into a shaggy ball on my mother's side of the bed. It was the first time I could remember that he had not slept the night in my bed.

I thought for a moment that I would seek out my father wherever he had retreated to sleep without my mother, but this did not feel right either. I knew there would be no comfort for me there. Not yet. Tatty Glover, who had orchestrated my mother's service and the reception afterward because none of us seemed capable of even answering a doorbell, was sleeping over in the guest room in case she was needed in the night. But I could not go there, either. Tatty, though grieving, was so forthright and competent that I could not imagine snuggling up to her smartly angular body. I stood in the doorway of my parents' empty room, literally wringing my hands, and then I ran back to my room and pulled out the satin drawstring bag that had once held a handbag of my mother's and now held her hair, and ran back to her bedroom and crawled under the covers. With her hair against my cheek and Wilma sighing and snoring against me, I finally slid into sleep myself, the terror buried for the moment under bronze-gold coils and doggy-smelling fur. I slept until nine o'clock the next morning, and woke trying to hold on to the ghost of my mother's laughter, to echoes of her deep, gurgling laugh. The obscene fear came crawling back, and I ran barefoot and in my pajamas into the kitchen, where I heard voices and could smell cooking and feel warmth emanating from behind the closed double doors. My hands were shaking so that I could hardly open the doors and when I did, they were all there, my father and Tatty and Flora and Emma. Jeebs, shaken and silent, had gone back to Groton earlier that morning.

My father was drinking coffee and staring over Tatty's head out the kitchen window, where, in the back garden, wisteria now shawled the trees in purple and birds whisked around the little fountain. He did not seem to see me. Tatty Glover, in a soft, flowered cotton housecoat, sat across from him, red and swollen of eyes, with a yellow legal pad and a pen on the table in front of her. She did not notice me either, but Emma and Flora did, at once, and whirled at me with milk and fresh toast and jam. There were silver snail's tracks of tears on both their dark faces, but they managed smiles for me.

"You sit right down here and eat your breakfast, Lilly," Flora said. "You didn't eat no supper, and you gon' need your strength. You the lady of the house now."

I looked wildly at Tatty. It hadn't ever occurred to me that I would become "the lady of the house"; surely no one would expect that of me. Somehow I had thought that among them, Tatty and my father and Emma and Flora would see to it that life went forward. Who in their right mind would place their trust in a shivering thirteen-year-old in an unseen diver's helmet whose sole proficiency was swimming underwater?

"You do need to eat something, Lilly," Tatty said, briskly crossing out something on her legal pad that had obviously been accomplished. *#34, Lilly fed?* I thought. I still looked at her mutely.

My father turned his head toward me. I knew, suddenly, what he would look like when he was very old. All the life was gone from his eyes, life not lived, but drained away.

"Your mother would certainly not want you to starve, baby," he said, stumbling a little over the word "mother."

"I'm not hungry," I quavered.

"Well, of course you're not," Tatty said impatiently. "Nobody's hungry. But life has to go on, and the first step is for you to sit down and eat your breakfast."

She looked at me more closely. "Are you all right, sweetie? I mean, are you feeling sick? You're white as a sheet."

"I . . . I woke up in the middle of the night and couldn't find anybody," I said thickly. "I couldn't find Wilma."

"I knew I should have slept in your room," Tatty murmured. "But we all thought, after having to deal with all those people and everything, that you might want to be by yourself. Never mind. I'll stay another night or two. It was a bad idea—I see that now."

"It's okay," I said. "I found Wilma in Mama's bed and I curled up with him. You don't need to stay, Aunt Tatty."

Tatty Glover was not, of course, my aunt, but my mother had always referred to her as such, so I did, too.

"No," my father said, his voice stronger. "I need to take over my house now. Lilly needs to come to me if she's . . . lonely in the night."

He didn't say "afraid," but somehow I knew that he knew what had dragged me out of sleep and flung me into the hall in search of warmth and safety.

"Wilma's a good sleepover friend," I said, trying for humor over the terrible trembling in my limbs and voice.

"Wilma's a dog," my father said. "I'm your father and I love you and from now on I sleep in your room. Or at least in the room next to you."

"George, do you really think—" Tatty began.

"Yes. I really think," he said.

She fell silent.

"I've made a little list of things you'll want to get done right away," she went on finally. "Notes that simply must be written, decisions to be made about where all those checks should go, setting up the foundation, deciding about Lilly's immediate plans, whether you'll keep the house, hiring someone to come in and act as a companion to Lilly. I simply can't do it with Charlotte still at home, but there will have to be someone she can go to, someone who can sort of—steer through her teen years at least until she's at college. Things a woman should know, things only a woman can help her with."

"No," my father said even more strongly. "Lilly and I together will handle all those things, and if she has a companion, as you call it, it will be me. We'll make mistakes. I'll make enormous ones, I'm sure, but they'll be Constable mistakes because that's who we are: the Constables. Not that it isn't lovely of you to think of it all, Tatty. We could never have pulled together a service and a reception so tasteful and beautiful as yesterday's by ourselves. I don't think we could even have ordered a pizza. Nobody who was here will ever forget it, Lilly and I most of all. If you'd just leave us the list we'll start on it right after breakfast. Well, no, but right after Lilly's home from school."

"George, don't you think it would be more seemly if she stayed home a few more days? It's customary—"

"Her mother would want her to go to school," my father said, and I knew he was right. I could almost hear her. "Get your behind in gear, baby, and start living *right now*. I won't have any tiptoeing around and weeping in corners in my house."

I smiled weakly.

"I ought to go, Aunt Tatty," I said. "I've got swim team practice this afternoon."

"Oh, the hell with swim team." Tatty sniffed. "Don't think I didn't notice the black straps of that bathing suit you had under your lovely white linen dress yesterday. I can't imagine what people thought, except that you were wearing black bikini underwear or something."

"I didn't notice it, Tatty, and I doubt anyone else did," my father said. "If it makes Lilly feel better to wear her swimsuit under her clothes, I say let her do it. Isn't that what this little conference is about? Making Lilly and me feel better?"

"Of course it is," Tatty said, standing up and gathering up her pens and pads. "You must do what's best for you. I just thought some guidelines—Lilly's still a very young girl, you know. But I'll always be here if you need to talk. I hope you'll remember that."

I saw that my father had offended her, and he did, too.

"Don't think we aren't grateful, Tatty," he said. "I meant it when I said it was the loveliest memorial I can imagine. Elizabeth would have loved it."

She smiled, mollified.

"You have my number," she said, and went out of the kitchen.

My father and I looked at each other.

"You'd better get dressed if you're serious about school," he said.

I got up to go to my room and dress and the great terror flew at me again, almost knocking me to my knees.

"I . . . Daddy, I don't think I can go by myself," I whispered, clinging to the back of my chair.

He did not question me.

"Then," he said, rising himself, "I'll take you. And I'll pick you up and bring you home, too."

When he stopped the car in front of the Cathedral School, I found that I could not seem to get out. I sat studying the small surf of girls surging into the school, the new green trees, the flowers and shrubs rioting in borders. Then I turned to my father.

"I don't know what to say to anybody," I said.

"Well, they'll probably just say they're very sorry about your mother, and you smile and say thank you."

All of a sudden I was angry, at him and all the faceless students of the National Cathedral School and at myself for being frightened and at my mother for dying and putting me through all this.

195

"I don't see why I have to smile," I muttered, glaring at him. "They *should* be sorry."

"It's the right thing to do, Lilly," he said, rather crisply, and I knew he was angry too, though most likely not at me. At my mother? But that was impossible.

"Okay," I said, dropping my eyes. "I'll see you back home."

"No. I'm picking you up, remember?"

"You don't have to do that! Almost everybody takes the bus—"

"I don't care about almost everybody," he said. "I'll see you after school."

"I have swim team practice—"

"Then I'll watch you practice. I've never done that, have I?"

"Daddy, nobody's father watches swim practice," I said desperately.

"Then maybe I'll start a new trend."

When I walked out onto the pool apron from the dressing room that afternoon, there he sat, halfway up the metal bleachers, his hat on his knees and his briefcase at his feet. He saw me and smiled and waved. The other team members and our coach looked at me, then at him and then back at me, but no one said anything. The whole school, that day, was tiptoeing around the girl whose famous (well, almost) mother had just died of cancer. I turned to the team and we took our marks and waited for the whistle. When it came, I dived deep, so grateful for the cooling, chemical blue water that I could have stayed there forever. It was not until practice was over and the swimmers were scattering that I looked up again. He was still there, smiling. He made a little circle with his thumb and forefinger. All of a sudden I was smashed by a wave of love for him; almost drowned in it. My person. He was there for me. With him I would be safe.

Emma and Flora made one of our family favorite dinners that night, a tuna casserole that my mother once said owed a large debt to the Campbell Soup Company. I did not care. It slipped down, warm and cheesy with just a hint of sherry, heating the cold core of me to languid comfort. The crumbled potato chips on top were browned and crisp. There were some sautéed green beans, too, and hot rolls and cold milk. I doubted I could eat anything; I ended up eating everything. Flora and Emma beamed. My father, who did not finish his meal, did too.

After dinner he said, "Sit with me for a while," and I followed him into the sitting room, where a large fire crackled, even in the warm spring dusk. He took his accustomed deep leather easy chair on one side of the fireplace, and motioned me to the faded brocade wing chair that sat opposite it. I hesitated. It had always been my mother's chair.

"She'd like to know you were sitting in her chair," he said. "And this way I can see you better. It strikes me that I haven't really looked at you for a while. You've turned into an amazing swimmer, haven't you? And all without your mother and me watching it happen, or encouraging you. Somehow I guess we never took it very seriously. I'm not going to let that happen again. I intend to really know my daughter from now on."

Something inside me tightened. Would he be able to see the diver's suit and helmet if he observed me closely? What on earth would I say about it? Surely no father in his right mind would want a daughter who walked around in a diver's suit and helmet day after day. Perhaps I could begin to leave it behind me some of the time. But the fear that hit me after the thought pinned me motionless in my mother's chair, and I knew that I could not walk unprotected in the world. Not yet. I would keep the diving paraphernalia, and if he should discern it, we would talk about it then.

I looked across at him, in his chair under the circle of light cast by the old bronze floor lamp that had always stood there. Firelight flickered on his face.

When had he grown so old? I thought in alarm. *I never noticed. Had it all happened since my mother?* But the lines in his face, and the slight sag to his jowls, and the little mound that was now his belly could not have happened overnight. The bleak, sunken eyes, yes, and the gray pallor, but not the rest. His slim athlete's body was still slim, but it had softened, and his erect spine seemed to have bent a little. I knew that he seldom worked out in the basement gym now that I was so far gone in swimming, but I had noticed little else about him. We both needed to really look at one another. I did not want to lose the sense of my father. I had already lost my mother; my sense of her would always be what it had been before her death. I would not see it grow, or change. I did not know if that thought grieved or comforted me. I could not seem to feel much at all about my mother and wondered bleakly what that said about me as a person and a daughter.

"Perhaps we should talk about your mother," my father said slowly. "Tatty says we should, as soon as possible, that we can't start to work through our loss until we do. Would you want to do that?"

"No sir," I said, dropping my eyes. "All I know about her right now is that I miss her awfully. I don't know what else there is to say about her."

"Me either," he said, smiling faintly. "I guess when the time is right we'll know. I did think the service and reception went well, didn't you?"

"Yes sir," I said, relieved that I did not have to begin to parse my mother. "It was beautiful. Everybody said so."

And it had been. Even I could see that. Through the intervention of Tatty Glover, who said that she and my mother had talked about it many times, my mother had indeed been cremated, and her memorial service was held in the little Episcopal church on Connecticut Avenue where she and my father were married. Her bronze urn had been placed in the church's new columbarium, in a wall niche, and the service itself was small and dignified and yet with an upward tilt of joy. One of her painting subjects, a lyrical black soprano, sang "Deep River" and "Morning Has Broken." Some of my mother's closest friends stood and recalled their fondest memories of her; many of these were downright funny, and there was real laughter among the real tears. My father had decided not to speak, Jeebs couldn't because he could not stop crying, and I had threatened to run away from home if anybody tried to make me. I insisted on leading Wilma in on his jingling chain, and for once he behaved with (for him) doggy propriety. For some reason, Wilma made more people cry than any of the eulogies, and I was proud of him, even though I heard Tatty Glover, at the end of our pew, give a great, rattling sniff of disapproval.

Afterward, at home, Tatty and Emma and Flora had made magic happen, had managed to make the old high-ceilinged rooms a glowing, polished, and light-filled arena for my mother's last party. There were flowers everywhere, though we had asked, in the funeral notice, that gifts be made to the Elizabeth Constable Foundation, to benefit women in the arts who were working for social change. There had been a small deluge of checks, too. My father looked at them helplessly, laid neatly on his desk, and Tatty took them away, saying we would go to the bank and the lawyer's office and set up the fund after a few days had passed.

One of the bouquets, a glorious fountain of pink, blue, and lavender anemones, came from Jacqueline Bouvier Kennedy, though, of course, not from the White House. The accompanying note said. "We can scarcely afford to lose the glowing gifts and souls of women like Mrs. Constable." Tatty was literally high on the note, and placed it, with the flowers, on the round table in the foyer so that no one could miss it.

"And," she burbled to my father after the reception was over, "you *did* speak to Mrs. Graham and Mr. Bradlee, didn't you? So thoughtful of them to come."

We stood at the door, my father and I and Tatty, speaking to everyone who came and departed. I thought there must have been hundreds, most of whom I did not know. It occurred to me only then that my mother had a rich, separate life from mine, lived with people who were fond of her and of whom she was fond, without my knowing anything at all about it. It gave me a strange feeling to nod and mumble to all these people, who seemed to know me but who might, as far as I was concerned, have arrived this day on a spacecraft from Uranus. It felt as if my mother had been leading a secret life, one hidden from me, as if I were not deemed fit to become a part of it. I looked anxiously up at my father, who stood stiff and formal beside me, shaking hands and kissing cheeks and murmuring thanks to the population of this other world. If he did not know who they were, he gave no sign. I felt like a changeling in the drawing room I had grown up in.

Once, looking out onto the front walkway, I saw Canon and Mrs. Davenport waiting in the queue to come into the house. My heart fell into my stomach. I started like a pony bitten by a deerfly, and made as if to flee, but my father clapped his hand on my arm and I stood still, heart thundering.

"Peaches sends her love and condolences," Mrs. Davenport said to me when she reached me, leaning over to kiss me on the cheek. She smelled powerfully and dustily of violet bath powder. "She's at Madeira and simply couldn't get away—finals, you know. She was very sorry. She admired your mother very much."

I nodded, looking at my shoes.

"Please thank her for us," my father said, and the Davenports moved on.

We did not sit very long before the fire that first night, but while we did I was oddly comforted—or at least anesthetized—by the warmth and light and presence of family, even diminished family. In truth I could feel little, and I finally looked at my father and said, "I can't feel anything, Daddy. It scares me. I should be like Jeebs, I should cry or something. I can't cry. Do you think there's something wrong with me?" I had never spoken to my father of anything that went on deep inside me, of my secret joys and sorrows and fears. In the world of my childhood, kids simply did not. It did not seem remarkable to me now that I did. Much had changed.

"No," he said, smiling slowly at me. Some of the young father I had always followed into adventure was back, just for a moment.

"Dylan Thomas wrote something once I've always remembered," he said. "He said that 'after the first death, there is no other.' You've had your first death, Lilly, a long time ago, at Edgewater. It doesn't mean that you don't mourn your mother, and always will. It just means that the awful surprise of the first one isn't there. Once we've been through the first one, I think we build walls so that the next one, and the next, won't simply kill us. You've done that. You started doing it the night we . . . lost Jon. Your mother and I saw that. It's all right. We do what we have to do not to simply . . . sink."

A brief explosion of grief and shock, a sense of drifting fog and feet pounding up a gangplank, swamped new acid tears. I simply pushed it away.

"Will it ever be different?"

"Of course. When you're ready for it to be."

He smiled at me again, a bit more broadly.

"You're a brave girl, Lilly," he said. "Your mother always said that."

"She did?"

"She did."

We did not speak much after that, and suddenly I was so drugged with food and firelight and this strange new communion with my

201

father that I fell asleep in my chair, and woke only when he shook my shoulder gently.

"Time for bed," he said.

I stumbled up the stairs and into my room without thinking of where I would sleep—in my own room, of course. Where else? Wilma followed me up and settled himself into the crook of my leg. In my parents' room I heard my father moving about softly, and saw that the light from the bedside lamp in their room went out. I did not wonder for a long time after that what that first night without her in the bed they had always shared must have cost him. Where else but there would he sleep? This was right too.

In the morning there was light and warmth and Flora and Emma in the kitchen, and the smells of french toast and sausage, and then my father and I walked to the car and he drove me to school.

"See you after school," he said.

"See you," I said.

I did not realize it then, but that first night and the day after it laid down a pattern we would follow for many years. Perhaps we always would have; many people do cling to what they have as long as they can, and don't seek anything more. Literature is full of them. I see now that I might well have done just that. It was just a safe and comforting life, for both of us. The time came when we clung to each other and our routines out of more than love and comfort, but that was in the future.

My father took me to school and picked me up afterward, or after swim practice. He came to all my meets. We had dinner at home, or sometimes he would take me out; to the little Chinese restaurant in Chevy Case Circle that we had always gone to on Sunday nights, or to the Marriott Hot Shoppe at the Key Bridge, or to the Chevy Chase Club. But mostly we ate at home, the dinners that Emma and Flora had cooked us, and sat in the sitting room afterward and talked over our days, or I did homework and he read and listened to music on the phonograph, and Wilma twitched and snored and groaned happily and grew old before the fires.

Outside the house on Kalorama Circle, the world caught fire and flamed; crowds shouted and ran and threw bricks and bottles and sometimes a bomb; good men who stood for sanity were shot and died; an unimaginable war half a world away wallowed on in the virulent heat and mire and wet of bloodied jungles; flags were burned and furious people marched and were beset by dogs and police and fire hoses; scandal and treachery leaked from our own federal heart; hemlines soared and music shouted and jangled and railed; smoke from cigarettes changed and sweetened; academicians exhorted the young to tune in, turn on, and drop out and the young did just that; city streets that once had been busy and lamp-lit and alive were now dark and dead places where faceless danger slid through shadows, waiting; the pill that was supposed to liberate young women enslaved a generation with rote sex that many of them did not even want yet; hippies and head shops and smoke-fumed rock festivals and deadly summers of love bloomed on televisions that fed it all to us; Wisconsin Avenue became a street few mothers would let their daughters travel alone. For the young, it was all largely intoxicating and enabling; for the no-longer-young it was often downright terrifying.

My father became one of the latter. Given different circumstances, I might have been one of the former. As it was, cloistered away behind paneled walls and automobile doors and Cathedral's seemly stone and mortar, and most of all swathed in cool disinfected green water and the suit and helmet, I was only remotely curious about the world outside. It had about the same immediacy as an engrossing history book, or a gripping serialized novel. But still, there was a pull; only later I realized that it was a small, buried urge simply to be young that was as immutable as the thrust of a green shoot toward the sun.

At the time, I buried it. Because not long into it I realized that my father had become not just solicitous for me, but desperately afraid. Afraid that something would happen to me, some harm come to me when he was not with me, afraid of losing me, too. It was painful to see and somehow shaming, and so I stayed close to him, dutifully and then willingly and then gladly. For I had become afraid, too. Afraid of the world outside my small arena, afraid that it would take me away from him, afraid that it would take him away from me. Those few years of my growing up, I see now, were for both of us a seemingly endless pas de deux of love, and fear. We were artists at it.

I was pretty and knew it; he never tired of telling me so, and on the occasions when my Aunt Tatty dragged me shopping for clothes, I could see it in the mirrors of many chic small shops. I was still slim and small, like my father, but I had my mother's blooming fullness, too, as well as her ocean gray eyes and her hair. I wore it long because my father loved it so; Aunt Tatty would urge me periodically to have it cut into a smart Carnaby Street bob, but when I mentioned it to my father he was so genuinely stricken that I abandoned the idea. Secretly I loved the mass and swirl of my bronze and gold hair. Sometimes I took my mother's hair out of the bag I kept it in and held it up against my own; they were the same.

But I had no real sense of how others viewed me, and was surprised when one young man or another asked me out to the movies or to a St. Albans dance, or even asked me to dance in the evenings at the club. My father would say, "Do we know his people? I don't think we do. Why don't you bring him here for dinner, or let me take you both somewhere fancy," and I would refuse the invitation. So far I had no real wish to go out. The thought vaguely threatened. Would we get lost and end up in the dark part of town where the shadows were alive? Would my escort get drunk and desert me, or worse? Would someone see the helmet?

I have no idea what sort of reputation I had among the young of Washington at that time. They were almost a different species from me, erratic and brightly plumaged and apt to fly off and do anything at all. I doubt that they gave the reclusive girl on Kalorama Circle a thought, except as a silent, slightly awesome swimmer.

Aunt Tatty kept her oar in. Somehow she never completely despaired of us, the eccentric Constable *père et fille*. She was forever at the ready with suggestions for clothes, social events, projects, vacations. Her own daughter, Charlotte, had, by the time I was in my junior year at the Cathedral School, vanished into Sweet Briar in a swirl of clothes and invitations and friends—the right kind of friends, her mother exulted.

Tatty Glover's world had shrunk considerably. Her husband, Uncle Charles Glover, had died on the back nine at the Chevy Chase golf course several years previously, and though he had a grand funeral at the Cathedral and burial at Arlington, having been a three-star general attached to NATO in Europe for many years before retiring to Washington, I had little sense of loss. I had known him only as a gruff, beige-all-over man who occasionally shared dinners with us at the club and vanished immediately afterward to play poker dice in the men's bar with other retired generals. I assumed he was genuinely mourned by his wife and only child, but had little sense of their loss, either. All I knew was that Aunt Tatty had, as a miffed Flora once put it, done moved in.

She had dinners with us perhaps twice a week, and she and my father would sit in the sitting room afterward and talk, he in his chair, Tatty in the one that had been my mother's and was now mine. I did not know what they talked about, as I could not bear giving up my chair and felt vaguely annoyed that she roosted so comfortably in my mother's. So I went to my room, ostensibly to study, but usually to watch television and read. I know that I read a great deal of folklore and many scurrilous best-sellers, but I don't remember much of the television, except for having a vague crush on Peter Gunn. When Aunt Tatty left I would go back down and make hot chocolate for my father and me, and we would resume our comfortable communion. The rest of Washington society might, as Aunt Tatty said, find our way of living strange, to put it mildly, but I found it as comforting as sliding into warm water. I didn't even know who Washington society was.

I thought perhaps Tatty and my father talked mainly of comfortable, trivial things because, whenever I left my room, I heard their talk rise and fall gently, as on a mild surf. But there was one night when it broke its seemly boundaries and they were almost shouting. I crept out of bed, shushing Wilma, who was jingling and shuffling in anticipation of a late night snack, and positioned myself on the stairs to spy, as once I had, obsessively, on my mother.

"She's almost seventeen," Aunt Tatty hissed. "Has she ever had a single date? Does she have any friends? So far as I can tell, what she does for fun is that eternal swimming and sitting here by the fire with you in her mother's chair, chatting. George, can't you see that you're making her into a pale little version of Elizabeth—or is that the idea?"

I could not hear my father's reply, but I heard the anger in it. I didn't blame him. The idea was—unthinkable, terrifying. But for a long time afterward I wondered secretly if, when he smiled at me across the hearth rug, he saw her.

". . . do some things for her," Aunt Tatty went on. "Arrange some invitations to cotillions. The dancing class was a success, after all, wasn't it? She's a good dancer, and you don't have to talk a lot while you're dancing if you don't want to."

I would never tell anyone what agony those strictured and structured evenings at Miss Crenshaw's dancing class were, but I did emerge
from them a proficient dancer, a skill I determined I would use as little
as possible. Aunt Tatty had won that round.

"Or let me have some little dinners for her and invite some of the
young men she should know. Everybody's mother does it. It can't take
the place of coming out, of course, but I can't imagine either of you
are going to let that happen. I do know that Elizabeth very much
wanted her to come out—"

"Come out of what?" my father asked, genuinely puzzled. I
cheered silently from the stairs.

"Make her debut. George, honestly. How can you have lived in
Washington all this time and not know that the girls in our families
are presented to society? Oh, for God's sake, why do I keep trying?
All right, then, let's talk about college. Have you even thought about
that? I thought she might want to look at Sweet Briar, or Hollins, or
Randolph-Macon; they're close enough so she could get home every
weekend, if she wants to. Surely you and Elizabeth talked about that.
I mean, you were always so sure about Jeebs . . . mathematics, of
course. And speaking of Jeebs, does he ever come home?"

"Jeebs 'alone has looked on Beauty bare.'" My father smiled.
Aunt Tatty looked confused.

"Jeebs is so far gone into numbers that when he does come I
expect equations to come out of his ears. I don't mind that, Tatty.
Certainly I miss my son, but I understand what passion for a life's
work can be. It's hard for him here without Elizabeth. And he has a
girlfriend. He promises to bring her home to meet us soon."

"Oh, wonderful," Aunt Tatty cried. "At least maybe there'll be one
wedding to plan. I don't suppose you've considered that Lilly will marry
eventually. That is, if you ever let her out to meet anyone suitable."

"We haven't talked about it," my father murmured. My ears and cheeks flamed. Marry? Who could I marry who wouldn't rip me out of the tapestry my father and I had created? As a matter of fact, who would want to marry me at all?

"So school . . ."

"She'll go to George Washington, of course. We have a very fine English department, if I do say so. Lilly is wonderful at English and literature."

"So this is okay with her? It's really what she wants? Elizabeth mentioned Wellesley once. And Bennington . . . though, of course, I mean, *Bennington* . . ."

"That's months away, Tatty! And that's enough of this talk for now. My God, you'd have been a great success in the KGB."

Aunt Tatty was offended, as she should have been, and took her leave in a huff. But she was back by summer, apparently having forgotten or decided to forgive. That year we took our month's vacation at the Cloister at Sea Island, Georgia, and Tatty came with us.

"Lovely," she said, approving of the beautiful old hotel and its lush, perfect grounds and seemly beach club overlooking its seemly beach. It was thronged with attractive families and children, though I saw few people my age. So I had long beach walks with my father, and swam in the adult pool or the ocean while he read his book in an umbrella chair and Aunt Tatty napped, and we met for decorous cocktails before dinner in the dim little ballroom, and I danced with him to the tunes of the current Lester Lanin trio, and we had a lovely dinner at our usual table with our usual waitress, and then played bingo, and finally had graham crackers and milk in the lobby and were off to bed in crisp, lavender-smelling sheets, me with Aunt Tatty, he in the room next to us.

It was a vacation almost identical to the ones we'd taken over the years at the Greenbrier, and the Grand Hotel at Point Clear, and once even the distant and exotic Broadmoor. I didn't really mind where we went as long as I could swim.

The spring I turned eighteen, the one before I was to enter George Washington in the fall, Wilma died. I went to sleep that night with a blanket thrown over the two of us against the spring chill, and he snuggled into my side as he always did, groaning his pleasure, and did not wake up again. I think I knew even before I came fully up out of sleep; my father and Flora and Emma heard my cries even before I was aware I was making them and were in my room when I came fully awake. My arms were around Wilma, and he was cool. He had the same goofy, glad-to-see-you smile on his face, but he was cool.

All the grief I had held in for my mother, carefully folded away somewhere inside me, came tumbling and spewing out. I cried desperately, crazily, inconsolably, for days. I could not eat, and there was no question of school, as I broke into tears as easily as I breathed. My father, his own face streaked with tears, held me and comforted me as best he could.

"He had a grand, long doggy life, baby," he said. "I can't imagine a happier life for a dog. And he just . . . went to sleep. It's just the way he'd have chosen, all snuggled up with you. We can get another dog—"

"*No!*"

And we did not. Never, as long as my father lived, did we have another dog. I could not have loved it, and I could not have borne losing it, either. He knew that without my saying so.

Aunt Tatty came over and tried to take charge of me.

"Darling, you've simply got to stop crying," she said, hugging me. "We have to go on; it's what people have to do. I don't think you cried like this for your mother."

I had not, of course. Wilma was the one who turned that key. My endless tears were for her as well as for Wilma. It was the last great gift he gave me, the ability to mourn my mother.

We buried him under a great, drooping hydrangea bush in the back garden. It already had a Wilma-shaped depression in the dust under it; it was where he dug himself in and slept on the hottest days. When my father finished digging his grave and we laid him in it, wrapped in a favorite old comforter from my childhood, yellow strewn with pink daisies, my tears stopped. They simply stopped. And from that moment, something was different in me. Something that wondered, if it did not speak the wonder aloud, what the green lawns of Wellesley would be like. What the weathered old walls of Bennington, so far away in Vermont, held within them.

Who I would be if I was . . . not me.

I did not speak of this new thing to my father. But I knew that it would emerge of its own sooner or later. How could it not? More than my childhood had gone with Wilma.

Two weeks later, when I was still mourning him, my father said he would take me to dinner someplace special, someplace we had never been. Tatty would go, too. I was to choose. I remembered a small, darkly lit Italian restaurant on Wisconsin Avenue that I had passed several times; it always smelled wonderful, and I always heard sounds of laughter from inside.

"I want to go to Luigi's," I said.

"Darling, Wisconsin Avenue?" Aunt Tatty said.

"Luigi's it is," my father said gallantly. "I'll make reservations for Friday night."

On Friday afternoon he called to say that he had a late faculty meeting he could not miss and was sending a taxi to pick up Tatty and me and would join us at the restaurant. So, in the violet spring twilight of Georgetown, Tatty and I alit from the cab and made our way into Luigi's. Rock music was booming into the street from inside, and louder laughter followed it. Tatty looked at me.

"Are you sure, Lilly? Grenville's is just up the street."

"Positive," I said.

We walked in, Tatty behind me. When I stopped dead, she bumped into me.

The loudest laughter was coming from a knot of young men at the bar. One of them, with a laugh like a triumphal cry of Renaissance brass in the last notes of an opera, turned and looked at me. He was still laughing; joy and exuberance and pure maleness ran off him like honey, like smoke. He was taller than the rest, and lean and tanned, and his hair was long, a silky red blaze to his shoulders, and he had a neat goatee and mustache of the same wildfire red. His teeth flashed white in all that bronze.

"My God, Bitsy! Bitsy Randolph! Come here to me! Where have you been all this time, you gorgeous creature?"

And he started toward me, arms outstretched, laughing.

I walked toward him, as unconscious of moving as a robot. I felt my own mouth curve up into a smile.

When he was only feet away from me, he stopped and said, "Oh, God. Sorry. I got the wrong girl."

His arms were still stretched toward me.

"No, you didn't," I said, and walked into them.

Cam

CHAPTER

12

W hat do you remember the most about your wedding?" Kitty
Howard said to me a couple of years ago.

We were lying on our stomachs on the old dock that rambled
drunkenly from Kitty's bed-and-breakfast inn, on a spit of swampy
land that bordered a sort of hiccup in Chesapeake Bay, near Ware
Neck. Why anyone wanted to sleep and eat cinnamon buns on this
beautiful but desolate and mosquito-haunted piece of Virginia earth
remained a mystery to me all the long days of our friendship, but
somehow Kitty's charming little pre-revolutionary house, leaning
precariously toward the bay, seemed perpetually full of wayfarers
eager to get away from Washington or Richmond or even Williamsburg. Most were young families in SUVs, eager to give their bored
children a firsthand look at their country's birth state as it was before
malls and ye-olde-colonials moved in, or groups of gray-haired ladies
wearing no-nonsense walking shoes or Wellingtons and studying bird
books at breakfast. I don't think Kitty made a lot of money off them,
but it was enough to keep the Ware Neck Inn open and enough to
allow Kitty to pursue her heart's passion, which was painting. If she
wasn't very good, she wasn't bad, either. I had several of her landscapes in our house, across the peninsula on the James River near
Claremont.

I turned my head and looked at her. Her face was resting on her arms and the aqueous stipple of light from the slow green water below us made her look fragile, mythic, drowned: a lady o' the lake. Nothing could have been farther from the truth; Kitty Howard was full bosomed, loud, sometimes bawdy, always funny, and loving in the extreme. She was as loyal and nurturing a friend as I ever had, and if her loving-kindness often extended to some of the husbands of our strange, archaic plantation society, I couldn't have cared less. Many of the women of our part of the Tidewater cared, though, and consequently Kitty had few women friends except me. I spent a great deal of time with her, for I was alone much of the time when Cam was out of town on a project and the girls were too young to leave. Kitty was wonderful company. I couldn't say as much for most of the other women in Cam's crowd, which, of course, was now mine. I thought they were vain, shallow, and self-righteous. They thought I was a rather elitist hermit. All of us, I think, were right, at least in part. It was a situation that might have made me restless and unhappy, for I had lived much of my life here and might have found that life isolating and unfulfilling. But I didn't. I never had. I had Kitty and the girls and my sculpting. And I had Cam. Always I had Cam. I could not imagine wanting anything more.

"Let's see, what do I remember most?" I said to Kitty on this September day, when the sun was warm on our faces and forearms but promissory cool breathed in with the tide. It was utterly still and peaceful; tiny golden motes danced above the water in the slanting sunlight, and water bugs skated on its green surface, and the bay itself slapped and wallowed peacefully in the reeds along its shore.

"Well, *that*, of course." Kitty grinned. "But I mean the ceremony itself."

"I remember that some errant insect got up under Cam's kilt and he nearly bolted like a spooked mule, and I had an asthma attack literally at the altar. It was the wedding of the century in Carter's Cove." Kitty turned over onto her back and laughed joyously. I thought her rich, deep laugh might have been heard far inland.

"I'd give anything to see Cameron McCall in a kilt. Those humongously long hairy legs under that little skirt, and those wild, Scot eyes. He must have looked like the original highland barbarian. *Braveheart*.

"Well, you could have had the big Tidewater wedding and reception at McCall's Point," Kitty continued. "Six hundred well-bred guests and little black boys in white aprons serving drinks in the gah-dun, don'cha know, and the family silver shining like new money on a bare behind. Mama McCall would have loved it. She might even have come to like you. But no, you had to run off to some cabin on the rocks in Maine."

"Edgewater isn't some cabin on the rocks, as you well know, seeing as how you come up every summer. And Mama McCall wouldn't have liked me if I had been deb of the year and had a dowry of five hundred elephants and trunks of gold," I said. "Did you know that when Cam told her we were married, she said 'You two?' She was holding out for Beatrice Custis right until Cam and I said 'I do.'"

"So was Bebe Custis, and all the assorted Custises who've been haunting this river for all these hundreds of years. Just think what vigorous new blood would have meant to that tribe—not only a fresh shot of McCall money, but blood, and blue blood at that. Not much money or blood left in the Custis coffers these days. Been marrying cousins too long. They look like a school of flounders, all those flat noses and lips and eyes out on stems. I bet they just couldn't stand the idea of the family's savior hooking up with a woman who was not even from the Tidewater, but D.C., for God's sake. They think nobody lives in D.C. but lobbyists and little guys with plastic penholders and slide rules in their pockets. Oh—and of course maids and gardeners and things."

"Oh, come on, Kitty. Most of them go to parties and dances at the embassies and clubs all the time, and to the White House, too, come to that. And lots of Georgetown dinner parties. Not all of them can still think D.C. is—déclassé."

"Oh, it's okay to party with 'em, but marry one of them? For that you've got to have a Tidewater plantation girl. Only trouble is, there aren't any left who aren't as inbred and fish-faced as the Custises. I can't imagine what everybody said when Cam first brought you home to meet the family and the few hundred assembled neighbors. You with that hair floating all over the place, and those oceany eyes, and those boobs that weighed more than most of their firstborns."

I raised myself on one arm and looked down at my chest. Under my Washington Senators T-shirt, faded no-color now with age and washings, my breasts looked flattened from the boards of the dock and wet with sweat from the sun and the occasional surly little splash from the bay.

"'Alas, poor Yorick,'" I said. "'I knew him, Horatio.'"

"You do okay for an old broad of fifty-six, married thirty-eight years and with two grown kids," Kitty said, complacently regarding her own spectacular, beetling breasts. "But of course compared to mine, yours aren't even in the ballpark. These are the jugs that launched a thousand ships, or a thousand Chevy backseats, anyway. They're semi-retired, but they still do an exhibition game every now and then, anyway."

"You wish," I said fondly. Kitty was still a formidable-looking woman, but she was six years older than I—Cam's age—and she wore the extra years in folds around her waist and stomach and her massive brown upper arms and thighs. Almost every inch of her in plain view was freckled. Her red hair was still a bonfire on her head, also like Cam's, but she did not often bother to have it cut or styled, and it had a frothing, sometimes belligerent life of its own. The oversized tortoiseshell spectacles she wore magnified her hazel eyes into something exotic, if slightly buggish. I often wondered why it all added up to such a forcefully attractive whole, but the truth was that Kitty Howard still turned heads and elicited spontaneous smiles wherever she went.

"She's everybody's nanny and mother and favorite aunt and first lay all rolled into one," Cam said once. He had known her since they were both children at the same country kindergarten, a rather tony one I gathered, since Cam's mother would have sent him to no other sort, and Kitty's family was as rich in land, if not dollars, as Cam's. There was little about each other's provenance they did not know.

"Did you ever date her?" I asked him once.

"God, no. I'd have bored her to death. She knew more about sex in the first grade than I did in the eighth. By the time I was running around with cheerleaders she had worked her way through the entire United States Naval Academy. I think they once considered putting up a bronze statue of her boobs on the parade field."

"But she never married," I said thoughtfully.

"I think she did, once," Cam said. "When I went off to architecture school she just . . . vanished for a couple of years. Her parents said she'd gone west to school, and she may have; Berkeley would have suited her perfectly. But somebody or other said they ran into her at the Top of the Mark in San Francisco around then, and she was with a dark little man with a mustache she introduced as her husband—a Greek or something. He didn't talk much. But she came back here without him a couple of years later, and refused to live with her parents, probably to their secret relief, and bought the old Eaton house and turned it into a B-and-B, and there she's been ever since. I don't know where she got the money to buy it. Not from her folks, I'm sure of that. They never did approve of her, and while she was gone they sold the old plantation to that resort development those beer people are putting up and moved to Palm Beach. I think they still live there, and I know there's still a bunch of money in the family. My dad talks to hers sometimes. But I doubt she'll ever see a penny of it."

"Was it all those men that did it? There doesn't seem to be a man in the Tidewater she doesn't know—biblically, I mean."

"No. It was probably Berkeley. They could handle the screwing around; every family around here has one or more Kittys in it. But by God, nobody has a liberal."

I snorted. I knew this only too well.

"So what happened to the mustachioed Greek?"

He shrugged. "Nobody knows. I think he just . . . vaporized one night in the sack with her. She's something else between the sheets, I hear."

"You hear?"

"Yep. By the time I might have been tempted to see what it was all about, I'd met you and the screwing situation was taken care of."

"Cam!"

"Well, it was. After we finally did it, I knew you'd always be my one and only screw."

"I swear to God, you sound like that's all we ever did."

"Well, for a while it was. Especially after we got married and didn't have to do it in the backseat of that old Porsche, or, even worse, on that grungy mat in your basement that was under the trapeze. I knew your dad was listening at the heat register. I once thought of trying it out on that trapeze itself, but it wasn't a good time to bust my ass. What with us just getting started up. But sanctified joy is much better than sneaky screwing."

"Sanctified joy?"

"It was what the first missionaries to Hawaii called married sex. If God is for you, I guess you can always get it up."

"And you know this how?"

"Girl I used to know told me about it. I think maybe she was pushing for the sanctification before the joy."

"Whatever became of that one?"

"Don't remember. Just remember about sanctified joy."

It was no secret even to me by now that Cam McCall had had more girlfriends than a shah. He told me himself right at our start, I suppose before I could hear it somewhere else. His friends had teased him about it when they were with us, and Kitty Howard had filled me in on all the details when we first met.

"Never more than one at a time," she'd said, "but he started early. And while he was with a girl, he wouldn't let her out of his sight. Just glued to her. It was almost scary. But none of them lasted. I asked him why once and he said that none of them ever really fit him. I didn't know what he was talking about until he met you. He told a bunch of us at the country club that he'd found the only girl who'd ever fit exactly into his arms and up against him. Under him was implied."

"The hell you say. We didn't . . . do that until the night before we got married. And when we did do it we decided to get married right away, as soon as possible, the next day, and a honeymoon on the Friendship sloop my father had, way out into the Gulf of Maine and up as far as Campobello. It was a wonder we didn't drown on that honeymoon. We let the sloop just drift for hours at a time."

"It's a wonder you ever got married at all," Kitty said. "With the combined forces of the Tidewater and Kalorama Circle against you, I wouldn't have given a plugged nickel for your chances when I heard you-all were married. I was in Italy then, for a year in Florence, or I would have come straight home and stood beside you on the ramparts."

I looked at her. Not get married? Of course we would marry. We both knew that while I stood in the circle of Cam's arms at Luigi's the night we met and when he leaned over and kissed me before he even knew my name.

"I'm Cameron McCall," he'd said into my hair. "I live down on the James River and I'm an architect. Do you think you might marry me?"

"I'm Lilly Constable," I said against his shirt, feeling the heat and strength of his arms and his solid, tall body against mine. Safety. Utter safety.

"I live on Kalorama Circle and I'm starting at GW in the fall, and I think I might. Marry you, I mean."

Kitty had been right about the outcry, though. The first came from Aunt Tatty, who stood in the door of Luigi's and watched in disbelief when I ran into the arms of a big red stranger and kissed him. I don't think she moved until I disentangled myself from Cam and turned and led him over to where she stood, iron faced, with two hectic red spots on her cheeks.

"I didn't realize you were meeting a friend, Lilly," she said icily.

"I'm not," I said stupidly. "Or not until just now. Aunt Tatty, this is Cameron McCall. He's an architect; he just finished his graduate studies at GW. He lives out on the James River. Cam, this is my Aunt Tatty Glover. Well, not really my aunt, but—you know."

"I'm very pleased to meet you, Mrs. Glover," Cam said, putting out an enormous red-furred hand.

"Lilly, they're holding our table, and your father will be here in a moment. Come along now," she said, looking only at me and ignoring Cam's outstretched hand.

She took me by the shoulder and started to march me away. I

gave Cam a despairing look and he laughed. It was the same joyous, piratical laugh I had heard before. Then Aunt Tatty turned.

"Are your people by any chance the McCalls who live at McCall's Point? Out near Williamsburg?"

"Yes ma'am. That would be us."

"I believe I've met your mother. At the Sulgrave Club, I think," Aunt Tatty said in a different tone. It was a silky, lilting tone. I stared at her and then at Cam.

"I wouldn't be surprised," Cam said. "It's one of her hangouts."

"Well, perhaps you'd join us for dinner," Tatty said. "It's just Lilly and me and her father, who's a bit late now. He's a professor at George Washington. English. You may have heard of him."

"Professor Constable," Cam said. "Of course, who hasn't? He's a legend at GW. I tried twice to get into one of his undergraduate classes, but they were full both times. I've always regretted that."

"Well," Aunt Tatty said, and smiled. "Let's sit down. While we're waiting for him you can tell me how you and Lilly met. I can't remember her saying a word about you, but Lilly can be rather vague at times."

"We just met tonight," Cam said, grinning. "About ten minutes ago. I thought she was someone else. I'm very glad she wasn't."

"Oh," Aunt Tatty said in a strangled voice. "Well."

We were just sitting down, Cam pulling out first Aunt Tatty's chair and then mine, when my father appeared in the door. He scanned the room for us, spied us, smiled widely, and then stopped in his tracks.

Oh God, I remembered thinking wearily. *I can just imagine what we're going to have to go through now.*

Guilt flooded me then. I had never thought such a thing in my life about my father. Ever since my mother's death, and longer, really, he had been my lifeline. My refuge, my future. Could a person really change as drastically and swiftly as I felt I had when I met Cam? Was it even possible, or was this whole thing a magical delusion born of a laugh, a pair of arms? It sounded absurd, impossible, and sometimes it feels so to me even today. But I knew in some down-deep way that it had indeed happened to me, and the world that had so threatened and confused me for so long was simply gone, and a world that contained Cam and laughter and love and physical longing so acute that it weakened my wrists and knees had been born. The rubber suit tore and peeled away. The helmet went spinning into forever. Before was then. Cam was now.

I knew that my father saw it too, and pain and guilt so flooded me that I simply wanted to take my father and run away from this place and Cam, back to where we had been before. But only for a moment. I took the only way possible for me now.

"Daddy," I said, when he had come slowly over to the table trying so hard to look merely pleasantly interested that his face muscles bunched with the effort. "This is Cameron McCall. He just graduated from architecture grad school and he lives on the James River, and—I really hope you'll like him."

It was a foolish statement and it implied untold disastrous consequences should my father fail to do so, and I fell idiotically silent.

"Why on earth should I not, darling?" my father said, smiling the stretched smile at Cam and putting out his hand.

"George Constable, Mr. McCall. It's a pleasure. I meet so few of Lilly's friends."

"It's because I never really had any until now," I heard myself blurt to Cam, and on my left he smiled an I-don't-believe-that-for-a-minute smile at me and said, "The pleasure is mine, Dr. Constable. I tried and tried to get into your undergraduate English courses, but they were always full and grad school didn't leave me any electives at all. But I surely knew who you were."

"Well," my father said. "That would have been nice. I'd like to have known you earlier."

"Instead of having you shot at me like a cannonball in an Italian restaurant," he did not say. But I thought we all heard the words anyway. Aunt Tatty dropped her eyes, and I saw the flush that meant she was upset rise from her neck and stain her face. Cam's smile stayed in place, but he looked at my father quizzically out of his blue eyes shuttered over with thick red brows. It was, I thought, a look of pure, if polite, assessment. *Are we going to be friends, we who both want this girl? Am I going to have to fight you for her?* My father smiled at him. A difficult smile, I thought, a brave one, a smile of acknowledgment. The old warrior facing the young challenger.

I'm going to hurt him, I thought, and felt anguish. *I'm going to hurt my father terribly. I don't know how not to.*

And in the whole of the rest of his life I sometimes felt profound sorrow for him, and guilt, but never ambivalence. Cam and I were a fact from the moment we met. I knew I could never make my father see that. Tears burned in my eyes and I looked at Cam. He looked back, and then nodded slowly. From that moment on, I think, we conspired together in the small murder of my father.

I don't remember what we had for dinner, or what we talked about. It was like dining in the midst of a maelstrom. The unsaid dived and pecked at us ceaselessly, and by the time we finished dinner and my father had signaled for the check I was almost physically sick. My head nearly burst with the need for fresh, cool air and space. When Cam said, "If it's all right with you, Dr. Constable, I thought Lilly and I might get a bite of gelato at Piero's and then I'll bring her home. By ten, at the most," I smiled and nodded gratefully. Only then did I look at my father. His face was bleached and rigid; he was a man I did not know.

"Not tonight, I don't think," he said levelly. "Lilly has school to-morrow. She's at Cathedral—did she tell you? She's only eighteen."

"George," Aunt Tatty almost hissed, "will you come out to the lobby with me? I can never get a cab in this part of town—"

"We'll take you home, of course, Tatty—" my father began.

"*George.*"

He gave us a sort of despairing look and rose and followed her out into the lobby. I stood too. I knew that the evening was over. Cam did not stir.

From the doorway I heard Aunt Tatty's urgent whisper: "McCall! Don't you know who they are? The McCalls of McCall's Point! Oh, George, of course you do; don't be dense! Best families in Virginia . . . tons of very old money, and the plantation is an original king's grant."

I did not hear my father's reply. My ears were roaring with embar-rassment. I looked at Cam and whispered, "I'm sorry, my father's a little overprotective; we've lived alone since my mother died. Aunt Tatty's just plain nuts."

"Don't apologize. My family makes them look like Ward and June Cleaver."

He reached over and took my hand. My whole arm flamed with his touch.

"There isn't anything or anybody who's going to keep me from seeing you," he said. "You don't know me well enough to know that I always get what I want, but I get it in the nicest possible way. I'll try my best not to upset your father, but I am going to see you again no matter what it takes."

"I don't even know where you live," I said in a voice with little breath behind it.

"Pretty soon I'll be back at the point. I've been sharing a place with Chris, one of the med students you saw when you came in, but he's starting an internship in Atlanta and I don't have the money yet for my own place. But I will soon. As soon as I pass my boards I'm going to set up an architectural practice, maybe here or maybe in the Tidewater, and then I can live where I want."

"Won't your parents help you out?" I asked, thinking of Aunt Tatty's fervent whisper.

"God, no." He laughed. "They'd see me in the gutter before they'd lend me a penny. I was supposed to go into the family law firm. I'm the only male McCall in over a century who hasn't. But it doesn't matter. It's only an hour or so drive from there to your house. I'm going to lay siege to your father like a nineteenth-century swain right out of Edith Wharton."

"You read Edith Wharton?"

"I read everything."

My father and Aunt Tatty and I were mainly silent on the drive to her house. As she got out of the car, she said, "I hope we see more of your young man, Lilly. I thought him very nice."

"So did I," I said weakly. My father said nothing at all.

When we got home he went into the sitting room and lit the fire and smiled at me. I was hovering in the doorway, not quite certain what to do next.

"Why don't you fix us some hot chocolate," he said. "We all skipped dessert. And you've had a big day. I'd like to hear about it."

But I knew that I could not talk to him about Cameron McCall. What could I say? That I had half agreed to marry a man I knew next to nothing about? A man I'd picked up only hours before in an Italian restaurant in Georgetown? The impossibility of it hit me hard and suddenly; there was no one in the world now with whom I could talk about Cam. I could have, I knew, with my mother. But, failing that, there was simply no one. It was the loneliest feeling I had ever had. I wanted to go upstairs to bed and pull the covers over my head. I wanted Wilma.

227

"Daddy, I'm really tired, and I've still got about twenty pages of History to read. Will you excuse me? I promise we'll have cocoa with whipped cream tomorrow night."

"Of course, baby," he said. "One night without you isn't going to hurt me."

He laughed.

I turned and went up the stairs.

It would hurt him, I thought. I could hear the hurt in his laugh. I skinned into bed without washing my face and pulled my comforter up around my ears. I thought I would think of him downstairs alone in the sitting room with his fire and his *Washington Post* and his pain, but instead, I thought only of Cam.

CHAPTER

13

W e called it the Siege of Kalorama Circle," Kitty told me one September afternoon when the thermometer hovered at ninety-six and iron-blue, relentlessly sunny skies pressed down on us. It had not rained in weeks. Even the ferns and reeds along the bay and rivers were shriveled and brown. Dust lay in strata in the air like fog. We were sitting on the edge of our swimming pool, at McCall's Point, dangling our feet in the exhausted September water while my girls played listlessly in the shallow end. I knew the pool water was too tepid to be invigorating. I swam every morning, early, before the others were up, and even at five-thirty the water had seemed inert and somehow soiled. I did not swim long.

"I'll just bet you did," I said. We had been talking about Cam's and my courtship, which by now, I thought sourly, was surely the stuff of legend in the Tidewater.

"Oh, not around him," she said. "And we hardly knew you at all. But for sheer tenacity and tactical brilliance, he outshone Rommel. Every move he made, every time he went calling at your house, got back to us. Our crowd at the country club talked of nothing else. I don't think our parents did, either. It was the hot topic of that spring and summer."

"You people never have had enough to do," I said grumpily. "Why did you care if we dated?"

"We cared about everything Cam did," she said. "He was our icon, our legend. It was a pretty tame life then for kids down here in the Tidewater, you know. We hung out together because we really didn't know many people in D.C. or even around here, except us. Heaven forbid we should socialize with the townies. When I think about it, I can see that we were all really pretty much alike. Even I was, then. I didn't get wild till later.

"But Cam . . . Cam was something else. He did things we never quite dared to do, he said things that shocked even us, he had a real plan for his life from the very beginning. He always wanted to be an architect. Even as a kid he knew who the cutting-edge architects of the decade were, what and where they did their work. We grew up listening to him talk about Le Corbusier—Corbu, he called him—and his pilgrims' chapel at Ronchamp. Or about Mies van der Rohe, or Frank Lloyd Wright, or Bruce Goff out west, or Eero Saarinen. I can't remember him talking about many contemporary American architects except Paul Rudolph. He always said *he'd* be the one people talked about. And look at him. He is. With that new hotel in Costa Rica he's on the big map we all knew he would be.

"And besides, he was just plain larger than life, even as a kid. This tall, flaming redheaded pirate, with blue eyes that could bore a hole in you and a smile that could get your panties off—and did, probably more than we knew. We called him Eric the Red sometimes. I always called him Vlad the Impaler. I think he was the only one of us who knew what that meant. He liked it."

I splashed water on my sweaty face and neck. Somehow this fugue about my husband annoyed me. I knew all that; I did not think that there was anything about himself Cam hadn't told me. But I always did wish I'd known him as a boy. He was never anything but a man with me, even though sometimes a boyish one.

"And so whom did he impale, exactly?"

"Oh, God. Everybody. Every girl from Norfolk to D.C. and then some, I think. He was always attached to somebody: there was always some dippy girl with her hands all over him. Every one of them, we thought, would turn out to be the one because when he was with them, he was just so totally—*with* them. Sometimes you just had to look away. But in the end none of them lasted. One day they'd be there, crawling over him like kudzu, and the next day they'd just be gone. He never talked about them. He never said why. We never asked.

"And then you came along, and you *were* the one. We took bets on you for a long time. Nobody had ever heard of you. You lived at home with your daddy and never went out. You were some kind of hotshot underwater swimmer. To us, swimming was mostly something you did to show off your new Rose Marie Reid bathing suit. We were swimmers from birth, practically, but we couldn't even imagine anybody being serious enough about it to make a—career, I guess—out of it. It wasn't cool. *You* weren't cool. But there you were, a year, two years later. The stories of how he finally got you away from Daddy were mythic. You can't imagine how romantic we all thought it was."

I suppose it might seem so. Those first few weeks did rather sound like something from Edith Wharton or Henry James. The evening after we met, he rang the doorbell on Kalorama Circle, and when my father opened it, there he was, looking, as my father said later, like Rasputin with his red beard and mustache and long hair, holding a bouquet of flowers and smiling his wide, vulpine smile. He was dressed in a tweed sport coat and gray flannel pants, and he wore a neat striped tie. The faint odor of mothballs about him testified to the fact that he had not worn the coat and slacks for a very long time, but they were just right for calling on a young woman in a big house on Kalorama Circle.

"Well, Mr. McCall, is it," my father said formally. "And to what do we owe the honor of this visit?"

I was just behind my father, wanting desperately to kick him. He knew damned well to what we owed the honor of Cam's visit.

"The flowers are beautiful," I squeaked inanely.

"From my mother's garden." He grinned, looking at me over my father's shoulder. "Cut them on my way out."

"Goodness, I hope she won't mind," I said, wondering desolately where this stupid voice, these stupid words, were coming from.

"She won't miss them," Cam said. "She doesn't do the garden herself. She's got a guy who does it."

Still we stood there, we three, my father and I stiff with awkwardness, Cam respectfully at ease.

Then my father said, "Well, please come in, Mr. McCall. Lilly, take the flowers and find a vase for them. Flora will know."

Cam came in and handed me the flowers, smiling. Then he followed my father into the sitting room. I don't think they spoke; I could not hear their voices. I went into the kitchen, where Flora was stirring something in a pot and humming contentedly to herself.

"Well, ain't they pretty," she said, looking at the armful of flowers, which were beginning to droop now. "Where they come from?"

"A boy—a man I met last night brought them," I said. "He's in the sitting room with Daddy."

"Oh, Lord God," Flora said. "I hope your daddy don't run him off. It's past time you had a beau. Emma and me talks about it all the time."

"He's not a beau," I said, heat flooding my chest and face. "He's a friend. I just met him last night."

"Friends don't bring no flowers," Flora said serenely, taking the bouquet from me.

Numb, I went back to the sitting room and sank down on an ottoman before the fire. My father sat in his accustomed chair. Cam sat in mine. For what seemed a very long time, no one spoke.

Finally Cam said, in a voice as even as if he were telling someone the time, "Professor Constable, I would like your permission to call on your daughter. I know that she's only eighteen and you know nothing about me, but I can assure you that if I could visit once in a while, I would be extremely careful of her welfare, and respect any conditions you might want to set on my visits. I believe our families must have met at one time or another, at the Chevy Chase Club, or the Metropolitan, and I believe that my mother and Lilly's mother were both members of the Sulgrave Club. I'm just a few weeks away from taking my architectural boards, and when that's done I hope to establish a practice, either here in D.C. or closer to home, in the Tidewater. In either case, I have no plans to relocate away from the area, or be away on long assignments. My interest is in the architectural vernacular of the region. I want to build for these people and this place. Whatever your answer, I want you to know that I have the greatest respect for you and your daughter."

He stopped and looked pleasantly at my father, but not at me. I felt my face flame deeper; I could hardly get my breath. It was a remarkable speech. I could not imagine a young man of this time and place making it to anyone. My ears rang so that I could hardly hear my father's reply. It was a long time in coming.

Finally he said, "I appreciate your . . . delicacy, Mr. McCall, but I'm afraid there can be no, er, dating for Lilly yet. Her studies are the most important thing for her now; she will be starting at George Washington in the fall and needs to enter with an outstanding academic record. And then her swimming takes a great deal of time. I don't want her distracted from either just now."

Cam looked at Dad, his eyes narrowed.

"Sir, this is the latter half of the twentieth century, and Lilly is eighteen years old. Don't you think she should have some say in the matter?"

"Lilly is my daughter," my father said, ice crackling in his voice. "Don't you think I have her best interests at heart?"

"And what would those interests be, sir?" Cam asked pleasantly. But his eyes narrowed further. I saw, suddenly, two formidable adversaries, circling, circling.

"School, of course. And then a promising academic career, or perhaps an editorial or curatorial one. She has many talents. Washington has a number of fine outlets for them, and of course I am not without contacts."

"So she would live here all that time?"

"Of course. Where else? This is her home."

"Is that what she wants, sir?"

My father did not answer. There was a long silence. Then he said, "Well, Mr. McCall, it's almost our dinnertime. I'm afraid Flora did not cook for a guest. Will you excuse us? Perhaps some other time you might join us?"

"I'd like that," Cam said. He smiled and nodded to me, and then to my father, who didn't meet his eyes.

I heard him let himself out the door, very quietly; I looked at my father. He would not meet my eyes either. I whirled and ran upstairs to my room and shut the door. For a long time I simply lay in the dark and stared at my ceiling. I cannot remember to this day what I was thinking.

He didn't follow me, or call after me. In about half an hour Flora came up with a tray for me.

"You eat this supper, now," she said. "He get over it. Your young man just came at him sort of sudden."

I knew she had been listening from the kitchen. I did not care—about that or about anything. She left softly but I did not eat my supper.

A long time later Aunt Tatty came briskly into my room without knocking. She switched on the overhead lights and I sat up and blinked at her.

"Your father is very worried about you," she said. "What on earth is going on? He won't even talk about it."

Sudden tears blinded me. Stammering and scrubbing at my wet cheeks, I told her. Before I could even finish she had steamed out of the room. I heard her footsteps, very fast and hard, going downstairs.

For what seemed a very long time there was only the sound of shouting from the sitting room. Both of their voices were raised. There was real anger in them, not just annoyance. I dove under the covers and stayed there, trying to hear, trying not to hear. I missed Wilma with every fiber of my being.

I did that, I thought in horror and pain. But deep inside me, someone I did not know smiled my smile. *I did that.*

My father and I were silent on the way to Cathedral the next morning, except when he asked me what time I would finish swim practice.

I had forgotten swim practice. I had not even brought my swim things with me. All of a sudden the thought of cool, chemical dimness made me sick. What I wanted now, I realized with a stab of something that was half dread and half wonder, was air. And light and the sound of voices, and the touch of other flesh. Cam's flesh.

"Practice is canceled today," I lied facilely, without a qualm. "Teachers' makeup day."

"Well, then, I'll pick you up after school and run you home."

"Daddy," I said, the words thick in my mouth, "I'm going to ride home with Cornelia Royce. She lives one block over, and she gives a bunch of people rides. She's got a new Mustang; she got it for her eighteenth birthday. She's said lots of times she'd be glad to drop me home."

He shot a sidewise look at me. I made myself look straight ahead and keep my face pleasant and natural. All of a horrifying sudden it seemed as if the rest of my life hung on his reply.

"Is that safe?" he said.

"She got an Excellent in driver ed and her father won't let her drive on any of the main streets. Just around here."

"Do we know the Royces?"

"I know Cornelia. We started Cathedral together. She's president of Latin Club and got early acceptance to Wellesley."

He was silent for a while. Then, as we turned into the grounds of National Cathedral, he said, "I hope you'll go straight home. And call me when you get there. I don't think Flora or Emma come until around five, do they?"

"I don't really know. I'm hardly ever there when they get there."

"Well, lock the door and don't answer the doorbell. I'll try to be home a little early tonight."

A small flame, a thin plume of smoke, started up in the pit of my stomach. By the time I had gotten out of the car and started for classes, anger was blazing away in me as strongly as a new-laid fire. I sucked in deep gulps of sweet spring air and ran lightly up the steps. I did not look back. After a moment I heard his car start, and then move slowly away.

That afternoon I came into the empty house, feeling as timid as if I were entering a strange home uninvited. Had I ever been in this house alone? I could not remember. I walked from room to room, seeing afternoon sun flooding the kitchen and dining room, fingering small objects on desks and tables as if I'd never seen them and putting them back, seeing as if for the first time the moving explosive paintings of my mother's, the dimmer, seemlier ancestral oils that had come to us with the house, family photographs in which Jeebs and I were blank, featureless infants and my mother and father, tanned and laughing and very young, people I had never known but had, perhaps, read about. A portrait of my mother hung over the mantelpiece in the drawing room. I think it was painted about the time of my parents' wedding; she was younger than I had ever known her. Always before, she had, in the portrait, seemed a stranger to me. Now, in the silent sunlight, she seemed, suddenly, me. Was this what my father saw when he looked at me, across the sitting room in her chair?

I walked closer to her, leaned my forehead against the thick, ridged oil paint.

"Tell me what to do," I whispered.

"You're doing just fine," she said inside my head.

When my father came home, all the doors and windows stood open and fresh April poured into the house along with the slanting sun, and I was in the sitting room arranging the huge bunch of azaleas I had plundered from the back garden. They were a small festival in the house; dust and winter gave way to spicy summer. I had pulled my rebellious hair back and bound it with my mother's tortoiseshell headband, and I wore a pair of her coral linen slacks and my pale seashell cotton sweater. The pants fit perfectly. I had never owned anything like them.

He stood silently for a long time, watching me. Then he sighed.

"You look pretty, baby. The house does, too. I've always been afraid that one day you might look so exactly like her that I couldn't bear it. But you don't. You look like my daughter who looks very much like her mother. When did you get so grown-up, Lilly?"

"Night before last," I wanted to say, but instead said, "I guess it just happened in such tiny little ways that you don't notice until one day they all add up. I've thought about that, too—my looking like her. I was always afraid it would hurt you. I've tried not to."

"No, it's nice," he said. "I still have her and I have you, too. It's like having both of you in the house."

You always did have two of us, I thought. And I thought of all those nights by the fire when he would lift his eyes and smile over at me in my mother's chair; whom had he seen? For a moment I felt as if I were merely visiting.

"Your Mr. McCall phoned me at the office this morning. He said he hoped he might call on you tonight. I said no"—my heart plummeted and my face closed—"that you and I had some talking to do. But he is coming to dinner tomorrow night. Tatty will join us."

I nodded, trying to appear as if I thought this was simply an ordinary statement by an ordinary father to his daughter on an ordinary evening. But under my feet the earth cracked, and what rose up from the fissure was not the rancid breath of an abyss but sweet air, smelling of new-cut grass and, oddly, the sea.

"That will be nice," I said.

The next night we sat out on the terrace after dinner. The air was so thick with mimosa and the big magnolia tree in our neighbor's yard beyond the brick wall that you could get drunk on it.

Sitting in my chair at my mother's little mosaic table, sipping coffee and nibbling at the lemon cheesecake Emma had made, I felt so intoxicated that I thought if I stood up I would stagger, fall down. There was a patchouli-scented candle in a glass pillar in the center of the table, and in its light, Cam, in a blue blazer and blue Brooks Brothers shirt, looked like some sort of red Viking god, visible only when the clouds of his Asgardian stronghold parted. My father wore a seersucker suit identical to several others he wore in the warm weather. Aunt Tatty looked exotic and pretty in a boldly printed silk sundress.

"Peter Max," she said, giggling. Peter Max? Giggling? I was not the only one drunk that evening.

"We have decided," my father said, looking first at Tatty and then at me, and only then at Cam, "that you may call on Lilly on the conditions that you visit here most of the times, and there are no late evenings. Also, that she may accompany you to certain activities we feel would be of benefit to her: a concert here and there, a play, an art exhibition. I believe there are some outdoor performances around the mall and other places that we all might enjoy. She will need her afternoons for her studies, of course, and I believe you said you will be busy studying for your architectural boards. I will of course want to know where she is at all times."

When did "we" become my father and Aunt Tatty? I looked from him to Tatty, who rolled her eyes and mouthed silently, "We'll see about that!" I looked at Cam, who was smiling agreeably. When he turned his eyes to me I could see clearly in them what we would do when we could manage to be alone. My face flamed. The heat seeped down into the core of me, and I felt that I could not *wait*, could not *wait* for the time when he would touch me.

"Thank you," I said, smiling at my father and Aunt Tatty. And for most of that endless summer, Cam and I sat serenely with my father and Aunt Tatty, talking of more things than I had known were in the world, often about architecture.

Cam burned with it. When my father asked him what he wanted to build and for whom, he said, "Anything, providing it's around here or down on the river or bay, and for anyone who'll see what I'm trying to do and won't interfere with it."

"Won't interfere with it?" My father raised his eyebrows. "Where on earth do you intend to get your clients? Surely they'll want some say in their own—structures."

"We'll talk about what they want first of all, before I even do a

239

sketch. After that it's my show. As a matter of fact, I've already got a client. My grandmother, who lives with us in the big house—it's her house, actually—wants a little house and garden on the grounds, with the river and woods a part of it, and a little guesthouse, and a kennel. She raises Maltese dogs, for God's sake. I've almost got the elevations done. I hope to break ground in early June."

"Are you licensed for that? Where will you get the money? Is she paying you? Do you have partners in mind?"

I was appalled at my father. Tatty hissed and opened her mouth to speak.

Cam grinned. "I'll be licensed as soon as I pass the boards, and that's in a couple of weeks. Grandmother's paying me. She's got more money than God. And she's backing me to start up my own practice. She isn't going to lose any money on me and she knows it. We've been partners in crime ever since I could understand what a trust fund was. She wants me on the site till the whole thing is done, which should be early fall, if all goes well. I'm bribing my foreman well. After that I'll be moving into D.C., I think. It's the best place for the practice, even though I'll keep the old house on the James. That's hers and will be mine. It's just as well; nobody else in the family wants it. It costs the national debt to keep that old monstrosity standing."

For the rest of the summer we talked decorously on the terrace or at the Chevy Chase Club and kissed hungrily and hard in the cramped Porsche, and occasionally did more; soon there was not an inch of my hot flesh his hands did not know, and not an inch of his red, sharp-angled body that mine had not explored. It was as if we were both starving, both dying of thirst, and could not quite slake it with just our mouths and hands. But I knew that one day we would. I knew that a time would come when making love with him would be the only thing in the world, and that when we did, nothing in either of our worlds could keep us apart.

And so, "Not now. Not yet," became our mantra. And "Soon. Oh, God, soon."

And, locked against him in the Porsche, my body and heart cried, "Safety. This is safety."

I was never once afraid, and never stopped to think that, given the past few years, I might well be. Everything we did seemed familiar, as if we had been tutored, though, of course, I had not been, and Cam had no need of tutors.

The first time he kissed me was the night, early on, when I took him downstairs to the basement, to see the gymnasium. Aunt Tatty and my father were upstairs before the fire in the sitting room, because a blustery April storm had blown in suddenly, and we had been talking about my father's and my prowess on the bars and trapezes.

"No kidding," Cam said. "Did you really? Were you good?"

"Not as good as my father, but not bad," I said, shooting a look at my father where he sat in his old chair, across from Tatty.

"Actually, Lilly had a real proficiency for gymnastics," he said, not to Cam but to Tatty. "She was light and flexible with extremely good balance, and she loved the high bar and the trapezes. She was totally without fear, if I recall."

That sounded strange to my ears. Had I ever been without fear? I could scarcely remember a time I hadn't attempted to drown it in water.

"Do you-all still do it?" Cam asked.

"Oh, no. I think I'm quite past it, and of course Lilly found swimming. She has little time for anything else."

"I'd love to see it," Cam said, smiling at my father. "Would that be possible?"

My father's sandy brows knit. "Oh, I don't think so," he said. "The place is bound to be a mess; I don't think anyone's been—"

"Oh, let Lilly show him, George," Aunt Tatty said lazily, smiling at my father. "I expect he's seen a dirty basement before."

She looked pretty in the firelight, as she often did nowadays. I wondered how she was doing it. Charlotte was at college, and she had all day to choose dresses and practice makeup.

"I always thought basements were supposed to be dirty," Cam said. "I've never seen a clean one. You should see ours. My father sometimes puts the whole pack of hunting dogs down there when it is cold."

"Don't be long," my father said as we went out into the hall where the stairway from the basement opened. "Dinner in a few minutes, I think."

As we opened the door to the stairs I heard Tatty say, "At least half an hour. Honestly, George. Sometimes I wonder why Mr. McCall bothers to call on Lilly at all."

We could not hear my father's reply. I looked at Cam, who was grinning evilly.

"What they don't know won't hurt them," he said, and we went down into the dusty darkness.

The basement was pale and musty and yellow-lit by the only light fixture that still worked, the hanging bulb over the big balance bars. It could not have been more than forty watts. The room smelled of mold and dust and stale sweat that wafted from the floor mats and the pile of soiled white towels in the corner.

"Ughh," I said. "I didn't realize nobody had been down here in so long. I think the last time it was used my father came down here on the afternoon of my mother's memorial service."

I stopped. It sounded, simply, sad and tawdry. He put his hand on my shoulder and squeezed. I reached up and laid mine over it.

"It used to be bright and clean and sort of airy," I said. "It was fun to be down here. We played records, and we worked hard, and Mother brought lemonade down."

"If you could do these, you must have been really something. When did you give it up for swimming?"

"I don't quite remember. Once I thought people had always been able to fly and some could still if they tried hard enough. I wanted to fly more than anything. But then, I guess I got good at underwater swimming, and it felt sort of right to be down there."

I didn't tell about the diving suit and the helmet, not then. My family was eccentric enough as it was.

"What were you so afraid of?" he whispered into my hair.

A great salt lump bloomed in my throat, and tears prickled behind my closed lids.

"I was afraid of everything," I mumbled.

"You don't have to be afraid anymore," he said, and turned my face to his and kissed me. At first it was a soft and questioning kiss, and then something turned over in my stomach like a little leaping fish, and I put my arms around him and pulled his head down to mine, and the kiss exploded.

When he let me go, I was trembling all over, and he was breathing as if he had run a race.

"Not bad for a first kiss," he said, smoothing my hair back from my flushed face.

"Who said it was a first?" I whispered, starting to pull his face down to mine again. I wanted more, I wanted him to kiss me forever, there in that dim, rancid basement.

"I meant for us," he said, and removed my arms from around my neck gently.

Little do you know, I thought, and wondered where on earth my response had come from. I had assumed you had to practice kissing for a long time before you got good at it. Could it be some genetic legacy, perhaps, from my mother?

"Well, it's apt to be the last," he said, pointing at the heating duct that opened over our heads. Listening, I could hear Aunt Tatty's voice in its familiar lecture mode.

"I asked Quentin Savage, you know, who handled all our affairs at the bank, what he knew about him . . . probably billions, but nobody really knows . . . private bank . . . she's spent the fortune on primping the place up, but I think she's got her own gardening and household account. None of it's hers, of course. . . . Was a girl he met on the Jersey Shore when he was home on leave from the war . . . very beautiful, of course, but New Jersey?"

I opened my mouth in anger, but Cam put his hand over it.

". . . young man has his own trust fund from his grandmother, who I hear can't stand Patty Ann—*Patty Ann*, did you ever?—rich in his own right, and will undoubtedly inherit. There's only his older sister, and she married a Maryland Carroll and doesn't need a *sou* from Papa . . ."

I snorted with fury and jerked Cam's hand away. He put it back.

"If we can hear them they can hear us," he said, grinning widely.

At that moment my father called loudly, "Lilly! Dinner's ready. Come on up now."

At dinner, Aunt Tatty chatted easily with Cam, but I was stricken to stone with embarrassment, and my father seemed lost in his own thoughts.

After dinner I walked Cam out onto the porch. The Porsche sat like a carbuncle beside Aunt Tatty's elegant new Mercedes.

"You really want to go to that thing at the Phillips?" Cam asked, pressing a kiss on my cheek quickly and primly. "We never just sit somewhere and drink coffee and talk. Let's skip the opening and say we saw it. I'll take you to Martin's."

"Okay," I said, agreeing to betray as easily as I might accept another piece of toast. "Do you think you might kiss me again?"

He laughed. "Don't you know the guy is supposed to ask that? Of course I will. So much, in fact, that we may come home having not said a word, with red hickeys all over us. That ought to seal my fate with your father."

"I'm not sure my father knows what a hickey is," I said seriously.

"Cut the man some slack, Lilly," Cam said. "He was young once. He isn't old now. What do you think he and your mother did before they were married? She was spectacular, if she looked like her portrait. And he was a good-looking young man. I don't think they played canasta all the time, do you?"

"I guess not." At the thought of it, my chest tightened and my face burned. Why had I never thought of them that way before? I had certainly seen my mother in her Jeanne Moreau striped sailor's jersey mode up at Edgewater when I was a child. It was easy to see, even then, that other men wanted her. Of course my father would have, too. Then he was lithe and daring and laughing. I supposed I had forgotten that. I had not seen him so in a long time.

So we skipped the Phillips. Cam ran in and got a program, and then we went to Martin's on Wisconsin Avenue, a tavern with a storied reputation in which, I was sure, my father had never set foot. Once there, I could not imagine why. True, people were drinking and smoking and laughing, but I had often seen a lot more drinking at the Chevy Chase Club. We drank coffee and we talked. We talked endlessly. Of course we kissed, too, later—desperately, gasping, in the car before he took me home—but mostly we talked and we talked and we talked. I don't even remember now what we talked about that first evening, but on all the following nights that summer and into the fall, we talked about almost everything we had ever done, or been, or thought, or remembered, or hoped, or loved, or hated. Talk spilled out of us like mercury from a broken thermometer. And with each evening we spent so, when we felt that we could get away with bypassing this event or that, or when I was supposed to be in the library, I came home feeling light and easy and somehow wanted, included, in a world larger than Cam's and mine. It was as if a huge burden of unsaid words had clogged my throat and weighted me down for a very long time, and, evening after evening, the heaviness flooded away and I walked more lightly.

The humid, breath-sucking Washington summer passed, and we talked. He labored along with his crew on the new buildings he was doing for his grandmother at McCall's Point, but at night he came and we talked. I wanted to see the house, or at least some drawings, blueprints, elevations, but he would not show them to me.

"Not till it's done," he said. "Probably in early October. I've got a good crew, and good subs, for once. I want you to see what it means, and that won't be really clear until it's up and comfortable in its site. Then you'll be the first to see it—after Grandmother, of course."

"You talk like you've been building forever," I said. "And you just passed your boards in May. Does it feel, you know, strange, to be actually doing what you've studied so long for?"

"No," he said. "It feels just like I knew it would. In my mind I've built every project we had in school, board by nail by stone. Sometimes I'm still surprised they aren't standing somewhere so that I can go and see them, see how it is for the people who actually live in them or work in them."

"I can't imagine being so sure of myself," I said honestly. "Or having some talent that I felt so sure of."

"Not even swimming?"

"I don't even want to swim anymore, Cam. Not underwater, not competitively. I don't need it anymore. It's air I need now."

"Anymore?"

So I told him about Jules Verne, and the suit, and the helmet. And, of course, the great fear, though nothing of what started it. He assumed it began with my mother's death, and I let him. I could go no farther back than that.

"My God," he whispered when I was done. "How could you stand being afraid for so long? Didn't you tell your father? You should have, Lilly. He should have done something about that when it first started."

"He was afraid too. It took me a while to see it, but he was so afraid of losing me, and I of losing him, that we just—stuck together in the house like burrs. For almost six years, that's just what we did. It was only when I met you that I could see what else there was. And all he could see was that he might lose me. That's what's been the matter with him all along. He doesn't dislike you. He's afraid I'm going to leave him."

"Jesus, poor man! But of course he must have known he'd lose you sooner or later. He didn't expect that you'd just live there with him for the rest of his life, did he?"

"We didn't get that far," I said unhappily, because, of course, that was what he thought. And I let him think it, because in truth, it was what I thought, too. Love and safety. Love and safety forever.

I had never dreamed I could find both outside his house.

It was the source of a good bit of very real guilt and grief. But I shoved them both away from me. I would make him see. On a steaming Sunday afternoon in early September, two weeks before my father and I both were to start George Washington, we sat with my father and Tatty on the back terrace, seeking what shade could be found under the mimosas. The tips of grass and leaves were browning. Late summer flies thrummed from the end of the garden. Many natives think a Washington summer does not reach its blazing apogee until September. I remember hating the start of Cathedral because even our light uniforms were binding and stifling, and there was no unseemly air-conditioning.

But not this year, I thought. *This year I can wear pretty much what I please, and three of my classes and the student union are air-conditioned.* I looked forward to them like a man who was dying of thirst seeing, at least, the long-promised oasis in the desert.

There were a couple of old photograph albums on the table; Tatty had insisted that Cam see what an adorable baby I had been. Because my baby pictures were a little short of moronic, I was irritated with her, and restless.

Suddenly Cam leaned in close.

"Is that a Friendship? The one anchored at your dock at—I guess that's your Maine place, isn't it?"

He looked over at my father. I had told him about the Maine house, but little more than that we had one and had not gone there since my mother's death. "It just didn't seem right after that," I'd said.

"Yes, it is," my father said now, bending over to look at the faded photograph. "It was my father's."

"Did you—do you sail it?" Cam asked eagerly.

"Yes. Yes, I did. Do you know Friendships?"

"Oh, Lord, yes. My uncle had one that he kept at our place on the river, and I loved it better than anything in the world. He taught me to sail it when I was maybe ten. My father sold it when he died, though, and I've always missed it. Is yours still there?"

"I assume so," said my father. "I had it put in storage at the local boatyard when . . . we left. I get a yearly bill for its upkeep, so I suppose it's still seaworthy."

"Can you tell me about it?"

"Well, it's old. It came from Bremen, I think, around 1890-something. William Morse from Friendship built it. It was a lobster boat till about 1910, and I think my grandfather bought it and redid it around then. It's always been around Edgewater, as long as I can remember."

"Oh, man," Cam breathed reverentially. His face, turned to my father's, literally shone. He looked like a small child hearing a wonderful story about a miraculous treasure he had not believed existed. He turned his face to me.

"Can you sail it?"

"I could. I do when my father is with me—or did. It's been a long time now. I don't even know if I'd remember how."

"But you sail, right?"

At that moment I would have told him I could take the *Queen Elizabeth* across the Atlantic under sail. I would have given him the Friendship and anything else I had.

"I—" I began, and then stopped. I had not thought of the Beetle Cat for a long time.

"Lilly and Jeebs had a little Beetle Cat when they were smaller," my father said. "Jeebs never cared much for it, but Lilly could sail it blindfolded with one hand. It slipped its moorings in a storm and we never found it."

Across Cam's blazing red head we looked at each other, my father and I.

Is this all right with you? my eyes said to him.

Yes. This is the way it will be, his said back to me. The first lie we had ever conspired in hung heavy and odorous between us. And then it simply floated away on the light September wind on our terrace, and forever after, or almost, that was what had happened to my Beetle Cat.

"Did you get another one?" Cam asked, expectation lighting his already luminous face.

"Well, we haven't been back in a long time."

"It was so much her mother's place," my father said, "somehow we just haven't wanted to go back."

A wild, honey-sweet joy filled me. I could do this for Cam. I could give him Edgewater.

"Daddy," I said, my voice trembling with the effort to make myself believed, "I want to go back. I want to go back now, before school starts. We have time. We could open it up easily. I—I miss it, Daddy. I want Cam to see it. Please, couldn't we just go? Tatty could come with us."

I stopped and watched his face. It was still. We did not speak for a long moment. I realized that I was holding my breath.

Slowly, he nodded. He was still not looking at me, but over my head and back up at our house.

"I suppose we could," he said. "I guess it's time."

I ran to him and threw my arms around him, hugging as hard as I could. It struck me that it was a child's gesture, and I let go. But he hugged me back, as I could not remember his having done since, perhaps, I was very small.

"Thank you," I whispered, tears stinging my eyes.

"If we left tomorrow," Cam said tentatively, "we could have a good long time there before Lilly starts school. Maybe over a week. Would that be possible?"

"I don't see why not," my father said finally. "We don't need to pack much. I think we still have summer things up there. Maybe just a jacket and sweaters. It's not very nippy yet. I could call Seth and he and Clara could open the place and get us in a few groceries. Lilly, could you be ready by then?"

"Yes," I whispered. "Oh, yes I could."

"Tatty?"

"Do you really want me to tag along?" Her face was shining, too.

"Yes," my father and I said together.

"Then I better go home now and see what I've got that's Maine-worthy."

"It's not the North Pole, you know." My father smiled at her. "Or the wilderness. You won't need heavy boots and a machete. We don't wear much of anything but pants and shirts and sweaters. Bring sneakers if you've got them. I don't want a mahogany deck I've spent half a lifetime polishing scratched."

I could tell that he was excited also—just a bit, but excited.

It was an enormous step we were taking, but I believed then that he and I were the only ones who knew that.

Cam kissed my cheek and pounded my father on the back and hugged Aunt Tatty briefly.

"Got to get back to the river," he said. "Stuff to go over with my foreman. And I want to get some stuff together."

"You really won't need much," I said.

"I'll only bring what I need."

CHAPTER

14

We got to Edgewater after dark, just as the huge blind eye of the Harvest Moon slid from behind Mr. Carl Forshee's towering promontory and flooded the bay and surrounding islands with molten silver, as far out as Great Owls Head Island. It was as if someone had thrown a switch and turned the world on; far to the right the spires of the Deer Island Bridge stood out like a child's Erector set. The roofs of all the summer cottages in Carter's Cove were etched starkly against the moon and sky. There were no lights in any of them except one, a little way down from ours, and seeing the porch light on at Edgewater was like falling, falling precipitously into a well-remembered and well-loved dream. It had been so long since I had seen the house like this, yet it might have been only last night. I almost expected to see the darting shapes of children playing Kick the Can on our moon-flooded lawn, hear their cries and laughter, my own among them.

"Well," my father said. He was the first to speak.

"Here we are. I see Seth has turned on the porch light, and the lawn's been mowed."

"And somebody put the flag up," I said faintly, watching it whip against the sky as it had on so very many nights, so long ago.

"It looks as if somebody's here besides us," Aunt Tatty said, not getting out of the car. None of us seemed quite able to leave it yet. It was too sharp a transition.

"It's the Davenports' house," my father said. "I didn't know they still came up; Mrs. Davenport is almost totally crippled with arthritis. It's pretty late for them to be here, but I don't think he takes services anywhere anymore, so there's really no need for them to go back. They must have somebody to help them, though."

He stopped. So did my breath. "Peaches" hung heavy and throbbing, an infection in the air between us.

"I don't think it's the granddaughter," Aunt Tatty said. "I heard at the club that she'd already gone off to Randolph-Macon. I think they have a young man who lives in."

I breathed again, and turned to Cam. He was staring at the house and bay as if he'd never seen a house beside water before.

"So what do you think?" I asked, suddenly anxious. I had never seen it, but McCall's Point was purported to be one of the truly grand plantations on the James River. This old house surely paled beside it.

"I think," he said in a near whisper, "that I've died and gone to heaven. I've only been to Kennebunkport a few times when I was a kid, when Dad and Mother visited somebody or other on the point there. And Camden once. Both of them were wall-to-wall traffic and tourists milling in the street like sheep. I realize now that I've never really been to Maine."

I saw the corners of my father's mouth curl up in the dark, and knew that it had been absolutely the right thing to say. I felt my heart squeeze with love for Cam. I felt that at least there was something I could give him that he didn't have.

As if at a signal we all opened our doors and got out of the car. The wind off the bay was still soft and freighted with pine and fir and salt, and kelp, but the tops of the trees sang with a note I had never heard before. It was a winter song. "I'm coming, I'm coming," it crooned, far up in the treetops.

I shivered.

"You cold?" Cam asked, putting his arm around me. It was warm and strong, and I leaned into it.

"Not really," I said. "It's just different in fall somehow. I guess it's because most of the houses are empty."

We walked across the grass to the steps. There had never been an outside light here, but no one had ever needed one. Our feet could find their way in the dark, and had, many times. Even now, as if of their own volition, mine sidestepped the hollows where the rain always pooled, and the holes made by the skunks foraging for grubs, and the formidable rocks, children of the great glacial boulders, that no one had ever thought of digging out. Behind me, Cam was surefooted, but Aunt Tatty stumbled once or twice, and I remember with annoyance and amusement that she wore high-heeled sandals.

"You're going to break your neck in those," my father had said when we picked her up.

"I have tennis shoes in my bag," she said. "I'm just going to be in the house when we get there."

"You've got to *get* to the house," he said shortly, but did not pursue it. Now he took her arm and walked her firmly to the steps, and we went up and across the big porch and my father pushed the door open. It was unlocked; Seth or Clara again, I thought.

My breath caught at the familiar smell of perpetually salt-damp rugs and upholstered furniture. Sour, years-old dust from mold and old books and the ghosts of fireplace embers and, somehow, Wilma. And perfume. In the thick air of the recently opened house, a note of the fresh, bitter-green scent my mother always wore. When my father lit the big lamp on the table by the old tartan sofa and the room bloomed into dim sixty-watt light, I looked at him. Did he smell it, too? It was as if she had just walked out of the room. But he gave no sign that he did. He continued around the living room turning on lamps, and we stood for a moment in a small knot, Cam and Aunt Tatty and I, inhaling summers out of mind and the skin of people long gone from us.

The room was immaculate; floors were polished and the fireplace cleaned and stacked with new apple-wood logs, and the smell of furniture polish and Clara's Murphy Oil Soap and a warm, buttery smell from the kitchen washed over me like a tide. I closed my eyes and stretched. It was as if the very air welcomed and embraced me. I was where I was wanted and loved; there was no other place I should be but here.

"It's a lot bigger than I remember," Aunt Tatty said, peering around in the dimness. I wondered how the house looked to her, how it would look to a stranger seeing it for the first time. I could not imagine that. No matter what anyone did to it in the years to come, I knew I would always see it through the eyes of the child I had been. Tatty vanished into the dark kitchen, and I saw the light flick on. My father was contemplating our small pile of luggage, and Cam was simply standing, hands in pockets, rocking slightly and looking around. The faint smile on his face was, I knew, unconscious.

"There's some kind of chowder," Aunt Tatty said, coming back from the kitchen, "and a pie. Looks like blueberry. And a plate of muffins."

"Clara." My father smiled. "It's what we've always had the night we got here."

"Well, let's get our bags put away and I'll heat it all up," Tatty said. "Maybe we could have it on trays in front of the fire. George, where do you want me?"

I saw bewilderment on my father's face, and knew he had not considered this. Where would we all sleep indeed?

I started to speak up, to say that I wanted my old room back. But he spoke before I could.

"Tatty, you take Jeebs's room, at the back corner of the second floor," he said. "It has the best view of the water, and the bathroom is right next door. Cam, I think the real guest room would be good for you—it has the best mattress and the newest bedcovers, and there's a dumbwaiter in the closet that goes down to the kitchen. Never can tell what you might pull up. Front room right, other end of the hall. Lilly"—and he looked at me—"I want you to take your mother's room."

"Daddy, no—that's yours, too," I protested. I did not want my mother's spare, soft-lit room. I wanted my own, with the chipped iron bedstead and the spavined mattress Wilma and I had curled up on so many nights, and the pentimento of each passing year pasted over the one before it: posters, a dreadful painting of the house leaning lopsidedly over the bay that an aunt had painted, a small watercolor of the dock and the Beetle Cat and the Friendship my mother had done over my spindly desk, and sagging shelves full of crumbling paperbacks, dried and lusterless shells arrayed on the bureau and the mantel.

"I can't sleep there," my father said matter-of-factly. "All her clothes are still there. I'll take your room. I always liked it."

"We'll get Elizabeth's things packed up and labeled in no time," Aunt Tatty said. No one spoke. I thought that I would throttle her if I saw her with a pile of my mother's clothes over her arm.

"I'll take the bags up," Cam said into the silence. He picked them up, two in each hand, and swung them up the dark stairs as easily as he might have lifted grocery bags. I doubted they were heavy. His, in fact, looked to be the largest.

When he came back downstairs there were noises and wonderful, familiar smells from the kitchen, and my father was bringing in our old rattan trays, trailing curls of rotting wicker and laden with steaming blue pottery bowls, into the living room. I had touched a match to the apple logs, and the sweet smells of summer smoke curled into the room. I sat down in a corner of the old sofa and closed my eyes and let the house breathe into me. I remembered then that I had not run out to look at the bay, to listen to its breathing and feel my own synchronize with it. Somehow the breath of the house in my lungs was gift enough for now.

When we had finished eating, Cam carried our dishes into the kitchen and washed them before anyone could protest, and came back into the living room, smiling.

"It's like the best summer camp in the world," he said. "My mother would have her interior designer out here by dawn tomorrow."

"Well, it's not much—" I started to mumble, but he cut me off.

"It's everything. I think I'd shoot the first designer who put a foot in here. I know more about your family by just being in this house for an hour than I could find out in a month. It's a family to dream about."

Little do you know, I thought, but then I knew he was right. Ours had been, up until our last day here, close to just such a family. I could not have seen that then, but I did now. My heart flopped, fishlike, with loss and remembrance.

"What's on the third floor?" Cam asked.

"Attics. Storage rooms. Bedrooms for the servants we never had," I said. "And my favorite place on earth. My own special place. No one came in unless I invited them."

"Can I see?"

"Well, since it's you," I said, smiling at him.

We started up the dark, precipitous stairs that miraculously had never caused a major fall. I looked back into the living room. Aunt Tatty was smiling up at us. My father was not smiling, but on his face was written loss, and wistfulness, and a kind of acceptance that

257

smote me through. *He's lost too much,* I thought. *How can I go away from him?*

But I knew I would.

In the far corner of the attic, my retreat was still as I had left it, so far as I could see. The small, tattered rug was disheveled, from being wrapped around me that last night, and the old, faded quilt still lay in a pile next to it. When I switched on the dim old brass floor lamp I had confiscated for my hideaway, I saw that books were still spilled across the floor where I had jerked them from the shelves in the agony of that night. I had not let myself remember it until now. It flooded me, almost doubling me over, and then seemed simply to wash away on a wave of warmth. I smiled, standing in the beneficence as I might under a warm shower. Whatever was in this house, it wanted my well-being.

"Thank you, Mama," I whispered.

"It's a perfect kid's hidey-hole," Cam said, and I opened my eyes and looked at him. He was grinning. "I can see you here on rainy days, you and—what was it, Wilma? Did you ever invite anybody else up here?"

"Yes," I said, bracing for the pain, but it did not come. The sweetness in the room deepened, just a bit.

"But only one or two. I had a sign that said 'Lilly's Lair. Private. No admittance except by invitation.' I wonder what happened to it."

"Messy kid, weren't you?" he said, touching the spilled books with his toe. "Let's see: *The Golden Bough. At the Back of the North Wind. Norse Eddas and Sagas. Beowulf.* Beowulf? Jesus, Lilly, what did you read for fun, the Addams Family?"

"This was for fun. I loved myths and magic and folklore. I still do. I'm trying to see if I can manage to make a major of it at GW. I don't really know what I'd use it for, unless I taught it or something. But there's really not anything else I want to study."

"Does your father know that?"

I dropped my eyes.

"No. He thinks I'm going to major in English literature and minor in how to become a curator of something or other. I thought I'd tell him if I get it worked out. If I can't, then I guess English lit is as good as anything."

"I wish I'd known this as a kid," he said, looking around.

"Maybe you do," I said.

"Maybe I do. Listen, Lilly. There's something else you could do that would be better than magic and all that stuff. And you could still go to school and study whatever."

"What?" I said.

"Marry me," he said. "Marry me, Lilly. After that you can go back to school or not, or anything in the world you wanted to do, but Lilly, I don't want to be without you."

"Well, I thought we were going to, I mean eventually . . ." I stammered. What was he saying?

"No. I mean now. Marry me now."

"But my father—I'm only eighteen—"

"You'll be nineteen in just a little while. You're of age. What's he going to do, lock you in the house until you're twenty-one? I thought maybe he was getting sort of used to me."

"Oh, Cam, he is. Can't you tell? But who would live with him? And I don't know how to be a wife—I haven't even met your family. I have an idea they'd disinherit you if you brought me home. And Tatty, and all Daddy's associates, and Mama's friends . . . what would they think?"

"I can't really bring myself to care very much what anybody thinks," Cam said, pulling me against him. He kissed my hair. I felt my muscles unclench, and I sagged in his arms. His body warmed me from the top of my head to the bottom of my toes. There was not an inch of me that he did not shelter, did not celebrate.

259

"I can't cook," I whispered into his chest. His oxford-cloth shirt smelled sweetly of starch and soap, and more strongly of Cam. I thought his skin, his body, smelled wonderful. It had a rich scent that I could only think of as a red-gold, like his hair, like his mustache.

He began to laugh.

"I can cook just fine," he said. "I learned at school, in self-defense. I'll cook and all you have to do is just lie in bed and wait for me to wash up."

I lifted my face to his, and said, in a voice that clogged my throat, "I always wanted to marry you. You asked me when we first met. I said yes. But I always thought that it was . . . ahead, somehow; it never felt like a thing we would do now. I thought that later something would change in me and I would know I was old enough to get married, I guess, and then we just would. It scares me, Cam."

He lifted my chin. I could feel his breath warm on my forehead.

"Are you afraid of me? Afraid that I would change my mind, or not take care of you, or stop loving you? Because that will never happen in my lifetime, Lilly. I know that as surely as I know how to breathe, or walk."

"How do you know?" It came in a whisper.

"I know. I *know*, Lilly. I know because the idea of living my life with you, every day of it, makes me happy in a way I've never been happy before. And I know I want that to start now. I simply cannot wait for one or two more years. It would be like waiting to breathe for that long. Goddamit, I want to make love to you, Lilly. Now— not in a suite at the Greenbrier two years from now. *Now*."

I began to cry. I did not know why and I could not stop. Neither could I stop laughing. He would think I was insane. *I* thought I was insane.

"Then what's stopping you?" I hiccupped.

As it turned out, nothing was.

I had imagined the first time we made love in literally hundreds of scenarios. None had included a squeaking, dusty floor in an ill-lit attic with books bumping against my hips and thighs and a lopsided sign at the corner of my sight, before I closed my eyes and gave myself totally to him, that read, crazily: LILLY'S LAIR. PRIVATE. I had always thought I would be afraid, or that there would be pain, but it was not like that. Not at all. It was a long slide up, a white explosion, ecstasy, and down again, an exchange of bodies and what felt like souls. I'd had no idea. Simply none.

When he lifted himself away and propped beside me on the rumpled rug, there were tears in his eyes and on his cheeks. He grinned.

"So what do we do now?"

"I sort of like what we just did," I said, laughing in joy and a kind of sensual fullness that seemed to fill every crevice of my body. "When can we do it again?"

"Not quite yet. I'm good, but I'm not that good. Do you feel you're old enough now, Lilly? Are you still scared?"

"Oh, God, no. I will marry you now, Cam. I would do it this minute if I could. I don't know how to go about it, but we can find out. What should we do first, get blood tests or something? And who would marry us, and where?"

"First we go down and tell your father," he said. Panic flamed for a moment, and then the prospect of simply having him, having him forever, flooded the panic away, and I rolled over on the bunched-up, Wilma-hairy rug, and said, "Okay. Will you talk first?"

"I'll do all the talking if you want. It might not be a very . . . fun thing, Lilly. I don't want you to start feeling sorry for him and back-tracking. He knows it's going to happen; he must have always known. There just isn't any good reason not to do it now."

I nodded silently, and he reached down and pulled me up, and we both straightened our clothing and took a deep breath, and started down the dark steps of Edgewater to change my father's life.

The next day, a Saturday, at four o'clock, I stood just inside the front door at Edgewater and waited to marry Cameron McCall III.

He had been right. It had not been a fun thing when we sat in the lamp- and-fire-lit living room and Cam cleared his throat and said, "Sir, I'd like to have your permission to marry Lilly."

My father stiffened.

"Marry Lilly . . . well, Mr. McCall, I think the time for discussing that is still far in the future. She's scarcely had time to know you, much less your family. And you really know little about ours. Perhaps in three years, when she's twenty-one, we might talk again."

"No sir," Cam said pleasantly, his white smile just this side of piratical. If you had not known him, you might have thought he was baring his teeth. Perhaps he was.

"I mean now. Very soon. As soon as we can find a place to get our blood tests and someone to marry us. I've been looking at the peninsula telephone book, and there are justices of the peace in Ellsworth, and the Blue Hill hospital has a lab. We both hope with all our hearts that it can be here, in this house, with you and Mrs. Glover to bless us. And I—we hope that for a honeymoon we might take the Friendship out and sort of island-hop for a few days. We'd be back in time for you and Lilly to start school, but if that doesn't work out, I have to tell you that we're going to do this anyway."

The silence in the room was total, except for the snicker of the fire. Somehow it didn't bristle with unspoken anguish, or with anger, though I knew that my father must feel both. His face, as he looked first at Cam and then at me, was gray. But for me, the benevolence of the house still prevailed.

"Lilly," my father said so softly that his voice was barely audible, "if you do this thing it will break my heart. It would break your mother's. You are simply too young, you are not ready for commitment such as marriage, your education is the most important thing you have ahead of you—can't you wait until you have graduated, or at least until you are twenty-one? Where would you live? Who would look after you?"

I felt tears starting in my eyes, and my heart literally wrung.

"Daddy, I—" I began.

Aunt Tatty spoke suddenly, sharply.

"Lilly," she said, her eyes literally bulging, "is this something you *have* to do? Lilly, are you—" She stopped, simply staring at me.

At my stomach.

Anger thickened my voice.

"I'm not pregnant, Aunt Tatty, if that's what you mean," I said coldly. My father made a small, garbled sound. I looked over at Cam, whose face was perfectly still and neutral behind the flaming beard and mustache. Incredibly, he winked.

"We'll live at the point with my grandmother for a while, Dr. Constable," he said agreeably. He had not yet lifted his voice, nor had anger furrowed his brow. But I knew he felt the same outrage at my Aunt Tatty's question as I did. I had, once or twice, seen him really angry. I did not want my father to see that face. It still shocked me.

"I planned a guesthouse for her at the new river house I'm building for her, and the guesthouse has turned into a really great little waterfront cottage. I thought when I was designing it that I would like to live there, and when I met Lilly I added another room or two and a little garden, and I think it will be a fantastic first house. When my grandmother passes away the big house comes to me, and though God knows it needs fixing up, it's a beautiful old house. We'll live there, then. Mother and Dad can't wait to get rid of it so they can

263

move to Georgetown. The new house and cottage should be ready about the time we get home."

"That's hours away from GW," my father said incredulously. "How on earth could she get to school from there?"

"Well, I've got new office space in Georgetown, at the end of Wisconsin right over the river. It has a small apartment that we could use in a pinch, but I can make the trip from the river house in record time. I know all the back roads. You'd see Lilly every day at school, anyway, and if she likes we can stay in town sometimes. Or she can come spend a night or two with you. And I assure you I can take care of her. I've already got four commissions waiting for me, and a trust fund from Grandma I haven't touched yet. See, here's the thing, sir: I do not want to be away from her even a day more. She feels the same way. We're going to make that happen."

My father looked at me, tallow faced.

"Lilly?" he whispered.

"Yes, Daddy. I do feel the same way."

My father stood up suddenly. He moved like an old man.

"We'll sleep on it. That's the best thing. Everybody's had a long, hard day. We'll all be clearer in the morning."

I started to protest, but Cam put his hand on my shoulder and said, "Good idea, sir. You're probably right."

He and I climbed the stairs silently and parted at the top for our separate bedrooms. He kissed me softly, chastely; even so the aching fire in my stomach sprang up again.

"Good night, Lilly," he said mildly.

"But Cam, nothing's decided."

"It's all decided, Lil. Just give him time to digest it."

"But . . ."

"'Night, baby."

"Good night," I croaked, near tears. I went to my mother's bedroom and climbed beneath her flowered duvet in my underpants and T-shirt, deathly tired, and lay waiting for the tears and the guilt, and the long, sleepless night to start.

But they didn't. I shouldn't have been able to hear the water from here, but somehow I could, and its breathing was calm and strong and sure. I felt my own fall into its rhythm; I felt sleep tug at my eyelids, and just before I dropped off I thought I heard a soft sound that was not of the sea: "Shhhhh, Lilly. Sleep."

"All right, Mama," I said, and did.

The next morning I got up late, dreading the day ahead, dreading my father's agony, dreading my own mingled threads of anguish and guilt and desire. The first thing I heard when I went out into the upstairs hall was laughter, coming from the kitchen. Laughter? It was. My father's, Aunt Tatty's, Cam's and Clara's. I ran downstairs in shorts and a tee and bare feet.

They were sitting in the kitchen, drinking coffee and eating the blueberry scones Clara had brought. And they were, indeed, laughing. I simply looked from one to another.

Aunt Tatty was wearing a pretty flowered sundress I had never seen and had her hair pinned up on top of her head. Her cheeks were flushed and she looked . . . young. My father's color was back, and he smiled at me, chewing scone.

Cam was glowing as if someone had plugged him in.

"We have decided," Aunt Tatty said, "that if you are going to do this, we are going to do it right. We called Canon Davenport last night and he will be delighted to perform the service this afternoon at four. He says don't worry now about the blood test; he knows the people to call about that. Mrs. Davenport is bringing armloads of flowers from her garden. Clara is making you a splendid picnic basket to take with you. And Seth has come and gotten the Friendship, and is freshening it up and putting some sleeping bags on deck, and a tarp for cover. All you need now is to look in your mother's closet for something proper to wear for a bayside wedding. There's some lovely things; we'll find just the right ones."

"But . . ."

I looked helplessly at my father.

"Lilly," he said formally, "Tatty is going to move into our house with me, and act as my hostess and companion. She will sell her own; it's much too big for just one person."

I could do nothing but look from him to her. Was he saying he was going to marry her, or what?

"George should not be alone," she said serenely. "Elizabeth would not want that. I'm glad to do it. Now come on, Lilly, and let's get started on your wedding dress."

I drifted up the stairs behind her, feeling as though the diving helmet were still in place and I was moving through water. But it was warm, serene water, and I knew that just outside the helmet such a tsunami of happiness waited for me that I could not face it yet.

"Do you love him?" I asked, watching her flip through my mother's closet, which also smelled of Vetiver.

"There are so many things more important than love, Lilly," she said, her voice muffled in fabric. "You can't possibly know that now, but you will. One day you will."

"No, I won't," I said, but she did not hear me.

By her fiat, I did not see Cam for the rest of the day until four.

"Bad luck," she said. "We'll spend the day on you."

And after I had bathed with my mother's bath salts and oil, she found lacy underwear among the sachets and offered it to me, and smiled when it fit beautifully. I did, too. I had never worn anything remotely like it in my life. *No wonder every man my mother knew was after her,* I thought. And then wondered how many of them had seen her in it, and blushed.

"Aunt Tatty," I said. "How is he, really? Daddy? I can't believe everything has been so easy. It would break my heart if he was covering up, but he seems okay about it."

"To tell you the truth, Lilly, I think he's a little relieved. It's terribly hard work, fighting so hard and so long what will be, in the end, a losing battle. Now it's over and he knows you'll be taken care of, and so will he. Relax and be happy."

At four o'clock, dressed in a long white pleated silk skirt of my mother's and a white silk tank top of my own, with a circlet of field daisies in my newly washed and Tatty-styled hair and an armful of Mrs. Davenport's late pink roses, I walked out of the house on my father's arm and stood for a moment on the porch, looking. Simply looking. The angle of the light was lower now, in September, and at this hour the bay glittered like an ocean of diamonds from midbay out to Owls Head Island. The pointed firs and pines arched against the still-blue sky. Across the way, the promontory where I had once thought a boy could fly was catching the late-slanting sun. I felt a stab of pain looking at it, and the soporific warmth of the house stole back and I merely smiled. The air was sweet with salt and pine and flowers, and I looked up at my father, and he smiled at me, and said, "Here we go."

Overhead a lone osprey wheeled and cried. "Thank you," I whispered to it.

And we went across the porch and down to the terrace, and there, at the beginning of the long dock out to the Friendship's mooring, I saw Cam and Canon Davenport standing, smiling, waiting for me. Canon Davenport had put on his full Episcopal regalia

267

for the occasion, looking like the Lord Canon of somewhere in eighteenth-century England.

Cam wore a kilt.

It was a full kilt: the McCall tartan, I had no doubt; the heathery short tweed jacket over the dark red and blue and green plaid, and knee socks on his strong brown legs, and the bag called, I thought, the sporran dangling from his belt; and also in his belt a small, sharp knife that I knew had a name, but I could not think of it.

He should have looked ridiculous. Instead, he looked magnificent, splendid and near barbaric, both regal and feral. His long red hair and beard were fire in the slanting sun, and his smile was broad and white and only slightly manic. I could see the flash of his blue eyes from where my father and I stood. I could only think of William Wallace and Robert the Bruce and Culloden and bone-chilling war whoops. For an instant I was almost afraid.

"He brought it with him," Aunt Tatty whispered as she fell in before me to walk down to the dock. "It's what he had in the big bag. I'm glad we're doing it here. Can you imagine that in the National Cathedral?"

I began to laugh. I laughed until tears ran down my face, no doubt streaking Aunt Tatty's carefully applied mascara. I tried not to laugh aloud, and bit my lip and held my breath. I did not want Cam to think I was laughing at him. I loved this half-wild laird who was waiting for me by the sea. I was just laughing at everything.

I straightened my face as we reached the canon, and my father stepped back as Cam and I moved to stand side by side before him. Behind them I could see the Friendship, shimmering like a boat in a fairy tale, roses tied to her bow, bobbing gently in the freshening afternoon breeze. I looked at Cam and took a deep breath—and could not get it.

It became the most important thing in the world to me, not to let anyone see I could not breathe, was choking to death at my own wedding. I stared straight ahead as the canon intoned the service, holding my face still by sheer will, waiting for the moment when I would simply sink to the dock and die. "Poor Cam," they would all say. "Just before she said 'I do.' Can you imagine?"

My eyes began to fail; darkness seeped in at the edges of my sight. I felt myself sway.

And then Cam whispered in my ear, "Listen to the bay, Lilly. Breathe with the bay. Breathe, Lilly."

And suddenly I could—could feel my breath sigh in and out with the water of the bay—and my vision cleared, and strength flooded back into my arms and legs.

"Lilly?" Cam said into the silence.

"Yes," I said, smiling at him with gratitude and all the love I had in my heart.

"You're supposed to say, 'I do,'" he whispered.

"Oh," I said. "Oh, I do!"

Everyone laughed, even the canon, and Cam kissed me, and I looked down to see that he had slipped a ring on my finger, a very beautiful old ruby and diamond ring, set in chased gold. I looked up at him.

"Grandma's," he said. "Come on, Mrs. McCall," and he turned and grabbed my hand, and we ran, both skirts swirling in the wind, down to the sloop, and he swung me aboard. Bags and boxes and the wonderful smell of something in a hamper curled up into the salt of the ocean wind.

"Thank you," I whispered to Cam.

"What, for marrying you?" he said, as my father moved onto the dock to cast us off.

"No. For telling me to breathe with the water. I really thought I was dying."

269

He gave me a hard, deep kiss, and then said, "Did I say that? I don't remember." And then, "Look out, Lilly, we're off. Let's get this sail up before we lose the wind."

And we scrambled for the line, white-silked and kilted and ridiculous, and the luffing mainsail filled and snapped, and the Friendship headed into the wind.

And so we were married.

CHAPTER

15

Many times when I traveled with Cam, in the pre- and post-small-child stages of our marriage, I woke not knowing where I was; indeed, even what we were doing there. Was it the Marriott in Shreveport, where Cam was working on the Grace house? The small inn on Point Reyes, where he was just starting construction on the beautiful earthquake-tracking facility for the U.S. Geological Survey? The Ritz in Boston, where he was deciding if he could ethically design a condominium on a wild stretch of shore near Marblehead? He couldn't.

"I'd have to blow it up when it was done," he said.

"You and Howard Roark," I said, hugging him under the Ritz's sea foam of white down comforter. I was glad. I'd hated the idea of him being responsible for a condominium on that empty, gull-haunted beach.

It would, however, have put both the girls through college, as he pointed out.

"Time they got scholarships and found jobs," I replied, only half teasing. The girls were showing the first warning signs of approaching Princesshood. At fifteen, Betsy was lobbying for a strapless black satin dress for her prom, and Alice, two years younger, refused to go to dancing school until her father bought her a designer dress.

"And I don't mean Laura Ashley, either." She sniffed.

"You have a point," Cam said, rolling over and reaching for me. "Man, there's nothing like a Ritz fuck, is there?"

"It's all this goose down." I grinned. "Cushions all your sharp angles."

The sixteen years that had passed since we'd lurched off into our married life on the Friendship sloop at Edgewater, Cam had, if not changed, then evolved. The Viking-red beard and long hair were gone, though his hair still flopped over his forehead and curled on his neck rather more than I would have liked. But he still had the riverboat-gambler mustache, and the coppery sun-baked and freckled hide, and the blue eyes were still as keen and sometimes dangerous as when I had first met him.

He had not slipped into early middle age with anything like a paunch, any slackness at all in his long muscles. Cam dressed or partly dressed was still breathtaking. Cam naked looked to me, as he always had, like a marionette being manipulated by a manic puppeteer. His long limbs were sharp-knobbed and loose, and he moved with unconscious lopes and jerks that, when I had first seen him without clothes, reduced me to convulsive laughter. Now he had his marionette act down perfectly, and it still made me laugh. Thank God, I often told him, that I was the only one person apt to see it.

"You wouldn't have many clients," I told him.

"That's what you think." He grinned.

But on this morning, my first alone at Edgewater, so early that the sky over the bay was still pearled and the crows were only just waking up, I knew beyond certainty, even not quite out of sleep yet, that I was in my old room, in my small iron bed, and the house held me warm inside it, and that endless summer days stretched out ahead of me like a July field sweeping toward the sea. I stretched greatly, and felt a warm, knobby lump in the middle of my back, and mur-mured sleepily to Cam, "Get your elbow out of my back."

"*It's my foot, not my arm,*" Silas said in a sleepy snarl. "*Cats don't have arms.*"

It was not our bedroom, Cam's and mine, the big one that had been my mother's and then ours for all our summers in Maine. And Cam was not in bed with me. My mind scrambled frantically, and found him in the urn on the mantel over the living room fireplace, where I had put him last night.

I fell precipitously into darkness.

Anyone who has lost a love to death can tell you about that fall. You wake from a hard-won sleep and lie there warm and groggy and consider engaging the day. And then you remember. Half of you is not there, and never will be again. The person who focused all the disparate parts of you into a whole is gone. The agony is too much; you almost welcome the great slide ahead of you. But there is no oblivion in it. Only blackness and an endless well of red pain.

At the very first, the effort to haul yourself out of the pit hand over hand seems impossible, and, indeed, unnecessary. What is there up top for you? But somehow you begin; I know few people who have truly surrendered to the blackness, even at the beginning, when a leftover life seems to hold nothing to give you light. Many of us have other lives, other beings, that wait for us to minister to them, and on their shoulders we toil, finally far enough up to begin to stumble forward. I do not know what happens to people who have no family, close friends, or animals. Perhaps they simply do not come back up. Or perhaps they are steelier souls than ever I could be.

Ridiculously, the first handhold I found was Silas, now grumping at me in the narrow little bed, needing breakfast. I thought of a line from a poem I had read once, Edna St. Vincent Millay, maybe.

Listen, children, your father is dead.
From his old coats
I'll make you little jackets; . . .
Life must go on;
I forget just why.

The sucking needs of others will pull you out eventually. Then I thought of the girls, back home in New York, stabbed through their hearts with grief, for they had adored Cam. True, they had husbands and one had children, but they had, now, only half a set of parents. I had become to them, instantly, a troublesome woman to whom they could not run because they considered me quite mad, not Mother-who-belongs-in-the-set-with-Daddy, who together anchored the world for them. I knew they were very angry about that. I didn't blame them.

"Somebody else is going to have to look after them for a while," I said to Silas. "I don't know if I've got enough left even to take care of you."

"Hop to it. How much gumption does it take to open a can?"

I pulled myself out of the great hole and waited for the blinding naked agony of daylight and ordinariness to twist my guts, but it did not. Oh, there was pain. Terrible, near-mortal pain. But the house put its arms around me and the pain became like pain perceived through a haze of opiate, still raging, but behind glass.

I looked out the window. The sun was gilding the world. Wonderfully, miraculously, a pair of ospreys swept in from the bay and dived, coming up empty-footed and sweeping away again, jeering.

"Your ospreys are back," I said to Cam, downstairs in his urn. "I don't know where the nest is, but I'll find it and let you know."

Talking to Cam was a great help. If it meant I was delusional, so be it. I didn't think it did; I had always talked aloud to myself at

times. But it terrified my children, so I would have to remember not
to do it when they were around.

"What's with you?" I said to Silas, turning over to look at him. His
narrowed yellow eyes were only inches from my face, and the white
scar that cut, Harry Potter–like, across his forehead looked disreputable, lower class.

"Any old port in a storm, is it?"

Last night, when I had finally stumbled, foggy and bone weary,
upstairs to bed, I had found Silas curled in the middle of the big bed
where Cam and I had always slept. He raised his bullet head and glared
at me.

"I'm not sleeping there," I said to him. "Not ever again. If you
want company you can damn well come into my room with me."

"Like that's going to happen."

"Suit yourself," I said, feeling my heart wrenching because I
knew why he was there. It was where Cam had always been. Silas
was Cam's cat to the marrow of his shambling bones, and had been,
ever since Cam found him shivering at a construction site as a kitten
and brought him home in his pocket. His first act, after he had come
out from under the refrigerator and decided we might work out as
a family, was to toil his way up the length of Cam's body, stretched
out watching the Senators play, and shove his nose into Cam's neck.
He sniffed, great, rattling sniffs, his spiky tail stuck straight out and
quivering, and then curled up in the hollow of Cam's neck and went
to sleep. It was where he had slept for many of his nights, whenever
we were home or at Edgewater, even after he had become a large and
cumbersome cat with a great mass of abdomen and sharp small feet.
Cam finally gave up pushing him away. Silas always sneaked back
in the night, and would wake both of us in the morning, his face
buried in Cam's neck, his startling, vacuum-cleaner grumble loud
in our ears.

"I told you you smelled strange. Nice strange, but not like any-body else," I told Cam.

"How many other necks have you smelled?"

"Well, Silas smells it, too."

"Then I must smell like Kitty Rations seafood dinner," he said, naming Silas's favored brand of sustenance, which stank so horribly I could barely feed him sometimes.

"I wouldn't even be in the same house with you if you did," I said, sniffing his neck, pushing Silas's big face away and putting my face into Cam's neck.

"Move your fat face," Silas growled.

"I'm bigger than you," I replied.

Last night I knew I should have cajoled and comforted him. But I could not seem to do anything about it. This morning, he stared at me and wriggled as though he could not get comfortable, and looked into the hall and back at me.

"He's gone, Silas. He can't come back. But I'm here."

"Well, I know that. Do you think I don't know that?"

But he still seemed uneasy and a little truculent, kneading the bedclothes fussily with his big hooked claws.

"We can't sleep in that bed anymore because he died there, just a little over a week ago," I said to him. "Or at least I can't. You can sleep wherever you want, but I hope it will be with me. I need you, you mangy old tub of lard."

Silas sat up and stared at me greenly.

"What do you mean he died there? What was he doing up here? It wasn't time for us to come up here yet."

"I don't know. I think he was working on a surprise for me. But that's the thing I need to find out. Can you hang with me, do you think?"

"Oh, I guess so."

Cam's death at Edgewater was a world-blasting thing for all of us. The death would have been enough; to lose him so suddenly on a silky June night when the Tidewater lay at the bottom of a globe of stars was pain enough to shatter lives and heave them in bizarre directions, like an earthquake. But to lose him when he was all alone in a place where he was not supposed to be, or at least one that was not his avowed destination, was anguished lunacy, madness making.

"*Why?*" we wept over and over. "*Why?*" I can still hear my daughters' voices spiraling up into the razor-edged panic of childhood. "I don't care if he didn't tell you! Why didn't you *know* where he was?"

Sick and stunned myself, I could only answer, "I thought he was in Green Bay. It's where he said he was going, to work on that Unitarian church up there. He always uses his cell phone, so I do too; I talked to him only a few hours before, and I thought he was in Green Bay . . ."

Cam's reputation as an architect had grown to the point that he could choose his projects, and they took him literally all over the globe. So on the rare times I was not with him, we simply used our cell phones. He could be anywhere at any time I talked to him, I realized, but why would he bother to mislead us? I could think of no other reason but another woman, and that notion was simply too ludicrous to entertain. I went with him on the majority of his trips after the girls were old enough. He had always been adamant about that, and since I did not like being without him either, I went whenever it was possible. Indeed, the first and only time I chose not to go was the occasion of the biggest and most rending, searing fight we had ever had. I didn't make that choice again.

"The only thing I know about it is that it was very sudden, an aneurysm, the doctor thinks, and he had just enough warning to call 911," I told my daughters. "He was lying on our bed when he called, and they found him there. He died before the EMTs could get him to the hospital in Blue Hill, and the doctor there was about to call me when Toby Halliday came running into the emergency room. One of the EMTs knew that Toby and Laurie kept the place up for us, so he'd called Toby. It was Toby who called me. I'll always be grateful for that."

"Why?" Betsy shrieked, struggling out of her husband's arms to come and stand before me, fists balled. "Dead is dead! Why the hell should you care who called you?"

Kitty Howard came up and put her arm around Betsy's shoulder and led her, none too gently, back to her husband.

"Because when you lose somebody you love it helps a great deal to be told by someone who loved them too," she said to Betsy. "I hope you won't ever have to find out that way, but if you do maybe you'll see what I mean."

Kitty was right. I think the clipped downeast accent of a young doctor I did not know bearing the news of Cam's death would have been like drowning in icy water. Toby, who loved Cam, had both pain and iron in his voice. It was right.

"Lilly," he'd said, "it's Toby Halliday, up to the cove. I have some real bad news for you, honey, and I want you to sit down. Is there anybody with you?"

"Yes," I said. "My friend Kitty Howard is here; you remember her, don't you? She helped you and Cam haul that branch off the roof after that storm—"

I was chattering. Worse than chattering. I could hear my own voice chipping out the words, knowing that Toby's voice held more than regret for a damaged roof or a break-in.

"I know." He cut me off. "Listen, baby, there ain't no better way to tell you. Cam was up here in the bedroom at Edgewater and he . . . he felt bad and called the EMTs, far as we can tell, and they lost him before they could get to the hospital."

"Lost him? How could they *lose* him?" I was screaming. I could hear it. Kitty got up from her chair and came swiftly and put her arms around me.

"He died, honey. The doctors say there wasn't anything more they could have done. Aneurysm in his brain; could have been there since he was born. They don't think he suffered. Anyway, I wanted to tell you that I'm going to bring him home."

"Bring him home . . ."

"Come on the plane with him. You can meet us when we get in and tell us what you . . . want us to do. But I'm not letting him come by himself."

I had started to cry.

"Why was he up there, Toby? He was supposed to be in Wisconsin."

"Well, don't know. Nobody seems to have seen him or talked to him. But the EMTs found a rolled-up drawing on the bed beside him, and some specs. They were labeled 'a sculptor's studio on the coast of Maine.' Real pretty, looked to me. Looked right out over the bay toward Sunderson's Island, where the ospreys nest. Figured it was for you. Looks like it was a surprise, don't it."

"Yes," I sobbed, sagging against Kitty. "It was a surprise. I've always wanted one. I just never thought it would kill him . . ."

"Hush, deah," he said. "This thing could have happened anywhere, anytime. I'm glad I was here to be with 'im."

"Oh, Toby, so am I." I wept, and was still weeping drunkenly, monotonously, leaning still on Kitty, when the early morning plane from Bangor touched down at Dulles with my husband and our friend on it.

I must have drifted back into sleep on this first Maine morning without Cam, because when I woke for good and all the midmorning sun was pouring into the open window of my childhood room, riding on a piney, kelpy little breeze, I could hear the clanging of the sail lines from the Friendship, and somewhere far off a lawn mower sang its summer song. I was out of bed in an instant, finding in my drawer an oversized faded T-shirt of Jeebs's that read GROTTIES RULE. I pulled it on over the jeans I had left in a heap on the floor the night before. I padded barefoot out into the hall and down the front stairs, the seagrass carpeting just as spongy and malodorous as it had always been. I began to trot, Silas grumbling at my heels. I could smell coffee and blueberry muffins from the kitchen, as I had every summer morning I could remember, and there was laughter. They were all there, my crowd of summer henchmen, and I was late.

Just before I reached the door I stopped. I had not really heard laughter; I knew that, but it shivered in the air as laughter sometimes does when it is over, leaving little surges of warm motion and particles of itself, like sparkle dust. I had always known when someone had been laughing at Edgewater.

I stood still and silent, listening, remembering. I was not ten or eleven and no one waited for me to lead a forbidden adventure. My small summer cadre had scattered long ago, and I stood alone in the big house on the morning after I had brought my husband's ashes here. The reality of it washed over me like cold water, but even though I tightened my muscles against it, no pain came. I felt a huge, warm, diffuse protection around me, the kind a child feels on a summer morning when nothing seems wrong and all things seem possible. I had felt it last night, too. Something in this house, perhaps the house itself, knew I was here; was looking after me. I had thought being alone here would be the hardest thing; I had never been alone anywhere. But I was not alone. I knew that as certainly as I knew the smell of coffee and blueberries from the kitchen was real.

"*Open the damned door! Did you bring me all this way to starve me?*"

"It's a thought," I told Silas, and pushed the kitchen door open and went in. I would consider the source of my well-being later. Or maybe I wouldn't. Wasn't it gift enough, when I had thought to have only pain and loneliness?

The coffeepot was plugged in and perking, and there was a plate of blueberry scones on the kitchen table. It was Laurie Halliday, I knew right away; since she and Toby had taken over for Clara and Seth, early in our marriage, we had had scones and not muffins.

"They're good, but they're not a patch on Clara's muffins," I'd told Cam. "I grew up on those muffins. Every kid in the cove did. My gang always got here early so they could get them while they were hot. One way or another, we fed every kid in Carter's Cove all those summers."

"I wish I'd known you then," he'd said, buttering another scone. "From what your father says, you were all wild as woods colts and you were the leader of the pack. I'd love to have met your partners in crime."

"I wish you had," I said then.

Now I said, to myself, "But of course, in a way you have," and poured a cup of coffee and opened the tin of Silas's food. The smell knocked me back a step or two.

"How *can* you?" I said to him from across the room.

"Well, since it's all you ever give me . . ."

"Don't start with me," I said to him. "We've bought you every kind of cat food on the market. You turned your nose up at everything but this. Remember the time when your daddy offered you filet mignon in wine sauce and you ran like a scalded—whatever? And the time I gave you vitello tonnato and you took one bite and threw it up all over the kitchen? And *that* had tuna in it."

"I recall nothing of the sort," he growled with his mouth full of stinking seafood cuts.

I found a note on the table, propped against a small glass vase full of lupine. My mother had always loved lupine.

Call us if you need anything at all, Laurie had written. *I'll check with you later today. We are heartbroken.*

And I thought they really were. They were as good friends as we had in Carter's Cove, and certainly up the road in the colony, where people seldom sailed or went junking or shared dinner with their housekeepers and handymen. I knew people talked about us, but then, they always had, first about my mother and now about my family. Cam's affection for Toby ran deep; he would have loved knowing that Toby had brought him home to me and got right back on the plane and went all the way back to Bangor. I'd begged him to stay, but he only said, "You'll be wanting your family around you now. I've already said my good-byes. And I hope we'll see you-all this summer. Ain't gon' be right without Cam, but it'd be a thousand times worse without you and the girls, and without your daddy and his wife, too."

I'd never told the Hallidays that Tatty was not my father's wife, though she lived with him in a pretty stone retirement community north of Reston and took, probably, better care of him than my mother ever had. They were inseparable, and few people knew they were not married. Not that it would have mattered much, though Tatty never ceased to press for legitimacy.

To this my father, who was drifting as comfortably into Alzheimer's as he might have into a sweet calm on the Friendship, said only, "We are married, dear. Don't you remember that awful affair at the church in Georgetown? I can't recall the name now, but Lilly will know—must have been a hundred degrees in the shade."

Whether or not he thought Tatty was my mother at times we never knew, but he was affectionate and serene with her, and we blessed her feverently. I suppose she worried about inheriting; I don't think the general left her much money, but Jeebs and I had decided to leave her our share of my father's estate when the time came. My father had given the house on Kalorama Circle to Jeebs, and there he lived quietly and absentmindedly, doing work for the government so esoteric that we could not have comprehended it had he told us about it, with his wife, a pale, nervous, hair-twiddling, distracted woman named Virginia whom he met at MIT and whose IQ was, if anything, higher than Jeebs's. She did a great deal of consulting work, but she had always stayed home with their three boys, all thin, bespectacled replicas of Jeebs at that age, who bade fair to grow up and follow their father and mother into inner—or outer—space. All of them were, of course, Grotties. Since Virginia was apparently incapable of getting a meal together, we did not see a lot of them except when I lured them out to our house on the James, where they twitched and fiddled until it was time to go back into their cave on Kalorama. My girls couldn't abide Jeebs's boys, and the girls terrified them, so it was with relief that we finally all decided to observe holidays and such with only a few kin and friends. We had the girls, of course, and their friends, and my father and Tatty and Christmas and birthday fetes, and Jeebs and Virginia had a small covey of pale geniuses who sometimes looked around the table in surprise, having forgotten it was Christmas.

It was I who most loved the holidays in our beautiful old James River house. The furniture and silver and crystal gleamed with the efforts of the small, quiet cadre of help who had, apparently, come with the house. We moved into it when Cam's grandmother died, about three years after our marriage. Cam's mother and father took all their vast holdings and shinnied off to a townhouse in Georgetown so storied and beautiful that tour bus after tour bus slowed down passing it, and there was always a cluster of ladies with notebooks and pens in front of it.

It might have been a rather awkward situation, because Cam's grandmother had left him the house and a small trust fund and the senior McCalls found themselves suddenly homeless. But they were eager to go, Cam's father because Georgetown was closer to his banks and his clubs, and his mother because she had never really liked living on the river anyway. The bugs bit her and the humidity ruined her hair and her nail polish almost never dried, and in Georgetown she could command whole ranks of society instead of luring them in small batches out to McCall's Point. All the beautiful, rather shabby antique furniture belonged to Cam and me, but that was apparently all right, too. Mrs. McCall bought an entire English village's worth of antiques and proclaimed them finer and more distinguished and expensive than ours. They probably were. Neither Cam nor I minded. So McCall's Point was, as they say, our primary residence, and I never thought of it as anything but home. My girls grew up scratching the furniture and heel-marking the priceless pine floors and burning wonderful old silk velvet chair coverings with their brief forays into smoking. Our succession of dogs contributed their own homely damage. Silas, when he came, peed on everything until he considered the house properly marked, and then he selected a Philadelphia Chippendale sofa as a scratching post. I simply tossed a gypsy shawl over it. Cam would not have let me punish Silas anyway. By that time they were all but joined at the hip.

There was little or no inherited money, except the trust fund that at least paid the taxes, but we required little, and by the time the girls discovered clothes and status and schools, Cam was making really quite a lot of money. And I was beginning to.

I did, indeed, get my degree from George Washington, though in English, not folklore, for the school offered no such. I soon got pregnant with Betsy, and after that with Alice, and working was out of the question for a long while. Cam adored the little girls, both of whom looked almost amazingly like him, except they both had my gray eyes and crops of my two-toned bronze and gilt curls. I was pleased to see a little of myself and my side of our family in them, because from the moment they were born, almost, they were Cam's creatures and no one else's. When he had to be away on work, as he did increasingly in those years, they were inconsolable, and when I could not accompany him as I had done through my first pregnancy, he was short-tempered and anxious, and seemed to me almost afraid.

"You know I can't go and leave them," I would point out, reasonably enough, I thought.

"Can't your dad and Tatty take them for a little while?"

"Cam, Alice is still nursing. And Daddy's just plain past having a houseful of children. I absolutely have to stay here and look after them. There'll be plenty of trips after they're grown-up enough to leave."

"And who will look after you?" he said. His face was white and drawn. We really were going to have to talk about this when he got home.

"I'll look after myself. I'm a big girl now. And there's Daddy and Tatty and the whole staff, and the Cardins just downriver, and there's always Kitty."

"Kitty's what I'm afraid of," he said sulkily and left before I could ask him what he meant. But after that, when the girls were small and he had to go out of town, at least he did not fuss openly, though I know he was never happy about it.

CHAPTER

16

It was on the beach at Edgewater, when the girls were toddlers, that I found what I wanted to do, work for both my hands and my heart. We had a small crescent of sand, as well as pebbles and boulders, and the sand was where we made sand castles and filled pails with seawater. I was always shivering when the rushing tide caught my bare feet and legs, but the girls apparently never felt it. They had to be pried off the beach at twilight, purple with cold and yelling lustily.

One day I was reading on an old blanket while they piled up a castle and dribbled wet sand for its turrets. I was reading about centaurs, and almost as if my hands knew before my mind did, I scraped together a rough, primitive horse's body and made a manikin atop it, and dribbled him a mane and tail. Tiny clamshells were his eyes, and seaweed was his beard. The girls were enchanted. I told them about centaurs, and when Cam came in from sailing the Friendship, he looked at it and laughed with pleasure.

"It's good. It's really good, Lil. I always thought centaurs were nasty, warring creatures, but this one is a charmer, a Disney centaur. You could make a living doing this."

About that time Betsy launched herself onto the centaur's back and his legs crumbled and the sea caught him, and I took her inside, howling. But I did not forget what Cam had said. The primitive little sculpture felt right. I could do other things; there was the whole pantheon of Greek gods, and then the Norse ones. And from that afternoon, slowly, the thing that I do best and love took shape.

On this first Maine morning I buttered a scone and went into the living room, where Laurie had opened the windows to the sea air and put another pitcher of lupine on the old coffee table.

I looked up at Cam in his urn. Silas had settled himself on Cam's old sweater on the corner of the sofa, turned around three times, and gone to sleep.

"It's a gorgeous day," I said to my husband. "It's your kind of day. You know every year about March when you always say 'Washington is where I go to wait to come to Maine'? Well, this is the kind of day you meant."

I thought about the morning, waking up without him, expecting to feel agony and feeling, instead, the arms of Edgewater around me. I thought about the laughter I had almost heard, the laughter of children. The laughter of that last summer, with a new laugh in the mix.

"I felt for the longest time this morning like I was ten or eleven or so," I told him, "and breakfast was waiting for me, and everybody was downstairs waiting for me to plan the day, and I thought I heard them laughing—no, I didn't hear it and I wasn't remembering it. It was like I was feeling somebody else remember it. I thought it might be you, because I think I feel you close to me up here, keeping me safe. And I don't mean I think you're a ghost. I just think you've left a chunk of yourself here, and it's your presence that was remembering. It was always your favorite place on earth. But it couldn't have been you because you didn't know me when I was a child up here."

And then slowly the knowledge came.

"But you did know us, didn't you? You found out all about us that time you came up here by yourself after the storm, and I wouldn't come with you, and we had that horrible, stupid fight about it.

"That's when everything changed . . ."

Though we had had other squabbles like any other couple, senseless, meaningless collisions that were forgotten almost as soon as they passed, we had never had a fight like this. It was a terrible fight, a wounding thing. It divided time.

It was early spring in our twentieth year of marriage, and Cam came in early from the office, his forehead furrowed.

"Toby called this afternoon. That last nor'easter took off the roof of the kitchen wing and a tree went down over the bedrooms at that end. They can't be fixed; we'll have to rebuild. I made some sketches for you to look at on the way—you always hated that kitchen anyway. We'll do it right this time. Can you be ready to go tomorrow morning? I've already called Kitty and she'll come over and stay till we get back; it shouldn't take more than a few days."

I was silent, and he stopped talking and looked at me.

"Cam," I said, "I just can't go. I'm maybe two days away from finishing the *Green Man*, and the parks department wants him in place when the children's exhibit opens. There's just no time."

I was working on my first large civic commission, though I had done pieces for private homes for years. This one was to stand at the entrance of a special area set aside in Rock Creek Park for children, with exhibits and nature trails and a picnic house. They wanted figures of mythological and folklore creatures scattered about, and had come to me. The Green Man came to mind instantly, that most ancient of semi-deities who symbolized the meeting of the spirits of the forest and of man. Rock Creek Park was wild in places, and I thought a traditional Green Man, with his satyr's face and legs and arms of green branches, might well frighten the youngest children.

So I had created a chubby, smiling figure who knelt half in and half out of the woods crowned with leaves and twined around with vines. You still got the idea, but he didn't frighten. The parks department loved him, and loved the sketches I had given them for the other figures for the park. I worked hastily and with love and total absorption. I had thought Cam knew how important this was to me.

He looked at me in silence.

"You're saying you're not coming with me."

"Well, yes. I guess that's what I'm saying."

His face whitened and the muscles around his mouth stood out.

"I want you to come with me, Lilly. I need you with me. There's no reason for you not to come."

"I have a deadline!" I shouted. "You know about deadlines, don't you? Those things you have to meet or they fire you? Lord, the whole world stops when you have one, but just let me get within spitting distance of my first one—"

"You don't know what you're doing to me!" he shouted back.

"I'm not doing anything except trying to finish my work on time, as per contracted. God almighty, Cam, you've been to Edgewater without me, and other places, too."

"But never because you just chose not to go. There was always a *reason*."

"There *is* a reason!" I shouted again. "What's the matter with you? You sound like I'm letting you march into the valley of the shadow of death all by yourself. You said yourself it's just a few days!"

He stood looking at me for a long time. The fury came off him in waves; I had never seen him like this. He was trembling. And I could have sworn there were tears standing in his eyes.

I opened my mouth to say that of course I would go, something, anything, but he made a motion at me that meant shut up.

289

"I'm going tonight," he said levelly. "There's a plane out of National to Boston at nine. I can make it if I hurry."

He turned and went upstairs toward our bedroom, and I started to go after him, and then stopped. I had nothing to apologize for. My reason for staying was as logical as his for going.

But I felt tears start in my eyes, too.

In a few minutes he came back down. I was in the kitchen starting dinner for myself and the girls, a dinner I knew I would not eat, and I did not see him. But I heard him. He went straight through the kitchen and hall and to the front door. I heard it open.

"Cam, call me, please," I called after him. "I don't know what this means, but I can't stand all this anger."

The door slammed shut. I waited until I heard his sleek BMW purr into life and glide away, and then I ran to the phone and called Kitty.

She let me spill it all out to her before she said anything, and then she said, "Well, he's acting like a horse's ass, of course. A spoiled horse's ass. I expect it has a lot to do with his sister, don't you? He probably doesn't even realize it."

I was silent, and then said, stupidly, "His sister? We don't ever see Deirdre; she and her husband cast their lot with Cam's folks, and we hardly speak. He doesn't even *like* her."

She took a long breath and let it out slowly.

"He hasn't told you about his little sister, has he?"

"Little . . . no. He hasn't. Nobody has. I didn't even know he had one."

"He doesn't, now," she said. Her voice was thick and dead, not at all the vibrant shout I was used to.

"You're going to have to tell me," I quavered. "You know you are, Kitty."

"Yes. I know. I'll tell you. And when he gets back and out of his snit I'm going to wring his neck. Cam's mother had a little girl when he was about five. She was a beautiful little thing; like a doll. Mrs. McCall played with her exactly like a doll. Dressed her up in frilly clothes, painted her nails, took her everywhere, like a toy poodle. Deirdre was old enough so that she had her own crowd and her own activities, and Cam was all boy and had his own pack, too. I don't imagine they were jealous of all the attention the little sister got, but they had to have noticed. Carrie—her name was Caroline—was just as spoiled and headstrong as you might imagine, growing up with all that attention and adulation. Even the old man paraded her around at parties and things, though I've never been sure he knew he had two other children besides her. Well, one afternoon Madame McCall was late to have her nails done, and she called Cam in from the river, where he and some of the little black kids from downriver were crabbing, and shoved Sister Carrie at him in her little yellow sundress and matching sandals and told him to watch her till she got home, not to take his eyes off her, not to leave her alone for an instant. So of course, because he wasn't quite eight at the time, Cam did take his eyes off her for a minute, just long enough for her to run straight down into the river. The boys dived for her as long as they could, but the current is strong there, and she was found way downstream."

"Oh, my God," I breathed.

"Of course, his mother had hysterics that lasted about two years," she said, "and his father was so angry at him that he sent him off to Episcopal and boarded him there. He didn't really come back home until he started architecture school, and he lived away from home then, too. I think he saw his grandmother quite often, but to his mother and father he was the little bastard who let their darling drown. We all knew it; he was our playmate on his holiday breaks, and we simply and completely loved him, and hated his parents. Even our families felt sorry for him. But he never said a word about it. There simply isn't anything you can do about a thing like that. I can't imagine why he hasn't told you. It's the thing that's shaped his life."

"What do you mean?"

"Well, I've told you that whenever he had a girl before he met you, he would never let her out of his sight. He was with her every second he could be. Then she'd fade away and another one would come along and it was the same thing. When you finally appeared, we watched like hawks to see if you were going to make the cut—you know he never wanted you to be anywhere but with him—and when you did, we all cheered. We thought now that he had someone he could really be with all the time."

"Kitty," I said as levelly as I could manage, "are you saying that Cam married me because I reminded him of his dead sister?"

"Oh, shit, of course not, Lilly. You were so beautiful then that you stopped breath, and you were funny, and nice, and—I don't know—absolutely unspoiled. Not naive, exactly, but kind of . . . untouched. Any man would have wanted to be the one that touched you. I'm just saying that we hoped he would finally stop beating up on himself for the drowning. Although I really think it's a subconscious thing with him now."

"Kitty, *he was only seven years old!*"

"Yes. Yes, he was. And my advice to you is that you sit him down and talk this thing out the minute he gets back. He had no right to keep it from you."

I spent the rest of the weekend working furiously on the *Green Man*, hardly pausing except to get meals for the girls and eat myself. I worked so late into the nights that I fell into bed without time to think, too tired even to dream. When Cam's behavior and my talk with Kitty did batter their way into my mind, I simply had to sit down with the weight of it and stare into space at nothing. When I thought of Cam I saw no face. When I thought of myself, I saw only a child so small and helpless that she was, to me, repugnant. Almost all couples, I thought at one point, have one or two secrets they keep from each other. But not the ones that defined life, skewed souls. Cam's secret was almost literally who he was. I thought there must be something in me that kept him from trusting me with that pain.

He came home on the third day, earlier than I had thought he would. I had not heard from him, and I had not called him. For those three days I felt he would forever be a stranger to me, and I'd wondered drearily how one made a life with a stranger who had not been a stranger for the twenty years that went before.

He came into the kitchen just as I was boiling water for pasta. The girls were upriver at a friend's birthday party, and I thought just pasta and butter would hold me nicely. I had just heard his quiet feet when I felt his arms go around me from behind and his lips fasten and linger on my sweaty neck. I froze for an instant, and then all my muscles, not knowing that there had been a quarrel, loosened, and I simply leaned back against him, feeling the sweet warmth of his body flow into mine like honey, like wine. I dropped my head and began to cry. He turned me around in his arms and pushed the hair off my face and looked at me, and then tears came into his blue eyes, too. He pulled me back against him.

"I'm so sorry. Just so, so sorry, Lilly. I don't know what got into me and I can't believe I let it spill all over you. I was afraid to call you because I thought you might have just—packed up the girls and left. And I didn't answer the phone because I was so afraid I'd hear the same thing."

"I didn't call." I hiccupped into the front of his shirt. "I didn't know who would answer."

He rocked me in silence for a while, and then said, "I promise never again to be such an asshole, to you or anyone else. But especially to you. I can't bear the thought of you not being with me, Lil."

"Me, either," I said, hugging him hard. "But at some point we need to talk about it, Cam."

"You're right. At some point we will. Christ, I need a shower. Is there time for a drink before dinner?"

"Yes," I said, reaching up into a cabinet to get out the martini pitcher. I heard him open the door to the bathroom, and then pause.

"I met somebody who knows you," he called. "Or used to, anyway."

"Who?" I asked, unscrewing the top of the vodka bottle.

"Her name is Roberta Singleton, but she said you'd know her as Peaches Davenport."

By the time I could get my breath back I had spilled half the vodka. I stuck a forefinger into it and licked it absently. I decided then and there to drink a great deal of it.

"Well," I said, in as bright and offhand a voice as I could manage. "Ol' Peaches Davenport. Is she still so beautiful that people stop and stare at her on the street? Does she still pull the wings off flies?"

"She said you didn't like her when you were kids. She also said it was with good reason. She said she had done a terrible thing that summer, something she never got over. But she also said what a magical place Edgewater was then, and how all the kids just ran wild on their bicycles and in their Beetle Cats and played outside under the stars, and swam in the bay—all the things she had never done before. You know her parents had died the year before in a car accident, and that she came to Edgewater with her grandfather and grandmother. I gather they raised her. It couldn't have been much fun for her. I think she envied you; she said you were wild and pretty, like your mother, and leader of the pack. For the first time I got a real sense of what you kids and the summer must have been like."

"So is she still the lady of the manor?" I said sarcastically, pouring vodka over ice.

"Not so's you'd know it," he said, his voice muffled in the towel. "Her grandparents are dead, and they left her the old Maine house— she was up looking it over, to see if she wanted to sell it, when she saw my car at Edgewater and came over to meet me—and I think she got a little money from them, but her husband died of prostate cancer five years ago, and she's got a young teenage girl with cystic fibrosis, in a special school near Monmouth, and a younger girl at home. They live in New Jersey; her husband taught theology at Princeton. She's not bad looking, but she's thin and frail. She works in some government job to keep her girls in school."

"I'm sorry," I muttered, having no idea whether I was or not. It was a sad story, but with Peaches you could never really know the truth. My heart was pounding as if trying to leap out of my chest. I did not want to remember any more of that summer.

I took the drinks out on the patio that faced the twilit river and sat down at a little wicker table. In a moment he joined me, comb tracks still in his damp hair and a fresh blue oxford-cloth shirt rolled up his tanned arms. He smelled of the lemon-sage bubble bath I used.

He lifted his glass and tapped mine with it. I gulped mine down.

"So is she going to keep the house?" I said.

"Don't know. I went over and looked at it with her, and she cooked supper for me, and we talked for a long time. She has fond memories of the house, she says, but she could get a good price for it if she put it on the market. I looked it all over. Just needs cosmetic work. I get the feeling that she'll sell. I don't feel that she thinks there's anything there for her now."

"There never was," I said mulishly, not looking at him. I could not bear the idea of Peaches Davenport playing the poor wounded victim of cold fate with Cam. Peaches wasn't a victim; Peaches *made* victims.

He drained his drink too, and made us both another. Then he

looked at me across the flickering candle I had lit, both for light and to ward off the shoals of strafing mosquitoes boiling in up out of the river.

"Why didn't you tell me about Jon?" he said.

I felt a surge of fury so profound it took my breath. I felt as if someone had taken the deepest and most intimate part of me and ripped it out and held it up to the light. God damn Peaches Davenport. Was one death not enough for Jon?

"Why didn't you tell me about Carrie?" I said coldly.

He sighed. It was a deep, defeated sigh.

"I knew Kitty would get around to it," he said heavily.

"Why not you, Cam?" I was near tears. "Why couldn't you have told me in the very beginning? Why carry that awful thing around with you all these years, when I thought we knew everything there was to know about each other?"

He didn't speak for a long time. When he did, his voice was thin and small, like a child's.

"I thought you would hate me for letting my sister die."

"How could I hate you? I *love* you! Did you honestly think I would blame you for that? My God, Cam, you were only seven years old! How could *anybody* blame you? Why did your mother leave you alone with your sister at that age, anyway? Didn't anybody ever think to blame her?"

"I don't know," he said dully. "Nobody ever talked to me about it again. I was plopped into Episcopal before I could get my breath, and when I came home I stayed with Granny in her wing. She was furious with my mother and father, but she didn't talk to me about Carrie either. They had consulted some psychologist or something, and he said the best thing would be for us simply not to discuss it again. So my sister drowned twice. Once in the river and once on our frozen tongues."

"How did you feel about all that?"

"You know how I felt? At first I felt as if I wasn't fit to live on God's earth anymore. And then I began to be angry at my sister, and after a while I came to absolutely hate her. If it weren't for her I wouldn't be a walking dung heap. And then, finally, I just forgot her. If you think it has escaped me that I hover over everybody I love, that I live in terror when I am away from you, it hasn't. I hoped it would never come to the point that it smothered you, but of course, it had to. My God, when you refused to go with me to Edgewater I was so angry at you I could have wrung your neck."

"What got you over that?"

"Well, Peaches did. She could tell I was upset, and somehow over dinner I just told her everything. She's easy to talk to. So she told me about Jon, about everything, about her part in it, and how awful she's felt ever since, and suddenly I had the answers to some things I've always wondered about you."

"Ah," I said. "And they would be?"

"About how you virtually disappeared into your father's house after your mother died, and about burying yourself in swimming and never dating, about being so naive and vulnerable for your age. I saw that you had been fighting the pain the only way you knew how, just like I had."

"I believe you said some *things* you'd wondered about."

He dropped his head. "Lil, I always felt when we met, and that— that absolute bonfire sprang up between us, and you came to love me so easily and naturally, especially after the way your father had raised you, that it was like you'd—oh, it was like something you'd done before. You just knew how to love me without stumbling and stuttering. I loved it, of course. But I wondered. And when Peaches said that she'd never seen two people of any age so much in love as you and Jon were—"

"Damn Peaches!" I shouted, beginning to cry. "I was eleven years old, Cam! Jon was twelve! We didn't even know each other more than a few weeks! What the fuck is it that you thought Jon and I did?"

"Nothing, really," he whispered, tears on his face catching the flickering candlelight. "I knew you, I know you, I know you haven't loved anybody but me. I dishonored you even to have it cross my mind. I just wish I'd known. Maybe I could have saved you some of that pain."

"Cam, did you marry me to save me because you couldn't save your sister?"

"Jesus, no! I married you because I couldn't wait to be with you for the rest of the days I have on earth, and because you were so beautiful you stopped my heart, and because you were smart and funny and almost a princess locked up in a tower—"

"That's what I mean! You just wanted to save me."

"Bullshit," he said at last, beginning to grin a little. "It was just easier to get you away from your daddy than from twenty-five other guys buzzing around you. It just meant that I could fuck you a lot sooner. But if you'd rather have done it any other way . . ."

"No," I said, still crying but smiling, and stood up and held out my hand. "Let's go do it the same old way. And Peaches Davenport is *not* invited."

"I should hope not," he said, taking my hand. "God help me."

I dreamed that night, a dream that frightened me more than any I had ever had, and even today I cannot speak of it. I dreamed that Cam and I were at some sort of county fair—maybe the yearly Labor Day Blue Hill Fair, which we both loved—and there was a booth that said, KISS YOUR GIRL AND WIN A PRIZE. The midway was thronged with people, but Cam took me into his arms anyway, and kissed me so powerfully and long that I felt myself start to sag against him, and returned the kiss hungrily.

A bell jangled, and from behind the stage on the booth Peaches Davenport's head appeared, painted on metal or plastic or something, one-dimensional and terrible, somehow, beyond imagining.

"Kiss her again and you'll get two prizes," she intoned tinnily, the great, stretched smile not moving.

Cam kissed me again, this time so deeply and intimately that I felt the familiar heat start up in the pit of my stomach, and moaned, and thought, *We can't do this here in front of all these people!* and tried to pull away, but he wouldn't let me go.

The bell clanged again, and Peaches' insane painted face popped up again and shrilled, "One more time and you get the grand prize!"

The kiss this time was different; it began almost tentatively, a soft searching for my mouth, and then becoming deeper and deeper and scaldingly sweet, and I lost my breath and felt the fire explode in my stomach and could only stand there, held up by his arms, gasping for breath and throbbing with completion, too ashamed to raise my eyes. He took his hand and lifted my chin and then I did look at him. It was Jon.

"You win it all!" screeched Peaches. "You win everything!"

I came awake gagging for breath and trembling and running sweat all over. I hadn't ever read much Jung, but I knew without a doubt that this dream meant something enormous to me, and I would see it if I examined it. I would rather have cut my own throat than do so. The nearly full moon, the Egg Moon, I think, rose very late that year and it flooded me with its silver light just as dawn cracked the world and its pink yolk showed through. I scrambled as far away from Cam in the big bed as I could. I was afraid the violent trembling would wake him.

It did. He rolled over and put his arms around me from behind and said, "You all right? You're shaking like a leaf. Come let me hug you till it stops."

"I'm okay." I quaked. "It was just a dream."

"Some dream," Cam said. "You'd better tell me about it or you'll carry it around with you forever, and that's no good."

"No," I said, pulling away from him and sitting up on the side of the bed. "I don't even remember what it was about."

"Okay," he said after a moment, and turned over on his side and burrowed back into sleep. I dug myself deep under the comforter and buried my head in my down pillows, but I didn't sleep. I knew I wouldn't.

Dawn was well on its way when I finally got up and went to make coffee.

Always, until tonight, there were two secrets between us, I thought drearily. *And then there were none. And now there's another, and I made it. I guess the second time is easier.*

Off Season

CHAPTER

17

I got up off the old couch at Edgewater, feeling all of a sudden new and shriven and young, like a forgiven child. I wanted to dance, to sing, to be everywhere at once in my most-loved world, to touch and experience everything Edgewater had meant to me. At first I did not know where the impulse came from; it would have made far more sense to revisit the places that Cam and I came to love and make our own, after we were married. After all, I had come here to celebrate him and find a permanent place in my mind and heart for him, a place I could live in when I had to go home. Home: how strange. This was home. It always had been. Funny that I had never seen that before.

And then I realized that what I wanted to do was show Cam my childhood world—all of it, not just the pieces of it sullied by Peaches Davenport.

I did the first crazy thing of many I would do that summer, or so anyone who saw me would have said. I found a small, heavy ivory envelope that I recognized as one of my mother's embossed Crane informals, and opened the urn, and very carefully shook a little cloud of Cam into it, and sealed it, and put it in the pocket of Jeebs's old shirt.

"You know your Edgewater like the back of your hand," I said, "but you don't know all *my* Edgewater. We're going to take the Grand Tour." I started up the stairs.

"Where are you going?" Silas said.

"I'm going to show Cam Edgewater like it was when I was a little girl," I said. "You want to come?"

"You're crazy as bat shit," Silas grumbled, but he unwound himself from the sweater and stumped after me, muttering grumpily.

We started with the rooms on the second floor.

"When I was little this was the guest room," I said to Cam, indicating the light-flooded front room facing the sea that Cam had made into his studio. "I remember there were always people in it, or nearly always, but I don't remember who they were. Well, Aunt Tatty was one. Daddy hated it when she visited. He always used this bathroom and she left powder all over the sink and hung wet stockings on the shower-curtain rail. He had to share the bathroom that went with his and Mother's bedroom, and that was just as bad. Mother had a lot of stuff to put on her face lying around.

"This was Jeebs's room, when he was in it. But he stayed gone a lot, visiting his pre-Grotty friends. Clara sometimes used it for an ironing room.

"This was my room—well, you know that. I'm staying there again. Silas and I simply can't sleep in the bed where you died. It's just too sad. Maybe in a week or two—my beds are awfully small, and Silas has the biggest, knobbiest feet I ever saw on a cat."

Silas bit my ankle.

We reached the back room, where Mother had had her painting studio. I pushed the door open; during our marriage we had used it as one of the children's rooms, with pretty twin beds and my grandmother's old lace curtains, limp and yellowed now. Both Betsy and Alice had loved it, chiefly because it was so far away from ours, and it was mostly where they slept. There was a faint scent of bath powder and sweaty little girl in it, as well as a later smell of flowery cologne and stale face powder. Under it all, there was a strong note of my mother's Vetiver and the acrid sweetness of old oil paint.

"This was Mother's studio," I told Cam. "I know you know the story, but this is where I walked in on her one day with her top open and that awful old man with his hands crawling all over her boobs. I always did think he gave her cancer. She was looking at him and smiling. I can still see it."

"I've done the same to you," I thought Cam might have said, with a leer on his face.

"And I've seen you naked so many times I can't count," Silas said indifferently. *"Women's boobs are no big deal to me, I can tell you."*

"That's the last time you watch me undress, you old satyr," I told Silas.

"Big deal. Now if you had six of 'em, it might be a different story."

I went out into the hall and climbed the musty stairs to the attic. I walked more slowly, because I was suddenly afraid that the attic would have changed, my special lair dwindled and cramped and banal. I didn't think I could bear that. My retreat and I were too closely connected; if it had shriveled, so would I have, in the deepest part of me. I stood outside the attic door for a long moment, and then pushed the door open.

There it was, at the far end of the long, dark room, under the big circular window, glowing as if a fire were lit somewhere near. The cool morning sunlight spilled over my old easy chair and the bookcases my father had built for me, crammed still with disorderly books. The rickety little table beside the chair was still piled with old legal pads and stubs of pencils and a kerosene lantern that I remember I had used on rainy days. On the floor, still, lay the dusty, once beautiful old rug where Cam and I had first made love.

"You can't have forgotten this room," I said to him. "It's where we first did the dirty deed, as I believe it was called in our youth."

The air was plangent with silent laughter.

"*Yuck,*" said Silas.

I turned around and around in the patch of sunlight, feeling the dust of childhood sink into my pores, breathing in the dander of discovery and delight. Suddenly I wanted to sit cross-legged in the sunlight surrounded by piles of my old books, leafing through this one, dipping into that.

"Oh," I said, spying a book high on a shelf. "I want you to see this. It's where I first came across the Green Man. If you think Frazer's is scary, you should see this guy."

I wedged the book out of the shelf.

"Drop that book!"

It was more of a hiss than a whisper, almost silent. But I heard, and dropped the book to the floor. A huge brown spider came scuttling out of the spilled pages and made for the molding in the corner. I didn't even have time to squeal before it was gone. I have always feared and hated spiders.

Silas sprang after it, then stopped and sat down.

"Do your duty, O mighty hunter," I said to him.

"*I draw the line at brown recluses. If it bit you you'd lose a chunk of yourself and probably worse. Their bites almost never heal. You want that one out of here, call Orkin.*"

Sweat sprang out at my hairline.

"I don't suppose that was you, was it?" I said to him weakly, but he had fled down the stairs, leaving me alone with living spiders and ethereal protectors.

"Thanks," I said to Cam in my pocket. "You really know how to look out after a girl, don't you?"

The air smiled silently.

I went out onto the porch and looked at the dazzle of the bay, summer-blue and still. The wind, I knew, would come up with the changing afternoon tide. I heard its tranquil breathing and felt my spider-pounding heart slow and my lungs fall into its rhythm, just as I had last night, when I had thought I was choking and the soft, clear voice told me to get up and go out, that the fog had lifted and I could hear the water breathe once more. I smiled into all the swimming blue and sunlight. Home. Home to Edgewater. Just as it had felt every summer when I had first come here as a child. My blood bubbled and a small giggle, pure joy, caught in my throat.

"You know the first thing I used to do when we got here? I used to just take off down these steps and run all the way across the lawn and down to the end of the dock and back again. If Jeebs or anybody was with me, they never beat me. I always won. I'll show you."

And I catapulted off the sagging bottom step and raced down the path the sunlight made across the big lawn—I had always thought of it as the Yellow Brick Road when I was small—and out to the end of the dock, and turned and pounded back again.

I heard the jingle of a chain behind me and yelled back, "Wilma is a pussycat!" and heard the scrabbling paws drawing nearer until I bounded up the step again and slapped the back screen door.

"Last one's a rotten egg!" I called.

I leaned against the door, head down, gasping for breath, happy in my skin under the sun.

"Lilly?"

I lifted my head and looked into the kitchen. Laurie Halliday stood there behind the big wooden table, her hands busy with dough, looking at me in alarm.

In a breath it all dissolved. I was nearly sixty, not eleven. Wilma slept under the ferns and azaleas a thousand miles to the south. And my husband was in my pocket.

I felt my face whiten and tears sting my eyes.

"Are you all right, baby?" Laurie said, coming to me and drawing me into the kitchen, one arm around my shoulders.

"I heard you running and yelling, sort of, and I didn't know what on earth— Look at you! You're dripping sweat. Sit down and let me wash your face off, and tell me about it."

I leaned back gratefully against the kitchen chair and felt the benison of the cool washcloth on my forehead. I didn't want to get up. I didn't even want to talk. But of course I had to. Otherwise she would think I was mad as a hatter and call the girls.

"I'm sorry, Laurie," I said. "I was walking around the house showing Cam how it was when I was a little girl, and then I remembered this thing we always did first when we got here . . . and I kind of got carried away."

She was silent for a while, mopping my face and staring at me.

"You were showing Cam?"

"Well, of course, not Cam really," I said. "It's just that I feel him so strongly here at Edgewater—it's the place he loved best, you know. It's like I still have him with me."

She sat down opposite me.

"Lilly, do you think it's a good idea for you to be here by yourself right now? I could come spend the nights with you. Or you know one of the girls would come."

I reached over and hugged her.

"I have him here, Laurie," I said, patting my heart and my shirt pocket both. "I don't mean he's sneaking around the corners or rattling chains or anything. I know better than anybody that he's gone. It's just that somehow it's better here. I love being here alone; I've never been anywhere alone in my life. I wouldn't dream of pulling you out of your bed at night. And as far as the girls go, that's the main reason I came up here, to grieve on my own. And I've got a million things to do; I want to inventory all Daddy's books, and go through all the old chests and trunks, and maybe get a little work done on the house and just— do the things I've always loved. Riding my bicycle and swimming and kayaking, and reading all night if I want to . . ."

She smiled.

"You've got it coming, I guess," she said. "It's just, well you know, you hear things."

"What things?"

"Idiocy, mostly. You know how some people will talk about a house where someone has recently died. Don't have enough to do, I always say."

"*Laurie.*"

"Oh, well, just little things. Consider the source, I tell everybody. Lorna Harris's no-good boy Curtis got drunk—again—the other night and she'd locked him out of the trailer, so he jimmied a windowsill and crawled into your house and passed out on the sofa. Not before he'd built him a good fire, though. Long about dawn he came banging on his mother's door hollering that he waked up and saw water falling on the fire just like somebody had thrown it out of a bucket, and the fire went out, and Curtis went with it, tail between his legs. Didn't stop him from blabbing all over the village that your house is haunted, though."

"And he was drinking what?" I said, smiling.

"I know." She smiled back. "Nobody believes anything Curtis Harris says. But you know, the other day, before you got here, I came over here to start putting things in order, and when I left I went out the back door and locked it, and forgot and left the front one open. Then came a hard thunderstorm, and I ran back over here to close it, and it was already closed. And locked."

"Laurie . . ." I didn't know what to say. "Don't you think you could have closed and locked it yourself, you know, just absentmindedly?"

"It was locked from the inside," she said.

"And then I sent the two girls who help me when I'm opening cottages, you know, Carlene and Dorothy, not a brain between them, over to straighten up your bedroom and change the sheets and all after—you know—after Cam left. And they came running and squalling back and said they hadn't got half through before they heard someone say, clear as day, 'Sloppy.' Quit on the spot, not that it's a great loss to me. So of course I went back and did it right, and I don't know, Lilly. I could swear I heard somebody kind of laugh and say, 'Thank you.'"

"Well, whoever or whatever it was, it sure wasn't Cam," I said. "He never in his life made a bed, or cared if anybody else did. Laurie, you don't really think my house is haunted, do you?"

"No," she said, after a while, smiling at me. "I think it's a very happy house and sometimes that—happiness—just sort of overflows."

"Bless you," I said, hugging her. "Now quit worrying about me and tell all those blabbermouths that they're welcome to come and spend a night on my couch anytime."

"I will. But you keep in touch with me, Lilly. It's not a time to be too much alone. Come to supper tomorrow night with us; Toby's hauling his traps in the morning. I'll cook us some lobsters."

"I'd love it," I said. "And I love you."

"We love you, too," she said. "You know that. And we loved Cam . . ."

"I know. Everybody did."

Presently she went home, leaving me fresh bread and a blueberry pie. She sat in her old Chevrolet a long time looking at the house before she left.

"You never did know when to keep your mouth shut," I said to Cam.

It was a strange summer, even to a woman who chatted with her husband in her pocket and argued with an old cat. There was a radiance to it, a kind of light around everything that seemed to come from within. Sound carried clear and pure for miles around; I heard the cries of eagles, the soft coughing of deer, the strange little barks of foxes in the night, the neck-prickling cry of many loons out on the night bay, usually when it was foggy. There were a far greater number of loons in the little cove at Edgewater than I ever remembered. Seven or eight pairs, at least. I remembered having only one pair at a time in the other summers. One pair came several years; we named them Arthur and Clare de Loon, and grieved when Clara said she'd heard a fisher had gotten one of them. We never saw the other again.

But this summer's loons were sleek and verbal and many. I never tired of looking at them, their strong, thick necks and the red eyes and natty black-and-white-checked plumage.

I mentioned the largesse of loons to Laurie one morning.

"Yeah," she said. "We've got them over to the cove, too. It's a two-moon year. You'll probably be seeing some mighty strange and wonderful things."

"A two-moon year?"

"Supposed to be an old, old Indian belief. I've heard it goes all the way back to the Red Paint people. The year of two moons—it's when two moons are visible in the sky in one month, the Wolf Moon, and the next moon, the Snow Moon. That doesn't happen much. Powerful magic, so they say. Last one I remember was when I was a little girl, about eleven."

Laurie was the same age as I. Yes, my eleventh summer at Edgewater had been full of magic. Some of it the darkest kind of magic, but magic nevertheless.

"What else can I expect?"

"Well, you never know. Wild things come closer to people and don't seem to be afraid. Carlisle saw a young moose behind the library right up in town the other night, and they don't hardly ever come this far south, and never in the summer."

Carlisle was Laurie's son, a silent, industrious, talented carpenter, and an avowed teetotaler. If Carlisle Halliday said he saw a moose behind the library, he had indeed seen a moose.

"You keep watching," Laurie said. "You'll see some of the critters we usually just don't see. I've seen young foxes dancing in the moonlight around an old apple-tree stump in the front yard. Lots of bear sightings too. You don't want to mess with the bears in case some of them have young nearby, but in a two-moon year they're supposed to be tame as house dogs. The deer will almost come up and let you pet them, though they'll eat your flowers and shrubbery, too. Awful nuisances, but nobody shoots them in a two-moon year. And porcupines, and battalions of skunks, and every kind of seabird—quite a gift, don't you think?"

"Have you just sort of always heard about the year of two moons, or what?" I said. "I've read a lot of the New England myths and legends and I've never heard of it."

"I don't wonder. Some folks say it's been passed down in their families since forever, but most of us first heard about it in a book a crazy lady from Boston wrote and published, forty years ago. She claimed to be a folklorist who had discovered some wonderful old tales and legends from hereabouts, but most of us had never heard of them, and it's common thinking that she made half of them up. Went naked out there in the woods when the moon was full, and made these god-awful noises, said she was communicating with the old spirits and elementals. She was mental, all right. Her daughter from Providence came and got her when she took to wandering up around the old Comfort Chapel on choir night, as naked as a jaybird."

"Wow," I said, laughing. "Maybe I'll take to shucking my clothes and dancing around the flagpole in the moonlight. Thank Toby for putting the flag up, by the way."

"His pleasure. No, you keep your clothes on. And stay inside at night. You can watch the sky stuff from the porch just as well as from the top of that old cliff yonder."

"Sky stuff?"

"Great August and September meteor showers in the two-moon years. And if you're going to see the aurora borealis, this is the year you'll see it. That would be later, though. After it's gotten good and cold."

"Oh, God, Cam would *love* that!" I said "Maybe I could manage—"

"No." Laurie wasn't smiling anymore. "You need to get on out of here before the cold comes and the dark drops down. It'll be early this year; always in a two-moon year. I want you good and gone back to Virginia beside your own fireplace, with your own girls, by then."

"Why on earth? I mean, I'm sure I will be; I'm going home right after we have the . . . the ceremony for Cam. But what would hurt me here in the cold that won't in the summer?"

"Nothing but yourself. But you listen to me, Lilly: The long, cold nights are not the times to be alone. Your head gets full of stuff you don't need in there, and if you got a sorrow it'll eat you up. Now it's all right with me if you want to handle your sorrow the way you are right now, riding that bicycle everywhere and kayaking and singing and talking to that old cat—it's your way. But the long dark will change that. Toby and I are going to send you home, ready or not, if you're still here when winter starts."

"Well, don't worry. I'll be home listening to my girls boss me around and Silas grump at me, trying to find a way to live, before the first frost."

"You'll find a way to live, dear," she said. "Look at how well you're doing now. I could swear you've been happy."

"I have, Laurie. It doesn't make any sense. I guess it's denial or something. But this place and this house just seem to care about me. Take care of me. I feel . . . loved."

"You are loved, baby. Not a soul in the village but doesn't think of you as one of their own. Your family has always been one of us. So was Cam. And so are you. When you come back in the summers you'll be coming home just as surely as if you were coming back to Virginia."

"I've always felt this was home way more than Washington or Virginia. Cam used to say that Virginia was the place he went to wait to come to Maine."

"Well, we'll always have part of him, won't we?" Laurie said, her eyes gleaming with tears. "Both in our hearts and in our bay. I love it that you'll be scattering his ashes there. Toby was so touched when you asked if he'd sail you out on the Friendship."

"It was always a toss-up whether Cam loved me or Toby or the Friendship or the bay more. He's getting the whole deal," I said, hugging her.

"When are you thinking about?"

"Oh, gosh. I'm not sure, Laurie. I wanted him to have one last summer here—"

I broke off and looked at her. She looked back at me levelly.

"I guess I mean I wanted one last summer while I still feel him so near," I said lamely. "I won't have that anymore when I come back next summer."

"I know."

Later, when I thought of high summer at Edgewater, the word

numinous always came into my mind. I knew that it meant, roughly: spiritual, supernatural, beyond understanding, and that was indeed part of it, surrounded as I was by my loving dead. But the word sounded in my ear like *luminous,* too, which the air and light certainly were, and somehow always brought to mind the hypnotic, trancelike state that the phrase "bee-loud glade" evoked. Or the old, clichéd "music of the spheres." That summer was never silent: Eagles called and the bay breathed and songbirds warbled, especially a wood thrush that came each evening and poured his gold over us; ducks honked, seals splashed, deer huffed, and the katydids sang and sang and sang in the trees at night. They were so loud once that I went down from the porch and followed their song into the little clearing above the driveway where, I believe, Cam was going to put my studio, for it had been partially cleared. And there, in the white moonlight, I saw the young foxes, four of them, leaping, playing, barking softly.

Dancing.

I stood there a long time, crying for joy. And then I went home.

"Thanks," I whispered into the dark of my bedroom.

"Don't mention it" came back. I more felt it on my ears than heard it, and might have thought I imagined it, except that Silas raised his craggy head, cocked it, looked at me, and tucked it back into my backbone.

I didn't hear Cam so much now. Instead, I felt him. He was often so near that I thought if I turned quickly, he would be there. I never did; I did not want to startle him. Cam sat beside me on the dock when I dangled my feet in the water, as I drank my morning coffee there, watching the plumes of mist and fog curling around the islands like dragon's tails in a Chinese painting; when I sat on the old sofa at night reading, with Silas in the bend of my elbow. He was never not there. It was a peaceful, dreamlike feeling; I was never alone, he was there; he would be there. Talking could wait.

For about a week I had been hearing the shrill piping of the ospreys, so close overhead that I thought they must be fishing our cove, but I never saw any.

One morning I asked Laurie if she thought Toby would get out the old Beetle Cat we had bought for our girls, which had been stored for the winter.

"Sure," she said. "I'll ask him at lunchtime. Where you planning to go?"

"I thought I'd go over to Sunderson's Island," I said. "I've heard the ospreys every day, lots of them, but I never see them. I thought I'd check in on the nest. I used to love to do that."

She looked at me strangely, and then said, "Sit a spell. I never get a chance to talk to you. Let's have some coffee."

I sat and accepted the coffee and waited to hear what she had to tell me. I did not think I was going to like it.

"Lilly," she said, "the ospreys are gone. They've been gone a couple of years. Their tree was cut down. I hear they've built a new nest over on Little Deer Isle, but I just haven't had the heart to go see."

"Cut down . . ."

"Some people bought the island from old Mr. Sunderson's heirs and are going to put a house there. A real showplace, I hear. Had every crew within fifty miles hired to work on it."

"A *house*? You can't put a house on that—"

"I know, baby. But it's theirs, fair and square. Not anything we can do about it. Nobody likes it. Nobody likes the people who bought it."

"Who would do such an obscene, awful thing?"

She reached over and put her hand over mine.

"I was hoping I wouldn't have to tell you this," she said. "A couple named Surrey, from Massachusetts somewhere. They're planning to live year round on it, if it ever gets built."

"Surrey . . ."

"You knew the wife as Peaches Davenport, I think," she said.

My mind was a white explosion. Only afterward was I aware that I had been screaming "No, no, no, no!"

"I know," Laurie said. "Everybody knows what she did that summer. Not many will speak to her, even at the post office. She doesn't seem to care. She had one husband die on her, and then, about fifteen, twenty years ago, she married some bishop of something or other and brought him up here to see this place, and they bought the island on the spot. She's got two grown girls and a boy in school somewhere. When she first got here she asked me to tell you, if I saw you, to give her a call."

"And you said?"

"I said I didn't think I'd be seeing you, and she said, 'Oh, well, I'll look her up next time we're here, then.' They're not here often. The house has kind of pooched."

"Did they run out of money, I hope?" I said.

"No. Got plenty of that, I hear. Thing is, no workmen will stay more than a day or two."

"Why?"

She took a deep breath and looked out over the bay. The afternoon wind had come up, and the rich blue was ruffled and glinting in the sun. The light was lower now. The water had a pewter cast.

"They say they keep getting attacked by ospreys," she said. "Hear 'em shrieking and diving around their heads, feel the wind of their wings. A couple of men have deep cuts on their necks and arms."

"But the ospreys are gone."

"Yes," she said softly.

"Laurie," I whispered, "I hear them all the time."

"I know. I do, too."

317

"But if they're not there, what are we hearing? What are those men hearing? What's attacking them?"

She sighed and looked away, up into the woods that lay behind our house. Color was beginning to tinge them now; the mountain ash trees, always the first to turn in the fall, had glowing patches among their dense green. Some of the small swamp maples were fiery red and orange. When had fall happened? Why had I not noticed?

"Lilly," Laurie said wearily, "you've been coming here since you were born, and your folks before you, but you're still from away. When your folks have lived here three or four generations, like a lot of ours, you learn not to ask too many questions, or think too much on things you don't understand. Maine is a wild place, at least this part of it is. Wild things happen, things beyond ken. Mostly, we don't question them and just enjoy them. We're not meant to know all the answers. I think that's why some people who really love it here, and want to live here year round, end up going somewhere else. The world has got to make sense to them and when it doesn't, they just can't stay."

"I never saw anything I couldn't understand," I said. "At least before this year."

"Two-moon year." She grinned at me and then grew serious again. "Most of that kind of stuff happens in the fall and the long dark, after you all have gone home."

"That's when Maine gets . . . haunted?"

"Oh, for God's sake," said Laurie, who never swore. "That's when it's too dark and cold to do much but watch TV and drink liquor. I never heard of a haunting that didn't start with a bottle of Old Forester."

"It wasn't cold or dark out on the island when the men heard the ospreys, or when you and I did."

"Well, that crowd out there was nipping from the first day, with nobody really to supervise them. And then I expect they just got bored. Ghost ospreys are as good an excuse as any to knock off work."

"But we weren't drinking."

"Lilly. Stop fretting and just enjoy the sound. It's a poor thing if you can only love what you can see."

I dropped it. She was right, of course. The blessings that fell on me that summer were, and remained, unseen.

Something strange happened after that, though. Something that puzzled me and made me vaguely uneasy. It seemed as though, with the mention of Peaches Davenport, a tiny drop of ink got into a still, clear basin of water and eventually stained it all with swirls. Cam was silent. Silas slept most of the warm afternoons away and did not argue with me. Where there had been magic now there was reality. I wasn't grief stricken about Cam; I still felt him near. But the throat-tickling exultation that had floated me through the early summer was gone.

I began to get restless, without knowing why. Odd things happened in my day-to-day rounds. At the post office one day, the first time I had stopped in that summer, the elderly, sweet-faced postmistress said, "Oh, Mrs. McCall, I was so very sorry to hear about Mr. McCall. We all loved him. He always had a joke and a grin, even when the weather was at its worst and nobody else would give you the time of day. And he plowed a few of us out when the snow was deep."

"When was he here in winter?" I asked. "I mean, I know he came up once a long time ago when a tree fell on the house, but—"

"Oh, now and again," she said, and looked away. I knew she would say no more.

But she did say, "I've been meaning to ask you. He's gotten some mail this summer, and I haven't quite known what to do with it. He used to have me send it to his office, but I thought you might want

319

it now. There's not much, just two or three letters; they're all post-marked the same place: Santa Fe, New Mexico. No address, just the postmark. I thought you might need to see them."

She handed me three battered envelopes. They were regular drug-store number ten envelopes, with, as she had said, no return address or name. I opened one. It said, simply, *C . . . thanks so much! D.*

Suddenly I did not want to know any more about D in Santa Fe, New Mexico. It was unmistakably a man's hand, but it still felt strange. Furtive.

"Thanks, Mrs. Ellis," I said. "They're nothing we need. Can you just toss them if any more come in? This D will hear sooner or later that Cam's gone."

"Of course, dear," she said. "Stop back in before you go."

"I will." I smiled thinly. I went home. I sat down on the sofa in front of the empty fireplace and thought of making a fire; the room had grown a little chilly. But I didn't. Instead I merely sat and stared at Cam's urn. Part of him was still in my pocket, but most of him was there.

"Who is D in Santa Fe?" I said aloud to him. "When were you up here in the winter? We said there weren't going to be any more secrets."

He sat silent. From the end of the couch Silas lifted his head and glared at me.

"Don't ask questions if you think you might not like the answers," he said.

"What did you say?" I goggled at him. It was not a Silas thing to say.

"I don't remember."

"It sounded like a warning of some kind."

"Will you put a sock in it? I was sound asleep till you came barging in here. A fire wouldn't hurt, either."

I built a fire and sat drinking some of the scotch Cam always kept in the kitchen. I had not done that all summer. I sipped the smoky scotch and watched the flames and thought.

Then I got up and went to the kitchen phone and called Kitty Howard. We had spoken during the summer, of course, but not of anything important; mostly she was trying to coax me home, or to relate the girls' latest laments. They knew better than to call me yet.

"I've decided that we're going to have Cam's ceremony on the weekend of September eleventh," I said. "Will you get the word out? Just you and the girls and their husbands—no children, please, and maybe Aunt Tatty. And anybody at the firm who's particularly close to him. I can't remember. I can sleep about ten comfortably and any number uncomfortably."

"Sure. But why so late? Lilly, it's time for you to come home now. John Corbett is bitching about getting Cam's will probated, and Betsy calls me every day to see if I've heard from you. Seems Deedee's little preschool—the one she *has* to go to if she wants to get into a decent college—has raised its tuition again."

"Her husband only makes about a gazillion dollars a year in bonds," I said testily. "She's just used to calling Daddy. Well, I'm coming home right after the ceremony, and I'm having it then because it's the weekend of the most fabulous meteor showers you've ever seen."

"Cam isn't going to care about a goddamned meteor shower," Kitty yelled, plainly thinking I had been there way too long already.

"Yes, he is. More than any of us. Don't you remember when he taught himself celestial navigation just because the stars fascinated him so?"

"Lilly . . ."

"Bye, sweetie," I said. "I can't wait to see you."

And I hung up.

CHAPTER

18

I don't care what he said! I don't care what you say! I don't want him just dumped into that damned dirty bay! Fifteen minutes later nobody will know where he is! You might as well just flush him down the toilet!"

My older daughter's face was red and corrugated, like heated tin. It had always been so when she was a child and in the throes of grief and anger. Tears leaked from her beautiful gray eyes, swollen shut now, and scrubbed red.

She sat across the living room from me at Edgewater in the bentwood rocker my mother had always loved, rocking furiously and sobbing aloud. She still wore the elegant earth-colored linen suit she had arrived in from New York, hardly two hours ago, and her narrow feet, in towering spike heels I could not have gotten across the carpet in, were crossed at the ankles. The bottom of her looked like the fashion editor she was, and the top of her looked like the child she had been. Her husband, Gary, of the booming bond career, sat beside her sipping scotch and patting her on the knee now and then. He might as well have patted a Bengal tiger. You did not stop Betsy in full spate. You simply waited it out.

Across from her, on the sofa, Alice, my younger daughter, leaned back against the cushions with her eyes closed. She had the knack of removing herself from uncomfortable situations simply by shutting her eyes and going far away somewhere in her head. I looked at her, spilled against my sofa, long and thin and graceful, her rich red hair piled up on her head, showing small ears with amber pendants dangling from them, her thrown-back head accentuating her long, creamy neck to perfection. She looked at the moment so like Cam when he wanted to be somewhere else that I almost laughed. Alice did publicity for a line of women's clothing and accessories the price of one of which an average family could have lived on for six months. I wondered if it was back to work she had gone. Her husband sat beside her, his hands clasped between his legs, looking at the floor and whistling absentmindedly through his teeth. Joe was a sports columnist for an august New York daily. I had always wondered at the attraction between them, but knew it was an honest one. Of my two sons-in-law I liked him best; Cam had too, even if he never said so to either of the girls.

"Feel free to jump right in," I said to Cam in my mind.

Silent laughter made a small wind against my cheek. "Nothing doing," I heard, deep inside me.

"They're yours, too," I said.

"Nope. All yours now. I did my best with them for a long time."

"You gave them everything they wanted!"

"But they won't expect that from you. Put your spine into it, Lil."

"That child is spoiled rotten. I always said so," Silas muttered.

"Thanks for your input," I said huffily to both of them.

"What did you say?" Betsy shrieked. "Were you talking to me? How could you say such a thing? My father is dead!"

"So is my husband," I said in exasperation. "I wasn't talking to you, Betsy. I was talking to Silas."

Everybody stared at me.

323

"He was growling," I said lamely.

"You want to hear growling? I'll show you growling," Silas hissed.

"I don't blame him," Kitty Howard said. "You didn't object to the plans your mother made when you first heard them, Betsy. Why now?"

"Because I saw that urn and I knew he was in there, and I wanted to keep him! I want to know where he is."

"That would hardly be hygienic," Kitty drawled. "And besides, you wouldn't know where he was if he was buried. Not the part of him that was . . . him."

"But I could go visit him!"

Betsy would not be consoled.

"Well," I said wearily, "you can come up here any time you want to and go swimming with him."

"I hate you!" she wailed, and got up and tottered out of the room on her looming Manolo Blahniks.

"Don't take her seriously," her husband muttered finally. "Of course she doesn't hate you. She's had a rough week. Deedee didn't get invited to the play group Betsy wanted for her, and she had to cut a piece for spring *Vogue* in half, and we just found out that she's pregnant again and we'll have to move, and she just finished decorating the East Sixty-third Street place."

"And now I'm going to scatter her dad in the drink," I said. "Nice about the baby, though."

"She's not thinking rationally. Let her have a nap and some supper and she'll come around. We all agreed it was a really good thing to do, and Cam wanted it."

He sighed wearily, as if he knew the drill well.

"Poor baby," I said contritely. "It's a lot on her plate at once. I'll talk to her after supper, when she's rested a little. Maybe she can help with the ceremony or something."

I knew that, to Betsy, I would forever be the one who cast her beloved father into Eggemoggin Reach. The fact was that now the event was at hand, I didn't want to do it either. The bronze urn had become the centerpiece of my life. I didn't think I could look at it knowing it was empty. I made a note to myself to snatch a bit more of Cam and put him in something larger and more permanent, like a locket, so that he could be with me literally as well as—what? spectrally?—all my life. Maybe if Betsy had some of the ashes . . . No, I was not going to parcel Cam out like vacuum cleaner dust for all and sundry. He wanted the bay. The bay it would be.

I looked back at Gary, who would not meet my eyes. There had been a rather nasty little scene between us when they first arrived, and I knew I was not forgiven. I had not forgiven him, either. And, as for Silas . . .

Gary had not been seated long, with a full glass of Cam's single-malt at hand on the old rattan table beside him, when Silas lifted his head, leaped off the sofa, lumbered across the floor, and was in Gary's lap with his nose plugged into his neck sniffing loudly, before I could stop him.

"God! Get this goddamned cat off me," Gary cried and pushed Silas off him and kicked him across the floor. Silas gave a surprised yelp. I picked him up and held him under my chin and stroked him. The creaking, rusty purr rasped out into the room.

I stared at Gary.

"Never," I said in a low, trembling voice, "never put your hands on Silas again. If you do, you're out of here. He's as much family as any of us, and more than you are, and Cam adored him. He was just trying to see if you smelled like Cam. He does that to almost every man who comes in. He wants Cam back so badly."

"It's disgusting! I have cat spit in my ear," Gary snapped, and I suddenly hoped the bond market was collapsing as we spoke. "And

I have scotch in the lap of a four-thousand-dollar Armani suit; that flea-bitten son of a bitch knocked my glass over!"

We all looked. Gary's glass lay on its side on the table and twenty-year-old single-malt scotch was indeed dribbling steadily into his lap.

"Silas didn't do it," I snapped. "He was across the room right here in my arms. You hit it with your elbow."

"I did not!"

"Then it turned over by itself, because Silas never touched it," I said.

Everyone looked at Silas and me, and then at Gary and the dripping glass. He got up and stomped off into the kitchen to try to rescue his Armani. There seemed to be nothing else to say. Just at that moment we heard a car crunch up the driveway and screech to a stop, bumping the front porch smartly.

"Get the door while I pee on the jerk," Silas said.

"Better let well enough alone," I said. "Scotch on your crotch is bad enough."

"I take your point."

I got up and went to the door. I hadn't realized any more were coming.

"Oh, I forgot to tell you," Kitty said as I passed her. "This awful woman in Cam's office, the office manager, I think, insisted on coming. She coyly refers to herself as his office wife. I think she thinks she's his real one. Junie Sternhagen—we all knew her in high school. She was just as awful then. Anyway, I told her if she was driving, she'd have to pick up Tatty, and I see she did. I'm sorry, Lil, but she'd have come anyway. Walked, probably. She's had a crush on Cam since fourth grade."

"I've never met her."

"She hides when you come, I think."

"Great. I'll put her in with Silas."

"Poor Silas."

I opened the door and greeted the two women. Junie Sternhagen was large and buxom and pinkly painted in a madras skirt and a T-shirt that said LIFE's A BEACH, apparently her idea of Maine coast attire. She wore thong sandals; the brilliant pink painted toes that peered out were already blue with cold, and there were goose bumps on her ample arms. Even this early, the nights were chilly. This one, I read in the paper, would be a record for early September.

"Please come in," I said. "I'm Lilly McCall. It was very thoughtful of you to come."

"Oh, I know all about you," Junie Sternhagen trilled. "Cam went on and on about you. And I've seen your picture on his desk. I must say you look—different—now."

"Lilly, dear, what on earth have you done to yourself?" Tatty said fretfully. She was very frail but in full possession of her considerable faculties. She had lived on in the little house she had shared with my father until he needed a nursing home.

"How do you mean, Aunt Tatty?" I said, though I knew what she meant. I had gotten the same dismayed question from my girls and Kitty.

"You look like . . . a very little girl. Are you eating at all?"

I had not really thought about my appearance until Kitty, the first to arrive, looked at me and said, "My God! You're wasting away to nothing! I'm taking you back home with me."

When I went upstairs to bathe and change before the others arrived, I had studied myself in my mother's full-length mirror. Except when I washed my face and brushed my teeth, I don't think I had noticed my appearance all summer. I was thin, though it didn't seem to me to be a sickly thin; I remembered I had looked so when I *was* a child, rangy as a yearling deer. My face was innocent of makeup and freckled, and I was deeply tanned from hours in the sun. My hair had gotten troublesomely long, and so I had begun simply to plait it into pigtails. I had on a T-shirt and cutoff shorts from the wardrobe in my room, and remembered for the first time that these clothes had been mine as a child. I had been wearing them all summer. There was a large Band-Aid on a cut on my knee, and calluses on my palms from kayaking. I winced. I didn't look like a grief-stricken anorectic; I looked like a child who had been sent up to wash before dinner.

I took a quick shower and slathered on lotion from my mother's bathroom. Her clothes were too big for me now, as were the ones I had brought with me, but I found a pretty, old flowered caftan in her closet, a one-size-fits-all thing, and in it and her gold ballet flats and chunky gold jewelry, I began to see myself emerge in the mirror again. I made my face up carefully, with lipstick and blush and mascara from her dressing table, and unbraided my hair and brushed it until it stood out like a vermeil cloud around my shoulders. A slosh of her Vetiver completed the transformation. I was much prettier, but apparently it did not fool anyone. I had still gotten cries of dismay from my daughters, and now from Tatty.

"I'm eating like a horse," I said to her, as I had to the others. "Just ask Laurie Halliday. It's just that I've been riding my bicycle all over the place, and swimming, and doing a lot of kayaking. I feel terrific."

Everyone looked at me strangely when I said this, and so I added, "Physically, anyway. I find it helps to keep moving."

That morning Laurie and I had swept and polished and made beds fresh, and hauled out and washed the best china and crystal, not that there was much of that at Edgewater. She had made a huge tureen of clam chowder from the clams she had dug the previous evening, and little buttermilk biscuits ready to go into the oven, and she had baked a blueberry pie. I ran and bought wine from the general store—they had a few decent bottles for the summer people—and fresh goat cheese and crackers. At the vegetable lady's house I bought dahlias and some of the last sunflowers, and small bunches of chrysanthemums to put on bedside tables. With the fire lit and candles glowing, Edgewater would look, if not glamorous, then festive and welcoming. I hoped that in the dimness—the sun set by five now—no one would notice the holes in the carpet where Silas had sharpened his claws or the mantling of cat hair over everything. I had polished Cam's urn, and it seemed to gather all the light into itself; it blazed out in the dusk like an amulet.

"Show-off," I said, coming back downstairs to where Kitty sat drinking scotch.

"Who are you talking to?" she said. "You look better, by the way. Sort of like a little girl dressed in her mother's clothes."

I did not tell her they were my mother's clothes.

"I was talking to Cam," I said. "He's shining like new money on a bear's behind," as Seth used to say.

She followed my eyes to the urn, and then looked back at me.

"You talk to Cam?"

"Oh, Kitty, of course I do. You know I talk to everybody and everything; I've been talking to Silas for years."

"Yeah, I know," she admitted. "Well, just so he doesn't talk back."

I started to answer her, but then did not. It was not the time. Perhaps the time would never come, though I longed to share the simple, joyous fact of Cam's presence with someone. With Kitty.

Silas came up to me and wound himself around my ankle.

"*Dinnertime,*" he said.

"Yeah, let's get it over with," I said. "Otherwise we'll stink up the whole house."

"*Shit happens,*" he said, and marched out of the room, tail high.

"What did he say?" Kitty said curiously.

"He said it was dinnertime," I said.

"Well, it is," Kitty said. "What have you got to nibble on until everybody else gets here?"

I brought in the goat cheese and crackers and the scotch bottle. We poured our drinks and she lifted hers to the mantel and I followed.

"To you, Cameron McCall the Third," she said. "We miss you."

"And to you," came back clearly and silently. "I miss you, too, Kitty Howard."

I quickly looked at her, but she had heard nothing.

"Ah, God, it seems a long road without him," she said, her voice trembling.

"The longest," I said.

We did not speak again until my girls arrived and the clamoring over how atrocious I looked began again. I thought it was going to be a very long night.

But as it turned out, it wasn't. I suppose there are few things so tiring as gathering to toss one's father's and husband's ashes to the wind and water, and airline travel was impossible now, and many of us had driven long miles. Even my peripatetic Betsy had powered down to the point where she ate Laurie's glorious chowder in groggy silence, and then was taken off to bed, nodding, by her husband, who gave Silas a long look of hatred as he passed. I saw rather than heard Silas growl at him—at least his tattered throat vibrated slightly and I knew it was not a purr.

"Don't even think about it," I hissed at him.

"Yeah, well, you never know what a cat is thinking, do you?"

"I know what you're thinking, fur ball. I always do," I said.

"You wish."

I was sure no one had heard that exchange, but Kitty raised an eyebrow at me.

"He was going to pee on Gary," I said. "I told him not to."

Kitty stared from Silas to me and back to Silas. I saw her struggle with credulity, and then give up.

"Pity," she said, and we both laughed.

Shortly after the coffee and blueberry pie yawns ruled, and most of the rest of us trailed off to bed. I went into the kitchen to hug and thank Laurie, and came back into the living room with a cognac bottle and glasses. I was suddenly overflowing with what this summer had given me, and longed to spill it out to the one person who, at least, would hear me out. But Kitty was fast asleep on the sofa before the dying fire, with Silas jammed into her hip, so I woke her and took her off to the other little iron twin bed in my old room, where, I think, she was asleep before her head hit the pillow. I undressed and crawled into my bed, disappointed, but Silas burrowed into my ribs and began snoring and all of a sudden I couldn't keep my eyes open.

"You did well," I thought I heard as I slid into sleep, but was not sure.

The next morning we all slept late. It was almost eleven o'clock by the time we had eaten scones and sausage and drunk pots of walloping coffee and assembled on the front porch steps.

It was a day out of the morning of the world, I thought. There had been fog in the night, but it was burning off and the islands and sea were emerging as if from developing fluid. The autumn colors smote the heart. We in the south got nothing like this, even in the lush forests of the Tidewater. The sky overhead was a dome of the strongest, purest cobalt I had ever seen, and the sun climbing through the woods made paths of dappled gold and laid down rays in which motes of gold danced. To walk up our driveway to the road was to enter a world of flaming stained glass, to mainline light. I remembered the rich, mellow light of Maine in August, but now, in this untimely full autumn, it was simply supernatural. Everything was outlined in blue. The small outer islands seemed to float above the sea. I would not look at Sunderson's.

Numinous, I thought, and smiled.

Even the eight of us sprawled on the old wooden steps were blessed with light, outlined in it as if a miniaturist had traced us with his richest gold leaf. Betsy's beautiful head caught its fire. My quiet younger daughter, Alice, had her long legs stretched out to the sun, though the day was chilly and sweaters and even blankets had been brought out. So like Cam, I thought, looking at her long rangy legs and arms, with the small hairs turned to piratical flame in the light. I saw Cam's arms and legs, too, as I had seen them a thousand times before on these old steps, all knobby angles and blazing pelt. My eyes filled and I closed them. Behind them, suddenly, there were other arms and legs, brown knobby, smooth-skinned, with the hairs on them turned to white-gold wire by the sun. I opened my eyes and shook my head violently.

"What's up for today?" I asked the crowd at large. Nobody seemed to be contemplating moving from the steps.

"I just want to sleep," Betsy muttered. "I don't know what's wrong with me."

I remembered that she was pregnant, and thought of my own sleep-stunned early months carrying her and Alice.

"There's a hammock on the other side of the porch, in the sun and out of the wind," I said. "Go crawl in. I'll bring you a blanket."

She smiled gratefully at me.

"Thanks, Mom. Ahhh, what time is the—you know, the thing tonight?"

"About eight. It'll have been full dark for a long time, and the paper said the first of the meteors might begin around then. There'll be plenty of light, though. I'll light the flambeaus down on the dock, and you can watch from there or from here on the porch, if you'd rather. It's going to be cold."

"Why you had to pick off season for this . . ." she grumbled, the old Betsy back again.

"Your dad always said he wanted to be up here off season," I said. "And I see what he means now. It's enchanted. A different world from summer. On moonlit nights all sorts of wild things come out: foxes, porcupines, a bear or two, once even a moose. I'd be surprised if you didn't see my foxes dance. I'd like to stay forever."

Heads turned toward me, annoying me greatly, and so I got up and said to Kitty, "Want to take a little hike with me? I'll show you my special hideaway from when I was little. It's sort of a climb, but it's worth it."

"Sure," she said, getting up.

Junie Sternhagen turned her crocodile smile toward me. It was outlined in vermillion lipstick this morning, and she wore a fuzzy sweat suit to match it.

"Off-season Maine is lovely, isn't it? I'm so glad Cam got up here then as often as he did. He always had something new to tell me about when he got back."

I was silent.

She said, "I thought he might not have told you about the times he came up here, Lilly. I'm sure he didn't want you to worry about something being wrong with the house, or something. It wasn't all *that* many times. I made his reservations, so I think I've got a record of his trips somewhere, if you'd like to have them."

"No, thanks, Junie." I grinned back fiercely. "I usually knew where he was. I know something I'm absolutely sure he never told you."

"Well, I knew an awful lot about him." She bridled. "He always called me his office wife."

333

Everyone's head turned toward her in startled distaste. I heard Kitty draw in a great breath, and I laid my hand on her arm.

"But I bet you never knew what he wore under his kilt," I said, and the porch exploded in laughter, and Kitty and I walked off across the beach toward the beetling promontory, the illicit cliff we children climbed without a thought for the ANYONE SWIMMING ON THESE ROCKS WILL BE PROSECUTED sign posted at its base. It still reared its great head over the pebbly beach, shadowing it, and I still felt the faint, wicked thrill I always had when I approached it for the first time each summer.

"What a bitch," Kitty said, looking back at the crowd on the porch, still laughing. "You got her good, Lil. There's nothing she'd rather know than what Cam wore under his kilt."

"I didn't know about all those trips, Kitty," I said in a low voice.

"I'll bet you a year's worth of fancy lunches that she made three-fourths of that up. Don't give her the pleasure of knowing you think about it. By the way, what *did*—"

"Kitty!"

"Right."

We reached the top of the cliff. I took a deep breath and felt my breathing ease into the breathing of the bay. I had not had the awful chest constriction up here this year, except that first night, but still I breathed deepest and most fully with the sound of the sea.

"It's awesome," Kitty said quietly, almost in a whisper. "It looks like the dawn of time, doesn't it?"

We were surrounded by the same light-struck mist that I remembered hung here on many mornings. Through it, far away, the dark shapes of the pointed firs pricked the fog, and below it the sea, now a pewter glitter in the low light, unrolled itself out past Great Spruce Head and ended itself in a gunmetal line on the horizon. We stood, cloaked in bright, swirling mist. I heard the unmistakable sweet-shrill cries of hunting ospreys. I did not comment on them. I didn't want to get into this with Kitty.

She heard them, though, Tidewater girl that she was.

"Ospreys. Where are they? Is there a nest somewhere around here?"

Kitty loved ospreys. She had put up several nesting poles along her stretch of creek, and the ospreys always came.

"No," I said, as casually as I could. "There used to be over there on Sunderson's Island, but some people cut their trees down. I heard they have a nest over on Deer Isle."

"Then where do these come from?"

"I don't know. I never see them, only hear them. I'd think I was nuts, but Laurie hears them too, and now you. It's a great comfort."

She raised an eyebrow at me.

"Ghost ospreys?"

"Would you rather have ghost skunks? There are about a million of them around, too. They're what make those little holes in the lawn, in which I devoutly hope Junie baby steps and breaks her wedgie. They dig for grubs."

"No kidding. Where are they, if they're close enough to hear so plainly?"

I told her about the year of two moons, and what Laurie had said, and also about her theory that all off-season Maine hauntings had their provenance in whiskey.

"How much wine did you drink last night?" I laughed at her.

"I wasn't the one hugging a cognac bottle," she said tartly. "No kidding, do you hear them often?"

"Almost every day."

"Does it scare you?"

"How could the cries of ospreys scare anyone? It's like a gift from Maine to me, whether or not I can see them."

"I see what you mean. But, Lilly . . ."

She did not go on.

"What?"

"This place right now, it's like your feet never quite touch the earth. I felt it the minute I got up here. Don't stay too long, Lil. You need the earth."

"I've had the earth all my life. Right now midair is okay by me." I smiled. "And besides, we're coming home as soon after tonight as I can get some quotes from an antiquarian book dealer over in Ellsworth. I took a lot of Daddy's books over there a while ago, and he said he thought some of them might be valuable."

"Would you sell them?"

"No, but they're part of the estate. I need an estimate on them. Not much else in the cottage is worth anything."

"Will you keep it, do you think?"

"Of course I'll keep it. It's my favorite place on earth; it was Cam's too. It's the only place I feel him . . . near."

Her face was troubled, but she said nothing for a moment. Then, "But you're definitely coming home after that."

"Of course. I can't stay up here much longer. We're not winterized."

"I'm glad."

The gold-shot mist was swirling around us now. I knew it was breaking up.

"I used to think people could fly," I told her, smiling. "That we all could once, and a few of us still could. The last summer we were here when I was a child I was up here just about this time of morning and the mist was doing the very same thing, and I met someone who . . . who—I thought he had flown here."

All of a sudden my breath left me and I could not go on. I bent over from the waist, gasping, and felt tears running down my face.

My blinded eyes saw a carved golden face and very blue eyes and white-blond hair like living flame, and felt smooth tanned skin and callused palms from tennis, and smelled the damp, salty, smoky smell of an old sweater.

"Did you fly?" my eleven-year-old voice said through the roaring in my ears.

"Not the way I think you mean," his twelve-year-old voice, deep for his age, replied.

Jon.

I felt Kitty's arms around me from behind, easing me down to the dry grass on the cliff top. I felt her hands shaking my shoulders, and heard her voice, very far away.

"Lilly! Lilly! What is it? Lilly, *breathe!*"

From the air I heard a whisper, "Breathe, Lilly. Find the sea and breathe with it."

And slowly I did. I sat gasping, my heart racing, the tears drying on my face. When my breath steadied I looked up at Kitty's worried face.

"I'm sorry," I said. "I get this asthma . . ."

She looked at me levelly, then shook her head.

"That wasn't asthma, Lilly. I've seen your asthma. Who was he?"

"Who was who?"

"Oh, shit, Lilly, the person you met up here in the mist, and you thought he'd flown here—"

"How do you know it was a he— Oh, God, Kitty. His name was Jon. Jon Lowell. He had just come out for the summer; none of us had ever met him before."

"And you loved him."

"Yes, I did."

"What happened to him?"

"He died," I said, beginning to cry again. "He died right out

337

there in the bay. He took our Beetle Cat out in a fog and . . . nobody ever found him. They found the boat, but not him."

She drew me closely into her arms and let me cry wearily on her shoulder.

"And that's why you . . . lived the way you did. All shut up in your father's house or else at the bottom of a swimming pool, so nothing could get to you again."

"I guess so. Don't analyze it, Kitty. I was not quite twelve years old. He was not quite thirteen. It couldn't have lasted even if he hadn't died."

"Why not?"

"Because that sort of thing, at that age, never does! How can it?" I said angrily. I was breathing well and my tears were dry again. I wanted no more of this.

"Did Cam know?"

"He knew . . . most of it."

"But not the love part."

"Kitty!"

"Okay, baby. Let's go back, in case June Bug has decided to try and nick his toothbrush or something. I just—"

"Just what?"

"I just think it must be hard, losing both of them to the bay."

"I never even thought of that, Kitty. I never think about him. It was just today, and the mist and all. Look, don't feel sorry for me. I had my great love. I had it for a long time. I still have it."

"I know," she said, and we went down the cliff path and back across the beach to Edgewater.

"Weather breeder, sure enough," Toby Halliday said that night on the dock at Edgewater.

It was the most beautiful night I had ever seen. At sunset the last of the low sun had struck my headland to gold-vermillion; against the darkening purple sky it was almost frightening, eerie. I had the fleeting thought that it looked like the last day of the world. Well, in a way it was.

The dark fell quickly. We all bundled up in whatever we could find in the cottage and trundled down to the end of the dock, where the Friendship bobbed at anchor, scrubbed and fresh painted, her brightwork giving off sparks in the dark. Looking as far as I could see on both sides, I could make out no pinprick of light at all on the shore. I had never seen night like that here. This was what Laurie meant by the long dark.

The wind was still and the chill grew. I thought there would be ice tonight, inland, probably. I had lit the old summer flambeaus on the lawn, and set lanterns down the path to the dock, but beyond that the only light was that of the great, swollen stars hanging suspended like grape clusters in the velvet sky. Reflected in the still, black water, they gave ample light to see by. Down at the end of the dock, where the pilings sank into the rocks and then the bottom of the sea, phosphorescence winked and danced. I had never seen it so except on the hottest nights of summer. *Everything is conspiring to shine for Cam tonight,* I thought, hugging the urn close under Jeebs's old down parka. Instead of making me sad, the thought filled me with exultation.

"Watch closely. This is your big night," I whispered to him, both in the urn and in the small gold mesh pouch, once my mother's summer evening bag, that hung around my neck under my sweater. There was more of him there than there had been in the envelope. I had taken care of that days earlier.

I thought about the slacks and sweater, though. When I had gotten ready to dress for tonight, I remember wondering what one wore to fling one's husband into the Atlantic Ocean. And when I opened the closet in my room, there they hung: white linen trousers and a heavy navy blue cabled sweater. I had not seen them, I thought, in years. I certainly had not seen them hanging in my closet. And yet there they were, and I took them off the hangers and slipped them on. They fit perfectly. I looked in my mirror and saw a memory: a young girl dressing up for one of the first times in her life, with her hair piled up and her mother's blush and lipstick on her face. And a bit later, the voice of Peaches Davenport, saying snidely, "Isn't that a winter sweater? Gosh, you must be burning up."

"Okay," I said aloud. "All right. You want me to wear 'em, I'll wear 'em."

A small, warm breath brushed my cheek.

"Thanks."

Everyone was on the dock except Betsy, who was sobbing in her bedroom.

"I can't, Mama," she had hiccupped. "I just can't."

I hugged her.

"Don't worry about it," I said against her hot cheek. "You're not losing him. You'll see. He'll be with you always, right here." I tapped her chest, which would soon swell with food for her unborn child. Death and life . . .

"Really?"

"Really. I've had him with me every minute since he's been gone. He's not going to leave his girls alone. And he wouldn't want you to cry for him, either. You know that."

"I know." She blew her nose. "But still, I can't go."

So the rest of us stood quietly in the beginning of the long dark and waited. Presently we saw the first silver arc of a star falling far out over the islands. And then another, and another.

"Ready, Lilly?" Toby asked.

"Ready, Captain," I said, and he took my hand and swung me

aboard the Friendship, as Cam had done a thousand times, and my father before him.

By the time we ghosted out of the bay, the stars were blooming in the sky like winter snow, like comets with their sweet silver tails intact. Around the bow of the boat the phosphorescence danced. Toby had his running lights on, but we really did not need them. All the world was silver tonight.

We reached the spot where the wind usually picked you up if you were sailing, just outside the last great boulder on our cove's beach.

"Reckon this would do?" Toby said, his voice thick. "Cam always liked this spot. Called it Land's End."

"Then Land's End it will be," I said. I was calm with a serenity I had never felt before. Everything felt slowed up, underwater, but absolutely and incontrovertibly right. I smiled in the darkness.

Toby dropped the line and the mainsail fell still. The sloop rocked sweetly, outlined in phosphorescence. The sky rained stars, snowed stars. It was so beautiful that I felt as if I had been caught up in some great, godlike moment out of antiquity, a ceremony for a fallen warrior, perhaps, or the birth of a great king.

Toby cleared his throat. "There's something I always liked that I thought I might read, if you don't mind," he said.

"Of course not."

He took a small, tattered book out of his pocket and raised it close to his face. He cleared his throat and began, "'Sunset and evening star, / And one clear call for me! / And may there be no moaning of the bar, / When I put out to sea . . .'"

As he read the rest of Tennyson, I laughed silently, and then cried. Cam hated the poem, but he loved Toby.

When he was done, I walked to the rail of the Friendship and hugged the urn to me for a moment and then held it aloft and let Cam's ashes spill out and into the little night wind. The wind took them and whirled them, and the crowding stars lit them and the flickering phosphorescence in the water received them. For a moment the ashes glowed on the surface of the bay like silver dust, and then were whirled away on the water. I watched them for a long time. When they faded from sight, they were still glowing.

I turned my face to Toby's and saw that tears streaked his cheeks like silver snail's tracks. I reached my fingers up and wiped them away.

"Don't," I said. "He's still with us. We'll always have him."

"I know, baby girl," he said. "I was just thinking about your wedding day, when Seth brought the Friendship around for him, and there he was with those hairy red legs sticking out of that silly little skirt, falling all over you to catch the mainsail line before she foundered, and you with your pretty silk skirt hiked up over your head. I was watching from the dock; Seth let me come with him that day. I remember I was so impressed with that—what was it? That little knife? I know there's a Gaelic name for it—sticking out of his sock."

"It's called a Sgian Dubh," I said, beginning to laugh, too. "But he forgot his, and so he had to use a steak knife."

We were still laughing, though with tears falling freely, when he brought the Friendship back in. It was so cold that everyone on the dock had retreated to the house, but I stood outside for a long time, in a snow globe of swirling stars, and thought about my husband, with love, but not with loss. That came later.

CHAPTER

19

I woke the next morning to low, heavy gray light, but an ineffable sense of late morning hung in the silent air. So did aloneness. Sometime during the long, dreamless night and early morning, everyone had gone. Not even the lump that was Silas was under my tangled covers. I swung my feet out of bed and onto an icy floor, and scrambled for Jeebs's tatty old flannel robe, which I had appropriated. It was colder than cold, arctic. I had never felt such cold before. Part of it was the emptiness. Why had they all gone and left me alone?

I groped in my mind for Cam, but I could not find him. By the time I stumbled into the living room I was in a frigid sweat of panic. But Kitty was there, curled up under several mothy old Hudson's Bay blankets, drinking coffee and watching the fire sputter. A bony head, looking for all the world like a desiccated jack-o'-lantern, rose from the folds near her hip.

"Will you please tell this woman where the can opener is?" he grumped. *"She's been trying to hack into a can with a fork."*

I stared at Kitty. She had dark rings around her eyes and her hair was wild. She was wearing a heavy sweat suit and old Uggs, a brand of boots that I so detested but whose woolly warmth I would have cut her throat for this morning, and her packed bag stood beside the door.

"Kitty, where is everybody? Why didn't somebody wake me up?

343

There are space heaters all over the place, and dry firewood on the porch."

She knuckled her eyes and looked at me.

"Please feed this goddamned cat and then we'll talk. He's about to go for my throat."

I fed an ungrateful Silas, poured myself a cup of coffee, and ran back into the living room. My bare feet were numb; I thrust them under Kitty's blankets.

"Now. What?"

"When you came in from the dock last night we called out for you to come join us—it was a fine wake, Lilly. Cam would have loved it. But you just gave us this rhapsodic look—Joan of Arc comes to mind—and drifted on up the stairs, so we figured you needed to be alone and sleep. The girls and their husbands decided to get up very early and see if they could get an early plane out of Bangor that would get them to Boston, and then take the shuttle to New York. Everybody had critical projects lying on their desks, and they said they'd call you when they got in. I personally think they were all dying of the lack of little willowy guys in black bringing in their Kona coffee, and the sound of rarefied snits going on out in the hall. Junie lit out of here soon after; I don't think she wanted to spend another night in Cam's house with only you and no Cam. Tatty went with her, fretting about where they were going to stop for lunch. I'm not sure Tatty knew where she was all weekend. Everyone gave you their deepest love."

"And you stayed."

I was grateful to her, and vaguely angry with everyone else. Cam deserved better than this.

"I stayed. Just long enough to pack you up and get you out of here *this* morning. You can't stay here anymore, Lilly."

"I can't go until I've picked up Daddy's books and packed up the silver and china," I said, my brow furrowed. "I told you that. The plan is to pick up the books today, and Toby and Laurie will come over in the morning and help pack us up and we'll leave right after. Depending on the time, we might drive straight on in. Or stop in New Haven or somewhere. You knew all that, Kitty. What's wrong with you? Did you sleep out here last night?"

"I did. I got up about three and drug all the blankets I could find and built up the fire and conked out on the sofa. Silas joined me."

"Was it cold? Did I snore or something?"

"No, Lilly, you didn't snore. You talked all night to Cam, practically without stopping."

"I told you I talk to him sometimes. And I dream about him a lot."

"You didn't tell me he talked back to you."

I stared at her.

"Oh, yes. Mostly you were telling him about pitching him off the sloop, and how beautiful everything was, and how he shone brighter than the stars, and you said you were sorry about that awful poem Toby read, but you knew he loved Toby and wouldn't mind.

"And he laughed, Lilly. As clearly as I hear you, I heard him laugh. Or somebody. And then he whispered, 'It was the right thing to do. Thank you.'"

"And then what?"

"I don't know then what. I got out of there before I saw him. Lilly, nobody loved Cam McCall any more than I did, except you, but this is not right. It's not healthy. You can't stay in a house where . . . your dead husband is. It's like saying no to any more life at all. How can you go ahead with the rest of yours when you know he's—stuck here?"

"He's not stuck here, Kitty," I said, tears of relief and joy that at last I could talk to her about it filling my eyes. "He's here because I'm here. He's my true north, Kitty. Wherever I am, he is. He . . . takes care of me. I know that."

"Oh, God, Lil. Do you think he's coming back to Virginia with you? That he'll be all around McCall's Point now?"

"Yes. That's just what I think. He's always been with me. He always will be."

Kitty's face reddened and her mouth straightened into a tight line.

"He was never a saint, Lilly. Don't make him into one now. Dead or alive, saints will screw you every time."

"Cam never screwed me, as you put it! What are you *talking* about?"

"Nothing I'm going to get into until you're out of this iceberg of a house and home by your own fireplace, where you ought to be."

"If you know something about Cam that isn't—right, you'd better tell me now."

"Would you believe me?"

"No. And I want you to go on home now, Kitty. We'll be right behind you tomorrow or the next day. I don't think, even with the space heaters and the fire, I can keep the house warm any longer than that. I'll call you from the road and you can have supper waiting for me and Silas."

"And Cam?"

"I don't know if he eats or not. I'll ask him."

"You do that," Kitty said in despair, and got up to leave. When her suitcase was stowed into the back of her neat old 1998 BMW and she was firmly in the driver's seat, she looked at me. She was not smiling.

"I'm calling you tonight," she said. "If you don't answer I'm calling nine-one-one, the police, and Laurie and Toby—in that order. Don't think I'm not."

"I'd never think that," I said, and reached in and kissed her cheek.

"I love you, Kitty," I said.

She started to cry again.

"Oh, shit, Lilly, I love you too. Please, *please* take care of yourself."

"We all will," I said, and she backed the car out of the pitted driveway, turned around, and roared up the gravel road to the highway, tires spurting gravel. She did not look back.

Back in the house, I took a swift survey. The cold had crept into every room and bleached it frost gray. In the kitchen there was a pot of beef stew from Laurie and a note that said *Call us when you get back from Ellsworth. The radio says there's a nor'easter coming in day after tomorrow. We want you long gone out of here before that.*

"Yeah, yeah, yeah," I muttered, and began gathering up space heaters and moving them into the living room, where I arranged them strategically around the room. I moved all my and Silas's bedding onto the couch before the fireplace and added a pile of perpetually damp, salt-smelling blankets to pull over if needed. I carried in the last of the wood Toby had brought me and added a couple of logs to the fire, and put the others in the old bin beside it. I moved Silas's food and water into the living room and put them by the fire, and brought in apples and a chunk of rat cheese and some cold blueberry muffins and set the plate on the table in front of the sofa.

"Ready for the siege of Edgewater," I said to Silas, who eyed me yellowy and then curled up in his basket lined with Cam's old sweater. I turned on a couple of space heaters and added another small log to the fire, and these, with the old lamps burning brightly in the gloom, gave the living room an inviting, snug-harbor sort of look. In truth, I did not much want to go out into the rising wind, but my father's books were the last task I had left, and then I could burrow in with the fire and blankets and food and Silas and Cam. The prospect was, suddenly, magical.

I got as far as the deserted Blue Hill Fair Grounds, slowing up because I had heard several times that a young bear crossed the road there almost every day. I looked both ways, noticing only then that the stands of hickory and maples that wove through the pine and fir woods here were almost bare of leaves, and that more were whirling down in the wind. Surely there had never been such an early winter; surely this was not a typical off season.

It happened then. I felt a pressure against my chest and throat as if someone had physically pressed me back against the seat, and a gust of warm wind—or was it breath?—curled against my cheek, and was gone. I felt hollowed out, all vitals gone, weak and wounded and breathless. I had a quick thought—*Heart attack?*—and tried to breathe but couldn't.

In my ear, quite clearly, I heard Cam: "I'm sorry, Lilly. I just couldn't be alone. But I always loved you."

There was nothing after that. I knew he was gone. All the combined grief and terror and shock I had not felt at his death, I felt now. It doubled me over the steering wheel and blinded my eyes. I could not see. I could not breathe.

But then there was a whisper, "Breathe, Lilly. Imagine the bay breathing, and breathe with it. Breathe, Lilly. . . . Lilly, come home."

And gradually I did, and could at least force breath into my body. Was he not gone after all? What was he telling me? Was he saying he had to go back to the house? What? I could not feel or hear him, but I could breathe and drive, after a fashion.

It seemed to take forever to drive the fifteen or so miles back to the turnoff into Edgewater. Behind the forest that shielded the houses of the bay from the road, swollen purplish clouds were piling in, and small spots of something wet spattered on the windshield. It could not, could *not*, be snow, not in late September. But nevertheless it bit and stung me as I lurched from the car into the house, slammed the door, and stood leaning against it, bent over and gasping for breath.

Heavy, smoky warmth reached out and wrapped me close, and the fire crackled and popped happily. Space heaters whirred and lamps glowed. Silas raised his head to look at me, nearly cross-eyed with sleep.

"Is he here, Silas?" I whispered. "Did he come back here? I thought he had gone; he said—"

"Nobody gone as far as I can tell," Silas said thickly. *"But as you no doubt see, I have been asleep."*

"Oh go back to sleep, scussfuzz," I said angrily. "Why I depend on you . . ."

"Why, indeed," he muttered from between his paws.

Suddenly I was so tired I could hardly lock my knees to keep myself erect. I stumbled over to the sofa, threw myself down on it, wound Jeebs's fleece jacket and two or three blankets around me, and fell into sleep as deep as any I have ever known.

It was a long sleep, perhaps an enchanted one, certainly not a normal one. In it I heard voices: my mother's calling us in to supper; my father's reading some bit of folklore from Frazer to me in front of a different fire; Wilma's jangling chain and loving, witless woof; my own voice saying, "I'll never do that and nobody can make me"; the cloying voice of Peaches Davenport, honeyed with ersatz sorrow, saying, "I lost them both, you know."

Jon's voice, saying as he pressed my face into his sweater, "Don't look, Lilly. Don't look . . ."

I jerked myself awake about sunset, or at what would have been sunset if the great purple clouds had not thickened and lowered.

"Where's my box? I have to pee," Silas was complaining.

"So do I," I snapped, and dashed into the freezing black kitchen and pulled his litter box into the living room. I used the toilet in the alcove under the stairs that we had always called the guest bathroom, freezing my buttocks in the process, and dived for the sofa again. The sleep had been sweet and succoring; in it I had felt care and love and safety. I desperately wanted it again.

"Wait a minute! I'm starving!" howled Silas indignantly. I opened a can of his malodorous dinner and dumped it into his bowl and vanished up to my chin in blankets.

He must have come back here, I thought. *I still feel him, even if I can't hear him. He's keeping watch; all is well.*

The long-reported nor'easter came screaming in two days early. It must have been well past midnight when it hit; I could not tell because all the lights and the space heaters were out, and only the glowing embers of the fire lit the room. I was cold to the bone, so cold I did not think I could move. Huddled against me, Silas actually shivered. Outside I heard wind howling as I had never heard it before on this ocean, and the crashing of surf against rocks, and ominous creakings from the huge trees that leaned over Edgewater. I could see nothing outside but swirling white. Snow. My God, it was snowing, and we had no power. I was sure of that; the power on our cove went out if someone blew out a match, my father used to say. Wait a minute, weren't there oil lanterns? And oil? Somewhere in the kitchen or pantry . . .

I got up, threw the last big log on the fire, lit one of my mother's white tapers in a bronze candlestick, and stumbled into the kitchen. It took me only a second to realize that if the lamps and oil were there, I would freeze to death before I found them. I grabbed for the telephone; it was out. I had no idea where my cell phone was. There was nothing to do but wait it out until daylight, when surely Laurie and Toby would come in their Jeep with the snowplow and all would be well. We could last until then. Of course we could; anybody could.

The fire had flared up again and threw out a little warmth. Silas and I rolled ourselves Indian fashion into all the blankets we had brought, and lay down as close to the fire as was possible. It was still cold, but gradually warmth spread over us like hot water and I felt my muscles and those of the big cat soften and relax, and we slid back into sleep.

Sometime before dawn I felt the heavy weight of another blanket being spread over me, and did not wake except enough to murmur, "Thank you."

Shortly after that, there was a small thud on the coffee table and I opened one eye and saw two of the kerosene lanterns sitting there, filled and primed.

I smiled as I fell back to sleep.

"I never should have doubted you," I whispered.

"No. You never should."

Two or three times during the rest of the dark, I almost saw him. I would feel the displacement of air as someone moved past me and look up, and perhaps see a shadow, or a door closing. Once I thought someone was sitting in the old bentwood rocker, looking down on me.

Just at dawn came a loud, rending crack and then a crash, and I knew a great tree had gone down just outside. It was probably the patriarch fir that had shaded the driveway since before I was born. I held my breath but did not hear it grind into the roof. I did, however, see a tall, slender silhouette against the window onto the porch, looking out toward the tree.

I smiled again, and slept once more. True north. I would be cared for. We would be cared for.

Dawn had broken when there came a great rapping on the front door. I struggled to my feet: Laurie and Toby, surely. Hobbling to the door, I could see, through the windows, that Edgewater and its forests looked as if they had been caught in a war. Huge trees were down, their splits raw yellow in the winter darkness. Branches were everywhere. The flagpole was down, and the Adirondack chairs that always stood on the edge of our cliff were simply gone. The wind howled, moaned, screamed. White foam from the bay blew against the windows.

I jerked the door open. Not Laurie or Toby, but a boy, or a young man, rather, stood there in a yellow oil slicker holding a load of wood.

"Mrs. McCall?" he said politely. I stared.

"My mother saw your lights last night and thought you might be needing some wood. I'm David Surrey, but she said you'd know her as Peaches Davenport."

Still I stared. It was Cam. Cam as he had been when we first met, back in an Italian restaurant in Georgetown those many years past; he had a fiery red beard and mustache and eyebrows, wet now with melting snow, and Cam's piratical blue eyes, and crooked smile. Cam.

"C— Thanks!"

Cam.

"Thanks! David."

Cam.

"Mrs. McCall?" the boy said again.

Still I stared.

"I'll just put this over by the fireplace, shall I?" the boy said. "And I'll make your fire up again while I'm at it. Pretty cold in here . . ."

Still I stared, and then whirled and ran past him, into the darkness and still of the kitchen. Ran, stumbling and crying.

"Where are you, you son of a bitch?" I screamed.

I ran straight into a pair of arms, which closed around me and drew my face into the shoulder of a Shetland sweater. I knew without being able to see that it would be blue. It smelled of seawater and wood smoke and the sweet sweat of a boy, smells out of another time . . .

He pulled me closer, so close that every inch of me fit sweetly against him. His warmth was heaven, life-giving, life-saving. I felt it fill and melt me until I sagged against him completely, and he held me up.

"I can't breathe," I whispered, and he put his mouth to mine. I felt his soft, chapped lips and he whispered, "Take mine. Take my breath."

I did. I knew at that moment that I had never really known that total completion existed. Not this kind. Not in this world.

"It was you all the time, wasn't it?" I whispered, giving him back my breath.

"I've been here all along," Jon said.

Epilogue

The boy got into his truck to turn it toward home—his home, not his mother's; he went there only when he had to—and then put his foot on the brake.

A cat. There had been a cat, hadn't there? He cast back into his mind, to the second time he went into the woman's house at the urging of his mother, letting his eyes slide over the pretty woman where she sat at the table, head on her arms, gray eyes open but narrowed as if she had been laughing, slight smile on her mouth. In her curled hand had been a faded, dried osprey feather. He had started to pluck it out, then left it. It looked right.

He'd known he could not help her; he had called Laurie and Toby Halliday on his cell phone and the whole process of death in this house had started over again. She would now, he knew, be on a plane or train home to Virginia, and out of his life forever.

But a cat, in this weather, with no food. He slewed the truck around and gunned it out onto the road, followed it, and plunged down the driveway toward the McCall cottage. The big fir had been split and sectioned and laid aside on the lawn, and the one that had blocked the main road was gone, but there were branches and needles and shingles strewn everywhere, as if a giant had taken out its rage on a dolls' house.

The boy screeched to a stop in front of the house and ran inside. The door had not been locked. *No need, now,* he thought. He walked through the dark room calling, "Kitty, kitty—here, kitty, kitty, kitty . . ."

When he reached the kitchen he saw and then heard the cat. It was a big, clumsy bullet-headed cat with a chunk out of one ear and slitted yellow eyes. It sat on the counter by the sink, as if waiting for an appointment.

"It's about time," the cat said grumpily.

"Well, I just remembered you," the boy said.

"Thank heaven for small favors. Are we going?"

"You want to eat first, or go home?" the boy asked, not yet noticing that he was talking to a cat who talked back.

"Home," the cat said. *"So long as it's warm."*

"Well, it's not much, just a doublewide on a kind of cove down the bay a little, but it's warm and it's clean and it's full of stuff to eat," the boy said. "I'm game if you are."

The big cat clicked across the floor and launched himself into the boy's surprised arms. Instinctively he drew the cat close and wrapped his fleece parka around it.

"I'm sorry about your mama," he said.

"Me too. But she's okay now."

The cat buried his icy nose in the boy's neck, took two great, rattling sniffs, and began making a horrendous grinding, metallic noise that the boy only belatedly recognized as a purr.

Old Silas knew home when he smelled it.